Flight of
the Quetzal

Samantha King Mystery Series Book Two

Lloyd Mardis

To Andrew who has overcome all obstacles to be a fine chef!

Lloyd

Outskirts Press, Inc.
Denver, Colorado

Flight of the Quetzal
Samantha King Mystery Series Book Two
All Rights Reserved.
Copyright © 2009 Lloyd Mardis
v30

Outskirts Press, Inc.
http://www.outskirtspress.com

ISBN: 978-1-4327-3087-1

Outskirts Press and the "OP" logo are trademarks belonging to Outskirts Press, Inc.

PRINTED IN THE UNITED STATES OF AMERICA

Prologue

The February wind blew hard. The Texas sun deepened from gold to orange. Slender strips of dirty-blue clouds snaking south through the Hill Country unraveled like old ropes. Down near the ground the moaning norther whispered through the thick stand of acacia, live oak, and mesquite, some hardly more than shrubs, but dense enough to keep out prying eyes.

The white-tailed doe had lain in a warm bed of leaves all day, waiting. Her large sensitive ears swiveled constantly, listening for the sounds of a possible predator. Her moist black nose sampled the air. The season seemed new to her, although it was her second winter.

Something in her life had changed last autumn when she had felt the weight of an insistent buck on her back, clasping her with his fore legs.

Now she walked out into the open. She continued testing for dangerous scents. She came to a weathered and neglected wood rail fence, found some Spanish oak acorns, and a few stiff yellow stalks of wild oats still heavy with grain. A treat. The sun disappeared and all was clothed in a soft rose and purple light.

She sprang across, landed lightly, and bounded toward gray cenizo bushes near a gully.

Normally, she would have stayed in the open, but because the wind had not died completely, she walked in the canyon where it was quieter.

Two hours earlier, a young mountain lion weighing about a hundred pounds, his black-tipped tail nearly as long as his body, made his way carefully along the limestone ledges next to a pasture already in shadow. A new area for him. In a show of inexperience he had attempted to bring down a Longhorn calf that afternoon. The huge mother with a horn span of nearly six feet had charged like a rock slide. He had barely escaped, but carried a ragged hole in his shoulder for his efforts.

The hungry lion moved to the top of a bluff. The wind still blew as it had for most of the day. Some huisache daisies danced near his feet. He lay down near the edge where he could see what passed below, and tried again to reach the gash in his shoulder with his rough tongue. The tawny color of his fur blended in with the restless bunch grass.

As the red sun set, the young cougar waited. He could not run fast enough to catch any prey. He would have to ambush to eat.

Chapter 1

I'm nobody's prime rib. –From Samantha's Journal

In the late afternoon, Samantha King heard the diesel pickup ease up to her Land Rover and stop. A door opened and shut. That would be her Uncle Stu, ending the wait for the dreaded talk. Both had skirted the issue all week, and tomorrow she would leave the ranch to stay on schedule, talk or not. Nothing would change, but she wanted him to accept her decision.

She walked quickly to greet him as he climbed from the truck's cab. He opened his arms for his usual hug.

"Whoa darlin', you're certainly a welcome sight for these tired old eyes." Cowboy hat and boots, a fleece-lined vest, a red and black-checked flannel shirt, and well-worn jeans said "Texas." Exactly their intent. Samantha leaned against his massive chest, then looked up at him.

"Come in. Come in. I've moved a ton of stuff from Austin since the last time you came by."

"Hey, I like it. I like it." He stepped in, by-passing the colorful ethnic rugs, careful not to mar the pine plank floor. Stuart King took off his Stetson, and wiped his hand through iron-gray hair. Above him the vaulted ceiling reached up a story and a half. Through the large kitchen window he saw the winter-dressed trunks of trees standing straight, tall, and bare. He walked close to the thick pane of glass and looked at the Sabinal River, twenty feet below, and the naked knees of the rust-colored Cypress trees sprouting from its banks.

"That's the cleanest river in the county, I do believe. Just look at that water and those little waterfalls. Crystal clear, and those pools look like emeralds."

"Uncle Stu, you are getting poetic." She had already decided he would be the one to begin the serious talk.

"If I'd known how good this would turn out, I might have built down here myself."

"Well, I could trade it for your ranch house."

"Hey, that's good. Tell you what. If I get myself down to real skinny and little like you, you're on."

Samantha poured two cups of aromatic Sumatran coffee, and handed one to her uncle. Now comes the talk, she guessed. He eased his tall frame down onto a wooden chair, and placed his cup on the matching breakfast table.

"Tell me about some of the things you brought from Austin. Like what's this hanging on my chair? And what's that by the fireplace?" O.K, so he was not ready. He didn't want to face the talk anymore than she did.

"That's a horse blanket I got in Burma. The rugs on the floor are called kilims, and come from Iran and Daghestan. They date from the late 19th century. The pillows are scrunched up peasant skirts from Rajastan, and in the corner, a Kurdish baby carrier from southeast Turkey, and those salt bags are from..."

Her uncle's eyes glazed over.

"Tell me why in Sam Hill you want to go traipsing around in Honduras?" At last the talk.

"Because I have to."

"Nobody has to do anything except die, and that might happen to you if you go down there."

"Uncle Stu, you know I value your opinion, and you know I have to live my own life. I'm willing to face up to the consequences of my decisions. Believe me, this is something I just have to do. I need to stand where my dad died, and say I'm sorry."

"Sorry?"

"Yes, I could have healed our break. I knew that. I was stubborn, unwilling to confess I'd made a mistake with Blanchard, and sorry I'd let him down in the oil business. I thought I had lots of time, and we'd forgive and forget, but now he's gone, and I have nightmares about that crash almost every night. I wake up yelling for him to watch out, and I see his plane disappearing into the jungle."

2

"And you think going down there, and seeing there's nothing left of the plane, and knowing his ashes are in Oklahoma, it'll bring you peace?"

"I know you think it's unwise, but that's exactly what I've got to do, and I want you to accept me doing it. I love you Uncle Stu, and I need your support. Please don't let me leave here without it."

"But Good Lord, darlin'," the only name he ever called her, "you just got back from an earthquake in India, and being shot in New York. Don't you think you ought to rest before you take off?"

"Dad's plane went down last year, and I can't wait any longer. I had hoped it would get easier, but it hasn't. I'm rested. The bullet only grazed my arm, and it's nearly healed. I got worse scrapes when I rode my bicycle as a kid. I've got to go."

"Well, darlin' from what I hear, the crash happened in deep jungle; it will be hard to get to."

"I'll get a guide."

"I would hog-tie you to keep you from going on this wild goose chase if I could, but I know you'd bust loose before I could turn around. So, yes, I'll accept your going, and I'll wish you all the luck in the world. If anyone can pull it off, it'll be you." Samantha walked over and hugged him.

"Thank you, Uncle Stu, it means everything to me to have your support." Her uncle scratched at his chin, and looked up at the beams.

"The only person I know was with your dad before he went down was his friend from Air Force days, Jason Murdoch, a consultant with him in the Guatemala City office. He got fed up and resigned. I hear he went to Greenland to live with the Eskimos, somewhere past the Arctic Circle, and north of Thule. He wanted to get as far away from the oil business as he could, and back to a simple life. I'm not sure he'd shed any light on what Martin was doing there at the last. I tried to get some information once, but he wouldn't talk about it, so that's a brick wall. You'll be on your own."

He stood up, and kicked at the floor with his hand-made scuffed-up boots, but made sure he was on the hard tile squares first. Samantha wondered if John Wayne would have bothered being that thoughtful. Thoughtful or not, her uncle was determined to be an authentic Texas rancher.

Well, hell, did he not have 18,000 acres of prime Hill Country land? Cattle? Wild game? Horses? Biggest damn ranch house in the county? Samantha could hear him rehearsing his list of things judged essential to be a true Texas cowboy. She loved him.

They walked out to the pickup. The visit had come to an end. He climbed in, pulled his Stetson down securely, started the big Dodge Ram, and yelled above the diesel, "I'll see you in the morning, darlin'."

Samantha felt close to her uncle after their talk. That night the moon blocked out some of the brightness of the stars. Nearly full, a gibbous moon, it beamed down upon her from space, once a part of earth and now its child. For once, she slept without nightmares.

The next morning she stretched and touched the appliquéd designs on the coverlet she had bought in Delhi. The fabric gave her the impression of orange. Regardless of the color of any cotton cloth, it gave off an orangeness to Samantha.

She was a synesthete, part of a small minority of people in the world who experienced a merging of the senses. Her merging involved taste, color, and touch. She looked at it as an enhancement of life. Some synesthetes never mentioned this gift for fear of being considered abnormal.

Letters of the alphabet, and numbers, had their own colors and most of the time the colors were unique to a particular person. Some synesthetes saw shapes when words were uttered. A person's name could have the aura of a circle, or appear as a jagged mountain, or a flowing river.

Up until a colleague's death, she had found her synesthesia useful only in judging fine fabrics. When Ben died, a little over a month ago, she used it to solve his murder. She still thought often of Ben Kruger. He had been her soul mate. It was so hard for Samantha to accept that they would never talk, laugh, and joke together again. The tears started.

4

A hole in her heart. She wondered if it would ever heal. However, if healing meant having to forget him, she would gladly hurt forever. She dabbed at her eyes.

After a shower, Samantha looked at herself. It was a way of checking up on reality. She wasn't perfect, not really getting any better, but not exactly wasting away either. She recalled Gertrude Stein's letter to Scott Fitzgerald when his novel wallowed in non-sales. "...one does not get better, but different, and older, and that is always a pleasure...." A good way to look at her own body, thought Samantha, it was just different. Not better. Just different and older. Especially, she wanted to remember: "...and that is always a pleasure...."

Sometimes, she wished for brown eyes, like her dad's, instead of green. Wrinkles around her eyes, yes, but didn't they connote character? She glanced at the welt where a bullet had grazed her arm last month.

Samantha took a morning pot of tea to the deck in time to greet the brass sun coming up in the west. At the ranch, directions were always mixed up to her. No clouds today. Yesterday's wind must have blown them into Mexico, or Canada. The cold crisp air, and the hot herbal tea, proved to be a perfect sensuous merging of opposites.

Duchess, her black Quarter Horse, nickered quietly from the stable. After tea she would saddle up, and ride to the main house for breakfast, and a last visit with her uncle. She would thank him again for accepting her decision. Later, she would drive to Austin on her way to London, and yes, Greenland.

She put a saddle on Duchess, led the horse outside the small stable, and put her foot in the stirrup. The ride would take perhaps thirty minutes.

She enjoyed the big Sunday morning breakfast with her uncle, and all the ranch hands. There wasn't a cook in the county who could outdo Maria's steaming platters of huevos con chorizo with fresh salsa, and hand-made corn tortillas with cream butter. Maria bought fresh-roasted beans and ground the coffee herself. A steaming cup was always welcome on a frosty morning.

A few crows cawed in the distance, and a jack rabbit with long black-tipped ears, loped across the cold pasture into a lacy-white thicket of acacia trees and shrubs. A gray mocking bird sent forth a dazzling selection of trills and chirps. One offering sounded much like the squeaky gate Samantha had just opened and shut. The warm scent of horse and leather rose around her. Up ahead, near a bluff, three hawks circled. She looked again. No, they were turkey vultures soaring low, without effort. She would pass beneath the swooping circles. Something had died.

Duchess caught a scent she did not like, and began to rear and prance. This caught Samantha by surprise, but she quickly calmed the horse, talking to her, patting, and rubbing her neck. Reassured, Duchess walked on, but with smaller and hesitant steps. She snorted puffs of steam into the chilled air, as if to clear the disturbing smell from her nose.

Beneath the bluff lay the answer. A doe had been killed by something, and fairly well eaten. The head remained untouched, and the large brown eyes gazed with an open, almost philosophical look of acceptance, or perhaps of calm wonder. Duchess stamped. It was time to leave, but Samantha held her there. The unmistakable pug prints of a mountain lion shone on the soft patches of earth beside the scattered and bloody carcass of the doe. Samantha noticed a set of very tiny hooves near the doe's torn belly. A pregnant doe. A fawn stilled before seeing the land, the trees, the sunrises, and sunsets of Texas.

Nature appeared so ruthless at times. The world seemed to be built around violence. One either ate or was eaten. Was that the meaning of life? At the top of that food chain were human beings. All animals, humanity included, were hard-wired to survive, but nature seemed to have checks and balances. Too many deer would not be good Samantha supposed. Too many mountain lions not good either. Yet, a young doe and her unborn fawn, robbed of life, touched Samantha with sadness.

She wondered if the next time she bit into a venison steak, or a beef hamburger, she would feel sad too? If all animals were vegetarians, would we become upset over the possibility that a carrot had feelings too, and a right to life?

Possible solutions: mass suicide by not eating, or perhaps

learning to live on dirt and sunlight. Neither answer seemed appetizing.

She wondered about the lion. Maybe it was watching her at that very moment. Crouching just behind that clump of cenizo, and protecting the kill. While she was worrying about a carrot, she could end up being the entrée on the lion's breakfast menu. Samantha shook off the feeling. The lion would be far away by now, but a part of her said to watch out.

She knew her uncle, although a conservationist and friend to wild life, would not welcome a mountain lion in the same pastures with his high-priced foals, even though the mares could probably keep the lion from attacking. Besides, there were plenty of deer around, a mountain lion's favorite prey. And what about this doe? Where was she going? What thoughts had flashed before her, if she had thought at all, in those final horrible moments as the lion ripped the life from her? A necessary victim perhaps, but a victim, nevertheless. I will not ever be a victim, Samantha decided.

She allowed Duchess to trot swiftly away. Survival demanded vigilance. Nature didn't show partiality. Life could be brutal. Yet, it was what we had to work with. Mysterious. Wondrous. Terrible. Yes, beautiful too. Life was worth living.

"We laugh and we cry, and we can still eat a good breakfast," Samantha said aloud to herself.

———————

Soon, she would drive back to Austin to her apartment. She would concern herself with attending a reception for the Mesoamerican Archaeology Group, promoting Mayan culture awareness. The information could prove helpful, or not. There were some appointments to be kept concerning her real estate purchases for her clients, but nothing really urgent. Since the death of her boss, she had rearranged her life. The process was far from over, but she had a break and she planned to use it to find her dad's plane. Another month, and she might be in Honduras, or Guatemala City, or in Mexico. She wished she knew exactly where to go, and what to do.

Perhaps some of the answers could be pried from the enigmatic

Jason Murdoch in Greenland. She would see him first. If her uncle had been unsettled about the jungles of Honduras, Samantha wondered what he would think of her going to Greenland in the dead of winter? She decided he didn't need to know everything. She glanced back. The cenizo bushes and small ridges hid the doe.

Chapter 2

Jason Murdoch. I hope you have some answers for me.
Greenland. Honduras. When can I see you Emerson? Can I do
without you for another month? No way. –From Samantha's
Journal

On Sunday morning, mindful of the thin glaze of ice on the
streets, Julie Amber parked her year-old silver Porsche Boxster,
part of a hiring bonus from a now-defunct Austin dotcom company. She unwound her long jean-clad legs, eased out from the
leather seat, and minced her way across the snow-crusted sidewalk.

She held onto the cold wrought-iron stair railing with her left
hand. Her other hand clutched a white paper sack containing two
fresh multi-grain bagels. The aggregate-covered steps were dusted
lightly with white grains of sleet. The upscale new apartment
looked over Austin's Town Lake, actually, the dammed-up Colorado River.

Julie knew without a doubt that Trak Barber, her significant
other, friend, live in, or house-mate–whatever, would be in the
middle of the floor clicking away on his keyboard with reference
works spread about him like a teenager with a stash of favorite
CDs close at hand. He would be neck-deep in his archaeological
studies and fanatically preoccupied.

After attaining his Ph.D., a two-year target, he would either go
into research, or teaching, or both. The pull of an actual dig in
some impossible corner of the world had always appealed to him.
The Mayan sites in Mesoamerica captivated him. His dedication
made Julie love him all the more. It looked as if he were hooked
for life and she, hooked on him. Julie felt his disappointment at not
being able to help out more, financially speaking. He had hoped

for a raise as a graduate teaching assistant, but the extra dollars had not appeared.

In the meantime, Julie carried most of the financial load and was good to do it. Although the kaput dotcom had been exciting and creative, Julie had viewed her work primarily as a way of putting the bagels on the table. Perhaps someday, work and vocation would merge and she would breathe heavily over the task at hand as Trak did.

Luckily, she could work anywhere that had dependable electricity. High-speed access to the Internet would be nice, but she good make do with a good phone system, and she liked the freedom and the option of setting up almost anywhere on the globe.

A new business venture still hung in limbo, but since she had opted for cash when she first joined the failed company, she had a nice-sized conservative portfolio that made for a comfortable living until she decided what to do next.

Lately, Julie considered going back for her Ph.D in Computer Science and wanted to talk to Trak about it. She opened the door.

Sandy-haired Trak Barber sat cross-legged before the imposing brick fireplace facade which soared to the ceiling. A Scott Joplin tune, one of Julie's favorites, filled the room.

"Brr, it's nippy out there. Great music. I got the bagels. I'll get the cheese and jam. Did you plug in the pot?" She tossed her black leather jacket on the sofa and shook her long golden-brown hair. The question drew no response. Trak might as well have been lost in outer space.

"Hello, hello. Houston calling. Are you there? Bagel here. Fresh bagel. Come in for a landing in the kitchen station."

"Oh hi, guess I was pretty deep into this."

"You're always deep into it. I'm just glad you're not doing fertilizer research."

"Hah, good one. That's cool. O yes, coffee pot. Yes, yes, I plugged it in. My brain is entering the atmosphere. Let me get vertical." He stood, slim, muscular, and maybe an inch shorter than Julie.

Soon, bagels were sliced and toasted. Cheese and jam selected. Two large yellow mugs steamed with Colombian Supremo.

"Tell me again how we got these yellow monstrosities?"

"Take the we out of that question. You ordered them over the Internet. You should stick to Mayan temples and leave the Internet purchases to me."

"O yeah, they were supposed to be black. Oops, as the surgeon said. Maybe they'll grow on us and if we ever get married and have kids they can decorate them at preschool. Yum, this is a bagel worth chewing. You did good."

"That's not the only thing I'm good at."

Julie quickly left her chair and plopped herself in Trak's lap. With her thumb she wiped a bagel crumb from his chin, planted her lips on his, searched his mouth thoroughly with her tongue, made passionate groaning sounds, and rubbed her erect breasts, naked behind her thin t-shirt, against his chest.

"There, you had too much jam and cheese in there. Don't want you getting fat on me."

"So, that noise was a vacuum sweeper and not my beloved's primal moans of desire?" Trak grinned and took another bite. Julie pulled back and looked into deep brown eyes.

"I love you, my little Mayan addict. I love you. Prepare for some more vacuuming."

The mugs of coffee got cold. Julie and Trak took fresh cups in by the fireplace. Trak made room among the piles of reference materials for them to sit close together.

"There's nothing like a fire on a cold February Sunday and clutching your main squeeze, right?"

"Poetically put. Trak, what would you say if I went back and got my Ph.D?"

"Serious?"

"Serious."

"Well, I'd say do what you want to do. You've worked hard and you're not complaining about me not keeping up my end. If we can handle it financially, or if we have to get some place cheaper so you can do it, then I'm all for it. Did your dotcom thing have anything to do with it?"

"Yes, I guess it did. If it hadn't bellied up, I'd still be putting in my sixty or eighty hours. But since it has, this might be a good time to increase my intellectual worth. I may need it. And how about you? Are you still hot and heavy for the Mayans?"

"More than ever. I think I've found my calling. The research is just now taking off. UT could become the dominant player in deciphering Mayan writings. Some of my professors put it on a par with space exploration, and the discovery of the genetic code. It's one of the great intellectual adventures of the world. It's so exciting to be a part of it, I can hardly stand it."

Julie laughed.

"What a surprise. Just kidding. I'm glad it means so much to you. Whatever happens I'll be there for you. We'll work together. Who knows, maybe I'll even join you in a dig some day and help you with a thorny Mayan grammar structure I can figure out on the computer." Trak's gaze drifted up toward the exposed beams.

"Speaking of helping. Julie, would you go with me to a reception about UT's work in Mesoamerica?"

"Of course, unless I'm called to orchestrate the peace initiatives in Ireland and Israel. When is it?"

"If you're called to Camp David I'll understand. I won't be happy, but I'll understand. However, if you're free it's next Sunday afternoon at a private home. The hostess is involved with CHAAC somehow. A professor will talk about Palenque. A lot of faculty members are attending and some important Austin people who might do some funding."

"Boy, you are a fountain of information. What's CHA... whatever?"

"Sorry, Center for the History of Ancient American Art and Cultures. Just say chalk and you're close. So, can you go?"

"I thought you were going to do work at Copán in Honduras. Isn't Palenque in Mexico?"

"Right. Very good. And here I thought you were just a gorgeous dotcommer. The writing is similar enough so that all sites in Mexico, Guatemala, and Honduras can be somewhat interconnected. You'll get to meet some of the leaders in the field and some of my professors. You'll love it and I'd really like having you there." Julie felt just a tickle of anxiety wondering what the future actually held for her and Trak.

"I'm going to miss you terribly when you go to Copán next month. Yes, I'll go with you. If the president wants me to fly with him on Air Force One, I'll turn it down. Now listen very carefully to an announcement. Do I have your complete attention? Good.

"I have this overwhelming desire to have hot, extremely athletic and liberating sex with someone, preferably a budding archaeologist, who is near at hand, but who must be really horny. Do you happen to know of such a person, Mr. Barber? Someone who can tear himself away from the Mayan alphabet for say, a couple of hours, and could start a ravishing archaeological dig on this willing body immediately?"

Trak said he knew the perfect person who could fit all those qualifications, and yes, that person could start right away.

"Then to mix up the analogy, but not the underlying message, welcome aboard, Cap'n Hook. This ship is yours to plunder." It didn't bother Julie that she often instigated the process that led to sex. Well, maybe it did bother her a little. It would be nice if Trak thought of it first, sometime.

Chapter 3

Out on the road again. Up in the sky again. Hopping in bed with Emerson again.... Great songs different tunes. −From Samantha's Journal.

Samantha returned to her seat. Ten minutes later came the announcement to prepare for landing at Heathrow. The bright morning sun disappeared as the plane dipped into a thick bank of gray clouds. A few moments later, Samantha could see the darkened landscape below. Streaks of rain wormed across her window. It would be a dreary day in London. A bright spot: Emerson Jacque would be waiting to pick her up.

She wondered if the sleet had melted in Austin. The drive in from the ranch had been slow. Uncle Stu said he would keep an eye out for the mountain lion, although he figured it had moved on, since there wasn't much left of the doe to eat. Besides, one lion had been shot nearby. Maybe it was the culprit. The ranch manager took Duchess to the main stables to care for her until Samantha returned. At breakfast, her uncle informed her he'd be adding new horses to the string. The breeding operation was showing a profit.

While still at the ranch, Samantha decided definitely to go to Greenland. She did not tell her uncle. Her long standing habit: keep plans to herself as long as possible. That way people didn't "help out" with advice and dire predictions. Going to Greenland also allowed her to see Emerson Jacque in England.

She would do her best to find Jason Murdoch, a daunting undertaking, since he lived north of the Thule air base, probably at a winter Inuit hunting camp. Although Uncle Stu made it clear she would get no help from Mr. Murdoch, and had closed the book on it, Samantha had not. She would find out for herself. If she could locate him, surely she could persuade him to supply some information. Even a tiny bit could prove extremely helpful.

Samantha had great faith in her ability to persuade, ironic, since she didn't like anyone telling her what to do. Yet, she would do some coercing if it were important, a trait that came in handy as she negotiated real estate deals. She could be manipulative and calculating to get the job done.

A few weeks ago, she had worked her way into bed with an unsuspecting male, who thought he was doing the seducing. Emerson Jacque may have been a victim of her lusty plans, but from the beginning, she found it difficult to sort out what actually happened. She suspected later, that love had played more of a part than either had realized.

She would worry about that another time. Now, she focused on finding and persuading Jason Murdoch to help before she flew to Central America next month.

Samantha emailed her long-time friend and former client, Christina Madalora, at her home in Rome, and asked her to meet in London for a day. She also considered giving Amy Posher a call as well, then realized it could be awkward for her to leave her classes at Brighton. There would be time later to talk after Amy graduated. Samantha did hope her French Alps skiing buddy would want to come work with her. She could use the help, now that she was on her own.

She wondered how Babs, Mollie, and Kate were doing. Skiing with the younger women had turned out to be a life saver for her, after she thought Emerson had stood her up in Paris. And then, there was the French ski guide, Guillaume, but she dared not think of him this close to Emerson. A wave of rainbow-colored chocolate washed through her mind. Chocolate. Part of her synesthesia?

Thinking sex, having sex, anytime she was turned on, voila! chocolate. Chocolate of a thousand colors and tastes. The chocolate thing, in all its forms, she guarded as her secret.

Another idiosyncracy, however, could not be kept secret. During orgasm, her eyes would cross. Her former husband, Blanchard, had teased her unmercifully about it, and had tried to see how many times he could get her to do it. She had to admit he had been quite successful, to the point she would nearly collapse from utter exhaustion, damn him. Samantha made her mind shift gears.

She enjoyed attending the Mesoamerica reception. The home of the hostess was grand and filled with tasteful, valuable artifacts from all over the world. Samantha met a delightful young couple, committed to each other and obviously in love, though not married. Trak Barber impressed Samantha with his enthusiasm for deciphering the Mayan writings. He would be at Copán next month. Perhaps, she would see him in Honduras during the search for her dad's crash site.

Julie Amber had been quite taken with Katrina, a life-sized plastic skeleton in the foyer, done up in a pink chiffon gown, wide-brimmed hat, and high heels.

Samantha could tell Julie really wanted to go with Trak to Honduras, but the facilities at the research site wouldn't permit it, according to her boyfriend, and Julie didn't want to stay at a hotel by herself.

An idea took root in Samantha's head and the more she allowed it to grow, the more plausible it became. Perhaps, something could be worked out between her and Julie that would be mutually beneficial.

If they traveled together in Honduras, Julie could be of great help while Samantha put to use any information Jason Murdoch might provide. With her business and computer expertise, Julie could act as a temporary assistant who would give Samantha a better cover, and possibly be tax deductible, too. Julie could visit Trak at Copán while Samantha searched for the crash site. The more she considered Julie going with her the more she liked the idea. If she felt the same when she returned from England and Greenland, she would check to see what the young woman thought about accompanying her.

The plane rolled to a stop, and Samantha stood to leave. Soon, she would see Emerson. Her heart beat increased, and her breathing seemed constricted. Separated–how long? Just a few weeks? It seemed like months to her body.

It had begun in London, but nothing could equal the passion of that Parisian night and morning. Breath-taking, an inadequate description. Then, he was gone. Devastation. No explanation. And then, Guillaume. What would she ever do about Guillaume? Guilt? Certainly not at the time. She would have to see. Too much.

Then, Emerson showed up in India and told her he had been forced to leave her. Impossible to believe. And over it all, hung the terrible loss of Ben Kruger, her soul mate and colleague. Was her whole involvement with Emerson, and later, with Guillaume, simply a rebound from her devotion to Ben?

Samantha and Emerson had emailed daily after her return to New York. They had talked by phone and had run up huge bills just to hear each other's voices. They had tried to figure out their relationship and their future, but their efforts to find a solution had failed so far. He wanted her. She wanted him. But sometimes she wavered. Maybe he wasn't certain either. In a few minutes they would be face to face again. Though Samantha could hardly wait, part of her wanted to run away, while she had the chance. If she did, she would have to wade through some very deep chocolate, now beginning to pile up around her ankles.

Chapter 4

**...hand too shaky to write today. A big bed is a lovely thing. –
From Samantha's Journal**

Samantha leaned back against the Jaguar's deep-red leather
seat. The XK 140, Emerson's mistress, rumbled through the heavy
mist which still blanketed the mid-morning English countryside.
Just a month or so before, she had ridden beside him to London.
How much difference a month could make. Then she knew him
only as a competitor. Roger Bhatt, her boss, had decided Mr.
Jacque would make an excellent member of their team, particularly
in the light of having lost Ben. She recalled her feelings, negative
feelings, about what Roger had instructed her to do. She had
grieved for Ben, her dear Platonic friend. Sweet man.

Droplets gathered on the Jaguar's divided wind screen and
were whisked away by the wiper blades. Samantha looked out the
window. Had she not seen those same cows a month ago? She
shook her head, not about the cows, but about her changed relationship with Emerson Jacque, a change that continued to cause
flip-flops in her heart and mind.

At Heathrow he had swept her into his arms. She had surprised
herself with the sudden animal-like yearning to feel his lips upon
hers. Apparently, he had read her thoughts. He had kissed her
long and completely. She had wanted more, even in that public
place. Her body had signaled let's go. Her mind had said hold on
a minute.

Hugging and clinging to him, mouthing absurdities and affir-
mations, she had ignored all warnings. Why had she ached for him
so? Lust? Or the bonds of love?

In January he had met her at Great Fosters, an estate hotel

18

seven miles from London. They had been wary of each other, but courteous. They had gone places. Sightseeing. He had tried to kiss her. She had disappeared for two days. Then, they had talked and they had left for Paris and had made incredible love for the first time. It had turned her into a volcano.

She remembered that he had kissed her last just before she had boarded the military helicopter from Bhuj to Ahmadabad. Her face had been streaked with tears and dirt, her heart and body had been wrecked. No time to sort through his story. She had been hopelessly confused and hurt, yet the taste of chocolate, mixed with grit, had been undeniable.

Now a new chapter would begin.

"I can't tell you how much I've missed you. Even the Jaguar doesn't drive right unless you're sitting over there." He smiled, but she knew behind the joke he was serious. Amazing how well she understood him.

She remembered coming down the stairs at Great Fosters and seeing him standing there, six feet tall, brown hair combed straight back, decidedly handsome, neatly dressed, carrying an umbrella and apologizing for those ridiculous white athletic shoes. They had laughed at that. Her insides had warned her to watch out. Boyish, sincerely apologetic, and winsome, he had become her first step onto the slippery slope of romance, although she had not recognized it, and would have vociferously denied it, if asked.

"I'm glad the Jaguar appreciates me, usually a mistress can be jealous instead of supportive. Thank her for me at your next car-talk time." He reached across, touching her knee, then caressed above her knee. A chocolate-covered tingle went up her spine, and a slight catch in her breathing betrayed her. Samantha needed to have a talk with her shameless body.

They arrived at the small hotel she had reserved. There was a moment of indecision, quickly squelched. Samantha in control. Efficient.

"And now for a quick shower and a rest."

"Give me a call, um, I want to take you back to the Kew. Big surprise, the crocuses are just starting to bloom. Then, we'll have dinner at Langan's again, if that's all right with you."

"It sounds lovely. Emerson?" Mind deposed. Heart elected

to govern.

"Yes?"

"Do you have to go? I'll only be a minute. I believe I can rest and visit at the same time." So much for that talk with her body. Samantha felt her reserve, her rational decision to be cautious, running like storm water down a thirsty drain.

"I would like to stay. I always want to be with you. You know that. I'll wait right here."

Still slightly damp from the shower, Samantha wrapped a terry-cloth robe about her and stepped back into the bedroom. The robe fell open as she walked to the bed. She wrapped it again around her body, but she was too late to avoid his gaze. She could tell from his eyes that he wanted her as much as she wanted him. She could smell her own scent, warm and moist.

"Would you mind shedding a few clothes, and lying down beside me? Maybe we could snuggle, too."

Emerson pulled back the spread. Samantha lay down, and as she did, the robe parted above her knees, she attempted to cover them, but she knew, happily, that all was lost, conscious that in spite of her need to rest after the long flight, she had never felt more alive. Ten in the morning and she couldn't wait. "Please hurry, Emerson. Please hurry." Impatiently, she watched as he took off his clothes.

"I want you so bad. So bad." He lay down beside her and with some difficulty rolled a glistening translucent sheath over a very eager part of his body.

"I can't stand to have it slow, Emerson. Please understand. I need you in me now." It would not be slow. He pulled her to him with great strength. She felt light as air.

"Are you ready?"

"Yes, oh yes."

Her mind relived that first time in Paris. A maddeningly slow Emerson. So tender with his kisses and caresses until she knew she would die. So perfect and necessary. She was brought along until she was so ready for him she had cried out. She knew she could not bear waiting this time. She wanted to cry out already.

Samantha need not have worried. Hot demanding arms encircled her shower-cooled body. Hard muscles pressed against her.

She winced a little as his arm brushed the red mark on her arm. He saw her expression and immediately apologized and kissed her arm so tenderly.

"It's O.K., you made it well. But there's a lot more of me that needs quick medical attention, doctor. Please continue the full-body treatment." He covered her mouth with his, kissing her deeply.

Her long legs drew him to her unlatched door. She felt him there seeking entrance. She had but a fraction of a second to muse, to wonder, and to begin a smile before he entered her, pushing until they locked together like two snug picture-puzzle pieces. Her smile changed to an open-mouthed cry, a yell, as he moved away a little and plunged in again and again. She could not believe her hunger. She could not believe her eyes were crossing already. There were two ferocious Emersons pounding away, breaking down her defenses, and taking no prisoners.

She felt him straining, pulsing, inside her. Someday he would not have to wear a condom. Then she would experience his fountain spurting into the deepest part of her. That would be the day of commitment for them both. Oh, how in this moment, she loved him.

Chocolate filled the room. An ocean tide of chocolate crashing on boulders. Frothy chocolate. It washed over them, the bed, disappearing in the rich brown syrup, tumbling them as in a storm-tossed surf, rising, falling, sliding, drowning in chocolate. Chocolate-covered arms, legs, and lips. She opened like a chocolate flower, she wanted to enclose him—to shut him up inside her velvet petals, her secret places. Places he could not escape from.

He was a chocolate plucked from its protective wrapping, kissed, licked, and swallowed. Soft, hard, syrupy, nutty, fruit-filled and seeping with fine liqueurs. Samantha heard her own moans. Her raw emotion demanded satisfaction. Could she be heard? She didn't care.

Her eyes were crossing as they always did when her overloaded senses began exploding in sexual ecstasy. He loved to see her eyes cross. He kissed those crossed eyes as she tried to focus on his nose. Two noses. The intensity increased. She was coming yet again. She did not want to rest, although she knew she neared physical collapse.

21

Was it too much to ask Emerson to keep her eyes crossed until she died of exultation? What a great word. A great word for how she felt. Exulted. Ravished. Destroyed. Born. Alive.

Her arms dropped. She fell back against her damp pillow. Her eyes closed just for a moment then opened and fastened on him with an urgent appeal.

"I'm not through with you. Don't you dare leave me. Just give me a second more and I'll melt you into me. One more second and I'll feast on your beautiful body again." Emerson seemed quite willing to wait a second or two, as his chest expanded and depressed, accompanied by great gasps.

"I'm not through with you either. We may both end up jolly well dead on this bed today."

Samantha locked her arms about his neck and drew him down to her steaming wet breasts. She knew that the plaintive sounds deep in her throat would soon start again. She wrapped her body around his as he slipped inside her again and pinned her firmly to the bed. Samantha smiled then laughed. She clasped him to her with her long legs and went promptly cross-eyed. Soft moanings and gentle touches returned. Tender kisses were given and received. Satin skin to satin skin glistened in the morning light. Racing hearts began to slow at last.

"Wooee, I think I needed that more than rest."

"It was astounding. It's been too long. I love you, Samantha." He reached for her terry cloth robe and wiped her breasts ever so gently. She arched her back suddenly smacking her wet belly against his.

"Are you sure? Could be just plain old lust, you know."

"Could be. Guess we'll just have to keep on until we find out. In the meantime may I kiss your knees and anything else in that general vicinity?"

Samantha laughed and pulled this chocolate man to her.

"Yes, yes, I've got several places for you to kiss, so just start anywhere and don't miss anything. I love it when you cover me with kisses. Take your time, and as soon as I can get my breath back, I do intend to recapture and imprison a certain appendage of yours in solitary confinement, where it'll be squeezed with a vengeance, until I see two of you again, and pass out."

Chapter 5

When I'm with someone I like, then I like everything, no matter how mundane or extraordinary. –From Samantha's Journal

Emerson and Samantha drove to Kew Gardens. The lawns near the Temple of Bellona were covered with thousands of blue and white blooms.

"Even on a cloudy day, they are so beautiful."

"Yes, I must say, and in another few days there will be over a million crocuses in bloom here. I wish you could stay and see them."

"So do I. Maybe some day."

"And over here," Emerson pointed toward the Marianne North Gallery. "There will be camellias trying to out do the crocuses."

"I think the Temple of Bellona is exquisite."

"Named after the Roman goddess of war. There are plaques inside commemorating regiments that distinguished themselves in the Seven Years' War."

"The Doric columns are so simple and graceful. Do you think there will ever be a time when humanity gives up going to war?"

"That's a tough question. War seems to be a natural state of things. What do you think?"

"Surely we'll find a way to live without having to murder each other. Of course, we are still animals, and I think it will be a long time before our animal drives are mitigated, if they ever are. Kind of like our love making this morning. That's a powerful drive. I wasn't sure it was going to happen. I tried to reason it out, but once I got you in that room there was only one thing I wanted, and that was you all over and in me."

"Well, that's one animal drive I hope never goes away. I'm glad it overpowered you. I was a bit overwhelmed myself. Now we'd better stop talking about it, or we'll end up flattening a bed of crocuses."

"And flowers so beautiful shouldn't be spoiled. Perhaps I'll stop talking if you shut me up with a kiss or two."

They walked around for a time, then sat on a bench talking, touching, catching up, and remembering the last time they were at the Kew.

"Would you stay with me tonight? Cancel your room?"

"Oh yes, yes." Samantha felt her heart hammering at the thought of waking in Emerson's arms.

They remembered the last time in London when Emerson house-sat the luxury flat on the Thames. That time had been like walking on egg shells. Testing. Probing. Wondering. Now she would be in his flat. His home. She wanted to be in his heart as well. She wondered if he truly loved her or just her body? What a question.

Samantha liked Emerson's flat. Eclectic. She noted the painting she had seen last month, a painting Emerson had just purchased and couldn't bear to leave, even for the few days he had stayed in downtown London. The artist, Larry Smitherman lived in Austin.

Now, she saw another painting, surely of the same model, wrapped in a free-flowing white translucent shawl. The background colors were earthy and filmy, soft, dreamlike. Thick paint created great texture.

"Don't tell me you have another Smitherman. You are getting serious about him, aren't you?"

"Isn't it smashing? Took a bit out of my savings for this one. I really like it. I'll have to live on bread and water for awhile before I buy another."

For lunch Emerson prepared a garden salad, and chose a nice wine to go with it.

"We can drive directly to Langan's from here. I would like it a lot if we could sit exactly where we sat before."

"You are a romantic aren't you?" Samantha reached across the antique wooden table to pat his arm. Emerson put his hand on hers.

24

"I feel an animal drive returning. I hope that doesn't alarm you, but if it does, I'll head for a cold shower."

"What a coincidence," said Samantha. She looked straight into his eyes and gave his arm a hard squeeze. Love or lust, she knew her heart beat increased rapidly at the thought of bedding Emerson in his own bed. Maybe it would squeak. It did.

A couple of hours later, the Jaguar rumbled towards Piccadilly, and Langan's Brasserie. They did manage to get the same table where they'd eaten in January. The Venetian room was a perfect place for an intimate dinner.

Emerson lifted his glass.

"A toast to a woman who has ruined my life with indescribable desire and happiness."

"Hear, hear. Just change the gender and that can be my toast, too."

As dinner came to an end, they sat quietly with coffee and snifters of Mandarin Napoleon.

"I feel absolutely at peace with the entire world," Emerson said. "Do you remember what we talked about last month?"

"I think we were trying our best to be nice. As I recall we exchanged some of our globe trotting stories, didn't we?"

"Oh yes, I remember. I told you how I was killed and eaten in Borneo, and for you not to go there."

Samantha shook her head and suppressed a laugh.

"That was mean. I believed you were telling the truth, until you got to the last part. I felt like cooking you in a vat myself."

"Well, we've come a long way in a very short time. It seems like a miracle to me."

Samantha agreed and wondered in her heart if Emerson Jacque really would be her true love. At least he'd kept her interested so far. An understatement.

"So, what's the plan for tomorrow? Do I get to see you?"

"Of course, Christina Madalora is coming in. We're meeting for most of the day but she's flying out around six to get back to Rome. I'm all yours after that."

"Then, let's take the sleeper to Edinburgh. We can board the train from Euston Station and be in Edinburgh early in the morning, do some sight-seeing and have dinner at The Witchery. And guess what?"

"What?"

"A splendid B&B right above the restaurant. Very historical. Very posh. Very decadent. You'll love it Samantha."

"Well, we certainly wouldn't have far to go after dinner would we? Lets do it. We can come back to London the next day?"

"Indeed. Now let's go back to my flat."

"And your squeaky bed."

Chapter 6

Finding and keeping a good friend of the same sex is easier for women I think. –From Samantha's Journal

Christina Madalora arrived on the eight a.m. flight. Swathed in sweeping grays and blacks with calf–high boots and a bright red shoulder scarf, she could have stepped right off the modeling runway.

"Buongiorno, Samantha! Divine, you look most divine!"

"Buongiorno, Christina! You should be on the cover of a fashion magazine!"

Chattering in English and Italian, they brought each other up-to-date since they were last together in Florence and Rome in January. Christina said she worried "nearly out of my mind" when she learned Samantha lay buried in India. And then, "you were almost killed in New York, I must hear it again even though it is too scary for me to listen." Then, Christina held her at arm's length and peered at Samantha's leg.

"Earthquakes, buried, a man shooting, and you were limping on a hurt leg. I cannot believe it. Do you still limp my little cripple?" Samantha had almost forgotten the skiing accident in the French Alps where she gone to forget Emerson.

"No, no, Christina, it is entirely well. And you look lovely, like a fresh bloom. You bring high fashion to sodden England."

"And the man who brought you pain, did you kill him as he deserved?"

"You mean Emerson? I'm glad to report he is very much alive. And he had a good reason to leave me. If he hadn't gotten me out of that building when he did, I wouldn't be here talking to you now. We've definitely patched things up. I got in yesterday and we've been together ever since. And I'll be back with him tonight and we're going to Edinburgh. It is almost too much to bear."

"He's wearing you out. I know men have only one thing on their little minds. Tell him to let you rest. I will come beat him up and he will be sorry I am your friend."

Samantha shook her head and laughed. She tried to talk and had to laugh again.

"No, no, dear Christina. I'm the one wearing him out. All we do is make love. I can't believe I am so insatiable. If lust has anything to do with love, then I must be the most in-love person in the whole world. Yesterday at the Kew Gardens I wanted to throw him down in a bed of crocuses. If he ventures too close to a sofa, he's a goner."

Now it was Christina's turn to laugh.

"This, I can not believe it. A demon you have, I know it. A candle I light for you no, no, two candles and for you I pray. Also, I pray I don't meet such a man as Emerson. My poor body could not take it. You are a wonder." Christina squeezed Samantha to her.

Samantha knew the hurrying passengers must have wondered about the two attractive women standing in the terminal, seemingly on the verge of hysterics, gesturing wildly and hugging every few minutes.

At an airport bakery they filled up on pastries and coffee. That seemed to settle them, although one or the other would suddenly giggle and for a minute or two they would be helplessly out of control. Then, they talked about the new man in Christina's life.

"A tiny bit my Roberto is like Emerson, maybe."

"Watch it, I'd better start lighting candles for you. But wait, wasn't his name Rafael? What happened to Rafael?"

"His fat mamma. She I could not take. Into everything she poked her nose. Rafael, a mamma's boy, a child, how could I make love to a child, I ask you? Always he looked at his watch to be on time for his lunch with mamma. He is gone, gone out of my life like a poof! Roberto is much better, much better. Him I could marry, if ever I wanted to."

"And when that happens I'll be there no matter what the doctors at the nursing home say."

After the laughter subsided again, Samantha filled Christina in on why she was on her way to Greenland.

"I must try to find this Jason Murdoch and I just hope he can help me with some answers."

"Your uncle, is he not upset that you go to Greenland when it is so cold in the winter?"

"I didn't tell him, Christina. He thinks my trying to find the crash site in Honduras is dumb enough, and maybe it is. I haven't told Emerson about Greenland or Honduras, and I don't think I will. It's my business and not his. I don't want Emerson trying to talk me out of it."

"What about Ben? Do you still think of him as much and do you hurt still?"

"Yes, he is always present to me. And I don't want to let him go and I may never. He meant so much to me. He was so sweet and dear. He made dealing with eccentric buyers bearable. Real estate is getting to be a drag."

They had lunch in London and after a flurry of shopping it was back to Heathrow. The day was too short. They made plans for Christina to come to Texas for a visit soon.

Chapter 7

Sometimes it worries me I'm so obsessed with sex, but I'm not going to worry about it too much. –From Samantha's Journal

Christina boarded her plane for Rome. Samantha returned to her hotel for a brief nap and a quick shower.

Emerson had decided on Mark's Club for dinner, but changed his mind in favor of George, Mark Birley's newest restaurant.

"It's very 'in' but not so formal as his other restaurants. Great food naturally, good bartender and well lighted, and cheerful with huge windows, and a kitchen that's in full view."

"Is that good?"

"When the chef is Luca dal Bosco, it will be a treat."

The dinner was superb. The waitresses in long white aprons and black waistcoats, the fresh flowers, the profusion of art, all combined to make for a memorable evening.

"In Scotland we'll be in the land of Burns, Scott and Stevenson."

"Promise you won't let Burns rub off on you. As I recall, he had several affairs. He seemed to fall in love with anyone in a skirt."

"Yes, but he was honest about it. He was pure sensation, the people's poet. And don't worry. You're the only skirt I'm interested in."

Samantha and Emerson opted for the dark greenish blue 'nighterie,' a cozy place downstairs where they could sit close on a sofa, and listen to music until time to catch the Caledonian Sleeper. They could board by eleven get settled in their compartment, and arrive in Edinburgh early the next morning after a good night's sleep.

"We're not going to sleep all night, are we?" asked Samantha.

"Not if I can help it."

"I'll give you all the help you need." Samantha planned to be true to her word.

They awoke the next morning to snow on the ground.

"I just love Edinburgh. It's a magic place. I can hardly wait to wander along the Royal Mile."

Emerson yawned, grinned and began searching for his toiletry kit.

"Where do you get all your energy?"

"Come on sleepy head. Up and at 'em. You need a good Scottish breakfast," then she jumped up to beat Emerson to the small lavatory.

The day went by too fast. They began with the imposing Edinburgh castle sitting high above the city on its mount of volcanic rock. St. Margaret's chapel, the oldest structure in Edinburgh and built in 1090, proved to be the highlight of the day.

"This is so unbelievable that we're standing in a space over a thousand years old. I wonder what Austin will look like in a thousand years? Will there be any single building still standing?" Samantha took Emerson's arm.

After the castle, it was time to saunter down the Royal Mile. No one sat outdoors. Too cold.

"I like the cold. Do you, Emerson?"

"Well, if I lived in super-heated Texas, I'd probably enjoy a crisp breeze now and then."

"Hey, it gets cold in Texas, too. If you visit me in February, I'll take you to the Panhandle for a blizzard treat."

"Now you can understand why I like London. Gentle rains, just enough sun to really enjoy it, and no blizzards."

There it was. Although making a joke, Emerson would never move to the states. And Samantha could not move from Texas. How would they ever make the relationship work? Was she just kidding herself?

The moment passed. Samantha pulled Emerson into one of the many shops to look at tartans and bagpipes. Afterwards, they explored a narrow street known as a close.

"Let's stop in this book store. I wonder if they have anything

31

by Thomas De Quincey." The clerk pointed to a volume called Selections From De Quincey, published in 1901.

"Perfect. Just what I wanted. There's a piece in here where he describes the death of his sister that's heartbreaking."

"Is his Confessions of an English Opium Eater in there too?"

"Wait. Yes, here it is. What a stir that caused. Did you know he spent the latter part of his life in Edinburgh? Wrote for Blackwood's Magazine. So did Doyle. They just discovered a story Doyle wrote when he was eighteen and a medical student here in Edinburgh. Blackwood turned it down, but because Doyle had not included a stamp to have it returned it stayed in the magazine's files until this year, one hundred and twenty-five years later. The National Library is bringing it out the end of March. I certainly want to get a copy of that, too. Wait. Now I remember. The title was The Haunted Grange of Goresthorpe.

"Emerson, what an astounding memory you have. I remember reading the Hound of the Baskervilles. I'm still too afraid to walk out on the moors at night. I saw the movie, and I'll never forget that hound's howling. I feel a shiver even now, just thinking about it."

"Oh, look Samantha, here's Stevenson's The Strange Case of Dr. Jekyll and Mr. Hyde in an early edition. Guess I'd better get that too. Say, did you hear we've got sort of a Dr. Jekyll and Mr Hyde in England? Dr. Harold Shipman. They think he's murdered hundreds just for pleasure. Last year he was convicted of murdering 15 women over a span of three years. And talk about weird, he did it in a little town called Hyde. The media missed out by not nick-naming him Dr. Jekyll from Hyde or Hyde Hides in Hyde."

"Enough of this talk. Why are we drawn to tales of horror and murder? We are preoccupied with death and ghouls."

Suddenly Samantha realized she had been involved in several deaths recently. She shook her head.

"Let's get back outside and see what a neat place Edinburgh is." She grabbed Emerson's arm, and led him to join her in a skip along the snowy sidewalk.

"I think I'm in the middle of an old-fashioned picture post card at Christmas time." Emerson laughed.

"I expect you to start doing the Highland Fling at any moment. Yes, I know what you mean. And no more of the macabre, madam, I promise. Hey, I do believe it's almost time for dinner. Are you ready for a fine Scottish restaurant?"

"Ready and willing." That was a double entendre if ever she had heard one. Did Emerson catch it? Samantha thought she saw a smile.

They examined the menu in the Witchery.

"All of that bracing air has given me an excellent appetite and everything looks so good. I hardly know where to begin."

"Maybe we should offer each other a taste of everything including each other," said Emerson and grinned. So, he was playing the game.

Samantha finally decided on whiskey-cured salmon with caperberries and citrus dressing for an appetizer.

"I can't be in Edinburgh and not have a touch of Scotch whiskey."

They both chose the grilled fresh lobster and had two wonderful bottles of wine, plus a dessert liqueur to go with a warm dark chocolate torte with white chocolate sorbet. She realized she was smiling as they ordered. She knew she would end up with more chocolate later on.

"Enormously perfect," said Emerson.

"Perfectly enormous," replied Samantha, "but I enjoyed every bite. And to think, we have another sturdy Scottish breakfast to look forward to in the morning."

"Wait until you see where we are staying tonight, and thank heaven, it's only a few steps away."

The Old Rectory lived up to its billing—one of the most spectacular and indulgent suites in the world. Oak paneled and red fabric walls served as the backdrop for the lavishly draped bed created from an antique pulpit. Tall gilded bookcases flanked a marble fireplace. A separate sitting room featured trompe l'oeil draped walls. Samantha walked into the room as if she were on a tour.

"Oh look, Emerson there's a daybed for you, just in case I can't entice you into my pulpit."

"I'm enticed. Fear not my little one. And did you notice?

Another bottle of champagne. I may have to pass on that, or else I may be only good for snoring tonight."

"Then by all means, we'll keep it corked. Now, come here. I feel a need to have you kiss me. It's been hours."

Chapter 8

The better the sex the "worser" the fight! –From Samantha's Journal

Emerson and Samantha enjoyed breakfast in bed: hot scones with jam, fruit, granola with cream and lots of strong black coffee. They scattered crumbs on the huge unmade bed. If a dab of jam fell on a thigh, a chest, a knee, a willing mouth fell upon it immediately.

Waste not, want not, seemed to be the motto of the morning as each one kept the other scrupulously clean, no matter where the offending tidbits ended up, or how ticklish that spot turned out to be.

"This has been so perfect Emerson." Samantha laughed, then shrieked as Emerson dived into private territory for a grape.

She laughed again and tried to calm down for a second.

"You always come up with just the right thing to do. I never would have thought about coming to Edinburgh. I hate to have to go back today."

"Well, I was hoping you would feel that way. I have another surprise for you." Emerson tipped her over on her back and moved between her widening legs. He thoroughly searched her face with his lips then both sides of her throat, then down, down, kissing each breast and circling each pinkish brown bud with a demanding tongue until they stood upright, causing Samantha to squeal in mock protest.

"I'll give you until tomorrow morning to stop doing that."

"You had a crumb determined to escape. Wait, I think I see where it went." With that Emerson moved on down and kissed her deeply until her squeals became moans and the remodeled pulpit looked the other way. Afterwards, they lay comfortably, peacefully entwined.

"Samantha, by tomorrow morning we can be in another winter wonderland. Instead of going back to London today, I've got us tickets for the train to Inverness.   It's less than 200 kilometers. More snow and a great music festival await us. We can spend the week and go back to London next weekend. What do you say to that?" Samantha lay still.

"Oh Emerson, you know I would love to. But I can't.

Remember, I asked you if we would be going back today, while we were still in London, and you said yes?"

"I didn't think you were serious. But even if you were, what's the harm in taking off another week? Unless of course, you're getting tired of me." Heavily he moved away and sat on the edge of the bed.

"Emerson you know that isn't true. There's nobody in the world I would rather be with. I think I am falling in love with you."

"Well then, prove it. Go to Inverness. Shake up your schedule, for once. Put our relationship first, for once."

"That's not fair. And if there were any way I could take off another week, you know I would do it. Please let's not argue and spoil the time we've had together."

Emerson stormed into the bath. Samantha could hear him moving around, rummaging, showering. Should she tell him about Greenland? Why didn't she include him like she had Christina? She had already applied for and received permission to enter the U.S. air base at Thule, Pituffik, from the Danish Ministry of Foreign Affairs in Copenhagen. If she told Emerson he would try to talk her out of it or want to go along with her. The red tape involved would effectively cancel the trip.

Jason Murdoch, reportedly, was north of Qaanaaq somewhere around Siorapaluk, according to an official who knew him. It would be ticklish enough by herself to talk with Mr. Murdoch. Emerson's presence would not be a help.

Yes, it would be better to keep all this to herself. If Emerson couldn't handle it, so be it. She felt empty inside. Why did life have to be so difficult? Was she deliberately driving a wedge between them? Was her self-determination that important? At that moment she had to admit, it was.

The bathroom door opened and Emerson walked toward the bed where Samantha still lay.

"O.K., O.K., I'm sorry for hitting you with a change without talking it over. I just made the plans on impulse. A bad habit for a bachelor. Am I forgiven?"

"Yes, of course Emerson, and I'm sorry I seemed so obstinate."

"So, how about a compromise? We can fly to Inverness and then fly back to London on Monday. Surely, a weekend won't make that much difference in your plans, whatever they are."

A moment heavy with silence passed.

"I'm so sorry Emerson, I can't do that. I must return today. My reservations are set. I must keep the schedule."

"Haven't you heard of changing schedules? What could be so important that a couple of days would hurt? What could you possibly be doing on a week-end that would be so iron-clad?"

"I'm sorry, Emerson, I can't tell you."

"You mean you won't."

"All right then, I won't. It's something I have to do and I can't tell you about it now. I don't want to argue about it. I have to go back to London today. Everything I have planned to do including an important Central America trip hinges on the next few days."

"So what I hear is, you can't bloody well trust me."

"I think you would interfere and cause a hassle which I don't want, and can't stand right now."

"Well fine! I'll make sure I don't interfere. I'm going on to Inverness and you can go bloody anywhere in hell you want."

Emerson dressed rapidly, and threw stuff in his bag without saying another word. Samantha did not move. Crumbs and small splotches of jam, the fun props just a short time ago, were now just plain messy. She could not believe this scene. Like a bad movie. A soap opera. Emerson deserting her again, and this time, the disappearance would not be mysterious.

A hard ball began forming in her stomach and worked its way into her throat. She could not say anything. She watched him go. The door slammed shut. Suddenly, the room seemed unbearably overdone, cheap, and tasteless.

Chapter 9

Cold feet can take one's mind off a hurt heart. –From Samantha's Journal

Samantha tried to connect her mind to her body. In a few minutes, she would be landing at Pituffik, also known as Thule.

She could not believe the parting with Emerson had generated so much anger and despair. Anger for him, and despair for her. How could a relationship so sexually and intellectually exciting, so fulfilling and perfect, crumble so completely? Ever since they had made love that night in Janurary, life had imitated a ride on the world's most hellish roller coaster. She was up, down, and inside out, all at the same time. The flights getting to Greenland had been somewhat distracting, but a heaviness had refused to leave her heart.

The plane began its descent north of the Arctic Circle. Samantha saw large aircraft hangers, giant service buildings, and flat-topped buildings, presumably for personnel. A few pickup trucks crawled slowly along the grid-patterned streets. At one time, during the "stand-off" years with Russia, 16,000 persons called "Toolie" home. Six hundred and fifty remained by 2001, and the civilian support greatly outnumbered the military staff.

If President Bush succeeded in getting his defense shield program through Congress, the base would get a new influx of equipment and personnel.

Snow covered most of the ground and where it didn't, the dark barren earth showed its face. No trees. No bushes. The pristine and permanent ice cap, that encased most of Greenland, could be seen beyond a ridge she recognized from her research. An ice cliff jutted up east of the air base. The ice and packed snow extended north and south the length of the land. It sat so heavily on the land, it caused Greenland to be sway-backed, not something you could see, because the ice had grown into a great dome thousands of feet thick.

It had taken almost three days to reach Pituffik. Samantha would spend a night in the guest house before the helicopter ride farther north to the village of Qaanaaq, a quick ride, unless a storm blew up. Winds could reach over 100 mph in a matter of minutes and last for days. If that happened, she would have to wait until they died down, before going on.

As the plane touched down at Pituffik, Samantha felt invigorated. Soon, she would be close to some answers about her dad's crash. Murdoch would be cooperative. She knew he would. She was totally confident. She would sort out Emerson later. This last thought immediately brought a heavy gloom into her heart.

She gave in to the blackness for a time. Emerson had not been unreasonable. She was the unbending one. If he still hung around after all this was over, and if they could get back together again, it would mean they were surely meant for each other, although Samantha did not believe in an unalterable destiny. "Humans can decide some endings," she said out loud as the plane rolled to a stop. Emerson returned to the back burner of her mind with orders to stay put, though she doubted he would obey. She expected a visit from Ben, too, from time to time. She must remain strong, she must.

After a night in the guest house, and friendly welcomes from everyone she met, Samantha got stuffed with a tasty breakfast: pancakes, eggs, and bacon. Her new friends coached her how to grab a bite of mattak (whale skin)in her teeth, then saw it off from the main hunk with a sharp knife.

"Just think of chewy non-fat cheese." It helped prevent scurvy, she was told. She could do without scurvy, so she sawed away to the sound of laughter and yells of support.

She was questioned about her plans, and offered comments, not always backed by scientific investigation. She enjoyed the conversation immensely. It took her mind off Murdoch and Emerson and Ben. Although everyone agreed it was a broadening experience being in the north, they were eager to return to the states or Denmark.

None of them could understand why anyone would voluntarily fly to the air base at Pituffik. And where else? To Qaanaaq? To Siorapaluk? By dog sledge? Eight hundred miles north of the Arctic Circle? They couldn't believe it. These were places to the north they had never been to and barely heard of. Stories of stranded travelers, tales of blizzards, frozen hands, feet, faces, and noses proliferated as Samantha downed two more pancakes.

"Here, we have ropes between buildings so we won't get disoriented in a white-out. Up there, you'll just get lost and we'll find your body next summer, still frozen." "Unless a polar bear finds you first," added another wide-eyed youth. "And the Inuit won't lift a finger to help; it's every person for himself–er–herself."

"They'll probably want to marry you, then lend you out to strangers who enter your hut at night." "You'll fall victim to Fata Morgana, see a city big as life, just out on the ice a ways and you'll try to walk to it, or you'll see a big ship, or a forest of fantastically green trees...." "And don't forget Big Eye, when you can't tell what time it is, and you forget to go to sleep, and your eyes get big and bulgy."

Each speaker of doom tried to outdo the last one. It got to be funny, and soon, as gruesome as the tales had become, everyone began laughing. They all could see Samantha had not been swayed from her task. As a matter of fact, she seemed delighted with the stories.

The darkness gave way to the rising sun. Samantha watched transfixed. It looked like a huge flame of fire with a yellow center, surrounded by several shades of red, and framed in a graceful sheath of violet and purple. A most extraordinary and magical sight. It reminded her of the gigantic dome of an old world mosque, or a giant tulip blooming in all its glory. It would rest just above the ice for a brief time, slide a bit along the horizon and sink again until the next day.

Her table mates wished her well and shook her hand and gave her a hug. Then it was time to leave. The helicopter crew loaded her aboard and by late-morning in twilight, the copter whisked her away north to Qaanaaq.

Her final destination would put her only a few hundred miles from the North Pole. Perhaps, she should go on like the early explorers, and plant a flag or something.

Dashing from the helicopter after it squatted on a cloud of whirling snow and dust near the village of Qaanaaq, Samantha felt the knife-like cold, puncturing her clothing. And yet, because of the extreme dryness, it only seemed a bit below freezing, instead of 25 below zero. She shivered, nevertheless, and immediately went to her little red hotel, where she received another friendly welcome.

No tourists had shown up yet, so she had the pick of the rooms. And since no one else would probably check in, the bathroom would be hers alone. Tourists who did venture that far north, generally waited until July and August, just in time to watch the ice break up, and see the sculpted icebergs slowly drifting in the bay.

The brief summer of continuous sunshine night and day, with temperatures a respectable distance from freezing, could be described as a thrilling experience. Too, this far north and with the dry atmosphere, the mosquitos would be few. A definite plus. The hotel manager finished the lecture and urged her to come back during the official tourist season.

This said, the first days of March the temperature would be on the wrong side of zero. She might have reconsidered her schedule, once she learned that March could have the coldest weather of the year. But it was too late to worry about that now. At least, the sun would be making brief appearances each day, although not as much as at the air base she had just left.

Once situated, she inquired about the man who would take her by sledge north to the hunting camps. Surprise! It would be a woman. Aisa Avaalaaqiaq, already going to Siorapaluk, would take Samantha with her. Samantha liked her immediately although she didn't look anything like what Samantha expected.

"And the reason I don't look like an Inuk is because I'm not one. Before I married, I was Aisa Watson. I was born and grew up in Alaska. My husband, Philip, belongs to the Inuit. He too, was born in Alaska. We met at the University of Minnesota. So, you want to live the life of an Inuk for a few days? And please, call me Aisa, it's a lot easier to pronounce than Avaalaaqiaq." She smiled, showing bright white teeth. Lively blue eyes flashed, framed by golden hair, half-hidden behind a white cowl of Arctic fox. A long, wool parka opened slightly revealing hip-high seal-skin boots. There were other layers of fabric, probably wool, and another animal skin, caribou, Samantha guessed, beneath the decorated parka.

"I'm Samantha, and I'm so happy I get to go north with you. What gorgeous clothes. Are you going to dress me like that, too? I hope so. What a treat."

That seemed to please Aisa. She smiled broadly and extended a hand.

"Yes, of course, and I am happy you like the way they look. Your clothes from the outfitter are outside on the sledge. Give me a minute, and I'll bring everything in, and we'll have a style show." Through the window, Samantha counted 15 dogs unhitched from the sledge, but secured close by. Alert even at rest, the dogs waited with their own northern clothes: thick fur and bushy tails. Tourists were warned not to pet those magnificent animals.

A sledge dog in Greenland was more wolf than dog, and it took a strong driver to control a team. She read that dogs outnumbered people in Qaanaaq. Instead of an SUV parked in the driveway, a sledge and a bunch of dogs chained up nearby greeted neighbors, although now, most of the dogs were away pulling sledges on the ice field, hunting. Aisa came through the door and dumped an exotic pile of clothing on Samantha's bed.

"Try these on and if they all fit we'll jump on the sledge and go for a ride, so you can see how it will be. Does the cold bother you?"

"I did suffer some frost bite as a child, and my feet sometimes feel it, but all in all I think I can stand it. I promise not to complain, until I turn into an ice cube."

"There's no need to suffer if you don't have to. The Inuit are famous for suffering, and in the old days, the more suffering the better, but see what I have for you. Battery packs. We'll slip them into your boots. If your feet start going numb, you can turn them on. You might want to run with the sledge to increase circulation, but I'll have to make sure your breathing is protected and warmed or else you'll freeze your lungs trying to heat up your feet."

"There is so much to learn, but you have a very willing pupil, Aisa." Samantha pointed to a bundle she had gotten in Copenhagen.

"I bought this sleeping bag. I hope you approve." Aisa felt the bag and looked at the specifications.

"Perfect. Excellent product. You'll be warm as toast."

"Great. That's just what the clerk said." Samantha finished putting on what Aisa had brought in.

"These skins feel really warm. I thought the fox fur would be fluffy, but it's kind of stringy."

"That makes it even better. So out the door and into the wilds of Greenland, Samantha."

The ride was exhilarating. Samantha did not feel the cold at all. They didn't stay out all that long, but she felt at ease about going to Siorapaluk, and relished the prospect of an exciting adventure. Everything else slipped out of her mind, but thoughts of the next day's journey.

Chapter 10

Dogs pee in the snow and the sun looks like a giant multi-colored tulip. Food for thought. Sort of...neat. –From Samantha's Journal

Early in the morning, under the light of the stars, and the reflected light from the snow, Aisa and Samantha set out toward Siorapaluk, about 60 miles north. Samantha sat on the floor of the sledge where Aisa placed a seal skin, fur side up, and a dog skin for added warmth. Samantha fastened her goggles snug against her face mask. It was 25 degrees below zero. Surprisingly she did not feel uncomfortably cold, at least not yet. Aisa stood at the back, on the base transverse bar, grasping the oak stanchion of the sledge. The sledge was loaded with supplies for Aisa's husband in Siorapaluk, who had his own team and sledge there.

Aisa said the fastest way to get to Siorapaluk would be over the ice field, the frozen ocean. They would begin at the mouth of Inglefield Fjord, run between the shore and Herbert Island on Murchinson Sound, and reach Siorapaluk by entering Robertson Fjord.

The ice was firm enough to travel on and the weather reports promised good weather. Cold. At least 20 to 30 degrees or so below zero. Normal, for the first days of March. Even so, Aisa would watch for sudden storms and breaking ice. Usually the open ocean, or the ice edge, as it was called, would be several miles farther west. Hummocks near shore, caused by wave action, could slow them down, if they got too close to land.

Whether those jagged accumulations would be a problem near Siorapaluk, depended on the weather. Usually, the dogs would clamor over them, a truly remarkable feat of strength and will,

Aisa said.

"I hope it will stay calm all the way there and back." If things went well, Samantha would come back with Aisa's husband within a week. If things didn't work out, then Samantha would return the next day, after Aisa unloaded her supplies, and had spent a few hours with her husband.

For now, the trip seemed totally magical to Samantha.

The dogs fanned out in front, each dog pulled against its own twenty-foot seal thong trace fastened at the front of the sledge. A lead dog bounded slightly in front of the fan. Aisa used the whip to signal the dogs to begin, and shouted Aak! Aak!, which meant Forward! Then she shouted Assut!, which meant fast. But, the shaggy dogs needed no urging. The sledge slipped over the ice and snow with a swishing, and sometimes, grating sound as smooth ice alternated with rough.

At times, the sledge bumped on a slight pressure ridge, but mostly, it glided on flat ice. The dogs waved their tails in delight, and pulled as if this were the most important task in the world. Samantha could hear some dogs back in Qaanaaq, barking and howling, undoubtedly unhappy at being denied this adventure.

If the ice remained smooth enough, they could make the journey in one long day. Midway, the sun would appear for a very short time to the south, behind them, then move briefly just above the horizon. Each day it would rise a bit higher and stay a little longer, until it would stay up all day and all night. Until then, the rest of the day and night would be in darkness.

Samantha longed to see the Aurora Borealis with its undulating curtains of pink and green, but that might not take place for several more months. For now, she would content herself with the low hanging red-purple sun, and the glittering starlight bouncing off the ice. Not a bad trade-off.

The sun's colors were like her impressions when she touched the animal skins: Red-purple. Like blood.

The creak of the sledge as its leather bindings adjusted to the surface of ice, the white fog that drifted toward her, formed by the breath of the dog team, the stars and the ghostly light from the ice, all mesmerized her. She seemed to inhabit a deeper world.

She saw dark splotches on the ice. Dog excrement. The sharp smell of urine snapped her senses to attention. The team discarded that which it no longer needed. Was she carrying baggage that no longer had meaning? Why could she not let go of her dad's death? Would it haunt her all her life? No, it wouldn't, because she would find out what had happened. She would find the truth.

"I owe you that much dad," she murmured to herself beneath the woolen face mask.

Jason Murdoch would help her find the answers. Samantha revisited some troubling thoughts about her dad's plane diving into the jungle. Did it catch fire? Did he suffer? She could not accept the recurring vision of her dad running out of fuel. The crash site remained unexamined. Why? Too hard to reach, and, if found, what difference would it make?

Samantha could not believe the insensitivity and incompetency of the oil company executives. She had sought answers through channels. Her uncle had helped.

She had tried to put it to rest to get on with her life, but she had failed. Each month brought fresh pain. At last she could stand it no longer. She had to find answers. She remembered how Ben's death had been ignored, hushed up. She had found the answers, or at least some of them. The accident had become murder. It had nearly cost her life, but she had persevered. She learned never to give up no matter how tough things became. She would find the truth about her dad, and heaven help those who might stand in her way.

––––––––––––

Samantha moved her toes inside the seal skin boots. Not cold. Amazing. At 25 degrees or so below zero, she felt comfortable, cool yes, but quite comfortable. Alaskans and Greenlanders knew how to face the unforgiving north. Perhaps she should jump off and run with the sledge. No, she would save that for another time.

She leaned back for a better view of the stars, a brilliant can-

opy. The stars offered no advice. They just were. Neither
friend nor foe, but she counted them as friends anyway. They
were her stars or anyone's who wanted them. Despite her worries
it was a glorious night. Or maybe, it was still day.

Chapter 11

Defrosting a bite of frozen seal on my tongue...a gourmet delight. –From Samantha's Journal

Time stood still. The landscape, or rather the seascape, reached to the horizon on her left. To her right she could make out the bluffs and bald hills on the shore. Samantha could understand the melancholy that might seize a person traveling for hours in such a place. The dogs had ceased their barking long ago, and she heard only the scraping of the sledge, and the panting breaths that turned to fog from those amazing animals, pulling, pulling, hour after hour.

The ice had settled down a little. The gentle, but powerful wave action had created a rising and falling motion for most of the trip, almost lulling her to sleep at times. In years past, Aisa had said, the ice would be four feet thick this time of year.

The last few years, the ice had thinned and one had to watch carefully lest a patch of open ocean suddenly appeared. The sledge drivers depended on their dogs to smell the openings long before the dark waters were visible.

The knowledge that hundreds or thousands of feet of cold black ocean was under the ice had made Samantha anxious at first. Aisa had calmed her fears saying that it was still quite safe, if one were careful. That helped a little.

Shaking her out of her reverie, Samantha felt the grinding brake on the ice and the quiet but firm command to stop. For a moment or two, the powerful dogs continued to lunge ahead as the sledge dug into the ice. Finally they stopped and looked around at Aisa. She signaled them to rest, and immediately they curled into balls of fur. Tails curved around covering eyes and noses. It was supremely quiet.

"We are close to entering Robertson's Fjord, and we will soon be seen by the settlement." Samantha stretched and lifted her goggles. She squinted as the cold dry air hit her eyes. Aisa laughed.

"We want to make a grand entrance. The Inuit usually don't make a big fuss about arrivals, and sometimes one feels ignored, but make no mistake, everyone is secretly excited. All eyes will be on us as we approach. I want the dogs to be rested so we can zoom in at good speed. It will be all the harder for them to ignore us, but they'll still try.

"If Philip is there, he will be shaking his head, but I will say to him, if he had wanted a demure wife, he should have married an Inuk." She laughed again. Samantha liked this woman a lot.

"Climb off the sledge and jump up and down for awhile. How about a piece of frozen seal?" Again the laugh, even as Samantha felt her nose wrinkling beneath her face mask.

"If you stay here long enough in the cold you will eat more meat, especially seal, even preferring it to be over the hill, so to speak. The stronger the taste, the more you will crave it. You don't believe me do you?" Aisa's smile got wider and wider and her blue eyes danced. Samantha held out a gloved hand.

"O.K., O.K. give me a chunk of seal. If you can eat it, so can I." Aisa handed Samantha a small bit of the frozen pinkish meat.

"Hold it in your mouth until it defrosts, then bon appétit." Samantha lifted her mask and popped the frozen morsel in her mouth and moved it about to keep from freezing her tongue. They both laughed, Samantha at her ridiculous show of courage, and Aisa at the expressions that were obviously playing across Samantha's eyes.

"Ah, good, excellent. Soon you will be able to taste the true delicacy of the North."

"And what would that be?"

"Kiviaq."

"Kiviaq?"

"Each spring, the hunters go to the cliffs where millions of cute little auks nest. The birds are caught in nets as they swoop around. Once the hunter has caught say, 500 or so, he stuffs them into a sealskin bag which still has considerable fat left on the hide. The birds are not cleaned, nor plucked. The bag is sewn up and placed under rocks. The fat melts into the birds as the birds rot in the summer sunlight."

"Stop, stop, you are making me sick. Surely you don't think I could believe such a thing. You are really weird, Aisa." Samantha began jumping up and down and turning circles as though she were possessed. Aisa smiled.

"All right, all right, have your fun, but you may be offered one of those snacks. It's the favorite food to offer guests. Just tug on the little legs and the bird slides right out of its feathers, sort of a mousse consistency. Just think over-ripe fetid Limburger or Camembert and you have kiviaq. Samantha noted how much Aisa enjoyed teasing her.

"So, have you eaten kiviaq, without throwing up, that is?"

"Of course, that's why I told you about it," and Aisa smiled broadly showing her strong white teeth in the darkness. So, had she or had she not? Samantha laughed, not caring, but knowing kiviaq would never get behind her own teeth.

"And now, since you have chewed up your seal treat, climb back on, and we'll show the settlement how a real dog team enters a village."

The dogs jumped up eager to run again. The sledge jerked to the right and to the left to break the runners from the ice, then "Aak! Aak! Assut! Assut!" The dogs leaped and the sledge sped across the smooth ice of Robertson's Fjord. What a way to travel!

Soon, the settlement of Siorapaluk appeared against a barren and somber series of hills. The small cabins nestled on the edge of the frozen bay. Small figures ran about, pointing. As she watched, Samantha noticed the figures trying to slow down, trying to contain their excitement. They had a tough time hiding their glee.

Samantha wondered if Aisa's husband would be there. And maybe, Jason Murdoch. Briefly, Emerson's face popped into her mind wearing a very angry look. That was followed by an overwhelming desire for a crisp red McIntosh apple, or a tart Winesap, or a Golden Delicious.

She wondered if any of those people, standing in groups on the shore, had ever tasted a luscious Golden Delicious. As soon as possible, Samantha would devour a whole basket of apples. She wanted a mug of hot chocolate with whipped cream on top. Two mugs. Emerson's face came back, this time, with a knowing grin.

The sledge ground to a stop in front of the community building, which was set on pilings with wooden steps leading to the front door. Aisa Avaalaaqiaq and Samantha Callendar King had arrived! Just don't pass the kiviaq please.

There were only 50 to 80 inhabitants, and maybe 15 buildings. If Siorapaluk were anything like Qaanaaq, the buildings would be dark red, blue, green or yellow, quite colorful. Samantha was sorry the sun was not up.

"Picturesque, but don't count on any amenities, except some electricity. No TV, no cars, no ATVs, no snowmobiles, no supermarkets, gravel paths instead of roads, and used for walking and sledging," Aisa had said.

"Welcome to the most northern natural community in the world. The North Pole is only a few hundred miles away."

Samantha struggled off the sledge and removed her goggles and face mask. The frigid air buffeted her skin, but she wanted to give the people crowding around a chance to see she was a human being. Several smiled, gestured, and talked in a language Samantha supposed was Greenlandic. She caught a few Danish words, and remembered how to say hello in Danish.

Immediately, there were hundreds of unintelligible, but friendly sounding syllables thrown at her. She laughed and waved. Turning, she saw Aisa talking with a man dressed in bearskin pants, heavy boots, and parka; his dark face framed in white fox fur. Surely not Philip. Aisa faced Samantha.

"This fellow will see to our dogs for now and I'll come back to feed them in a few minutes. Lets carry some of our stuff in and get out of the cold."

Samantha needed no urging, glad the swarthy guy wasn't Philip. Grabbing up some of the bags, she pounded up the steps. The large room seemed warm. At least, it was above freezing. She smiled at herself for thinking anything slightly above freezing could be considered comfortable.

51

One more trip to the sledge and everything, except the supplies for Philip, were piled up inside. Aisa left to feed the dogs and to make sure the chains kept them safe from other sledges. Dogs would eat the bindings on blood-soaked sledges that had hauled freshly killed seal.

Curious, Samantha followed Aisa to watch her feed the team. Aisa chopped up frozen seal into chunks that the dogs could swallow without chewing, then tossed the choicest chunk to her lead dog and on down the hierarchy as the dogs watched.

A miscalculation as to which dog came next in the feeding chain could undermine the driver's credibility in the eyes of the team. Some dogs had a hard time swallowing the frozen seal, jerking their heads sharply to get the piece to slide down their throats.

Once in their stomachs, the seal meat would defrost and then be digested. One heavy feeding of frozen seal could satisfy a dog's hunger for up to two days if need be. With full bellies, the dogs curled up with their tails over their eyes and noses. It was time for a long nap.

Back inside, Aisa remarked that this was the first time she had been to the community building.

"I stay with Philip at his hunting cabin, but even so, I know this will be a very busy place shortly." She went on to explain the tradition of visiting, done more often in the cold and dark months. She told Samantha to expect a bunch of women and children to descend upon them soon, and that they had better hurry and prepare some food and tea, since eating and drinking always went with visiting.

"Most of the men are out hunting and fishing, and the women are starved for something new. And my dear, we are definitely something new." Tourists wouldn't be arriving until May at the earliest, and probably not until June or July.

"So we are the show. Prepare yourself for the onslaught. Actually, the women are quite nice, though you won't understand a word they say."

Samantha and Aisa set out various snacks, and put some water on to boil for tea. Half an hour later, the women and children began arriving. The women seated themselves on the chairs, talking and smiling. The children ran about casting glances at the newcomers, hiding behind their mothers, peeking shyly at Samantha and Aisa.

Aisa knew the dialect well enough to answer questions and describe the trip and the weather on the way. The women made many favorable comments about the visitors, and continued smiling and nodding their heads, as they helped themselves to the snacks and drank the tea. They left as suddenly as they had come. Aisa said the evening would be discussed for years.

"I'm staying here with you until Philip arrives. The man who helped me with the dogs said Philip would be coming in today. I can hardly wait for you to meet him. You will see why I am so much in love with him. His whole life is involved with these people, his people, in Alaska, Canada and Greenland, even Siberia.

He wants to do everything he can to guard the old traditions and at the same time bring the Inuit into the modern world. A big job, and he's much appreciated by all who know him."

"Well, if he is loved by you as much as you say, I will certainly look forward to shake his hand and congratulate him on finding you."

Aisa laughed and shook her head. Samantha liked her very much and felt they were becoming like sisters.

"We'll hang some skins on the chairs and make a small private room for you and your sleeping bag. You need not be concerned about anyone surprising you in the middle of the night. These are very honorable people, and if someone does come in, you will not be disturbed."

Later, the dogs began barking, which meant another dog team was arriving. Aisa put on her parka and pulled on her seal skin boots. She smiled at Samantha, and rushed out the door.

The blast of cold made Samantha realize how comfortable the room had become. When the door opened again, in swept Aisa and a dark young man covered in skins and gorgeous furs. He flashed a white-toothed smile and stamped his feet. Aisa was glowing. This would be Philip.

He was taller than most Inuit and quite handsome with blue-black hair, and a smooth, but frost-bitten face. Aisa waited impatiently, while he adjusted to the warmth of the room.

Seeing Samantha had been a surprise to Philip who learned about her only a few minutes earlier, as Aisa yelled the news to him above the barking dogs.

"I had no idea what she was talking about. I half-expected to see a skinned walrus in here."

Samantha noticed how easily and lovingly he touched Aisa, and how just as lovingly, she touched him in return. True love. She squirmed, as Emerson's face came back into her mind. Would he be her true love someday, she wondered? Probably not, if she continued acting like she had in Edinburgh.

They sat in chairs around the small stove to stay warm.

"So, you have come all this way to talk with Jason Murdoch," said Philip. "I hope you get the information you need from him. I get along fine with him, but then I never ask him anything. My feeling is that he doesn't want to talk of the past much. Actually, I know nothing about his past, but I can attest to his concern for my people and the passing of the old ways.

He's out there hunting and fishing now for the village. He never complains of the cold. Totally dedicated. A hard worker. No task is impossible for him, especially if he thinks some Inuit family might go hungry without his help. He'll be coming in tomorrow morning, bringing a load of seal and fish, then I think he plans to go back out as soon as possible to hunt walrus at the ice edge. You won't have a lot of time with him, if he'll visit with you at all. I wish you all the luck left in the North."

Samantha sat quietly, fully expecting this news about Jason Murdoch. She hated hearing it just the same.

"Thank you, Philip. Even my uncle back in Texas said Mr. Murdoch wouldn't want to talk, but I just can't accept that he won't help me resolve the death of my dad. Surely, he knows something that will help me put this behind me. I'll do my best to persuade him. If luck will help, I'll count on that, too."

It had been a long day. Aisa had planned to leave tomorrow, but hoped to spend one more day with Philip. Samantha would leave with Aisa, or later with Philip, depending on how cooperative Jason Murdoch turned out to be. Now, she could see that the young lovers wanted to be by themselves. They said their good-byes and headed for Philip's small cabin. Small, but cozy, she supposed, and just right for two people in love.

Chapter 12

If I could vote for the perfect couple it would be Aisa and Philip, hands down. –From Samantha's Journal

Dawn without the sun. No sunrise for several hours. When the sun did peek over the southern horizon, it would stay up a few minutes longer than it had the day before. Samantha waited eagerly each day for its appearance. She wondered how on earth these people could go for four straight months without seeing sunlight at all.

Indeed, Aisa had told her yesterday of polar hysteria. The Inuit word: perlerorneq. It affected women and men, although women were more likely to come down with it. It was described as the "weight of life," and also as being "sick of life." To Samantha it was like Kierkegaard's concept of ultimate despair which he called "the sickness unto death."

At any rate, it generally came upon younger people, but spared the very young, and the very old. There were stories, Aisa said, of women half-naked, grabbing a knife, slashing clothing, eating dog excrement, screaming, running onto ice floes, fighting anyone who tried to restrain them, possessed of tremendous strength, and finally collapsing from exhaustion. After a long sleep, they would awaken with no memory of the incident. Samantha could certainly understand such an outburst, when faced with several months of polar darkness, and the utter boredom of the long winter night.

During this period, "visiting" ranked right up there with spring or summer. A visit with the neighbors broke up the tedium. The retelling of old stories, eating in each other's homes, helped people get through the hours. In the polar night, people would visit neighbors three or four times in a single day, including the times they hosted others in their own homes.

Sometimes, nobody said anything and the visit lasted only a few minutes, perhaps one morsel of seal meat was eaten, and a small cup of tea sipped, then the visitor would leave for the next cabin, where the ritual would be repeated. Sort of an on-line chat room, often without chat.

At other times, someone might relate the story of a hunt, or an experience of unusual weather. No detail escaped scrutiny, no matter how trivial.

"It's a wonder to me that the whole village doesn't go mad," said Samantha, when Aisa had finished.

For maybe the tenth time, Samantha peered out the windows into the darkness, as if by doing so, she could will the darkness away. No such luck. Mother Nature would not be hurried.

She prepared cereal, using dry milk mixed with water, and brewed a pot of coffee, which helped her mood a lot. And she waited. A loud knock then a shout. Samantha recognized Aisa's voice. She sounded frozen.

"Are you up? Are you decent? May we come in?"

Samantha rushed to the door, on the verge of "polar hysteria."

Aisa and Philip breathed deeply of the coffee aroma that filled the room. Aisa headed for the stove, casting off her gloves and rubbing her hands together.

"Brrr, it's really cold today. That coffee smells divine."

Samantha poured two cups, handed them to her new friends and joined them close to the stove. Aisa and Philip made the appropriate noises of contentment. Samantha watched them and liked what she saw. She wanted to find out more about Philip and Aisa. Why were they here in Greenland? What were their plans?

Aisa laughed. "You will regret your curiosity. Philip is always ready to sow seeds and let loose his dreams on anyone who shows the slightest interest, so I shall defer to him. Don't say I didn't warn you. I myself have become a victim of his charms and now you, Samantha, are in grave danger of an Inuit conversion.

Philip's face was the reasonable facsimile of the rising sun. Samantha had seldom seen anyone with such animation and barely controlled energy.

Time seemed to stand still as Phillip explained how he felt driven to invest his life working with the Inuit.

Philip wanted to do his part in voicing the concerns of the Inuit to the world. To do that, he involved himself politically in Inuit affairs.

"There is so much to do and I feel there is so little time. I feel guilty when I take time to hunt and fish and raise dogs for races. Just last month the President of the Canadian Circumpolar Conference spoke at the U.N. about POPs in the polar environment and the danger they pose for the whole world."

"POPs?" Samantha had not heard the term before.

"Means Persistent Organic Pollutants. We're finding that because of the high meat content diet of the Inuit, these pollutants are sweeping northward and showing up in great concentrations in the mammals and fish.

The Inuit eat the contaminated meat and pass the contaminants on to their children through women's breast milk. The incidence of cancer is rising. This is a wake-up call to the rest of the world.

What is happening in the north, will be happening everywhere, unless we take steps now to reduce the spread of POPs. I hope to get a copy of the speech she made in January in New York."

"She?"

"Yes, her name is Sheila Watt-Cloutier. Besides being president of the Canadian Conference, she is vice-President of the world Inuit Cicumpolar Conference. That'll be held in Ottawa next year. Aisa and I plan to go."

"There should be at least two Philips to get everything done that he wants," chimed Aisa, looking at her husband with admiration and love. Samantha thought it would be marvelous to love like that.

"Aisa and I want to run the Iditarod in Alaska in a year or two. We are raising our dog teams. Another reason we're up here is to experience the way the Greenland teams work, which is quite different from how the teams work back home."

Samantha looked puzzled.

"The Iditarod is a race with dog sleds from Anchorage to

Nome. Twelve hundred miles of the most dramatic wilderness you can imagine. Philip and I may have to flip a coin to see who takes the team."

"We may have to hit the trail with two teams. I can't imagine either one of us not racing," said Philip, playfully tapping Aisa on the shoulder. Aisa jumped into his lap and they both landed on the floor.

"Promise? Two teams! I've got a witness. Hear that Samantha?" They rolled on the floor laughing and punching each other. Samantha wouldn't have minded rolling on the floor with someone like Philip.

The morning went by quickly, as they exchanged dreams and plans. Samantha told them more about her dad's crash in Honduras, and how she hoped Jason Murdoch would not be as secretive as Philip reported. Then, they ran to the window as the south began turning red.

"The sun is coming up," they chanted, sounding more like excited children than well-educated adults.

"Let's bundle up and go out," exclaimed Samantha. Outside they jumped up and down at the sight of the sun bathing them, and the fjord, and the hills behind them, in rose and gold.

"What a fantastic sight."

"Awesome."

Eager for a walk, the trio set off for the Lutheran Church. Clouds of steam puffed in the still air as they talked and laughed.

They were delighted to find the building unlocked and went inside to look at the small chapel. The walls and ceiling were painted white. At the front, a baptistry and white altar. To one side, the pulpit. Overhead, a series of white globes lighted the aisle. The wood pews on either side of the aisle could each seat three people. By adding a chair at the end of each pew, the chapel could hold about forty worshipers.

Philip explained that every village had a National Evangelical Lutheran Church, the state church of Denmark. He knew everything about Greenland, Samantha decided.

Sure enough, Philip regaled them with Greenland history on the way back to the community building.

"Largest island in the world. Gross GDP, one billion USD.

Fifty-five thousand population, eighty percent Inuit. Ninety-eight percent literacy rate. Great literary tradition. West Greenlandic is the official language. I wish it could spread throughout the world's Inuits. Still a lot of fishing and hunting, but tourism is gaining. Home rule since 1979. And of course, there is a darker side, but I won't go into that."

"Philip, you are a walking encyclopedia," Aisa teased.

"O.K. O.K., I can take a hint, so let's talk about something else. Samantha, if I gave you a compass, would you be able to find the North Pole?"

"Be careful, Samantha, up here things are not as they seem," said Aisa, with a watch-out smile.

"All right, I'll bite. I would turn the compass until N aligned with the pointing needle, like I was taught in school, so what could be easier than that?"

"Well, if you did that you would never make it to the North Pole," smiled Philip, his eyes grinning too.

"The needle of the compass points to the magnetic north pole and not the geographic North Pole, and if you are far enough south, say in Texas, it would make no difference, but up here, the magnetic north pole is due west of us and the geographic North Pole is at a right angle to it. So if you lined N up with the needle you would really be pointing west and the true north would be the E. So if you wanted the N to be in the correct position for the geographic North Pole then you'd turn the compass until the needle pointed west or W. But the easiest way is just to turn ninety degrees to your right from where the needle pointed and you would be right on target for the North Pole."

"Whoa, whoa! How awful, Philip." Then Samantha told them how she always got her directions mixed up at the ranch in Texas.

"So, now you're telling me even the compass gets mixed up. Now that's neat. I feel much better."

Aisa took off running, and dared them to race her. Arctic clothing was not made for running fast, and they were ready to collapse by the time they reached the steps of the community building.

As they came to a halt, nearly out of breath, the Inuk who had helped Aisa yesterday, stepped out from behind the building. "A sledge, with the white man you want to talk to, is coming."

They turned their eyes to the fjord shadowed in twilight; the sun was setting again. Far out on the ice small black dots slowly became a sledge and a team of dogs.

Samantha squinted. "How could he have possibly known that the driver was Jason Murdoch?"

"Good eyes," replied Philip. "Good eyes come in handy up here."

They stood watching the sledge, which seemed heavily loaded. The team of dogs slowly grew larger. The driver stood in back, but still too far away for Samantha to see him clearly. She could feel her heart rate increasing, instead of slowing down after her physical exertion, acutely aware that the beating signaled something else. It felt like dread.

Chapter 13

I sometimes wonder how different my life would have been had my mother lived. Usually, I don't care enough to wonder about it. She's a stranger to me. –From Samantha's Journal

Samantha and her friends were not the only ones watching the approaching dog sledge. Others seemed to know this was an important arrival. Not the same kind of arrival that stirred their interest when Samantha and Aisa arrived, but an interest and excitement caused by something quite basic: food.

A well-known fact: Jason Murdoch, an excellent hunter and fisherman, gave himself completely to bringing in sledge-loads of seal, fish, and later in the year, walrus. He did this to help the older members of the community have enough traditional foods to eat.

The sledge stopped near the meat racks. Several people crowded around the driver and peered at his load.

"Looks like Jason Murdoch has brought in a couple of seal, already cut up and frozen and there's a medium-sized shark, well I'll be, must be ten feet long. Bet he had a time keeping his dogs off it. And there's a couple of halibut, good size too, probably 40 pounds each, not bad for hole-in-the-ice fishing," reported Philip, seeing more clearly than either Aisa or Samantha.

The driver helped the people pull the seals and the fish off the sledge, and hoisted the catch up on the drying racks out of reach of the village dogs.

"I'll go tell Murdoch you're here. You might as well see what kind of mood he's in right away. If I know him he won't want to hang around long before heading out again. He could be gone for several days, so this is your only chance. I sincerely hope your trip is worth the blessing you are about to receive." Philip was half-smiling and half-serious.

"O.K., you're right. Go ahead. I'll stay here and see if they put you up on one of those racks along with the fish." Samantha thought she might as well join him in his dry Inuit humor. Not a bad way to approach life. Why get upset over small things? Up here the big things concerned survival. Everything else deserved a sardonic wink and a smile.

Aisa stepped closer to Samantha.

"We'll both watch you, Mr. Diplomat. Don't let us down."

Though it took Philip only a couple of minutes to cover the distance, it seemed like forever to Samantha. He arrived at Murdoch's sledge. She could see them talking. Murdoch towered over Philip.

"What's happening? Can you tell what's happening?"

"No," said Aisa, "I'm not too good at guessing the intricacies of the male psyche. For all I know they're discussing the weather and the weight of that shark."

The two men continued to talk. Occasionally, one or the other would help with a slab of seal, handing it off to a villager. Then the conversation appeared to be over. Jason Murdock continued unloading the sledge and Philip began walking back.

"Well?" Samantha and Aisa nearly said the word together.

"Not too good, but then, not too bad," again, the half-smile.

"Well?" they both said again, this time, impatiently.

"All right, all right. Let's go inside and I'll lay it all out."

Once the outer skins were off and the chairs were dragged to the stove, Philip cleared his throat.

"I don't suppose there's some coffee," he asked and was met with two loud groans. Samantha decided he was enjoying all of this attention too much. He was like a hunter who had to be teased into telling how well he had fared, despite privations, blizzards, crazy dogs, and a wrecked sledge.

"The good news first. Samantha, he knows who you are. I told him your name and he came back with 'Samantha Callendar

King?' and I said I didn't know your middle name, but maybe that was it. Then he wanted to know how you were, and how your uncle was, and then he said he knew your dad had crashed, and it had been, and still was, a big blow to him.

"Apparently they were really close. He couldn't imagine what you were doing here, but he'll see you although he doesn't have much time between trips. He'll come to the community house in about an hour after he takes care of his dogs and gets cleaned up."

"So that's pretty good, better than I had been led to believe. Thank you Philip for a job well done."

"Hear, hear," said Aisa, smiling at her husband.

"Uh, I should quit while I'm ahead, but I did say I had bad news, too, so let me get on with it and we'll see if you still think I did a good job."

Aisa and Samantha quieted down and leaned forward.

"In the first place, I may have made a mistake telling him that you thought the crash was no accident. I also told him that you had come all this way because you knew he could help you find the answers as to what really happened.

"Wow," said Aisa.

"It's O.K.," said Samantha. "He would have found out soon enough, maybe it was better he heard it from you, Philip; now he can stew about it for awhile."

"Stew, I doubt. He seemed like a lump of sea ice when I told him. He had been somewhat interested and even friendly, friendly for him, but when I added that last part, he clammed up and his face got really dark. He waited a long time to speak and when he did he sounded totally disinterested, detached, off in another world. Angry too."

"What did he say?" Samantha swiped at her eyes as if to ward off a dark cloud.

"What he said was, and I can't be sure I'm using his exact words, 'Tell Ms. King I'll see her as I promised, but I have no information at all about her dad, and even if I did, I wouldn't share it with her.

'It's over and done with, and she should forget it. I'm sorry as hell it happened, but it did, and there's nothing anyone can do to bring her dad back. She's got to let it go.

64

'That was another world and I don't want to, and I will not, go back to it. She has wasted her time, and now she will waste mine.' Then, he heaved some seal meat at a villager nearly knocking him over and turned his back on me. I left. That's it. I'm sorry."

Dark. Daytime, and still dark. Dark in Samantha's heart, too. It had been over an hour since Jason Murdoch's promise to come see her at the community building. She set out something to eat, and kept the water steaming for coffee or tea.

Samantha steeled herself from walking to the windows and looking out. He might see her peeking. Why that would be bad mystified her. Why couldn't she seem anxious? After all, wasn't she anxious? She was also disappointed, and put out, by his response to Philip.

Now that everything was in the open, and she knew how he felt, she was better prepared. She would persevere. If he had information she would get it out of him one way or another. So, why not look out the damn window? It would be an honest response.

After all, had she not come thousands of miles to see him? Had she not traveled, in the dead of winter, into northern Greenland, where tourists were barred until April? Why not let him know she was watching for him and ready for him? She didn't go to the window.

Sometimes, she was stubborn, just for the sake of being stubborn. When she heard the knock, her heart went into passing gear. She walked quickly to open the door.

"Ms. King?"

"Mr. Murdoch. Won't you please come in?"

"Thank you."

Samantha indicated the two chairs near the stove.

"Put your outerwear here near the heat and please sit down Mr. Murdoch. It was good of you to come. I realize this is your busy time of the year and I'll not keep you long. In the meantime, would you care for coffee or tea?"

"Tea would be excellent. I've been doing so many things since I arrived, I have neglected my tea. Fix enough for three cups, strong and hot. Listen to me, and my bad manners. I have been up here too long. Please, forgive me."

Samantha smiled.

"Quite forgiven, and after your trip I should think a request for three cups is not unreasonable in the least. Strong and hot, with more to come if needed." Jason Murdoch smiled back, or maybe not. Samantha couldn't be sure.

When she arranged his heavy parka near the stove, she had the sensation of blood-red and purple. With his black hair graying at the temples, penetrating green eyes and skin ruddy from the arctic wind, he exuded a great, volatile strength.

There was no doubt in Samantha's mind that here was a powerful man that age had not affected. He was as strong or stronger now at, say, sixty than he had been at twenty-five, she wagered. His step was quick, his eyes alert, his body ready for any emergency.

Samantha busied herself with the tea preparations, deciding to make the brew even stronger, gambling that she couldn't overdo it. She so much wanted this meeting to be a good one. It seemed to have started well. She would call on every psychology ploy she had ever learned, to keep this conversation moving in the direction she wanted. Manipulation? Perhaps. So what?

"Ms. King, there are some things I have to get off my chest before we start, and the sooner you hear them the better." Then, without waiting for her reaction, "I do not believe in what you are doing, trying to make a case that your dad met with foul play, if indeed, that is your mission, which is what I gathered from talking with Philip. If it is, I want you to know I think it a waste. It is dangerous, and fool-hardy, and I will have no part in it." He paused and looked directly into her eyes.

"I have no helpful information about our working in Guatemala City. I consider none of it worth your time and the sooner you accept that, the sooner you can get on with your life. Martin, your dad, and I were very close, as close as two guys can get without being brothers." Jason Murdoch shifted uneasily in his chair.

"I still think of him. I still wonder if I'd stayed with him things might have been different. But no one can bring back the past and change things no matter how much we try. Of course, I would like to find some answers myself, but it's not worth your life. I have lost a close friend. You have lost a father who loved you. He would never want you in harm's way, no matter what happened to him. I hope you can understand that." He paused to blow on his steaming cup of tea.

"Mr. Murdoch, you know what you can and cannot, or choose not, to talk about, and it would certainly be presumptuous of me if I thought I could change your mind or secure information you either do not have, or are unwilling to share. Thank you for getting those things off your chest, as you put it, and I'll certainly not press you on what you consider unhelpful, even though, I disagree with your conclusions. But as you said, there are answers you would like to have, and I can assure you I agree with you about that." Samantha took a breath to calm herself.

"Perhaps we can find some answers together. I certainly do not want you to think you are putting me in danger. It is my decision to make as to how much I am willing to risk. Nevertheless, I thank you for your concern and I respect your decision. I know you were close to my dad, and you must know how close I was to him, especially early in my life.

"If we can't talk about what may or may not have happened in Guatemala City, maybe other experiences you shared with my dad, would be helpful. I traveled a lot with him, until I went away to college, then we settled for holiday visits. Those times were always precious to me, as you can imagine."

Samantha and Jason Murdoch sipped their tea, then they began to reminisce about the times they had with Martin King on the various air bases and oil fields around the world. Their stories were like movies where the background music told the real story or, at least, carried the emotional side of the story.

It would have been easy to lash out at each other. He had, in a way, by telling her she was wasting her time, that she was being foolhardy. She bristled at his adamant refusal to help, under the guise that it was too dangerous.

Hah! She could tell him about danger. Try being buried at

Bhuj. How about holding a man until he died? Being shot at and attacked. Instead, she listened to another anecdote and waited her turn to share one with him.

She knew she must stay calm. Feelings too raw, too destructive to face, lay just below this civilized conversation. She had learned to deal with irrationalities. Her real estate buyers and sellers were full of distrust, and fear, and anger. She had learned to watch, to wait, to learn, to get below the outbursts.

Jason Murdoch had a lot of hurt eating at him. A lot of anger. Anger at himself? Others? She was alert to the slightest nuance. Maybe it was still too much for him to deal with what had actually happened.

"If we cannot talk of my dad in Guatemala, would you at least tell me something about your decision to leave for Greenland?" There was an uneasy pause. Jason Murdoch's face grew darker, then he appeared to relax.

"Of course I can share that with you. I got tired of the corporate lifestyle. The quest for the almighty dollar, along with corruption, politics, and constant intrigues caused me to leave for the simple life. I wanted to go somewhere as unspoiled by modern technology as possible and to be of use to my fellow man. I chose Greenland. As to finding the right place for my new life, I'll have to admit Greenland is not perfect.

"The country is in a state of rapid flux. Technology has been introduced and is becoming more important to the Inuits every day. That's not always a good thing. I keep moving farther north where the old traditions are still observed. I may have to go on to the great North East National Park and die an old man in the stomach of a polar bear. Is that helpful?"

Very. His facade was in place. Nicely constructed. But still false. He thinks it's real. Someday, Mr. Murdoch, the wind might just blow your facade down, then what? She sipped her tea.

"Yes, that helps me understand you better. I can imagine you and Philip have had some interesting conversations." Another sip.

"Since you were with my dad so much, did I ever meet you? I

don't remember."

"Yes, I remember you as a very little girl, a baby actually. You were much too young to remember me." Jason Murdoch held out his cup for another refill.

"Excellent. Strong. So often the tea here is not strong enough. The Inuit hardly flavor the water. Which is a wonder considering their taste for almost rotten meat."

"Thank you. Aisa Avaalaaqiaq told me about kiviaq."

"You are to be commended on pronouncing her name with such authority, most non-Inuits don't even try, and yes, kiviaq is a hands-down winner as an appetizer. Have you tasted any?" His eyes twinkled with the same devilish mischief Samantha had seen in Aisa's eyes.

"No, and with all the authority I can muster, I won't."

Then he laughed. She suddenly had a feeling of warmth to-ward this man who was so maddeningly, but charmingly uncoop-erative and who carried a damaged heart.

He would need her someday and then, smoothing her warming sweater, she thought she might need him too. A flicker of dark plum met her finger tips and some other color that came and went so fast she couldn't pull it into her consciousness.

A sudden realization. He'd remembered her as a baby! Her skin felt prickly. A drop of perspiration went sliding and rolling somewhere. Nerves. She took a deep breath and as off-handedly as possible, she turned toward the small stove and fiddled with the blackened tea kettle.

"Then you must have known my mother?"

Chapter 14

Reading between lines is an art and I'm pretty good at it. Thank you very much Jason. –From Samantha's Journal

Samantha moved her face mask a little to the left. That felt better. She was careful not to fog her goggles. Five in the morning and bitterly cold, not that the hour made any difference this time of year.

It was always bitterly cold, even for the brief time the sun showed itself in the middle of the day.

This northern sun would tease her, like a child hiding behind white skirts. She loved to gaze at it as it lighted the land around her, but it never brought a temperature change with it. Nevertheless, she felt warmer, and her mood would swing to the positive as the red and golden light bathed the sea ice.

The sunrise and sunset would be in front of her this trip, for the sledge was heading southward back to Qaanaaq. She counted out how many hours must pass before the horizon brightened with red, and the stars dimmed for a time.

For now, the stars glittered as the sledge creaked and groaned. The dogs, quiet again, sent back billows of steam as they huffed across the frozen mouth of Robertson's Fjord.

Part of the baggage for the return trip included the skins and furs Philip had been wearing. Aisa would get them cleaned in Qaanaaq. Most Inuit thought this unnecessary. They wore the same skins month after month. Philip believed they lasted longer and were more effective if given a rest and a good cleaning. Aisa had brought him a whole new outfit. She said he smelled better too.

Siorapaluk lay miles behind. Samantha's adventure in

Greenland would soon be over. She hoped they could reach Qaanaaq with some daylight left. The dogs pulled hard, urged on by Aisa's commands. A race south, and out of Greenland, perhaps forever, for Samantha. Aisa and Philip would leave soon for Alaska to welcome spring flowers, the long days of sunshine, and to see again the jagged snow-covered peaks beyond the valleys. Aisa could hardly contain her excitement at the prospect of serious dog training, and the possibility of racing in a couple of years.

"Just think, Philip and I in the Iditarod! It will be so awesome. You must come, see us off, and then go to Nome and welcome us at the finish."

That would be fun and Samantha wanted to go. Right now, as the sledge sliced along the ice beneath billions of far-off and furiously exploding suns, she had a lot to think about, grateful for this time to reflect and plan.

Her first thoughts centered on Jason Murdoch's visit last night. An interesting meeting. He had a strong personality and strong opinions, especially about her investigating her dad's crash.

Although she treasured the memories he had shared with her about her dad, she was angry at herself for failing to convince him to change his mind. Frustrating. Discouraging. Maybe he was right. The meeting had been a waste of time for them both.

The sledge hurried on and Samantha allowed the conversation to replay itself, recalling key sentences and words. She made a tentative list of positive points, instead of dwelling on the negatives. She began her critical review.

A waste of time. Foolhardy. Dangerous. He wouldn't help. If he had stayed maybe things would have been different.

That added up to a pretty impressive bit of information. He thought something didn't add up. He thought the crash had not been an accident. He thought someone might not like her finding answers. He felt guilty that he left, so something was rotten in Denmark (at that she had to smile). He thought he could have made a difference, if he had stayed. Perhaps, he could have changed things. Solved the problem. Warned her dad. Saved her dad.

What better information than that? At least someone else was yelling for justice. Well, maybe not yelling. What better information did she need than her dad's fellow consultant in the Guatemalan oil company voicing his suspicions? Those suspicions could mean serious crimes. Anyone investigating might be silenced for good. What mysterious crimes? Who committed them? Did her dad find out something? Was he blowing the whistle? Did Jason Murdoch believe any of that?

Samantha nodded her head against the face mask. Yes, she said to herself, he believed it. In so many words he had said it. As for the rest of the questions and answers, that's where she would come in. Her time with Jason Murdoch definitely was not wasted. Mr. Murdoch of the impeccable high-resolve hadn't wasted his time either. It had been a worthwhile meeting after all.

Samantha closed her investigative hearing for a brief rest. She let her senses meander for a time, sliding over, around and through the ice and snow. She felt a pang of sadness that Ben would never see this country, see the bright stars in the velvet darkness or the tulip-shaped sun sedately marching along the horizon. She missed him so. She remembered their talks at their favorite café in New York. She knew he would always be with her wherever she went. Samantha glanced at the night sky.

The stars had disappeared. For a moment the information didn't register. Clouds moved in swiftly and silently here. Had Aisa noticed? Of course she had. Not to worry. It didn't seem any colder. She pulled her mind back from the scenery and told it to go back to work.

She laid a firm foundation for her trip to Guatemala City and Honduras, then shifted to the end of her conversation with Mr. Murdoch. She smiled again at their using last names. She remembered doing that in Bhuj with Mr. Dewani, although looking back, she and Mr. Dewani became like daughter and father. He hadn't been that much older, but he had been like a father during their ordeal.

Maybe she and Jason Murdoch got closer to each other than either realized. He didn't seem a father figure to her. She wanted to call him Jason now. She would work on that some more, if the trip to Qaanaaq lasted long enough.

He had remembered her as a small child, as a baby. He might have known her mother.

"So you must have known my mother?"

Again, Samantha zeroed in on the words, the gestures, facial expressions, the subtext of their conversation. His voice almost dream-like or just disinterested? No, he had been interested, bothered, and flustered. She watched his hands fidget. She watched his eyes dart up and away and then down again, picturing, thinking, feeling. His tone, vague, fishing for words. Proper words. Words without emotion.

Clearly, he was uncomfortable, though he tried not to show it. Finally, he called her mother by name, Helen. He had a funny look when Samantha said she didn't remember her mother. Her dad had said scarcely anything about her. He carried her picture, a small one.

She had found a photo of her once, but it had disappeared later. Was she blonde? What color were her eyes? The photo was black and white. Yes, blonde, Jason believed, and blue, perhaps. Believed? Perhaps? Jason Murdoch knew! She watched him carefully. Yes, he knew all right. He didn't have to guess. Why did he distance himself so?

Something must have happened between them. But what? Shortly thereafter, Jason had left, so she didn't have much to go on. Maybe she would find out more later. It wasn't important, just interesting. Maybe Jason loved her mother. Maybe there had been an affair. Maybe Murdoch was her real father? A tragic love story. Samantha stopped her runaway mind. She shook her head. Give her imagination an inch, and it wanted to run a marathon.

She had thanked Mr. Jason Murdoch again and told him she'd be going back to Qaanaaq the next morning. At that time she had been disgusted with her performance, and with his. He had said he would leave for another load of seal, already caught and butchered, but he hoped they might meet again. There was an awkward moment. Samantha had thrust out her hand, and he had taken it in a firm handshake and then he was gone. She wondered afterwards if she would see him again. Would she also use the word, hope?

The wind pressure against Samantha's face shifted. The dogs pulled steadily, but the sledge slowed a little. Though her face mask and goggles protected her, she could feel an icy blast, pushing her back against the sledge.

Just like in Texas, or in Oklahoma, or in any of the Great Plains states, a day wouldn't be a day without the wind. Fifteen miles an hour was only a light breeze, what she felt was way beyond a breeze.

The sledge slowed some more. The team strained. Aisa called to the dogs, but her voice sounded far off. The wind increased. Snow filled the air. Samantha wiped at her goggles. Aisa screamed the command for the team to stop. Samantha felt the brake biting into the ice. The dogs needed no urging. Snow packed into their fur made them all white now. Immediately they dropped down curling their tails over their noses and eyes for protection. Aisa bent low over the sledge and yelled in Samantha's ear.

"Have to stop! Dogs blind! Ice in noses! Need rest! Wait out storm! Get off! Turn over sledge! Won't slide! Must put up tent! Need your help! Do what I say! We're O.K.!" The message came in gasps. The wind tore the words away.

Samantha nodded her head. She jumped off the sledge. They tipped it over. Aisa grabbed the tarp and together, they stretched it across the sledge, which acted as a shield against the wind. Extra skins and sleeping bags were spread out under the tarp, which shook and snapped, less and less, as Aisa tightened it here and there.

"Find the stove!" Aisa yelled. In a moment Samantha had it and set it up. The flame roared to life. She stared at the curiously welcoming blaze in the midst of chaos.

"We'll be all right!" and "Good!" and "That's great!" So spooky. Samantha had heard those words before, except in French. Words Guillaume yelled at her as they sought to find blankets, logs for the fire, and food at the deserted fire-damaged chalet the night they had been marooned by a snow storm. It seemed so surreal that Samantha had a hard time focusing.

Samantha remembered Aisa pointing to the shore earlier, and explaining that the couple of small cabins they saw there could be used by hunters, and that there were several between Siorapaluk and Qaanaaq.

"Very small and narrow and they really shake in the wind. There's no bathroom, running water or electricity. I'd rather stay on the sledge any day." Now, the cabins were invisible, hidden by the snow. Aisa got her wish. They wouldn't have to stay in a shaky small cabin. They had been traveling for ten hours. Surely, they were more than half way to Qaanaaq, but that mattered little in the middle of a storm. No one could see them out on the ice.

After a few minutes, things were better. Maybe the worst was over.

"I must see to the dogs. They have to be farther away. Once they have rested a little and melted the ice in their noses they are likely to begin eating the sledge fastenings which are made of walrus leather. Conceivably, if we stayed here long enough and they really got hungry, we could be next on the menu. I'll be back in a few minutes. Keep the fire burning so it'll show through the skin tarp and I can find my way back." After a few steps into the howling blizzard, Aisa disappeared.

Chapter 15

During the storm, Aisa told me she is pregnant! I told Aisa something that has been forever a secret. It felt right and good. –From Samantha's Journal

After Aisa left, Samantha felt the weight of being alone bearing down on her. She needed something to do. This was no time to panic.

She inventoried the sledge's contents, arranging and rearranging things into some semblance of order in the cramped space beneath the noisy tarp. The stove heated the small area quite well. The wind blew through small gaps providing ventilation, so there was no danger of a carbon monoxide build-up. She took off her gloves and her parka, and still felt warm. Though it was probably still below freezing inside the tent, the extreme dryness of the air made it quite bearable.

She wondered if it really snowed, or if the wind just picked up the old snow and hurled it across the frozen bay.

Samantha had read how the wind blew snow from the huge icecap that covered nearly all of Greenland. The snow, sand-like and abrasive, could cut exposed flesh in no time.

She heaped the extra skins, including Philip's to-be-cleaned clothes, onto the ice floor for further insulation. She found some tins of meat and a package of high energy bars. She considered making tea, but decided to wait until Aisa returned and got settled. But what if Aisa didn't return soon? How long had she been gone? Maybe five minutes. It seemed like hours. Samantha could think of nothing more to do except wait and feel the wind beating against the tent. It came in waves. First, like a heavy hand trying to flatten the tarp, then a brief interval before the battering returned. And in the background the eerie wailing.

A blob of white appeared through the opening of the tent. Aisa fell in onto the skins. Snow pellets covered her parka, glistening diamond-like in the light of the stove's flame. She shook off the coat and hood and wiped off the snow.

"That was a trip." She laughed, but sounded tired.

"The dogs are doing O.K. Got them all curled up and battened down." Aisa settled down in the mound of furs.

"Hey, you got it nice and warm in here, I'd bet it's in the high 20s, maybe nudging 30–a tropical paradise. Now, if I only had some tea."

"I was waiting until you got back. Hot tea coming up." Samantha moved around in the cramped space, found some of the ice they'd reserved for drinking and clanked it into a pan to melt on the stove. In a few minutes it began steaming.

"That's hot enough, I'm going to toss in the tea." Samantha found cups and soon they were sipping away and making appropriate noises of approval.

Two tins of frozen fish and more ice went into the pan. Again, when the steam rose, the tins were taken out and the lids peeled back. The still cold salmon came out in chunks which they ate quickly.

"Delicious. It just doesn't get any better than this!" They both laughed as the wind howled.

"What will the dogs eat?" said Samantha.

"No problem. They can do without food for awhile. They're eating snow for water. They'll be thirsty, but they'll survive. We won't make it in while the sun is up, that's for sure. We won't even see it. It's all milky–white out there. Pretty soon it'll be dark again, but maybe the wind will die down." Aisa took off her heavy outer sweater, leaving on a light knit pullover.

"This reminds me of a couple of months ago, when Philip and I were holed up in a hunter's cabin just north of Siorapaluk. We'd been out riding around, and a storm blew up fast like this one. We found a cabin, got our dogs fed, and went in and fired up our stove. It began to get too warm so we switched to an old-fashioned oil lamp. That warmed the place up so much we began taking off our clothes." Aisa stopped for a moment lost in remembrance. Shaking her head and smiling.

"Samantha, I'm pregnant," and her eyes had that twinkle Samantha liked. "Two months pregnant."

"Aisa, how wonderful. I mean, I guess it's wonderful. I mean, it is wonderful, isn't it?"

"Yes, yes, it's wonderful. We hadn't planned on a family yet, but I'm really glad. I haven't told Philip. He doesn't know. You're the first to know, besides me, that is," again the the smiling eyes.

"Anyway," Aisa went on, "I'm pretty sure it happened in that hunter's cabin. We took off all our clothes. Our shadows played against the narrow walls, dancing because of the oil lamp. We began to feel romantic, you know." Samantha definitely knew what she meant. Aisa smiled some more.

"The Inuit usually aren't too inclined until the spring comes, but Philip seemed ready enough. The only problem, I get kind of noisy. Inuit women are very quiet, because there may be other people sleeping in the same room, especially that was true in the old days, when there was just one room. So children, grand parents, guests, all snuggled in small quarters sleeping, or pretending to sleep. There might be fondling of breasts, maybe kissing her nose, and then wham-bam thank you ma'am, but all pretty quiet. Kissing on the mouth was considered disgusting.

"Well, thank the Great Bear, Philip isn't like that. I like to be touched, stroked and kissed all over, which is fine with him, but once I get going, he gets a little unsettled." Aisa hung her head, then looked up slightly, ready to share a secret.

"I don't know why I'm telling you this, I've never told anyone else. Maybe it's this tent. No, it's you. I think I've known you all my life. Maybe you're the older sister I never had. Anyway, I yell a lot. I mean really loud, long yells. It gets Philip excited, but it makes him so nervous, he can hardly stand it. That night, when I started yelling, he was sure some hunter would pass by, and come to the aid of a woman in distress. Talk about exciting! I yelled and yelled, and we had a really good time of it. I feel sure that's when I got pregnant. Such a romantic fucking." Samantha laughed and so did Aisa. It was Samantha's turn.

"Well I don't think I yell real loud, but I do enjoy making some noise. I'm so concentrated during that time I'm really not sure. I do know one thing. I go cross-eyed."

"Cross-eyed? How do you know?"

"Because I've been told, and sometimes teased about it, but I can't help it like you can't help yelling. I know the moment is at hand, when I start seeing two guys instead of one. It's a pretty good signal...." A heartbeat went by.

"I also see and taste chocolate." There, thought Samantha, I've said it. The one thing she'd never shared with anyone. Here in the middle of a white-out storm in Greenland with a stranger, but who didn't seem like a stranger at all, she had brought it out to share, as Aisa had shared with her.

Aisa gasped and hugged herself. Her mouth opened and shut and opened again.

"Chocolate! You actually see and taste chocolate during sex? That's fantastic! Oh, how I envy you. Chocolate is my favorite, when I can get it, and to have it when you're making love, too? Incredible! Incredible!"

Now, there was no holding back. Aisa demanded details and Samantha obliged, until both women were giggling out of control, and panting in mock seriousness, and maybe with honest desire. They agreed if a guy had stuck his head inside their tent right then, he would have had a story that his friends would never believe. If he had lived to tell the tale.

When the giggles had subsided, Samantha wondered about true love. Aisa and Philip obviously loved each other as much as any two people could. Would they grow apart, as she and her first husband, Blanchard, had? Probably not. Not with a little Inuk on the way. Would true love evade her all her life? Was Emerson the one? Would they always embrace in passion one minute and turn on each other the next?

Julie Amber and Trak Barber came to mind. They also seemed to have found soul-mate-lust-mate love. Maybe it was too late for her. Then, maybe, it wasn't. She would persevere in love like she did in everything else. Samantha King delivered. Could she deliver on love?

Samantha knew the lid needed to come off her tangled love life, and Aisa was the perfect person to help her. There was the Emerson story of love and abandonment. There was the Ben story

79

of platonic friendship. There was the Guillaume story. Aisa listened, commented and contributed anecdotes of her own. She found the Guilluame story really interesting and wanted to know how it ended.

"You were mad at Emerson, and you were going to take it out in furious sex with your ski guide? Did he know that?"

"No, and that was the problem. Just before he got to my room, I suddenly realized it wouldn't work. I wanted revenge. I wanted to receive, and give, angry sex. And then sitting on the edge of my bed, I knew Guilluame wouldn't do that. We had resisted each other in the burned chalet, and I knew how gentle he was.

I was scared to death Guilluame would really love me, instead of ravishing me. I didn't think I could stand being cherished. My heart was too torn up by Emerson for gentle loving. I wanted to call and cancel, but it was too late. He knocked. I let him in and hung the "Don't Disturb Sign" on the door, and then what I was afraid would happen, happened.

He cherished me all afternoon, all night, and all the next morning. And the funny thing about it, I felt released, and wonderful, instead of vulnerable. My anger got swallowed up in gentleness, and caring, and to this day, I have no guilt, and I don't know how I would ever explain that to Emerson."

Aisa hugged a fur. "I don't think you'd better explain it. Furious sex would be one thing. Beautiful, cherishing and loving sex is something else. I don't think he'd ever get over that."

"Yeah, I feel like that, too. I know I wouldn't want to hear a tale like that from him. Thanks. I wish you and Philip lived in Texas, or I lived in Alaska. We'd have tea every morning, looking at my river, or your mountains."

Chapter 16

There are times when Mother Nature just plays too damn rough. −From Samantha's Journal

The wind changed directions. At this time of year, the sea ice was supposed to be nearly a meter thick, and according to Aisa, the safest time of the year to be in the fjords, and on the bay. However, Aisa added, reports warned sledge drivers weak places in the sea ice had begun appearing earlier than expected, and to watch carefully, particularly, if the wind blew hard.

The storm had generated some powerful wave action out in the bay, and it began to reach them, rolling in beneath the ice. The ice rose and fell. Settled down. Rose and fell again. Creaking. Groaning.

"I don't like this. I don't like it at all," said Aisa. Samantha remembered the earthquake in Bhuj; the earth had come up and smacked her. The undulating ice made her queasy and Aisa's comment didn't help her peace of mind either.

A loud cracking sound, near the tent, jolted them both. The dogs began barking. The cracking sound grew louder, followed by a boom, like thunder. The dogs whined. Aisa grabbed her parka; threw it on.

"I'd better see what's happening. I don't like what I'm hearing. The dogs may be in trouble. Stay close and keep the fire going. The snow seems lighter now." Aisa slipped out of the tent.

The wind had stopped roaring, but still toyed with a corner of the tarp, making it snap. Samantha strained to hear Aisa, or the dogs. She could hear nothing, except the tarp flapping in the wind. She grabbed the loose end, secured it. She scrambled to a kneeling position, putting on her parka and gloves. She must be ready, but for what? How could she possibly help in this alien world of snow, ice, and black seas?

Her throat tightened; she could hardly swallow. Not sure what else to do, she looked out through the tent flap. The wind had slackened, but still blew. Her face quickly numbed without her mask, but she left it off, so she could see and hear better. Still no sounds. A sudden feeling of deep aloneness swept over her. She squinted into the darkness. Then she heard a scream.

Aisa! Samantha could not see her, but something automatic kicked in. She grabbed, and switched on a flashlight, and stumbled out onto the ice. The powerful beam got lost in the blowing snow. She lowered it.

"Keep it low like in a fog," she said to herself.

"Don't lose control. Now go. Go!"

Samantha lurched in the direction of the screaming. She screamed back that she was coming. A black hole yawned on her left. A black hole instead of white ice. Water. The sea! Waves washed against the jagged high edge of the white sea ice.

She raised the beam just enough to see how far the black went, and caught a glimpse of Aisa's hood, and a flailing arm in the sloshing water. She was close to the broken ice edge. She was fighting.

Samantha set the flashlight down so it pointed at Aisa, then she lay down on the ice and inched her way to the edge calling to Aisa to hang on. Why hadn't she brought rope? Did they have rope? They must have rope. Maybe extra walrus bindings for the sledge. Yes, that would have been just the thing, but she didn't have them. She couldn't return to get them. Aisa would go down before she got back.

She saw that Aisa had narrowed the space between them. She was swimming sluggishly toward Samantha. Samantha reached out as far as she could reach. The ice edge gently rose and fell. In what seemed an hour, but was maybe 10 seconds, their hands touched.

Samantha grabbed for her but her gloves were too big. She tore them off with her teeth and reached again. The frigid air on her wet hands was a knife slicing at her fingers. She locked her hands, hands trained in the martial arts and strong, around Aisa's wrists and pulled, but Aisa was too heavy to pull out of the water.

"We have to take off your parka. Now!" Samantha let go of one hand and between the two of them the parka finally came off. Aisa looked so small to Samantha, so defenseless, so utterly dependent. Samantha forgot everything except getting that marvelous, beautiful, mother-to-be over that jagged wall of ice. Nothing else in the world mattered. Nothing.

Samantha's arms ached. Aisa rose in the black water. Dead weight, but not dead!

"You–will–live! You–will–live!" Samantha yelled as a warrior of old would have yelled. Like a Viking. Like an Inuk faced with death and refusing it. Her strength might not be enough. She would die with Aisa before giving up. All feeling in arms and hands had disappeared. Did she still have hold of Aisa? Yes, she saw her hands still beneath Aisa's arms. Her face shone white, her eyes closing.

"Let her live, dammit! Let her live, damn you! Samantha fought against all creation. The creation bent a little. The ice shelf sank briefly. The jagged edge met the sea and Asia floated into Samantha's numb arms.

Samantha wrapped her parka around the freezing Aisa. She looked for her gloves, but couldn't find them. There was no time. She could feel the cold seeping through her sweater.

They struggled back toward the tent. Samantha half carried, half pushed, not letting Aisa stop for a moment. They fell. They crawled. They got up. They stumbled. Extreme exhaustion sent a siren call to "rest just little while." To rest meant to die. They reached the tent. Once inside, Samantha used her stiff fingers to strip Aisa, and herself, and buried the both of them in the thick fur-lined sleeping bag she had bought in Copenhagen.

"You'll be warm as toast in this," the clerk had promised. She would know soon if he had told the truth. Aisa felt like a block of ice. Samantha knew she must restore Aisa's core body temperature. The fastest and best way to do that was to hold her, skin against skin, sharing what little warmth they had left. Aisa shook and shuddered. Her eyes seemed wild, then blank, then wild again. The excruciating pain of awakening fingers and feet made both women cry out.

"My dogs, Samantha, I've lost my dogs. My poor dogs." Aisa sobbed as if her heart would break. Samantha rubbed her shoulders and her back and held her close. They drifted off for a few minutes of sleep.

Aisa awakened first. She shook Samantha.

"Wake up! Wake up! We have to get out of here. New cracks can start. We might get separated from the shore. We have to get out of here, now!" Samantha realized the sea ice still rose and fell from the wave action, although the wind had nearly died. She unzipped the bag, and felt her muscles rebel.

Aisa dressed in Philip's skins.

"These are a little large, but mighty warm."

"Am I ever stiff." Samantha put on her own clothes as fast as bruised fingers allowed.

They carried the sleeping bags, the stove, some food, and ice. Samantha wrapped a dog skin around her hands like one big mitten. Off to the left, farther into the bay, she spotted the flashlight, still burning, and started for it.

"Leave it," said Aisa. "There may be another hole out there. I'm not strong enough to haul you out, even if you got naked."

"You're right. Definitely not good swimming weather."

They walked toward the shore, a half-mile away. Aisa pointed out a line of pressure ridges they would have to scale before reaching land. After climbing over the fractured ice blocks, they would find one of the hunter's cabins and stay there to make plans.

"Well, so much for the sun we didn't see, and our destination that we didn't get to, but we're alive and I'm not complaining," said Samantha.

"We're not out of the woods yet, so to speak, but we'll just take one thing at a time. By the way, that was some prayer you yelled out as I sank into the briny deep."

"Yeah, Mother Nature plays a little rough and needs a talking to sometimes. Glad she listened."

They didn't talk about the lost dogs as they walked toward the low lying hills. The wind had all but stopped; they could hear the grinding, and the popping of ice, as the persistent waves continued to press against the frozen shore. They were careful to watch the sea ice for cracks. The glittering stars reappeared as if nothing had happened.

Chapter 17

**I'm amazed at the outcropping of joy in the meanest of places.
–From Samantha's Journal**

After reaching the small cabin, making tea on the stove, catching a few minutes in the sleeping bags, and running out-of-doors to relieve themselves, Samantha and Aisa settled down to plan.

"Qaanaaq can't be more than an hour away. We'll bundle up and walk in. Maybe someone there can come back for the sledge and the rest of our stuff," Aisa said, still ignoring the lost team. Samantha knew it was much too painful to talk about. All in good time. They needed to devote themselves to action, not therapy. At this point, action was therapy.

They warmed up some tinned meat, and made more tea before heading out. Keeping up their strength ranked number one on their to-do list.

Then they heard the dogs. Barking dogs. The lost dogs? No, they had drowned struggling against their tangled traces. Aisa had seen where the ice anchor had given way, close to the crack and the open water. Her throat tightened at the thought of her dogs drowning in the frigid seas. No, the dogs they heard must belong to a hunter. Maybe they could hitch a ride into Qaanaaq.

"Sam! Sam," are you in there? A voice boomed out above the barking dogs. Then another voice, "Aisa! Aisa, are you there? Are you all right?"

For the briefest of moments Aisa and Samantha looked at each other, frozen to the spot, then Aisa screamed and bolted for the small door. Samantha was right behind her. The other voice calling out Sam? No one but her dad and Ben had ever called her Sam. They were both dead. She was too excited to figure it out.

85

Clad only in boot liners and their sweaters, they rushed outside without thought of the cold. Aisa jumped into Philip's arms. They hugged and laughed. They screamed and cried. Samantha could not believe who she saw. Jason! He stood there grinning at her. Jason had called her Sam! He scooped her up in his big arms and hugged her to him.

"God, you're safe! We thought we had lost you when we saw the sledge. Now we've got to get you back inside before you freeze." The small cabin barely held them all. Everyone talked at once. Aisa hugged Philip hard and sobbed.

"Oh Philip, I lost the dogs. They drowned. They're gone. I don't think I can stand it." She sobbed and cried into his shoulder. He held her tightly, then shook her just a little.

"They don't look drowned to me. Look for yourself." Again, the women jumped for the door. The men came carrying parkas, which they threw on Aisa's and Samantha's shoulders. In Samantha's and Aisa's excitement, neither of them had noticed the extra dogs. But there they were, curled up with their tails over their faces.

First one, and then another, looked up at the foursome. Two dogs got up. Was it time to go again? Aisa was beside herself. She hugged each dog in turn. They were genuinely glad to see her. They had been in an adventure too, it turned out.

Philip and Jason saw them running back to Siorapaluk, the place of their last meal, and somewhat tied together in their traces. When they intercepted the dogs and recognized them as Aisa's team, they knew that somewhere south, the women were in trouble. Maybe they were injured. Maybe dead. Neither Jason, nor Philip, had voiced those possibilities. But why else would the dogs be running free? Had they sent them back on purpose? Surely not in their traces. The dogs had been in the sea. Ice clung to them.

Harnessing the dogs to their teams, Philip and Jason spread out across the bay in a desperate search. Two hours later the wind died and the snow stopped blowing. Jason saw a beam of light. It was the flashlight Samantha had left behind. The men had approached carefully along the ice fractures, and found the overturned sledge.

"But how did you find this cabin?" Aisa asked.

"We just followed your trail across the ice. You were dragging

86

something through the snow."

"Our sleeping bags...filled with our stuff," Samantha and Aisa said.

They all huddled together around the stove in the small building. The scent of strong tea filled the warming air. The tea poured and the first sip taken, Samantha began their story. Aisa filled in with the details. The men did not interrupt. At the end, Aisa leaned toward Philip.

"How did you know we were in trouble, while you were still in Siorapaluk?"

"We didn't know you were in trouble. But when we received the radio warning, it was Jason who said we had to find you right away, so we set out. We had to stop for awhile because the dogs couldn't see, and neither could we. I guess we were only a couple of hours apart the whole trip."

Samantha glanced at Jason, who hadn't said much. He caught her looking. She smiled her thanks to him before he could look away. So, Jason was more sensitive and caring than he had let on.

After tea and a bite of their tinned meat, Aisa and Philip took Philip's team and back-tracked to retrieve her sledge and rehitch her dogs to it. Aisa's team would need trace repairs, and Jason set to work on that project. Samantha watched.

Jason had a handsome knife and when the cutting was over, she asked to see it. Silver, gold, and ivory carvings, in a Viking motif, decorated the handle. A stylized winding serpent held its own tail in its mouth. The blade resembled an out-sized hunting knife with a slight curve upwards at the end of the razor-sharp edge. The blade was thicker than normal, appearing to be unbreakable. It was engraved with Viking runes. Blade tip to hilt must have been a foot long. An excellent knife for skinning and butchering.

As she touched it, staying clear of the knife edge, she sensed pink purple platinum from the blade and smoky blue silver plum color from the handle.

"Your dad had one just like it. We had them made when we were helping maintain the oil rig platforms in the North Sea. Martin had to get special permission because of the ivory. It's from a narwhal tusk." She felt the knife again, willing it to carry something from her dad to her. She handed it back.

"I never saw him carry it, and I guess it's lost by now. A lot of things happened later that I missed out on. I'm glad you were close to him." Jason returned the knife to its leather sheath.

———————

The small windows of Qaanaaq sent a yellow welcome to the four travelers as the sledges, in single file, slipped up the Inglefield Fjord. The dark mass of hills leading to the interior and the ice cap, provided a shawl-like cover, and an aura of protectiveness over the community. The yellow lights multiplied as their rectangles were mirrored in the snow. The teams pulled harder. The sledges picked up speed. Soon, the dogs would feast on great hunks of frozen seal.

Watching their tails sway, listening to their barks, Samantha felt a deep appreciation for the wolf-dogs who contributed so much and expected so little.

In a few hours, the sun would rise again, and stay a little longer. This time, they would see it. The three sledges came to a stop at Hotel Qaanaaq, where Samantha and Jason unloaded their gear. Aisa and Philip went on to their private cabin, just a few hundred feet away. They would return for dinner. Samantha and Jason had no trouble arranging for rooms, since it was still too early in the year for tourists.

Two rooms rented and four guests for dinner had the hotel owners beaming. In the meantime, Samantha and Jason ordered more hot tea. Jason invited Samantha to be first in the bath down the hallway, an invitation gratefully accepted.

"Take your time. Have a hot bath. Enjoy," he had said. She could hardly wait. Samantha did not think a five-room hotel with one shared bath could be so special to her. What an adventure.

So many things could have gone disastrously wrong, but here they were–really safe and sound, even merry. Life and death are often separated by the thinnest of margins, she decided.

Almost regretfully, Samantha parted with her parka, boots, and unexpectedly, the mittens found by Philip where she had dropped them. She laid out the traveling clothes she had worn from Copenhagen. Then as Jason had suggested, she took a long hot bath, shampooed her hair, flossed and brushed her teeth, and rubbed a generous amount of skin moistener on her body until she glistened and felt like silk.

Back in her room, she combed out her hair and dressed. She noted with pleasure that although the various furs and skins had kept her warm in the frigid air, they could not compete with her form-hugging traveling clothes. She patted her stomach realizing it was much flatter. A tough way to lose weight. A regimen never mentioned in the beauty/health magazines. She could do an article and appear on the cover.

Chapter 18

I do so love emails. It is a wonderful way to stay in touch and get something off my chest without being constantly interrupted. –From Samantha's Journal

The flight attendant handed Samantha another complimentary flute of champagne. Could it be that only three days before she had been in Qaanaaq with three new friends toasting each other and putting away huge amounts of food? So unreal. March 13. A sun-filled Tuesday, the sky, cobalt blue above her. Below her, a giant's ripped mattress spilling lumps of cotton batting all the way to the horizon.

Four days ago Aisa and she could have drowned in the black waters of a Greenland fiord. She looked around. Here she was, bound for New York in a sleek jet and sharing the first-class section with four other passengers. Did they have hair-raising tales to share? Probably not. And who would believe hers?

"Pardon me, but have you ever been caught in a blinding snowstorm off the northern coast of Greenland? Well, I was. There was this sledge, see, and we had to turn it over and then the ice cracked open and my friend sank into the ocean trying to save 15 dogs. I was lying on this tossing frozen slab trying to reach her. No? Well, let me say, at twenty below, it was no picnic."

Samantha sipped her champagne and smiled at how, sometimes, life was too bizarre to share. The others seated with her didn't seem eager to relate adventure tales either. Smart people. Samantha set down the delicate crystal flute. Her hands still felt bruised and tender. If she didn't stretch often she knew the deep muscle aches would return to her legs and back. Yep, it had really happened, and no, she wouldn't be telling her story to her fellow passengers.

Out her window she could see the shining wing behind her.

Brilliant. The brightness was difficult to get used to after so much half-light and darkness. Beautiful and wondrous as that Greenland world had been, she had missed the sun in a bright blue sky.

Had she stayed, she would have enjoyed 24 hours of sunlight in another few weeks. How hard to have the sun all the time, and then to lose it. She could understand why people there suffered severe depression as the sun began to leave in the autumn, and darkness covered the land.

Samantha had made a special request before boarding. First class had its advantages. And now after the second flute of champagne she was ready. She signaled the flight attendant, who brought a small basket, a plate, and a knife.

In the basket were three gleaming apples: one red, one yellow, and one green. She remembered her longing for apples as she had approached Siorapaluk, and the promise to herself to eat tons of them, as soon as possible.

She cut into the green apple first. Very tart. Juicy. Perhaps, a cooking apple. She ate it all, except the core, slicing it carefully and peering at each piece as one might examine a jewel. The yellow one came next. Luscious. Sweet. Intoxicating, with a delicate aroma.

She rested for awhile, savoring the experience, then sliced the red. The inside: white and firm–a taste treat fit for the gods. Perfect. She asked the flight attendant if she could keep the intricately woven basket.

"Of course."

The whole Greenland experience seemed tied to that little apple basket.

Although it made more sense to fly to New York from Greenland, she chose to go back to London–it was a decision made by her heart, not her brain. She wanted to see Emerson, if at all possible. In London, she had taken a room near Heathrow, and despite her resolve to contact Emerson, she had simply collapsed for most of the day. When she awoke, she had tried calling Emerson at his flat. No answer. No voice mail.

She had gone back to sleep.

Monday: a busy day. After trying Emerson again, without success, she emailed her uncle.

"Hi Uncle Stu: In London. Just back from a nice trip to Greenland and guess what? Found Jason Murdoch. We had tea together, he said to tell you hello. Not much information, just like you said, but going there was worth it. Met a neat couple from Alaska. They may race in the Iditarod. Maybe you will go with me and watch them win. Hope you are having a lovely Texas spring. See you in a few days. Love, Samantha."

She emailed the Krugers. She was determined to keep Ben's parents in her life. Christina, in Rome, was next on the list.

"Christina! Are you married yet? What fun in London. Back from exhausting trip to Greenland. Scary. Productive. Tell you all about it next time we stuff ourselves with pastry. I love you. Samantha."

She sent a message to Julie Amber. "Will tell you all about my adventures in Greenland, when I get back. Say hello to Trak, if he hasn't left for Maya land yet." Samantha went on to say how she wanted the young woman to go with her to Honduras and hoped she was seriously considering it. "Bet it's already getting hot in Austin. Greenland was cold, cold, cold."

An email went to Philip and Aisa. She didn't mention motherhood, since Aisa's pregnancy could still be a secret. She did say she wanted to come to Alaska, and if Aisa and Philip raced in the Iditarod, she would volunteer for the cheerleading position.

With a sigh, Samantha typed a short note to Emerson. She said how she had tried and tried to reach him, and that they had to talk. She should have gone directly to New York. Going to London had not worked. Perhaps, Emerson would never talk to her. Samantha sighed again.

The last email had gone to Jason Murdoch, in care of the Qaanaaq hotel. She didn't know when, or if, he would get it, but she wanted him to know how much their meeting together had meant to her, also how helpful he had been. She thanked him for coming to her rescue "like a true man of the north."

Why did she say that? For all she knew, a true man of the north would have remained miles away, hunting seal. It was the hardest email to write, because she did not really know Jason Murdoch. She didn't know whether to write him off as simply a person who supplied some information about her dad, or pursue some sort of relationship. Being a friend of her dad's, and even her mother's, didn't mean he had to be her friend.

He was an unknown quantity and quality in her life. She would need to sort that out later. He told her why he had come searching for her, and that had been unsettling. Yet, Samantha had felt detached as he talked. Maybe it had been too much to process at the time.

At the end, they both fought back tears, for different reasons. What to do about Jason Murdoch? Time would tell. She looked out the jet's small window. If it had been night, she could have looked at the stars. Always her friends. Always silent. No advice. Just acceptance.

Chapter 19

It just doesn't seem safe to have a decommissioned missile silo as one's "home sweet home." What if a rogue nation still thought you had a gigantic rocket in there? –From Samantha's Journal

The rest of Monday had been a whirlwind with clients, who seemed especially anxious. Maybe, it was just Monday. Samantha had given up long ago trying to figure out her clientele. It was nerve wracking, and even physically exhausting, to find the secret properties, to negotiate as if the fate of mankind rested on her shoulders, and then to see to it that every wish was granted. Occasionally, that could be a real challenge.

A case in point had to do with Abel and Mrs. Jorwoski. Samantha had procured a decommissioned missile silo in Vermont last year for the Jorwoskis. Actually, it had been a prototype Titan II missile complex, and had never been operative, that is, a missile had never been installed. The complex had been built to test structural components. It consisted of a buried control center of three floors, an entryway module with connecting cable ways, or tunnels, to the control center and the silo itself which was around 55 feet in diameter and 150 or so feet deep, designed to hold the 110 foot Titan missile. None of the hardware had been put in place, so the whole complex was just a series of shell buildings, all underground. Who would want a 15 story building that went down instead of up? Mr. Jorwoski. Samantha had received by courier, a list of "dos and don'ts" from Mr. Jorwoski. She sent back a proposal for turning the deep hole and adjacent structures into a "homey" space, and of course, a defensible fortress. The budget was set at ten million for plans and preliminary work.

Things were going smoothly until she received an email from Mr. Jorwoski while in London. The email was in code and instructed her to call him (he had signed as Tom Jones) using the prearranged secret touch-tone combination on her special phone that would automatically scramble their voices.

"Joyce, Tom here." (Even scrambled messages had been known to get unscrambled.) Joyce, her new name.

"You know that place we're working on? Well, I got a message the other day about too much water down a ways in it."

"Down a ways, uh...Tom? Could you be more specific?"

"Well, you know, flooding or anything like that, has to be on purpose the way that house was built in the first place. And I could use the number nine."

"Just nine or including nine?" Samantha racked her brain to find out if the upper floors had been flooded as well. It was the best she could do on the spur of the moment.

There was a long silence.

"Just," came the labored reply at last. Obviously, Mr. Jorwoski had also racked his brain over the prospect of giving out too much information.

"Jane," apparently Joyce had got lost. "You know yourself an accident is highly unlikely and if it is on purpose, then the deal is off and I'm pulling out and I'm ninety-eight percent pulling out already."

In normal real estate transactions, the broker would at this point calm nerves, appeal to reason, and assure the buyer that everything would be all right. The flooding hadn't happened on purpose, and nobody in Vermont even knew where it was, or what it had been. It had all been worked out at the very highest levels, and in complete secrecy. Losing the sale would mean the loss of a million, or so, in commissions and building-out fees. How Jorwoski had "heard" about flooding was anybody's guess. No use to question his sources. Maybe he had just dreamed it. Didn't matter. She had to handle it.

It had taken her years, but she had learned.

"Yes, Tom, the wise thing to do would be to pull out, there are other places. It wouldn't be worth the risk. I would have never thought such a thing could happen. I'm glad you called."

"Well, dammit, I liked that country and I had my heart set on it, you know. So, just check it out. Maybe someone is playing a practical joke. Maybe there's no water anyway. Thanks for hearing me out. I'll wait for your report. Have a good day and stay away from strangers, ha ha."

Soon, Samantha thought, soon she would have enough capital to open up a new business, working in the field of conservation and restoration. Preservationists were idealists, positive thinkers and lovers of tradition. She knew she would like working with them. She was counting the days till the changeover. First though, she had to get to the bottom of her dad's crash. If it had been an accident, she wanted to know so she could put it behind her. If it had not, then those responsible would be made to pay, or her name wasn't Samantha King...or Joyce or Jane.

Samantha watched the colors play on the wing's surface behind her. She could see a rainbow of color reflected off the shiny metal surface. She studied her fellow passengers: two single women and a couple. Husband and wife? Boss and secretary? He was the secretary? Parisian lovers running away? None of the above? She settled her head in the soft pillow and closed her eyes. Sleep did not come. But Jason Murdoch did.

Chapter 20

There's something wrong with me. I blame my mother for dying. Ridiculous of course. It's a small girl's reaction and I'm now twice as old as my nineteen year old mother. I have to work on that. –From Samantha's Journal

Unable to sleep, Samantha looked at the Atlantic, thousands of feet below, and began to replay her time with Jason Murdoch at Qaanaaq. Vanity had paid her a visit. Vanity. So? Damn, she had brought no make-up or perfume. She had slipped into her chic traveling clothes and walked into the small dining room to wait for Jason, Aisa and Phillip.

Jason Murdoch had taken a long time in the bathroom. Enjoying a hot bath in the north was indeed a luxury, but Samantha wanted company. At last she heard him coming down the hall.

Did he seem as shocked as she, when he entered the room? Shocked and pleased? First, she noticed he had trimmed his beard neatly in a Vandyke style. Very distinguished looking, with wisps of almost white here and there, contrasting nicely with the black. She realized the Arctic clothing had hidden a nice body. Jason was six feet tall and looked taller, because he stood so straight. He had been a full colonel in the Air Force. Same as her dad.

His eyes were a brighter green today, more expressive, as he looked steadily at her. She remembered that look when she had first seen him in Siorapaluk. Green eyes looked at green eyes. Broad shoulders and a narrow waist revealed not an ounce of extra fat. A striking man, no matter what age. When he smiled she noticed straight white teeth. Apparently he noticed her with approval as well.

A moment of silence floated between them, then they both

talked at once, the words spilling together, a brief respite, then at it again. Small talk to fill the void. How nice to have a bath at last. How good to change into other clothes. How wonderful that Aisa and Philip would join them soon. They sat down. The manager and his wife brought in tea and cups. Random topics seemed important and intensely interesting. Samantha realized they both felt quite uncomfortable in each other's presence. She sensed Jason holding back, maybe she held back too.

Aisa and Philip rushed in, rosy-cheeked, and out of breath. The food came and went. The four of them relived the details of their experience. Filled with cheer and thankfulness, they planned ways to be together again, sometime, somewhere.

The young, and very much in love, couple left soon after dinner. The manager and his wife cleared away the dishes. Samantha stood to leave.

"Samantha, please don't go yet. There is something I need to share with you. I was determined not to bring it up, but I feel I must."

And then he had told her about Helen, her mother, and how Samantha's father, Martin, and her young mother, Helen, had been such close friends of his. Jason and Martin had been buddies long before her dad had married Helen. They had first met her together, and then had become an inseparable threesome. At one point Jason had hoped Helen would become his girlfriend, but she had eyes only for Martin. Jason had accepted her decision. They continued their friendship. Later, Jason transferred to another base, but the three ended up in Enid again after their war stint.

"One night we were all at this club on the base and Helen wanted to call it a night, but Martin wanted to stay awhile longer and so did I. I volunteered to bring Martin home. We told Helen she could go on if she wanted to. Martin and I both knew she didn't want to leave by herself, but we badgered her until she did. I teased her more than Martin did.

"On her way home, her car went over a guard rail and landed upside down in a small creek. They said she drowned. Every day of my life I have replayed that night. In my dreams I warn her not to go. I chase her car.

Martin and I remained close, and though I blamed myself, he

would not hear of it. He felt responsible, too. After a few years even I began to think he was right.

We retired from the Air Force and went into the oil business together. You were just a kid. I was in and out of your life, but not too close. It was just too painful."

"You called me Sam."

"What?"

"You called out 'Sam' when you were about to find us in the cabin. Nobody called me that but a colleague and my dad. It was a shock to hear someone else say my name like that out in the middle of nowhere."

"I had forgotten. Yes, I knew you as Sam because your dad always called you that. He talked about how beautiful you were, how intelligent...how much he loved you."

Samantha remembered looking away when he had said those words. Tears had come to her eyes suddenly. She couldn't trust her voice. She had cried, staring out the windows in the little room. To learn that her dad loved her near the end and to learn of it in the cold darkness of Greenland was almost more than she could take. The story of her mother had been different. She had felt like a stranger, listening to a story that did not directly concern her.

She wondered about her feelings for her mother. She guessed it was because she didn't really know her. But she knew her dad, and the unspeakable pain at losing him had returned here in that Greenland hotel room.

Jason Murdoch had made no move to comfort her. No arm around her shoulder. She had appreciated that. She had suffered in silence.

"Sam or Samantha," she remembered him saying, "I'm really sorry about your dad. I miss him too. But the reason I came for you in that storm was because of what I did to Helen. Once more I was letting someone leave on a journey while I watched and waited. When I got the storm report I was like a madman. I relived that awful night all over again. I had to come. I don't think you can ever know what I felt when I called out and heard an answer from that miserable plywood hunter's cabin.

Samantha had gotten up from the wooden hotel chair and walked over to Jason. She had put her arms about his neck and buried her face in the side of his beard. He had circled his arms around her and drawn her close, and she knew there were tears in his eyes too, for a lost love.

Samantha needed to sleep. The plane would land at noon, and by that time it would have been a long day already. A small nap now would keep her going until bed-time tonight. Samantha allowed her head to burrow into the soft pillow. She slept. Bits and pieces of dreams played around the edges of her cataloging brain. She could not recall them as she awakened with a start. Back to sleep. More dreams. Bad dreams. Anxious dreams.

Chapter 21

It's really weird how I think of a room in the Stanhope Hotel as home and the concierge as almost family. Maybe I should blame my weird buyers and sellers for skewing my life...nah, I've always been weird. –From Samantha's Journal

Samantha caught a glimpse of the World Trade Center towers and their dominating presence. She wondered if her new head-quarters could be there. Nice address. She would look into it, but not now. Plenty of time. She would do some checking later.

On the ground at last. Snow threatened. It felt cold. Greenland was certainly much colder, but drier, and therefore not any more uncomfortable than New York with its humidity.

Samantha took a taxi to the Kruger's home in Queens. Ben Kruger's funeral seemed such a long time ago. So much had happened in so short a time. Almost three months had passed since his death. Suddenly, Samantha felt very tired and wondered how she could endure visiting with the Krugers. The taxi turned onto Main in Kew Gardens Hills. She saw the Kruger jewelry store and decided she must go in there one day. The taxi stopped before a narrow driveway and a solid-looking Kew Gardens Hills house. Mr. and Mrs. Kruger both came out to greet her as if she were their daughter.

With a good cup of coffee and the warm and loving welcome, she revived, and the fact that the Krugers appreciated her visit so much, made it all worthwhile. They talked of Ben. Old stories were shared. They laughed and cried. Ben's face became real to her again. She saw his thick glasses, the ready smile, remembered his subtle humor, his high principles, the burial service that emphasized his good name, her first Jewish funeral, and her realization of the closeness and love in the Jewish community.

After a second round of hugs and goodbyes she took a taxi into Manhattan to the Stanhope. She would be pampered and cared for as if she were family there, too.

Once in her room with the Chinoiserie and the Louis XVI furniture, she could at last relax. She would never take a steaming tub of scented bubbles for granted again. Pure heaven. Lounging on the bed in the soft terry cloth robe an hour later, she phoned down to the chef and put together a fabulous, but health-conscious dinner.

The chef had her favorite wine, Loupiac, a white Bordeaux-Chateau Verisse. And wonder of wonders, St. Marcellin cheese flown in just that very day.

She knew what she had to have for dessert, a tarte Tatin made with red Gala apples covered in a buttery caramel sauce. At the end, strong coffee from freshly roasted and ground Arabica beans. Perhaps some Mandarin Napoleon in a big pear-shaped snifter.

Samantha savored these good moments and enjoyed them. No matter that yesterday had been hell, and tomorrow would bring mind-numbing challenges. A night in the Stanhope. What could be better? Just what the doctor would have ordered. The soreness and chapping had nearly gone. Even her arm seemed well.

Stretching and massaging the sore muscles had worked magic. She wondered why she hadn't ordered a massage. She would save that treat for later. She looked in her luggage for a book not yet read, John Pohl's Exploring Mesoamerica. Soon, she would be roaming Guatemala and Honduras, lands of the great Precolumbian cultures. Long before "Chris" had sailed the ocean blue, the civilizations of Mesoamerica were in their glory "among the most sophisticated and spectacular of the ancient world."

Samantha was particularly interested in the Classic period of the Mayan culture, and especially the site of Copán in Honduras. Trak Barber would work there, and if Samantha could make it happen, she would enjoy the company of Julie Amber, Trak's significant other. Julie would be of great help to Samantha as she entered that world of mystery and intrigue.

It was a temptation to begin with page 91 where the site of Copán was investigated. But she resisted, knowing a good grounding before and after, would help her understand and appreciate that section better. Samantha liked the smell of her new book. She touched it sensing the colors of yellowish gold and turquoise with a hint of dark red, the latter color, coming from the spine surprised her. An animal involved? Blood again. Maybe just a holdover from the animal skins in Greenland. Interesting? Or foreboding?

She read for an hour before the book tented across her breasts.

Chapter 22

I have this crazy desire to move to Vermont. It's just beyond me why I like that state so much. Of course I'll never move there. It would destroy the attraction. —From Samantha's Journal

She opened her eyes to darkness. The book slipped to the floor with a soft plop. She swung her long legs over the edge of the bed and stretched as high as she could reach.

Her wake-up call was an hour away. But she felt rested, so why not get up? Her plane would leave La Guardia at 9:05. She could take her time. Crunchy toast, fruit, and black coffee had been ordered the night before, and would arrive by 7:30.

A tepid to chilly shower was a good way to wake up. She dressed, packed, and had time to read for forty-five minutes before breakfast arrived. She ate hurriedly, now impatient to get on with the day.

Originally, she had hoped for a leisurely stay in New York, perhaps making a few calls to the World Trade Center, maybe even a small tour if there were spaces she could preview.

A phone conversation with Abel Jorwoski, alias Tom Jones, had changed her plans. Now her day would begin with a short hop to Burlington, a drive toward the southeast near Waterbury, and a series of secret turns until she arrived at the site of the decommissioned missile silo to see if water had seeped, or had been pumped down, into the ninth subterranean floor.

She could have called her private contractor, Samuel George, and he could have checked. But Samantha prided herself in not accepting second-hand information. Her clients expected her to see with her own eyes, whether or not a problem existed. They tended to worry excessively. That went with the territory.

Samantha was one of the best in the business although she looked forward eagerly to the day when she would no longer deal with angst-ridden personalities. She would, in the meantime, do her very best to deliver on her promises, and uphold her reputation.

The plane touched down at 10:40. She picked up the Lexus rental and arrived at the site by 1:30. Since she had been so close, she had turned northward for a few miles and there, in a delightful meadow setting, with mountains in the background, she had stopped at the renowned Ben and Jerry's ice cream factory. She couldn't pass it up, but she did pass up the tour, opting instead for a big dish of several luscious flavors and concoctions. Hey, it was past her lunchtime anyway.

Samuel George had been with Samantha several years. She kept him and his crew busy and as far as she knew not a single scrap of information about those secret and far-flung headquarters, factories, homes, and what-nots had ever leaked to the public. Each site presented its own problems, and Samantha and Samuel had always found solutions. Often quite ingenious solutions.

The decommissioned missile silo would not be too tough, but Jorwoski had been somewhat of a pain, wanting to study at great lengths every suggestion. Now, he believed someone had spied on him and found his location.

Samantha pulled up at the guard house where two armed men in security uniforms and stiff-brimmed hats motioned her to stop. The prearranged code was given and acknowledged. A hurried phone call. A confirmation, and Samantha raised a slight dust cloud as she went up a small rise on the wide-graveled road toward a large warehouse.

So far so good. She had selected the security service, arranged for the large sign heralding the new home of an "acronym" research facility. A small second sign stated hiring would begin soon. It had an 800 number to call. The phone service had reported fifty-one calls already. In the surrounding towns PR announcements had been made and interviews given. Now, predictably, the neighbors had quieted down, and the work could continue on the project. Large trucks rolled in and out of the warehouse.

All employees at this point belonged to Samuel George. What the public didn't know: the huge store of materials unloaded inside would refurbish the underground silo, side tunnels, and command center, into a bunker the President of the United States would have been pleased to call home, during an all-out alien attack.

Samantha drove far into the warehouse to a small office. There, she greeted Samuel. To shut out the diesel engines of the huge trucks, and the beeping forklifts as they backed this way and that, Samuel escorted Samantha to the office and shut the door.

"Whew! Well Samuel, I can see you have things rolling." She explained her reason for coming. Since they knew each other so well, and had run into similar fears and buyers' remorse several times before, they shook their heads and smiled. Early in their relationship with each other, a situation like this would have caused angry looks and a stream of heated remarks. Now, each respected the other, and they worked together to solve buyer problems.

Samantha and Samuel took the construction elevator as far down as possible and continued with ladders until the bottom had been reached. No water. Indeed, no water even at the ninth level. There would be only ten stories of habitable space, with several of the floors having high ceilings. Samantha checked every floor. No water. Dry as a bone. That night she would report to Abel Jorwoski and get his go-ahead-decision. Actually, construction had not stopped. No need for that unless the unthinkable happened, and Mr. Jorwoski jumped ship. He never had before.

The construction looked great. Samuel had outdone himself and that delighted Samantha. She remarked to herself that if things continued this well, Samuel and his crew would share a handsome bonus when the job was complete. This, in addition to the generous pay they already received, three times greater than any other specialized crew in the world that Samantha knew of.

"Three months and we can wind this baby up. Won't go over another 150 million," said Samuel, with pride in his voice.

"You're doing a great job, Samuel, maybe your best."

They said goodbye, and she drove the Lexus out and down the hill and onto the small, two-lane black-top road.

In three months, the real fun would start. PR would circulate press releases stating the company didn't get funding. The warehouse would be torn down. The place leveled off. The guards would disappear. No trespassing signs and a for sale sign would go up.

A bogus buyer would buy the sizable acreage. Local contractors would be hired to build a modest house and some out buildings for the gentleman farmer who traveled a lot and would visit his "farm" sporadically. The arable land would be rented out to local farmers for crops and the meadows for pasture. The wooded area would be pruned occasionally to limit undergrowth. Handsome white fencing would go up around the property.

In all, the property would have a settled air to it and would operate as a very pleasing-looking Vermont farm. The house would be built right over the silo, and the local contractors would not have an inkling as to what lay beneath. If they had seen the luxuriously outfitted ten stories below, their eyes would have popped.

With the new home finally completed, Samuel and a couple of his crew would return and construct the connection between house and silo, then install and activate the surveillance system. All would be ready for the nervous Abel Jorwoski to arrive with his wife, hopping about the country-side in as circuitous a manner as possible, before darting in for a look.

Samantha knew they would like it for awhile, then the hunt would be on for a really, truly, safe place. And, if she were still in the business, she would sell the silo complex to another paranoid buyer. The number of hideaways stuck around the world had surprised Samantha. She still had the South Pacific atoll to work on. That would be a gigantic problem. She had to admit to ambivalent feelings. She was disgusted at the vast, unwarranted expense and yet stimulated by the almost impossible construction problems to solve. And it did pay well.

Driving back to Burlington the next day, after having spent the evening in a charming local inn, she drank in the Vermont scenery. Snow covered the ground and she knew the ski areas that dotted the hills and mountains would still be full of skiers and snow boarders, though the season neared an end.

She remembered her own skiing adventures in the French Alps

just a couple of months earlier. She wondered if Guilluame Minnon still skied there. If so, would he be taking out other broken-hearted women off-piste for glorious runs through the pristine powder? She bet they wouldn't get to spend the night with him in that deserted chalet.

Suddenly, fervently, she hoped they would not. She had passed up her opportunity and been glad at the time. But she didn't want others to sample what had been forbidden fruit to her. The never-to-be-forgotten interlude with Guillaume later at her hotel would remain priceless. No one could possibly understand how she felt about it.

"Damn you Emerson. Why did I fall in love with you, making my life miserable?"Samantha thought back to their last argument in Edinburgh. She pounded the steering wheel. Would they ever get back together? Not if she couldn't reach him. Did she really want to reach him? Heal the rift? She would send another email.

A rabbit darted onto the highway. Samantha hit the brakes and her car swerved. The rabbit's white fluff-balled tail disappeared in the snowy brush. No harm done. She saw the Burlington skyline in the distance, home of the University of Vermont, UVM Universitas Viridis Montis, University of the Green Mountains. She thought of Amy Posher, thousands of miles away at Brighton, trudging to classes and dreaming of a future as Samantha's assistant.

She must begin making plans how to help Amy develop her talents. The novice was intelligent and eager. Samantha wanted to help her use that intelligence, challenge herself, and keep that eagerness from slipping away. Amy would need to come to New York, and Austin, to find out whether her best suit would be research, management, or sales. At first, she would need to be trained to do all three.

Chapter 23

My friends in New York can't understand how I could live above a bunch of bars with loud music. I don't understand it either—or why I go happily at times skipping from bar to bar listening to that jangly music. Lovely jangly music. I'm a mess.
—From Samantha's Journal

Samantha's plane left Burlington for La Guardia at eleven, and arrived in New York at twelve twenty-nine. She lunched at the airport and did some emailing. She set up an appointment to talk about World Trade Center space. The agent tried to schedule for the following week, but Samantha, knowing they were not to appear too eager, wouldn't play his game. She got the appointment for that afternoon. She sat in the VIP club room at the airport and read for awhile, then took a taxi directly to lower Manhattan.

She had checked out of her hotel before going to Burlington and the concierge had made sure her luggage would be waiting for her at JFK for her flight back to Austin. She would be arriving at her apartment on Sixth Street just about the time the local bands began showing up for their evening gigs in the bars below her, and along the several blocks stretching from Congress Avenue to Interstate 35. Sometimes she liked listening, sometimes not. Tonight, after the stillness of Greenland, she would look forward to the musical cacophony. She might even go down and visit a few places.

The meeting with the WTC agent went well, and she got a tour of the kind of space she could lease. She wasn't sure she liked being that high somewhere above the 90th floor. That meant a lot of time in the elevator sometimes unnerving to an already nervous client. She would solve that later. She put a hold on a suite of offices, and would finalize the lease by phone, or go back and look at something lower down. Redecorating, computer set-up, and all the other details would not take too long. She should be able to set up shop in September. Her own office and at a prestigious address. She wondered if she could get Emerson to come to the grand opening.

Samantha watched the sunlight move along the facade of a building across from her Austin apartment. Home again. Nothing like waking up in your own bed. She stretched and lay there looking at the ceiling, out the windows, and at the decor of her apartment. She wondered whether the landlord would allow a window box. She could grow herbs. Maybe pansies. It was nine-thirty-one according to her atomic wrist watch, the morning of Friday, March 16, 2001. She liked orienting herself to the exact time and date. It put her on firm ground. A starting place. She would not leave for Central America until the twentieth or maybe later.

To not have a definite date of departure was unusual, but the reason for it was not knowing if, and when, Julie Amber could leave with her. Finding that out would be the first order of business. Soon she would see the slim entrepreneur again. She hoped Julie hadn't got herself tied into a job yet. Her dotcommer experience with a failed company probably had jolted her enough to keep her out of the clutches of another corporate commitment, at least long enough for a sojourn south of the border.

She stretched again. Last night had been a hoot. Rock, reggae, copy bands, country, swing, and jazz. There's no place like Austin for live music. She had wandered about listening until way too late, but had enjoyed every minute. She mused about the effect such a night would have had on Jason Murdoch or Aisa, and Philip, or the Inuk she first met when she and Aisa arrived in Siorapaluk.

She picked up her cell phone and called her uncle at the ranch. She had decided not to go there before leaving on her trip and she was hoping to persuade him to come to Austin for a visit.

"Uncle Stu, guess who?"

"Darlin'!" His booming voice making some cell phone tower

shake somewhere. "When did you get in? Are you in Austin? How the world are you? When can you get out here? Maria's been baking and stewing around for days, darlin'. How about today? You got to come. No arguing about it, just get in that Land Rover and get yourself out here!" The questions and demands tumbled over each other and Samantha just sat on her bed shaking her head. She had to laugh.

"I'm fine." she finally broke in, then added,

"O.K., O.K. I'll be there for dinner tonight." She should have known her decision to stay in Austin would be blown out of the water. Then a flashing light.

"I'm not sure, Uncle Stu, but if I can convince her, I'd like to bring out a young lady for you to meet. Would that be all right?"

"Darlin' you can bring all of Austin iffen you got a mind to, just get here. See you at dinner. Maria is a standing here just smiling all over herself, tell her howdy."

The Mexican house keeper and cook who spoke flawless English with not a hint of Texan came on the line. It was so good to hear her voice. The same questions were asked and answered and Samantha could tell Maria was as excited and concerned as if she had been Samantha's mother.

How blessed she felt with such caring people around her. It made her feel a little guilty for not sharing everything about her adventures with her uncle. He had not said "I told you so" about her Greenland trip. The gratefulness stayed in her heart. She would think about letting her uncle in on her plans later. Now she would call Julie Amber.

Chapter 24

At first I thought it was a fluke, but all my girl friends drive like they're on a race track. Why is that? Do I attract daredevils? Do I secretly want to be smashed in a terrible accident? Is my life so dull I have to hunt for thrills? Go figure. – From Samantha's Journal

Roaring up, over, and around the gentle hills southwest of Austin with the top down, and the heater on, was not the usual way Samantha drove to her uncle's ranch. Julie had said yes, enthusiastically, to the visit, but only if they would take her Porsche Boxster. Samantha wondered if Julie's excitement stemmed from wanting to visit the ranch, or from wanting to put the Boxster through its paces on the winding Hill Country roads. She remembered her wild ride with Christina from Florence to Rome in January. It must be fate that seated her beside race drivers. However, she admitted silently that Christina and now Julie knew how to get the best performance from a car.

The immaculate Porsche held the road as if the tires had been sprayed with glue. The seat felt like a warm glove. The outside temperature was bracing, and the warmth from the heater played excellent counterpoint to the March breeze. Hugged by a wool cap, which saved her hair from tangles, Samantha sat back and tried to relax on the roller-coaster highway. Both women were exhilarated, helped by the yells they sent across the canyons from time to time. The streaking silver sports car seemed alive, and as eager as any of the sledge dogs in Greenland to simply run, run, and run. Speed, the dream of dogs and men...or in this case, two women.

The massive gates of the ranch loomed into view.

This time Samantha held a state-of-the-art GPS to see if she could keep the directions straight as the ranch road began its two-mile meanderings.

A compass would have served her just as well, but the GPS showed all the turns, all the way from Austin to the ranch house itself, dutifully committing all to its memory bank. Samantha was tired of watching the sun come up in the west, and set in the east. The Global Positioning System would solve that for her once and for all, she hoped. She had read that synesthetes were easily disoriented. While she loved being a synesthete, she hated being disoriented.

Over a slight rise they saw the main ranch house, "biggest one in the Hill Country," her uncle had boasted.

Julie let out a yell of surprise.

"When you said ranch, I wasn't expecting this. Cool!"

"It's my uncle's way of proving he's a Texan, if not by birth, at least by heart, stone and wood. Wait until you see the birds."

"Birds?" was all Julie got out of her mouth before the big doors swung open and Samantha's bear of an uncle, his iron-gray hair slightly disheveled, came roaring out, his huge arms spread wide, followed closely by the ranch manager, Joe Bill Barstow, and he in turn, followed by plump, black-eyed Maria Gonzales, the head ranch cook and housekeeper, who with an ever-increasing staff of helpers, kept things in the sprawling ranch headquarters running smoothly, or as smoothly as possible, considering the erratic habits of Stuart King.

"Howdy, howdy, darlin'. You're a sight for sore eyes. Get out, so I can hug you." The next couple of minutes were filled with hugs and laughter. Tears of joy were shed by Maria. There were introductions, visual appraisals by all, with the consensus being everyone liked everything they saw. Samantha hastily added that Julie's true love was in Honduras, or else she would have brought him too. She did this pointedly, as she saw the appreciative look in Joe Bill's eyes and, surprisingly to her, in the eyes of her uncle.

She had to admit that Julie, with her thick golden-brown hair, now flying free of her cap, her brown eyes, and a figure that put the lie to skinny is better, could, and would, turn a male head, and that it was a good thing she did have a boyfriend. Now, Julie could relax and have a good time and so could Samantha. She wondered if she were jealous of the younger woman, and decided the male attention was due mostly to the fact that Julie was new to the guys, and not because she appeared to be a nubile nymph ready for plucking, euphemistically speaking, or a dance in the woods under a full moon. Samantha watched her long-legged friend lap up the warm male eyes like a saucer of warm barn milk, even though she did have a true love thousands of miles away.

Again the doors swung open and everyone trooped in to the hall of birds. With so many people coming in all at once, the special feathered friends of Samantha's uncle let out screeches of warning to each other. Perches were abandoned for the open spaces between the beams. A few feathers sifted down onto the protective plastic sheeting.

"Damn birds are taking over the house," shouted Uncle Stuart, as a dove circled his head and the myna bird in its black plumage from thirty feet up, advised raucously for the world to unite and fight for bird rights. A loyal congregation made up of red, yellow and blue parrots, green parakeets, white cockatiels, red-eyed pigeons, rusty-headed finches and a lost light-brown sparrow called out "amen" in bird talk.

"I love them damn birds, but there are days I want to shoot ever last one and have Maria make a big pie out of them. Come on into my office so we can hear ourselves think."

Uncle Stuart's office was big enough to swallow the entire floor plan of a 2,000 square feet suburban home. He herded everyone in and shut the door before a hovering dove could flit through with him.

Samantha was brought up-to-date about the ranch. Julie was included, as if she were now a part of the family. Maria excused herself and hurried back to the kitchen to oversee the evening's meal.

Before she left, she hugged Samantha one more time, and Samantha told her they would have a nice visit soon. The ranch manager, Joe Bill, also said goodbye, and that he would be back in time to eat. Self-consciously, he quickly shook Samantha's and Julie's hands before leaving.

114

Then Uncle Stuart asked Samantha how things were going, and if she still planned to go to Honduras, and also how surprised he'd been when her email had said she had no trouble meeting and talking with Jason Murdoch.

"You're a better salesman than I was. He wouldn't talk to me at all, of course, that was right after he'd decided to leave that company down there in Guatemala." Stuart King leaned back in his leather chair and rubbed his hands then looked back at Samantha.

"Well, darlin' I know you got to do what you got to do, and I just want you to get it done and over with so you can get on with your life."

Samantha decided not to tell her uncle of her suspicions about his brother's death. Nor did she see any reason to upset him with the details of her Greenland trip. It was enough for him that she had talked with Jason Murdoch and that she had been happy with the experience.

"Thank you for understanding, Uncle Stu. I really appreciate you. I know you will always be there for me." And Samantha meant it as she got up and went over to hug his grizzled head. He was so dear to her, even though she shied from coming under his too-ready advice and control.

"You're right about that, no matter how goldanged stubborn you've grown up to be. Now in case I forget after eating Maria's cooking tonight, I want you and Julie to promise to keep tomorrow afternoon open. Don't even think about skedaddlin' back to Austin before I have a chance to show you something really special. Agreed?"

Samantha looked at Julie, who nodded yes.

"O.K. Uncle Stu, count us in, but we have to go back to Austin sometime tomorrow to get ready for our trip south. Julie has decided to go with me, and we have a thousand things to do."

"That's great news. Wonderful. You going with Samantha and both of you staying for the show tomorrow. You won't be disappointed."

Stuart King clapped his big hands together and the birds in the adjoining room responded with enthusiasm.

Chapter 25

I really like being at the ranch. Of course, I love my uncle and Maria and the people who help run it. It is so "grounding" for me. A real stabilizing influence. I don't know what I'd do if I couldn't come out here and ride Duchess and jump in the river and listen to "them damn birds" up in the rafters of the main house. –From Samantha's Journal

Samantha and Julie left through the kitchen. The lovely smells of the soon-to-be dinner nearly overwhelmed them. Samantha had visited a little with Maria while the keen-eyed cook kept watch over the helpers who were running around, frantically, getting everything ready.

Samantha and Julie drove down to Samantha's cabin on the Sabinal to freshen up, before returning to the ranch house in a couple of hours. They had a chance to visit about the trip, and do some preliminary planning.

"We'll eat in the kitchen. Did you see that huge harvester table? Uncle Stu has invited some of his friends for dinner. We'll have a good time."

And Samantha was right. Maria and her helpers loaded the table down with chicken and beef quesadillas, tortilla soup, grilled shrimp, chicken and beef fajitas, fresh green salads, bowls of guacamole, relishes and salsas, chili rellenos, tacos, burritos, chalupas, corn tortillas and a big pot of frijoles. Mexican beer, Texas wine, agua fresca and strong black coffee made the rounds. For dessert, Maria served jalapeno pecan ice cream, ancho chocolate brownies and the classic Mexican flan. After dessert there would be more coffee, a selection of liqueurs, various old ports and cigars for any who wanted to smoke, but not in the bird room.

"Damn birds can't stand smoke."

Stuart King had invited three couples who lived nearby on ranches and two couples, friends of long-standing, reaching back into the government information years, although this would never be mentioned to the other guests. Stuart King never mentioned his government years either.

Tom and Jayne Waters had a nice home a couple of ridges away, near the Medina River, and stocked a few semi-wild Mustangs they hoped to ride some day in parades.

Last, were George and Christie Ormiston, both retired and now living in Medina. They planned to open a bed and breakfast. The ranch manager, Joe Bill Barstow, rounded out the guest list.

Topics ranged from cattle to politics and the conversations remained lively and friendly. Toward the end of the evening some philosophical and political differences began to surface and voices were raised a little. At that point Uncle Stuart slapped the table, grabbed a spoon and banged a glass hard enough Samantha thought it would break. He got everyone's attention.

"Before we tackle dessert, I have some news and an invitation. You know how fond I am of my niece. I could say she's my favorite niece, which would be true, even if I had other nieces." Heads nodded with polite laughter.

"Soon she will be heading for Honduras to locate the crash site of her dad who was also my brother and who went down a little over a year ago. We buried him in Enid, Oklahoma, beside Helen, Samantha's mother. It is sort of a pilgrimage you might say for Samantha to try to find where he died.

"It says a lot about her and her love for her dad. He raised her and did a damn good job of it too. I want you all to join me in a toast to her good health and the successful completion of her journey. We'll all be thinking of you, darlin'" He raised his glass again and motioned toward Julie.

"And let's toast this fine young woman, Julie Amber, who will accompany Samantha. Stay well both of you." Samantha noted that there was very little Texas accent during the whole speech, just the use of "darlin'".

Her uncle put down his glass, but remained standing and beamed at them, taking in each face in turn and smiling broadly until everyone was smiling back.

"Now, for the invite. Y'all know how much I like it here in the Hill Country and how much I enjoy y'all who're my good neighbors and friends. Some of y'all I'm just gettin' to know really well and some of y'all go way back. Well, if y'all can make it back here tomorra say around three, there's gonna be somethin' special happenin' here.

"After you see the show, I want you to hang around for an old fashioned Bar-B-Que featurin' axis venison, some of my best beef, goat, and a little feral hog, iffen you can stand it.

"Maria even tells me we got a few pheasant and quail tucked away, that she might trot out. So, let me see your hands if you can make it." There was an immediate show of hands from everyone present. Samantha couldn't believe the sudden shift back into Texan. Only her uncle. She smiled and shook her head at Julie, who winked back.

––––––––––––

The guests stayed for another hour, talking and mingling. Samantha and Julie enjoyed the attention and drifted about talking with everyone at one time or another. Tom Waters and George Ormiston seemed quite interested in Samantha's India experience.

Tom's black eyes took in everything. His hair, cut short, still had no gray, but his moustache and neatly trimmed beard had some whitish flecks.

"So, you never found out why some folks were so interested in what you brought back?" Apparently, Samantha's uncle had spilled the beans to these two and maybe to everyone in the room. These two gentlemen, however, wanted to talk about it. Samantha was pleased she had not shared all she knew about the textile she had picked up in India, nor about the promise given to Mr. Dewani, the Indian businessman.

George Ormiston, nearly a half-foot shorter than Tom Waters and with a very tanned bald head, leaned closer.

"We heard about your adventure from your uncle. It must have been terrible, being buried like that."

Samantha remembered her uncle stating once that both men

had worked with him in some sort of government covert operation, but not sure as to their motives, she agreed that her adventure had been quite nerve-wracking. She told them how torn she still was over the loss of her colleagues.

"I guess that's why I'm so driven to bring my dad's death to some sort of closure. It's almost as if I'm running out of time to get all the loose ends taken care of."

"Well," said Tom, his black eyes looking directly into hers, "we wish you the best. Just be really careful and come back to Texas safe and sound."

That night before turning in, Samantha invited Julie to go for a walk near the cabin. The stars were out and Samantha found out that Julie knew several of the constellations.

"Orion is my favorite. Ever since I was a little girl, I imagined Orion with his bow and sword as sort of my protector,"

"I like that," said Samantha, "how did you learn about Orion when you were so young?"

"My mother."

"My mother was killed in a car accident when I was very young and I don't really remember her at all, but if she had lived perhaps she would have told me about Orion too. You'll have to come back in the winter time, and we can see Orion again." They neared the pool. Samantha walked up to the edge.

"Say, how about a swim?"

"I'd love to, but I don't have anything to wear."

"Me neither." They both laughed.

"I do have two big terry cloth robes."

"Wouldn't someone see us?"

"No way, we're really private back here, and the ranch hands know not to be riding by while I'm visiting. Uncle's orders."

"O.K. you're on. Let's go back and get those robes."

They swam under the Big Dipper in the cold water until their teeth chattered. Setting on the back deck wrapped in robes, they listened to the Sabinal River below. Samantha told Julie about Aisa, Philip, and Jason and her Greenland experience, that almost

119

ended in tragedy. Julie shared her growing-up stories, which made Samantha wish all the more she had known her own mother. Samantha was so glad Julie would be going with her.

"Before I go off to Copán to see my dedicated archaeologist, maybe we could do a little sight-seeing down there," offered Julie.

"I would like that. I would like that a lot." Samantha realized there would be precious few moments of enjoyment on this trip, and Julie's suggestion was certainly welcome. She remembered her uncle's toast and wished it would come true.

Good health and a successful journey. In trying to find her dad, perhaps she would find herself as well.

Chapter 26

I just have to marvel at some of my women friends. Christina,
Amy, Aisa and now Julie. I feel so blessed to know them. They
are so full of life. It keeps me young to be around them. I
probably wouldn't trade them for any man, if I had to choose.
–From Samantha's Journal

In the gauzy early morning light, Samantha and Julie sat on
the deck with mugs of strong steaming coffee, and breakfasted on
scones, and huckleberry jam, the latter supplied by Julie.

"I got the huckleberry jam at a conference held last summer at
Jackson Hole. I was saving it for something special, so you're it."

"Delicious," said Samantha with her mouth full, "And I'm
honored, great flavor," she added. A sliced orange waited in a teal-
blue salad plate. The giant gray cypress trees rooted near the
river's edge stretched ghostly bare limbs into the thick blanket of
silver fog. The river tumbled and splashed against gray boulders in
near silence.

"Like living inside a pillow," said Julie. White foam mixed
and eddied with the dark jade of the deep pools, as the river wound
its way through the valley.

"It's so peaceful here. I could sit and watch and listen to that
river all day."

"Yes, when I'm away and things are hectic, I try to remember
sitting here. It really helps, and I can hardly wait until the next
visit.

"Spring is definitely in the air," said Julie.

"Yeah, already 50 degrees. Those trees will be waking up
soon. And before you know it everything will be green. A hundred
shades of green. I didn't realize there were so many colors of

green before I started coming to the ranch."

"Samantha, I have to ask this. I know it's none of my business, in a way, but since we are traveling together, I want to know as much as I can in order to be a really good assistant. Your uncle seemed concerned about your trip to Honduras to find your dad's crash site. Do you know exactly where it is?"

"Ask anything you want. You hit on part of the problem all right. I don't know exactly, just generally. I was hoping I could find out from the oil company he worked for, when I got down there. I'll have to get a guide and be prepared for a trek into the back country and that's what Uncle Stu is worried about. But it's something I have to do. He doesn't want me to go." Samantha picked up an orange slice and looked at it.

"He said he'd hog-tie me if it would keep me here. But I've got to find some answers. I've had nightmares about my dad's plane going down. I've got to see it for myself, if it's still there. By now, it could have been carted off and sold as scrap. No one seems to know for sure what happened. They think he ran out of fuel. I don't know what to expect. If I find the plane, it may not help. I want to know who found my dad. I'd like to talk to them. I know that's a long shot. They cremated him in Guatemala. That's about all I know, and it's not enough." Julie picked up an orange slice.

"And if you don't find the answers?" She asked.

"Well at least I'll have tried. I'll know that, and maybe it will be enough to bring some peace. It just gnaws on me Julie. I can't accept that it was an accident. He was too good a pilot."

"You can count on me to help in anyway I can. I wanted to go and be with Trak, but he said I'd be spending a lot of "alone" time in the hotel. So, you are certainly doing me a favor letting me tag along."

"And I'm so glad you're going with me. Now, how about getting into some jeans and boots, and going for a ride? There are two horses in that little stable over there. I bet they'd enjoy some exercise."

———————

Duchess, Samantha's black Quarter Horse, and Marian, a gentle light bay the ranch hands had brought over for Julie, indeed were eager to leave the stable when they heard the two women approaching.

"I like driving fast cars, but give me a slow dependable horse any day." Julie said, hearing the horses stamping in the small stable.

"And I bet, if you come visit me at the ranch a few times, you'll be asking for a high-strung stallion to tear around on."Once through the gate that set the cabin's grounds off from the ranch proper, Samantha and Julie crossed a wet-weather creek, and set a course that would lead through several meadows and lightly wooded areas, making a wide swing before heading for the sprawling ranch house and brunch. The horses stepped out smartly. Duchess tried out a few prancing steps before settling down to an easy walk.

"We'll walk mostly, but give them a chance to trot a little, too, where it's smooth and there aren't any holes." Julie sat her horse well and seemed to enjoy herself immensely.

Around them, clumps of dead grass, winter-killed, could not hide the bright green blades sprouting from them. The branches of small trees and shrubs were swelling with buds, ready to burst into flowers and leaves. The fog was beginning to burn off, and the sun was doing its best to poke through the mist. Patches of blue sky could be glimpsed. Cardinals sang out strident one-note territorial announcements.

In the distance, a mockingbird, the state bird of Texas, tried out a series of symphonic themes, repeating each theme two or three times before offering the next selection.

Then, rounding a copse of mesquite, they spied a Longhorn steer, with a horn span of five feet, eyeing them.

"Wow, will you look at that!" said Julie. "That must be the granddaddy of Bevo!" At the sound of her voice, the steer shook its head, bruising a flowering mountain laurel. A heavy oil-scented perfume enveloped horses and riders.

"That mountain laurel is strong stuff, like a batch of grape Kool-Aid flavored with diesel fuel. I like it," said Samantha, "As for granddaddy Bevo, we're hoping the next U.T. mascot will come from this herd. Believe it or not, this one's just average. You should see the really big ones."

"Wow," said Julie and laughed, "Never mind, this one's big

123

enough for me." The horses took no notice of the steer. Suddenly the Longhorn bolted, crashing away through the underbrush.

"Woo, that's scary. Glad I wasn't on the ground in front of him," exclaimed Julie, clearly impressed with the animal's quickness and speed.

Coming to a long level place, Samantha touched Duchess with her heels. The Quarter Horse took off like a shot. The long stretch of smooth trail ended too soon for both horse and rider.

Duchess came to a prancing halt. Samantha turned in the saddle to see Marian in a respectable gallop coming up from behind with wide-eyed Julie hanging on, exhilarated and scared at the same time.

"Sit up and pull back gently," Samantha called to the fast-approaching Julie, whose golden-brown hair streamed out behind her. Marian, needing no great amount of urging to call it quits and probably as surprised as anyone at her unexpected burst of speed, slowed quickly. The horse seemed perfectly happy to go from a mad gallop to a trot to a walk and then to a complete stop without a single prancing step.

"Wow!" called out Julie. "I guess, that's the only word I'm going to use all morning. But nothing else seems to come to mind. What a run! Didn't you say Marian was a slow horse?"

"To tell you the truth, she surprised me too. I'm not used to Duchess all that much either. I thought I would have her trot a little. I guess she decided we were after bank robbers, or competing in a rodeo. Whoosh, and she was gone. I guess I just let her run and when I stopped and turned around I expected to see Marian trotting sedately. A horse will surprise you sometimes. I hope it didn't startle you too much."

"I wouldn't have missed it for the world. So where's that high-strung stallion?"

During the following half-hour they spotted the rare scimitar oryx with the black markings on its upper legs, long straight upright horns and broom-like tail.

"That's the first time I've seen the oryx," whispered Samantha. "Isn't he majestic? Got to watch out for those lethal horns, though."

Julie saw a group of toy-like fallow deer, skittish, leaping quickly into the cover of some acacia trees, already thick with small golden yellow blooms. Three axis deer grazed under a live oak.

"There's no hunting season for axis deer," Samantha said in a hushed voice. Ranchers shoot them all year long, mostly to make sausage. We'll have some this morning. Delicious." Then she saw the look on Julie's face.

"You're not the first guest who couldn't eat something that looks at you with big brown eyes. Don't worry about it. I felt the same way, then I thought, where in the hell do steaks come from? I do believe we'll stop eating meat some day and just dine on plants. Life and death, kill or be killed, eat and be eaten. If we could develop green skins we could eat sunlight."

"And smell like a rose."Julie had to laugh. "Sorry to be so squeamish. I guess it goes with being raised in the city and never questioning where a 'happy meal' comes from. I'll try some sausage."

They rode near a bluff and Samantha remembered the young deer killed there not long ago. She pulled Duchess to a stop and looked around. The huisache daisies had grown taller and more numerous and the Mexican persimmon looked ready to bloom. She saw the bones, cleanly stripped, and already bleaching in the sun. Other animals had dined. Duchess and Marian didn't seem nervous. Apparently the smell of the mountain lion had dissipated. Julie had listened to the story in silence.

"A mountain lion? For real?" She looked at the bluff above her head with a worried expression.

"Don't worry, we're not on his menu, even if he were here, which he isn't. Uncle Stu feels sure he moved on. On the other hand, who knows?" Samantha felt herself smiling. Julie was trying to smile, but having a hard time at it.

"Believe me, Julie, if he were around, Marian would be half-way to the ranch house by now." Samantha told her how upset Duchess had been right after the kill when the smell of the lion had been so strong.

"This is like being in the wild, wild west. I love it, I think. One thing I know, Im getting hungry. Where's that chuck wagon?"

After brunch, Maria offered seconds on axis sausage, migas, tortillas, salsa, frijoles and coffee. Patting their suddenly convex stomachs and shaking their heads, the two women saddled up and had a leisurely ride back for a last swim before the big surprise that afternoon.

"Your uncle has got some cute ranch hands Samantha. Good thing I'm loyal and faithful to Trak."

"I know what you mean. I have a feeling the boys wouldn't mind you straying into some secluded corral."

"Samantha, whether you know it or not that blue-eyed ranch manager, what's-his-name...?"

"You mean Joe Bill?"

"Ah ha, so you do know. Anyway, he looks at you like its his birthday and you're the cake." Julie clapped her hands together at Samantha's momentary silence and look of incredulity.

"So, I'm a cake, you say? Only if I can be chocolate!" And laughed at her own joke.

So, Julie was steadfast in her love for Trak. That was great. Samantha was happy for her. She knew that she too would like to feel that kind of devotion. In spite of the ups and downs of her re-lationship with Emerson, she knew she would remain faithful and maybe someday there would be fewer downs to contend with. Cute as Joe Bill was, Samantha wouldn't be straying. Thinking maybe, but not doing anything she would regret later.

"I'm not so sure he could handle a whole chocolate cake."

To the south Samantha could see cotton-puff clouds forming. She knew it was south, at last, thanks to her GPS.

"Fair weather ahead for Uncle Stu's show."

Chapter 27

Julie pointed out that Joe Bill is sweet on me. I didn't realize this. In a short while I had a fantasy going. I thought I was a school girl again. What fun. If Emerson did that I wouldn't like it at all. Pooh on me. –From Samantha's Journal

At the ranch house the guests of last night were arriving or had arrived. Which was which could be determined by who had glasses in their hands. Maria's helpers were scurrying about, taking orders, and bringing out glasses containing liquids of various colors, some cooled by large ice cubes. Both Samantha and Julie requested white wine. Maria had set up a small table for hors d'oeuvres: peppers, sturdy nachos, a clay pot of melted cheese, and serving dishes filled to the top with ground beef, refried beans, jalapeno burritos, small sausages, and some green and red grapes. There would be the barbeque soon, and Stuart King wanted his guests to have plenty of room left for the "main vittles." What was offered in the meantime he considered light and non-filling.

Samantha noticed that Joe Bill stayed close. Funny, she hadn't noticed that before. He offered to get her more wine. He discussed Duchess, the weather, a rodeo coming soon, the ranch, anything. He was within touching distance, but he didn't touch. Maybe Julie was right.

Joe Bill had thick blond hair. He was slim and tall with hard muscles and wide shoulders. His western-cut shirt barely contained a body sculpted by grappling with spirited animals, lifting bales of hay, mending fence, and probably digging post holes. Yep, he could cause a vulnerable woman a heap of trouble.

What would he look like with his shirt plastered against his shoulders soaked in sweat, smelling of alfalfa hay? Maybe no shirt. Burned bronze by the sun. Good, strong-looking legs. Glutei maximi so well-formed it would be impossible to slip anything into a back pocket. Fine hands, hard but gentle she bet. Good teeth too.

Lost in a fanciful appraisal, smiling, looking, judging, signing the bill of sale, and accepting delivery. She was aware of silence. He had asked a question? He was waiting for an answer?

"I'm sorry, Joe Bill, I didn't hear what you just said." Thankfully, car doors were opening and shutting. Greetings yelled out. Laughter.

"I said how long you plan to stay in Honduras?" He shifted his weight easily from one boot to the other, standing kind of relaxed, but alert. Like a mountain lion ready to pounce? Was she a deer? Maybe she was the lion.

"I wish I knew. I'll stay as long as it takes to find some answers." Idly, Samantha wondered how it would be to have Joe Bill with her on this trip, fighting their way through jungles, rain and heat. Covered in sweat. She seemed to be really into sweating for some reason, and it wasn't even summer yet. What a perverse imagination.

"Your uncle's got something really important for y'all this afternoon." His blue eyes twinkled. "It'll be showing up here real soon."

Hell, Samantha was tempted. Tempted or just fantasizing? Where did one start and the other leave off? Would she really do it? That was the question. After all, she and Emerson weren't married. Not even committed. As a matter of fact they had split up.

Still, something blocked a fling. However, given the right circumstances, the right time, the right mood, and if she were romantically free...then, yes, this handsome ranch manager might have a chance to tame her heart. She could invite him for a swim in the pool some hot sweaty summer's night.

A heavy duty pickup with an outsized horse trailer rumbled along the ranch road, kicking up a plume of dust that blew northward across a small meadow. Four Thoroughbred mares raised their heads and tails, then galloped off to the farthest fence, wheeled, stopped, and stared. The pickup and horse trailer drew up to the group of people. The powerful diesel idled. Stuart King walked over to talk with the driver. The engine clanked and stopped.

"It's a horse, another horse, maybe two or three in that trailer. Why the fuss? Must be really special horses," murmured Samantha. She felt Joe Bill leaning close as if to catch her words. She caught the scent of strong soap and leather.

"Now it's my turn not to hear, except I know what's in there," and he grinned like a little boy who had brought something really shocking for show and tell.

"Are you going to tell me?"

"Your uncle swore me to secrecy, but I can tell you this much, you're right it being a horse."

"A horse, one horse, in that big trailer?"

"Yep, and that's all I can say. You'll see for yourself in a couple of minutes." Very lightly, he touched her elbow, and she felt a small electric shock to her system. As nonchalantly as possible, she allowed him to guide her to the rear of the trailer. It wouldn't be long now. Everyone was quiet. Waiting. Wondering. Samantha knew her uncle would consider this one of his finer moments.

The trailer shook as if it were caught in an earthquake. Samantha felt the vibration and heard a monstrous stamping. Instinctively she moved away, only to be jolted from behind as she backed into a granite wall wearing a western shirt. She stumbled and two marvelous arms encircled her and held her. Maybe those arms would hold her longer if she had sprained an ankle. No such luck. No pain. Damn.

"Uh, thanks, Joe Bill, uh, I'm fine now. I hope I didn't hurt you." Hah. Great line, Samantha.

"No ma'am, I'm fine. I was worried you were going to fall."

Samantha's heart rate had gone up. Usually, she didn't get this excited over a horse. She took a deep breath and let it out slowly, or maybe it was a sigh. Why couldn't Emerson ride up and save her from her foolishness?

She saw Julie grinning and motioned her over.

"It's a horse, one horse," whispered Samantha. Julie continued grinning.

"Yeah, I heard the noise and saw you nearly fall down. Good thing what's his name was there to give you a big Heimlich maneuver."

"Hush, he'll hear you. It was an accident."

"Yeah, an accident you really enjoyed. I told you he was bonkers over you. Was I not right?" They whispered back and forth. Julie giggled, and Samantha tried to look unconcerned.

The big doors creaked open and got everyone's attention.

Two men walked up a ramp and into the gloom of the interior. There were rustlings, snortings, and more stampings, then out came a horse too large to believe.

"It's a Shire," said Joe Bill to Samantha and Julie. Stuart King hurried over to Samantha.

"Well, what do you think of that?"

"I don't know what to think. I never dreamed a horse could be that big without being an elephant." Her uncle laughed, but not too loudly. He didn't want to spook the huge animal.

"This one's a Shire, known as The Great Horse Some say his ancestors carried the knights during the Middle Ages, except this one's a whole lot bigger. Nearly 20 hands high at the shoulder. That's over six and a half feet tall at the shoulder and his head is another two feet taller than that. Ain't he just about the greatest thing you ever saw, darlin'?" He was almost dancing, rising up and down on his toes and taking little steps this way and that.

"I've always wanted a Shire. A big one. The bigger the better, and this one's about as big as they come. Weighs more than a ton. Ever since I was a boy I wanted one, and now I got me one," using his Texas drawl.

The stallion stood quietly as if aware of the shocked and admiring glances from the people around him. The mighty head tossed repeatedly, threatening to touch one of the swollen gray clouds nudging each other across the valley.

The Shire's coat: russet red. Below each knee: pure white. And toward his hooves thick hair not only white but long and feathery.

The black tail coiled up in a bun. Blue and green bows fastened the black mane in small tufts marching up the mighty neck. And no question, this huge animal was a stallion. Samantha could not help but stare.

"Walk him around a little. Bet he could use a little exercise after bein' cooped up in that trailer all mornin'," the new proud owner said. The handler clucked a little at the giant and gently pulled on the strap. The first step pounded into the ground raising a small cloud of dust and sending gravel pinging into the side of the trailer and against blue-jeaned legs. Some of the onlookers were suddenly too close, but mesmerized and unable to move away fast enough before this mass of tissue and bone lifted and slammed another white-sheathed hoof into the driveway.

"That hoof's bigger than a cast-iron frying pan," said Joe Bill.

Stuart King walked alongside, detailing plans for the animal.

"Going to put him at stud. I'll fix him up with a couple of my breeding stock and get me some hunters, yessir. Going to ride him in parades, maybe get another one and hitch 'em to a little wagon and walk them around Utopia, so the kids can see what real horses look like." He rubbed his hands and patted the Shire's withers. The stallion took a turn around the small space and came to a stop.

"Come on over here, darlin' and give him a pat." Samantha walked up to the head of the horse and a great eye looked down at her. She held up her hand and the large soft muzzle brushed against it. With her other hand she touched the side of the mammoth neck and noticed some white showing in the eye near to her. She sensed a tense moment, but gently rubbed the hard muscle. The tenseness relaxed somewhat, but the eye looked at her intently. She felt a small ridge beneath the russet coat and rubbed it some more.

When the giant pawed the ground Samantha moved back a step. Again, she held out her hand and the muzzle returned to it and stayed for awhile. The eye looked into her eyes. No white showed this time. Samantha stepped away, filled with awe at her encounter with this giant stallion.

She confided to her uncle later that she believed this magnificent horse had been mistreated.

"Tell your ranch hands to use extreme gentleness in caring for him."

131

Snaking through the hills toward Austin in the silver Boxster, and in between whoops and hollers and trying to digest the full platters of barbeque her uncle had insisted on everyone eating, Samantha replayed to herself a portion of the visit to the ranch that bothered her, the brief conversation with Tom Waters and George Ormiston. Maybe they weren't former agents after all.

Tom Waters had probed a lot. She could still see those all-knowing black eyes. She had stuck to her story. Maybe Uncle Stu knew more too. It was all too much to worry over. She would tackle it later. There was another unsettling experience at the ranch she had to deal with: Joe Bill and his strong arms. Despite her fantasies, she knew she wouldn't bed the ranch manager. And it had nothing to do with Emerson.

Guilluame didn't count, because, well just because.... She had been over that and there was no contradiction in her mind. Now, back to Emerson. In spite of everything he had a hold on her heart.

In London and Edinburgh, Emerson had used condoms. Why hadn't they talked about it? If they were committed and tested, the condoms would be unnecessary. Neither of them had brought the subject up. Surely, making love would be far more intimate for him. For her too. Why hadn't she mentioned it? She had been only with Emerson after a long dry spell, if she didn't count Guillaume. But he had used a condom. To be sure she should wait at least eight weeks, since even condoms were not one hundred percent safe against disease or HIV.

Samantha wondered if Emerson had been sexually active with someone else. They could start counting now and then get tested. If they made up after this spat, maybe they could discuss it. At the longest, they both could be tested in two months, meaning neither of them had engaged in sex with anyone else for at least eight weeks.

She thought about that for a couple of miles. So, planning on tests and being trustworthy health-wise could also mean some sort of commitment. Funny, but the tests could turn out to be a bedrock of trust. Not too romantic, but effective. She wanted to email Emerson and tell him that in spite of the separation of thousands of miles and in spite of their fights and misunderstandings, they were stuck with each other until they called off fucking each others brains out. But that didn't mean she couldn't accidentally fall into someone's rock-hard arms and have to feel guilty about it. She smiled.

"What's with the big smile?" called out Julie leaning into a curve.

"Nothing. I was just thinking about what a good time my uncle's mares will have when that big Shire plows into them."

Chapter 28

I am so up for the trip to Guatemala and Honduras. Julie is perfect, so sensible and smart and fun too. –From Samantha's Journal

"Guess what?"

"What?" Samantha looked over at a smiling Julie as they entered the city limits of Austin.

"I think tonight's the last night of South By Southwest."

"And we mustn't miss it, right?"

"Right, it is our bounden duty to uphold the tradition of Austin's music. Just think, maybe a thousand aspiring bands have descended on our fair city and have been here for days making music. It wouldn't be right if we didn't show our appreciation." Samantha laughed.

"O.K. a night of bands. But first a nap, a shower and a salad. Drop me off and we'll meet later and do some clubs. And since it'll be pretty crowded around Sixth Street tonight, how about me driving over to your apartment around 10 or so and we'll go from there?"

Later that night while the music swelled all over Austin, Samantha and Julie squeezed into several places and had a great time listening to hard-working bands.

"No way we're going visit anymore clubs tonight. I'm ready to hit the hay."

"I swear Julie, I think my uncle has rubbed off on you, or did you grow up on a ranch?"

"No ranch, but I like the idea of riding around on that horse I was on. I might even slop hogs and milk cows if I could ride "Maid Marian" every day. That'd be really fantastic."

"Well, Uncle Stu doesn't have the typical livestock, but I bet he'd love to have an extra hand to muck out the stables."

"Yech! Me and my big mouth. One more beer and one more set and we're outta here."

By two in the morning, Samantha and Julie felt they had done their duty to the Austin music scene and admitted that a soft pillow seemed "mighty enticin."

"What say we meet tomorrow afternoon and do some planning?" It'll be quiet on Sixth Street. We'll do some Internet research and make a list of stuff to be done before we head south."

"Sounds good, I'll see you around four. It was a fun night, even if you didn't have that handsome ranch manager's arms steadying you."

"Now you've done it. I was wondering what would be on my dream channel tonight."

But instead of dreaming of Joe Bill Barstow, Samantha wanted to talk to Emerson. It would be around ten in the morning in London. She wondered if he would answer.

"So, how's your mistress?"

"I thought I'd never hear from you again after Edinburgh. I did get your email, finally. Trouble with the computer."

"I tried to call you as soon as I got back to London, but you didn't answer and your answering machine was on the blink. To tell the truth, I wasn't sure you wanted me to call."

After assurances that talking would be a good thing, they caught each other up with many apologies thrown in. Samantha explained why she didn't want him to know about Greenland. Emerson explained why he hadn't called sooner.

"What? An accident! Emerson, are you all right? What happened? You were in the hospital! A lorry hit you? Were you hurt?"

"Calm down, it's perfectly all right. I spent a couple of days in hospital and I'm having to do some stretching and swimming for sore muscles, but really I am in the pink, nearly. The Jag has a few bruises, scrapes and crinkles, but it's nothing serious, and the insurance will take care of everything. We'll both be good as new in quite a short while."

The conversation lasted for an hour. Samantha wished she

could hold him in her arms. She would help him stretch and rid him of those sore muscles. She would massage every muscle he had. She so much wanted to snuggle up against him and nuzzle his neck and touch him with little kisses. As they talked she raised her knee and kissed it, pretending.

"Oh Emerson, we must not fight again. Promise we won't fight. I miss you so much. Let's plan to be together as soon as I get back from Honduras."

"Honduras?"

"Why yes, I thought I told you. Maybe I didn't." She explained why she had to go to the jungle. There was a moment of silence.

"Emerson, are you there?"

"Yes, indeed, I'm here. Just about the time I think things are going swimmingly, you come up with a new bloody wrinkle." Now it was Samantha's time to be silent for a moment before answering.

"Emerson, if we are to have any kind of life together, I have to get this issue behind me. It won't take long, and I'll be thinking of you every minute. Please try to understand."

"What I understand is that you feel you have to bloody well handle everything by yourself. If, as you said, we shall be together, then what's the harm in letting me help out some..."

"Like you letting me help you when you were in the hospital? When was I to get a call...after the inquest?"

The independent streaks and strong wills were painted vividly onto both their lives. They recognized the barriers each threw in the face of the other. There was the unspoken question of who would submit, become the subservient one in the relationship. Regardless, it would be a bitter disappointment for the winner. And so they would fight and wait.

Again they murmured for time and the desire to find the answer to this conundrum.

Sunday afternoon Samantha and Julie made lists, divided up responsibilities. They decided what books to devour and when to get the shots needed to thwart a host of diseases.

"Listen to this. All we have to worry about down there are things like Yellow Fever, Cholera, Malaria, Hepatitis, Dengue Fever, Rabies, Chagas Disease and a bunch of other stuff with very long names that could do us in. Some things we can get shots for and others we just have to stay clean. And listen to this: 'Don't drink the water and don't let the flies and mosquitos bite.'

"If you sleep in a thatched-roof hut, the assassin bug will bite your face and fill you with parasites–that's the Chagas Disease. About a fourth of the Indians down there have it." Julie put down the list she had received from Trak before he left for Copán.

"I guess we're going to feel like a pin cushion after we get our shots this week. I'll arrange for my doctor to give them to us, if that's O.K. with you."

"Sure, let 'em stick away. I'm going to take some 100 percent DEET and shower in it everyday."

"I've heard if you use DEET too long, like for months at a time, you may end up with a mighty sick liver," said Samantha making notes.

"Yeah, Mother Nature's going to get us no matter what we do. We should be all right for a couple of weeks though. Since we're both going to be in the boonies, we need to take as much precaution as possible."

The research on the oil company Samantha's dad worked for showed that the corporate office was in Antigua, about thirty miles west of Guatemala City. She made flight reservations to Guatemala City and hotel reservations for Antigua. Once there they could decide when to get reservations in Copán for Julie.

They made lists of the important stuff they thought they couldn't do without; like good shoes and jungle clothing. Of course they would take a camera and binoculars, a phone system, Samantha's GPS, first aid supplies, and water pills. Julie got some more books on Guatemala and Honduras and the Mayan culture.

"Trak is going to be surprised with how much we know."

"After that meeting about what's happening down there, I'm eager to see the ruins at Copán. Wonder what it would have been like to have lived back then?"

"Maybe we would have been high priestesses."

"Way to go."

On Monday, they lined up some shots to take on Tuesday and Thursday. Samantha had a work-out with her personal trainer, sharpening her martial arts skills. Her muscles tried to rebel, but she stuck with it. Clothes were modeled and bought. Monday night, Julie suggested Dan McClusky's out by the Arboretum to catch a Beatles cover band. The restaurant was renowned for superb steaks, but they opted for a salad and white wine and later a beer as they listened to the music and watched as a few couples danced.

"Did I tell you my experience dancing, while Trak looked on?"

"What happened?"

"We were down in Lafayette, and there was a zydeco band playing outside the city limits. We knew some people and went out. I love zydeco. It's like Cajun music, although they don't admit it. The concertina is the main instrument and they hold it down near their balls and swing and sway with it. Really sexy looking. I kept thinking the musician would get something caught. Zydeco's got a really strong rock beat. You just have to get up and dance. Well, Trak and I danced some, but he doesn't really feel it like I do. Long story, short. This black guy comes up and asks me to dance. I said sure. He got really close, and we sort of got entwined if you know what I mean."

"Uh Oh, I think I know how this is going to turn out."

"You got that right. I glanced over at Trak and he had pain written all over his face. His face was like stone. When the dance ended I sat down, but he wouldn't talk to me, or even look at me. It took the rest of the weekend to get things back on an even keel."

"Really got mad, huh?

"Mad and forlorn all at the same time."

"So, you like to dance and Trak doesn't, and you have a conflict. So, what did you do?"

"I had to decide if dancing was more important than Trak. I decided Trak was, and I didn't want to see that look on his face again. Maybe someday he'll feel secure enough to let me dance with somebody. Maybe not."

"So you think it's worth it to give in?"

"Well, I don't think I would call it giving in, exactly. It's a compromise, so we can stay together. I know that dancing is O.K., a lot of fun, and it doesn't diminish my love for Trak in the slightest, if I dance with someone else. But if it's a big deal to him then I'll just not dance, if he's there. If he gets too possessive, I may have to rethink things, but for now, I love that guy so much I hurt."

Samantha was quiet, thinking about Emerson. Had she ever compromised? Had he? He did apologize in Edinburgh. He did offer an alternative. She had remained rigid about her schedule. She had thought there was no choice, but maybe she was afraid to meet him half-way. Maybe she was afraid to love him so much, afraid he would take advantage and try to remake her. Did she want to remake him? Julie had compromised, and she really loved Trak, but she might go only so far. Life was complicated.

Chapter 29

My uncle continues to surprise me with his sensitivity. I can't believe I ever thought of him as a "typical" male. He is so dear to me. –From Samantha's Journal

Tuesday morning Samantha's cell phone rang.

"I'm coming into town, be there around noon. I need to talk. You be there?"

"Of course, Uncle Stu, what's it all about? You sound upset and mad."

"You're damn right I'm mad. Too mad to stay here. I might hurt somebody. See you in a couple of hours."

"Now, don't you drive that fast. I'll be here. We'll get a burger and talk."

"Thank you, darlin', I knew I could count on you."

The weather was warm. Samantha had thought about a swim at Barton Springs, but she could do that tomorrow. While she waited for her uncle, she decided to read some more about Honduras. That didn't work. After every sentence her mind centered on her uncle. She looked at her list and saw she had time to buy some rain boots and a poncho. It was the dry season in Honduras, but it still rained in forests. She needed a good flashlight too and a small tent and a hat with mosquito netting. She drove out to the R.E.I. super sports store and was trying on boots when her cell phone rang.

"I'm taking a shortcut around Fredericksburg and I'll be there in an hour or so. And darlin' I don't want to go out to eat, I'm too blamed mad to be in public, so just get those burgers and a couple of beers into the apartment. I'll come straight on up when I get there."

"O.K. Uncle Stu. See you soon."

Samantha hurried with the purchases, made a stop to pick up the burgers, fries, and beer, her uncle's favorite food, and arrived at her apartment in forty-five minutes. She unloaded, ran up the stairs from the back and set the table, cleared away some things she had tossed over chairs, made a bathroom visit, and had just enough time to sit down and take two big breaths when she heard her uncle's heavy steps.

He knocked and opened the door at the same time. Samantha rushed into his arms and felt his rage.

"I'm so gol'derned mad I could, I could..." but nothing horrible enough apparently came to mind, so he just hugged his niece fiercely.

"Sit down, Uncle Stu. Here's some water. You're here now, and we can talk it out. Just tell me what's wrong. I've never seen you mad enough to bite horse shoes."

He stopped fuming and looked at her. Almost a smile and a big sigh.

"That's the damnedest thing I ever heard, but you're right. I don't suppose you got some around here I could gnaw on?" Then, he had to laugh in spite of himself. Then he sobered up again. Samantha paused at the kitchen.

"You want to talk first and then eat? How about a beer?"

"A beer would be good. And I don't know where to start so, I'll just barge into it. That fool cousin of Joe Bill's stuck my Shire with a pitchfork this morning! God! I could of killed that boy, and I still might! I had to get away."

Tears formed in the big man's eyes. His hand shook as he swigged at the beer. Samantha sat down facing him.

"A pitch fork? How awful. Why would he do such a thing? Joe Bill must feel awful about it, too."

"Yes, he does. I could hardly be civil and that made me feel bad. I was so mad at his sonofabitch cousin, I could have twisted his head right off his neck."

"But why? Why did he do it? Did he have a reason?"

"He said he was mucking out the stable, a job he hates. Hell, he hates any job. And he wanted the Shire to move over, and the

141

Shire didn't move fast enough to suit him so he hit him with the flat of the pitch fork 'hard enough to get his attention,' he said, and the horse pushed him against the wall so he stuck him with the fork. The Shire kicked him and broke the sonofabitch's leg.

"I heard him hollering and so did Joe Bill, and it's a good thing he got to his cousin first, or else he would have had two broken legs. Joe Bill got the story out of him and took him to our little clinic, and they set his leg temporarily and then drove him to Kerrville. It wasn't a bad break. At least no bones were sticking out.

"Joe Bill brought him back in this big white cast and the cousin commenced telling me I had to shoot the Shire because he was a man-killer. That's when I lit into him, but just with words, darlin'.

"Before he can be a man killer there's gotta be a man involved and as far as killing seems like you're still breathing, but if you keep on talkin' I might be able to do something about that breathin' part. You're fired and I want you off this ranch just as fast as you can drive your damned beat-up truck, and I mean right now. So off he went, with his fool dog, mad as hell and cussin' a blue streak.

"Joe Bill said he should have known better than to give his cousin a job and that he'd aways been bad news, but he thought he would change with a steady job what with Joe Bill watching and making sure he did the work right. I was real sorry I blew up in front of Joe Bill, but I just couldn't help it.

"While they went to the clinic I called the vet and he came right on out and gave the Shire some shots and cleaned out the pitch fork holes. Thank God they weren't deep, but the vet deadened them before he cleaned them since the Shire was still nervous. It's a wonder he didn't kill that boy. But horses don't do that unless they're really threatened.

"I soothed him and rubbed and patted him and that wild look left his eyes. I remember you told me to tell everybody to be gentle, and I did. I guess that fool cousin of Joe Bill's wasn't listening too good.

"When we got everything ship-shape, I started gettin' mad all over again, and the more I thought about it, the madder I got, and that's when I knew I had to get away, and here I am, and thanks for letting me get it off my chest, and where's that burger?"

"What if the cousin causes trouble? Maybe sues you?"

"Well, folks 'round there don't cotton to trash hurtin' horses. He'd likely go to jail. So, I kinda hope he does try to stir up somethin'. I'll pay him two weeks wages and the cost of the doctor and that's that. If he wants more he'll get a hell of lot more than he bargained for." Stuart King took a big bite of the sandwich, or was it the cousin's leg?

"Darlin' there's somethin' I need to tell you that might explain my behavior a little. You remember that my mom was gored by a Longhorn cow protecting her calf?"

"Yes, dad told me. It was terrible. She was only 42 and had her whole life in front of her."

"Well, you know we lost my dad in an oil rig accident not more than three years before. Losing mom on top of that was like the world had come to an end. Martin was there and got the cow away from her, but it was too late. Still, he kept his head. He was only 17. That was back in '58. She died five days later. I got there quick as I could. I was 21.

"Mom was still alive. I took down my shotgun, hunted down that Longhorn and shot her dead. I was going to behead that calf with a machete and leave it out there for the vultures. That's when Martin rode up and told me not to do it.

"Mom didn't want that Longhorn and calf hurt. The cow was just doing what she was supposed to do, protecting her calf. I was hotter'n and madder'n blue blazes, and I wanted them dead. "I rode in and mom cried when I told her I'd shot the cow. She opened my eyes to the creatures of the world and how they never get their say, and they're just tryin' to live their lives. I was angry, and I had killed that Longhorn with revenge on my mind. But mom got gored because that mother cow was afraid for her calf. Anyway, before she died, mom talked me into going back to college and finishing up the exams.

"I found that calf, and I raised it. I guess I've been trying to make amends to that old Longhorn cow and mom all these years."

Samantha shook her head. He had never talked about his family. It touched her. Her uncle was something else all right. He gave wild birds a home in his ranch house. He opened his ranch to exotic grazing animals, with no thought of letting trophy hunters have a go at them. His Longhorns and his horses filled him with pride and humility. The Shire having been mistreated earlier in its life received special handling. She suddenly felt so fortunate to have Stuart King in her life.

She wanted his support. And now she felt comfortable sharing with him. A new chapter in their relationship had begun.

"Uncle Stu, I don't think dad's crash was an accident."

Stuart King stopped in mid-bite. His face darkened.

"There's a lot of us feel the same way, darlin' and there's just nothing we can do about it. I was hoping you wouldn't get into it other than a quick trip to get over your grieving."

"So why haven't you demanded an investigation or some-thing?"

"We were told to stay out of it through channels that I don't want to talk about. There's a lot that goes on in this world that's not right because of pinheads in positions of power. I think that fellow Jason Murdoch thinks the same way. He almost said as much and then clammed up just like I'm supposed to."

"Does this have something to do with your intelligence work?"

"I'm sorry, darlin', I can't come right out and say that. Draw your own conclusions. Do what you got to do, but I can't do much to help you officially. But, I'll be there to back you up if you need me. I guess you know, Martin and I were real buds, and it has been a burr under my saddle to do nothin'. I guess I was kind of hoping you would sniff around a bit. No one can stop you. And I can still pull some strings while acting like I'm doing nothin'."

"Thank you Uncle Stu. That means so much to me."

She told him everything that had happened and her suspicions and how she planned to go to the oil company and walk right in, bold as brass.

"I'm pretty good at reading between the lines after dealing with my buyers. I bet I'll make a good snoop."

Later, they walked along a very peaceful Sixth Street. Every-one was still recovering from the big music, film, and Internet fest that ended the night before.

"Well, darlin' I'm feeling a lot better and especially I'm feeling good about you. I don't and won't tell you how to operate. I have faith in your drive and your intelligence. We could have used you in the department. So, I'm off to the ranch. Maria's probably getting worried. Thanks for listening."

"And thanks for having faith in me Uncle Stu. I won't let you down. Say hello to Duchess and the Shire for me." Samantha watched the big man go down the stairs. She wondered what else she didn't know about her uncle.

Chapter 30

I feel a heck of a lot better when my nails are done and my tummy's flat. –From Samantha's Journal

"And there's Tucson right over there." Julie looked out the jet's window at the green area bracketed by lavender and beige.

"My first time in Arizona. Thank you, thank you for twisting my arm."

"Well, we had a few extra days so what better way to spend them than at Canyon Ranch getting mentally and physically prepared for our foray into Central America?"

"Hear, hear."

"The van will pick us up and in a few minutes we'll be in heaven," Samantha stretched in anticipation. "I try to work in a visit at least once a year. You'll see. It'll be wonderful. Healthy food, massages, facials, the desert air, the staff.

There's nothing like it. The ratio of staff to guests is three to one."

"How will I ever come back to earth? I could have used this when my dotcom company went bye-bye."

"Better late than never. Besides, this will help us face the good times in the jungles of Honduras. Every time you slap a mosquito or side-step a big bug, you'll remember this utter luxury."

For the next four days, it was exactly that, utter luxury guaranteed to refresh body and mind. Body wraps with exotic herbs, aromatherapy massage, shirodhara (warm herbal oil treatment). Dozens of body therapies available, too many for the four days. After the day's hike, Samantha liked the Swedish deep tissue massage. Julie went for the Aloe Glaze.

They took in as much as they could: golf, tennis, swimming. Fresh fruits, vegetables, the finest meat and fish made every meal a treat. All meals custom-prepared for each guest's needs and desires. During the day and at night there were several lectures and seminars to choose from.

Julie and Samantha had a lovely southwestern casita with a covered porch. Guests came from all over the world. Quite cosmopolitan. Warm sun-splashed days and cool desert evenings with bright stars caused Julie to say, "Yes, I could live here."

Relaxing by the pool and reading about Guatemala, Honduras, and the Mayan civilizations one afternoon, Samantha closed her book.

"Do you think I'm too controlling?"

"What do you mean?"

"You know. Doing things my way. Like getting you to go on this trip, then to the ranch and now here. Did you feel coerced or manipulated?"

"Samantha, you have a strong personality, there's no doubt about that. But no, I didn't feel coerced in the slightest. I guess I was gung-ho about every suggestion you made. Remember, I really wanted to go to Copán, but I didn't want to go by myself. And I was bored in Austin, so a trip to your uncle's was welcome. Believe me, if I hadn't wanted to do that, you would have heard from me. Maybe we're too much alike for me to be objective. I can be a little controlling myself. If you had worked with me in my dotcom company, you would have found that out in a hurry."

"Two calculating, conniving women. The best kind."

They laughed together.

"Don't sell yourself short. You have things that are bothering you, but unlike a 'whiner,' you take action. Nothing wrong with that. If a man has drive and a strong will, it is generally seen as a good thing, while women have a mountain of prejudice to climb over any time we dare show a little kick-ass."

"Thanks, I needed to hear that. It's not that I want to override men, or women. I see a task and just jump in. I'm not too good with male relationships though."

"You seem to get along just fine with your uncle. I sense a

deep affection from both of you. I haven't seen you with anyone else."

"You're right about Uncle Stu. My uncle used to come across to me as controlling, but just a few days ago, I realized his strong opinions were just that, and he didn't intend to manage my life." Samantha put the Mayan book on the table.

"He is so supportive and he values me not only as a 'niece called darlin', but as an intelligent person who gets a job done and can take care of herself. He's there if I need him, but only if I need him. I hadn't understood that until last week just before we left to come here." Julie sipped her drink before answering.

"So, there you have it. You are being accepted."

Samantha thought of Emerson. She didn't think he accepted her yet anymore than she accepted him. Maybe what happened with her uncle would happen with Emerson. Time would tell.

"Let's go get a delicious wrap before dinner."

"You are coercing me and I meekly follow in your footsteps. Lead on, you mad manipulator."

Refreshed and glowing, Samantha and Julie arrived back in Austin ready to tackle anything life could throw at them.

Julie had called Trak. He had seemed preoccupied.

"Which I've come to expect. You know, I don't think that boy would look up from deciphering some Mayan chiselings even if I paraded totally nude in front of him. It's a good thing I have a healthy dose of self-esteem."

"Maybe he's feeling pressure."

"He mentioned again how we couldn't spend much time together. 'You'll be in a hotel all by yourself. It's hot and dirty here. I don't think you'll like it at all.'"

"Maybe he's afraid you'll be disappointed."

"So, I said, do you want to fuck me or not? Your call. And that really shut him up. I think I made contact at last."

"That's what I call cutting to the chase."

"Yeah, like parading nude, except over the phone. It worked anyway. He's dying to see me."

Samantha also got a call. She hoped from Emerson. But no.

"Joyce? Tom here."

"Tom?" For a moment Samantha drew a blank. Then it flashed in her mind. Abel Jorwoski. Before she could answer...,

"You know, Tom Jones and you're Joyce." A slight panic in his voice.

"Of course, Tom, good to hear from you. You want me to call back and use the special number? O.K will do."

Samantha entered the code and reconnected with Abel Jorwoski.

"Yes, Tom. How can I help you?"

"Thanks Joyce. It's like this, I'm close to that state, you know, where the building is, and I was wondering if I could jump the gun and have a looksee on the QT if you know what I mean. I know I said I would never do that, but I suddenly want to see it. Can we do it?"

Abel Jorwoski, a loose cannon, if he tried to enter those grounds on his own. Only one thing to do. Fly to Vermont, hold his hand and arrange for a short tour. Today was Tuesday. If all went well Samantha could get there and back in a couple of days. If things did not go well, it could be longer. Better to count on longer. She would tell Julie to be ready to go down south on or before Sunday April the first. April Fools Day. How appropriate.

"O.K. Tom, I'll call you from the airport in the state where the building is and meet you wherever you say. I'll make arrangements for your visit. Sound all right?"

"Perfect, what would I do without you? The missus says hi."

"Goodbye, Tom. See you soon. And say hi to Ms. Jones."

"Uh...who? Oh, yes, yes."

He hung up.

At least he didn't end up calling me Jane this time, Samantha thought. She explained the delay to Julie and then called Samuel George and worked out details for the visit.

Mr. Jorwoski hadn't said if Mrs. Jorwoski would be joining them, so, to play safe she would rent a nice sedan in Burlington. They would drive to the missile site. She wondered if they would like a scoop of something tasty at Ben and Jerry's.

Of course not. He would know for certain the ice cream factory had been infiltrated. That left the site itself as the main attraction. Back to Austin by the 29th, but she had two extra days for insurance. A good plan. And it worked. Samantha loved challenging situations. Mrs. Jorwoski had stayed home, wherever that was.

Chapter 31

**I travel a lot to developing countries. I need to stop being so
critical. There's a lot of problems, but I think economic problems cause most of the trouble. A full stomach can make a
revolutionary into a diplomat. I know it's not that simple, but
it worked in Rome, or did it? –From Samantha's Journal**

In the air and on the way to Guatemala City. The two women
were in high spirits. So far, the first day of April behaved itself. No
jokes. They were flying coach, so no complimentary champagne.
They ordered white wine instead.

"I can't believe that by noon today, we'll be landing in Guatemala, and Trak will be there. I hope it's sunny all day." Samantha
sipped and glanced out the window to check on cloud formations
for Julie.

"I imagine we'll have some clouds when we get there. That's
what the weather service reported, but so what? Meeting your
lover should be all the sun you need, Julie."

"Right. I really miss that little guy."

"I have two rooms for tonight in Antigua, then you can move
in with me when Trak takes the bus back to Copán tomorrow. It's
going to be a short weekend for you, but better than nothing. The
next two weekends will be much better."

"I'm looking forward to the street carpets in Antigua. But I
want to hear more about your quick trip back east before we land."

Without giving away circumstances and geographical details,
Samantha filled her in on the secretive client who would spend
millions to have a secure home.

"A missile One hundred fifty feet deep? Ten stories down?
And tunnels? Awesome!"

"Awesome is a good word. He was delighted with the progress and it looks like a go for the middle of June. I'll be going back two or three times before move-in day. I'll have to learn everything there is to know about the electronics and services so I can explain them and have a run through.

"The tedious part of this job comes from being on call in case of any breakdown. I have to get my private contractor out there after the client runs off somewhere to hide until things are repaired. If it's something huge, like the A/C goes out then I have to be there when my contractor arrives and fixes it."

"I didn't realize real estate was so demanding."

"Well, my specialty is more demanding that way. But any good broker realizes service is expected even after the sale."

Samantha looked quickly out the window.

"There's a treat coming. Watch over there. What do you see?"

"Lots of clouds. No, there's something else. Are those mountains poking up through?"

"Volcanoes. There are bunches of them down here."

Two dark cones pierced the cloud cover.

"Those two volcanoes are south of Guatemala City about 20 miles. So, we're almost there. I think there are over 30 volcanoes in Guatemala."

The cloud bank seemed to rise swallowing the plane's wings. Air currents bumped against them. A dreary landscape appeared as the clouds thinned.

"Lots of pollution down there, and if it's anything like the last time I came, it smells to high heaven. I don't understand how anyone could live there in a nice home and smell garbage burning all day and all night.

"Garbage burning in the city?"

"In the ravines around the city–where the poor people live. I visited down here with my dad years ago. Looks as if it hasn't changed much."

"Ugh."

"Ugh is right and also yuck."

———

They left the plane and submitted their bags to the customs agents. The officials opened each one and rummaged around. Finding nothing that was contraband, they allowed Samantha and Julie to head for ground transportation. Julie's cell phone rang just as she was getting ready to call Trak.

"What? Yes, we're here. Are you close?" There was a couple of moments of silence as Samantha watched Julie's shoulders sag. Bad news?

"I can't believe it? How long have you known? Why didn't you call? Never mind. I know, I know, my phone was off in the plane. I still can't believe it, and I guess I'd better not say what I'm really thinking. So now what?" Julie began shaking her head. Samantha could see tears forming.

"O.K, cool, see you next weekend. I'll come by bus on Friday. I'll get the reservations so don't bother. I'll call you when I get there and if you're too busy then, someone may send you home in a box. Bye. Me too. Bye."

"Not good news."

"Hell no, not good news. Some cockamamie story about not being able to get off from the ruins. Schedule too tight. Had to stay. The gal in charge demanded it. He was sorry and the bad part is, I don't think he was sorry at all. Why on God's polluted earth did I have to end up with a 'lover of the past' for a boyfriend? Now what am I supposed to do?"

"We'll call and cancel one of the rooms in Antigua. We'll get a car and go to the hotel. We'll check out Antigua and get drunk and to hell with boyfriends."

"Sounds like a plan." Julie wiped at her eyes. They opened the door. The odor of rancid butter and diesel fumes struck them in mid stride.

"Whew! You were right Samantha. This ain't good for our tender lungs." Julie wiped at her eyes, but Samantha knew all the tears there were not due to the poisonous air.

Samantha rented a Japanese four-wheel-drive pickup. This was not a country where you could take smooth highways for granted. In the rainy season some roads were impassible even for their truck. At least they would be able to claw their way through pot holes when they had to. But the truck had no air-conditioning.

The afternoon sun would melt them. The plastic covered seats had already reached baking temperatures.

Samantha went back and argued with the rental agent until he agreed to swap for an air-conditioned SUV with tinted windows and real smokey red plum blue leather seats, actually tan. It was beautiful and spic and span. The rental agent probably thought with a woman driver, it would be returned bent up. Well, she would show him.

———————

They drove in light Sunday traffic up Diagonal 12 in the direction of Antigua. Watching carefully for missing sections of the road, Samantha increased her speed. She opened the windows and left the A/C on.

"Smells better out here."

"If you'd let me drive we'd get there faster."

Samantha laughed at Julie.

"Spoken like the mad wild woman you are. But I have been here, and I know around the next bend or two there will probably be a chug-hole the size of the Grand Canyon. As she spoke, she saw the remains of a rock slide that had sheared off part of the highway. Samantha engaged the 4-wheel drive and inched and bounced through it.

"I'll bet that slide happened weeks ago, and it'll be several more weeks before it's removed. Mañana is a way of life down here. We have to leave speed and efficiency behind us."

In less than an hour they entered Antigua and the hum of their tires signaled cobblestone streets.

"This is a beautiful town. A historical place. Look at all those bougainvilleas. Have you ever seen so many gorgeous flowers? And look at those old Spanish colonial buildings. We've had some earthquakes here haven't we?" Rhetorical questions from Samantha, who knew some of the city's history.

———————

The day had cooled considerably. They found their hotel, a

lovely old Colonial home that had been turned into a gracious place to stay. Inside the massive gates that faced the narrow sidewalks, there stretched a beautiful flowered patio with covered walkways.

Above the open patio could be seen the active volcano Pacaya a few miles south and poking over 8,000 feet into the air. It spewed smoke and steam. The roof of the hotel framed the patio with earth-red tile, the walls of golden-rod yellow had windows set deep. Between the supporting stucco pillars along the covered walkway, Samantha saw lazy-looking hammocks calling to her and Julie. It had been a long day, and she could see them reclining and slowly swinging with a bottle or two of cerveza for starters. And that was exactly what they did.

"This is not a bad place at all."

"Right. If Trak had met us, you know, I wouldn't be here enjoying this beer and planning to climb up that damn volcano."

"Are you kidding ? Wait, I know you miss Trak and you certainly would be enjoying something a lot better than a cold beer if he were here. I mean, do you really want to climb that volcano?

"Yep."

"Mind if you have a little company? I need to find out where this oil firm has its office so I can drop in on them, but I'm free after that, so lets find a tour that'll take us to Pacaya and we'll conquer a volcano together."

"Cool." There was a moment of silence between them, then Julie sat up in her hammock.

"Hey, Samantha, thanks for keeping me from having a pity party. That was a low blow when Trak didn't meet us. Sometimes I just don't know how to take him. I love his dedication to his first love, Mayan puzzles, but I get to thinking I'm a caretaker more than his lover. Almost like I'm his mother, for God's sake, sending her little boy out to play."

"I know you don't want advice. I never did. So, I'll listen and empathize. Lord knows I'm the world's worst when it comes to romance. Since we are two beautiful losers, let's have another beer."

"I'll get 'em this time. Just lie right there and work up a load of empathy, cause I'm going to need a lot."

Dusk began to creep down the cobblestone streets, but the volcanoes still shone darker than the darkening sky. Soon the stars would be out. Maybe the moon. Samantha and Julie stayed in the hammocks and called out constellations to each other.

"Tomorrow, I'll tell you about my friend Christina and what she's going to think about our climbing up the side of a smoldering volcano."

Chapter 32

It's hard to keep up a break-neck pace in a laid-back society.
It won't be long before I'll be taking lengthy siestas and leav-
ing things for tomorrow. Ah!
   –From Samantha's Journal

Not a cloud in the sky. Bright blue everywhere. Samantha
looked over her map of Antigua to find the location of the oil firm
named GUASAUCO. Checking the Guatemala business directory
she found the nuts and bolts plant/office in Guatemala City which
made sense. The corporate office showed up in the Antigua list-
ings. That made sense too. If she were the head of the company
she would want to be here where the air was breathable.

Julie took off to explore the shops and stalls and would return
before noon. Armed with her map, Samantha wheeled the SUV
out of the hotel's gates and headed west. The street, although cobble-stoned, was wide enough for two vehicles.

She noticed several side streets that were quite narrow, as in
some of the villages in Italy she and Christina had visited earlier
that year. If two vehicles met, one would have to back out or else
both would use not only the street but the sidewalks as well to inch
by each other.

Traffic seemed quite courteous, however. After a few false
turns, she located her street and noted the address attached to a fine
old colonial-style home.

"Nice digs," she murmured. The home, now an office, apparently, took up nearly a whole block. The sides of the building
fronted narrow streets. A couple of windows, secure behind
wrought-iron cages, were high enough so that a vehicle could pass
beneath, even if it had to use the sidewalk.

A small ledge, part of the stucco wall, ran along beneath the windows. The building was painted in an apricot yellow with white trim here and there. The wrought iron railings were black and complex. Two intimidating wrought iron gates, large enough to admit vehicles, fronted the spacious main street. Samantha could see tire tracks leading up to the entry way. There was a smaller door and what looked like a knocker or buzzer.

"And it's a fortress." Samantha parked and decided on the spur of the moment to speed things up. There was a buzzer after all and she punched it a couple of times. In less than a minute, a Mayan Indian approached the see-through ornamental iron that made up the door and peered at Samantha. A gardener? Security?

Samantha decided to use Spanish, and it worked. But the results weren't promising. She would not be admitted. She would need to make an appointment.

The man seemed quite nervous and repeatedly looked across the street at the SUV. She checked to see if the number was correct. She handed him the phone number of the hotel along with a brief note saying who she was and why she wanted to talk to someone by tomorrow, if at all possible. Samantha could hear a dog or dogs making a fuss. Big dogs.

Back at the hotel, she shared her information with Julie who had just returned, too, definitely in a better mood after looking at and purchasing a darling hand-woven rebozo.

"You'll have to come look, Samantha. Everything is so colorful. I wanted to buy all the shawls and open up a shop in Austin."

"I know just how you feel. As if you didn't know after looking at my apartment and cabin."

"You are a little collector all right. That's cool. Let's grab something to eat and go climb a volcano. I got the tour bus and the tickets in my mountain-climbing hands. The driver said climbing would be no problem since I am young and strong. You may have to stay behind." Julie laughed as Samantha tried to land a mock karate chop.

"Don't you worry. I'll race you to the top and won't even be breathing hard."

Next week would be Holy Week and already the city's population swelled as relatives poured in from outlying villages and tourists filled up the hotels. Samantha and Julie were fortunate to have made reservations early.

The hotel appreciated their cancelling the extra room that Julie and Trak would have used. Next week there would be a tremendous increase in the processions, and the beautiful carpets, made of colored sawdust, plants, and flowers which together, would cover several of the streets with intricate designs.

Tourists, mostly young backpacker types, swarmed aboard the "volcano" bus, and soon off it went with the view of Pacaya looming through the windshield. One stop allowed a quick snack, and then a few more miles, and everyone got out to walk the trail up the flanks of the mountain.

The view was nearly obscured by the foliage. The trail began to narrow as the group resolutely trudged upward, eyes on the prowl for any wildlife not scared off by the noisy commotion of laughter and groans.

The weather was perfect. Not too warm. The foliage thinned a bit and Samantha and Julie saw that the undergrowth and some trees had been cleared for coffee bean fields. A slight mist developed, and the cone of the volcano once more appeared dead ahead, rising stark and dark. At the top, a plume drifted with the breeze.

"You still want to try to climb that thing?" Samantha stopped for a moment, and Julie mopped at her brow.

"Of course, remember, I'm young and strong. I see some of you old folks are dropping out."

Sure enough, the reason for the trail narrowing became apparent. Half the bus load had already called it quits and were laughing and snapping pictures and resting.

"I'm with you till the end. So lead on." With that Samantha went ahead and the march continued. Soon the base of the cone enveloped the trail. More people stopped and shook their heads. The trail now led right up the cone which was just a mass of cinder rocks like golf balls or ping pong balls but smaller.

Taking a step meant sinking into the rocks which now looked like some giant's black sand pile. Each step up became a struggle as the lava rocks gave way and half the stride slipped back.

"Whew, this ain't easy, my dear. How you doin' back there?"

"Better,if you'd stop sending those buckets of rocks down on me."

"O.K. I'll wait and we'll climb side by side." Ooh, I'll have to admit, I've found some muscles I haven't used lately."

"You wanna quit?"

"Hell no, even if it does look like that's what we're climbing to."

Above them yellowish smoke wafted about and they could hear a hissing sound.

"I smell sulfur, rotten eggs. That's what hell's supposed to smell like isn't it?"

"I don't know, but if it does, that's a good reason to go to heaven. Hey, how about that wind. I'm getting cold. Dante said hell was freezing cold, I think. Freezing cold and rotten eggs. I need a drink of water." Samantha stopped and took a couple of swallows and wrinkled her nose.

"Even the damn water tastes like a hundred-year old egg."

"You're getting hell and Chinese culture mixed up. I think you'd better slide back down to the old folks."

"I've come this far and I'll not quit until I look over the lip and into the cauldron."

Both women, along with a hand full of young backpackers, persevered until finally they reached the edge and peered over and down.

"Woo, we did it. Watch out, here comes the yellow poison. Hold your breath." The wafting cloud of noxious gases reached out to them causing both to gag. They took another look into the seething crater then down they slid back to the stragglers and to the bus.

A shower, a snack, a beer and they were ready to leap into hammocks for some rest. A girl from the lobby informed them there was a phone call. Samantha went to the office.

"Well, that was great. They'll see me in the morning at ten. Glad to meet with me and help anyway they can and so sorry about the sad trip I am on and they don't know much, but will share what they know."

"Good, Samantha. Want me to tag along?"

"Would you? I would really appreciate it. You might notice something I miss. And if they get rough, you can rescue me. Watch their faces when I tell them I want to visit the crash site. They don't know that yet. Do you think Trak will call?"

"I doubt it. He wants to keep expenses down as much as possible. I'll call him later tonight and see how he's feeling. Maybe I just read him wrong."

"Spoken like an understanding woman. Now, let's get something more to eat; Pacaya made me mighty hungry."

Chapter 33

I am so grateful for my upbringing which exposed me to so many different cultures and languages. How can we really understand the rest of the world if we don't make an effort? – From Samantha's Journal

At ten o'clock Samantha drove up to the oil company's executive offices. She punched the button. The Mayan appeared, still looking nervous, but seemingly eager to please. The huge doors opened electronically, and Samantha and Julie drove into the spacious patio area which was festooned with a multitude of pink and red bougainvillea blooms. There sat a gray truck mud-splattered with large knobby tires. Next to it gleamed a dark-blue pick-up and farther away two black sedans with tinted windows.

"Armored, too, I bet," whispered Julie as the smiling Mayan waited for them to open their doors. In the center of the patio a fountain sculpture of a robed woman holding a pitcher poured a never-ending supply of water into the wide circular basin below. The patio was paved with cobble stones.

Then, a jarring note. The low growls of two Rottweilers in a cage in the corner.

"Big dogs," Samantha remarked to the Mayan.

"Si, turn loose at night. Doors stay open, no problem."

He led them down a shaded corridor similar to the one at their hotel and stopped before a door: it opened it into a small foyer with three chairs, a small end table with a pewter-colored oil derrick on it, and a handful of magazines.

"You go in, por favor."

The inner door opened into a spacious work area with wall maps, filing cabinets, fax machine, copier, and two computers. A young man sat at a desk containing phones and a laptop. He immediately bounded up as Samantha and Julie entered and came around to greet them, all smiles.

"Ah, Ms. King I presume?" Looking first at Julie and then at Samantha.

"Yes, thank you." This from Samantha.

"Please be seated and I shall announce your arrival to Mr. Zayyat." He walked quickly down a hallway and out of sight. In a few moments a distinguished man with a trimmed salt and pepper beard and moustache walked from the hallway toward them. Large almond-shaped dark eyes peered through gold-rimmed glasses. His short stand-up dark hair made him taller, and he walked with the easy grace of one used to power.

"Ms. King, I am pleased to meet you even though you come in sadness." He looked directly at Samantha so, apparently, he had been coached as to whom to address.

"Allow me to introduce myself. Yusuf al Zayyat."

"And this is my friend and colleague, Julie Amber."

"So happy to meet you Ms. Amber. Now please come with me Ms. King back to my office. They passed three offices along the tiled corridor, one door was partially open, but not enough for a good look. Samantha couldn't help but wonder if her dad had one of those offices and maybe Jason too. The young man who had at first greeted them nodded as he met and passed them in the tiled hallway.

They entered a large comfortable office with white stucco walls and Guatemalan textile hangings in bright blue, red, orange and yellow. The furniture was of a russet-red leather and oak. Glassed in book cases of mahogany held leather-bound volumes. A deep-set filigreed window looked out on a thick wall topped with lush clumps of pink and red bougainvilleas. The mahogany desk had a selection of small sculptures and two miniature oil field derricks. To one side sat a laptop computer and a small filing cabinet. A high-backed leather executive chair in the same russet red hue completed the decor.

"Won't you please be seated," said Mr. Zayyat, motioning to the leather sofa.

"And would you care for some special Guatemalan coffee?

The beans are from my own fields."

"Ah, Mr. Zayyat, I would love some. And could I please request my friend join us. She will help me remember the information you have."

"Of course, I just thought this was a personal visit about your father's crash, and you wanted it to be confidential."

In a minute after a brief intercom conversation in Arabic, Julie appeared squired by the young Arab, who seemed to disapprove of Julie's short skirt although unable to stop looking at her long tanned legs.

Julie also was included in the coffee order and with cups in hand, the meeting began. Mr. Zayyat drew up a chair facing them over a low coffee table. His dark suit had an almost undistinguishable pattern in fine blue lines. His pale blue shirt and royal blue silk tie proclaimed a man of taste who enjoyed his life. Black patent-leather boots could have been construed as an effort to tie himself to oil, though they were much too fine for climbing about a rig. Samantha wondered if he even knew how to drive the powerful mud-caked truck in the courtyard.

"You are so very kind to be of help, and we do appreciate it," said Samantha.

"Thank you and how may I help you in your quest?"

Samantha went over the details of the crash and death of her dad as had been told to her. She asked if what she remembered agreed with his information.

"Yes, so regrettable. Your father was highly instrumental in helping the company achieve its goals. We were looking forward to a long relationship."

"It is just hard to believe that he crashed. You knew he was a colonel in the Air Force. A fighter pilot. I can't imagine him crashing. What was he flying?"

"Just a minute." He intercommed again in Arabic for the young man to bring the public file on Martin King. The one in the large filing cabinet. A flag went up in Samantha's mind. Perhaps there were more files? A secret file in addition to a "public" file? Mr. Zayyat would not know that Samantha could understand Arabic. Even so, perhaps she had an overactive imagination about more or secret files. Seated once again, this time with the file, Mr.

Zayyat opened it and leafed through the papers.

"Ah, here we have it. The plane was a Cessna Citation twin engine jet, a company plane. Perhaps, it was too much plane to handle without a co-pilot. The report says lack of fuel may have caused the crash."

"Did you recover the plane?"

"No. We thought about it, but the report from those who found your father's remains said it was totally destroyed. He must have hit very hard. Too, it was just at the time that the government was allowing bidding for oil exploration in the Peten region, and we made a business decision to use all our resources to get ready for the bidding. I know that sounds insensitive to you, but since we had Martin King's body, we didn't think it necessary or prudent to search for a destroyed plane. The insurance covered it. I hope this doesn't distress you too much.

"Were you successful in your bidding?"

"Unfortunately, no." Samantha glanced at Julie.

"Mr. Zayyat, I wish to hire a guide and go to the scene of the crash site. If you could be so kind as to give me the coordinates, I'll make my plans. I understand it is near the Celaque National Park close to the mountain, Cerro de las Minas."

"Ah yes, the coordinates." There was a moment of indecision, then he leafed through the file, and stopped at one page.

"I don't have them precisely you understand, but they seem to converge on the west flank of the Celaque mountain. So that would be roughly latitude plus 14 degrees 30 minutes north and longitude minus 88 degrees 50 minutes west. I must say Ms. King that is very rough country and very disagreeable to walk in to. This is the dry season, but it still rains there, and it is uncomfortably cold."

Samantha thought of the below zero weather of Greenland and decided central Honduras would not be so bad, relatively speaking.

"Thank you. You have been very helpful. I'll report what I find, if anything." Yusuf al Zayyat moved slightly in his chair in a way that connoted a mental uncomfortableness.

"There is one more thing I would like to offer. You are new to Guatemala and may not know of some of our ways, and I wish to mention it without seeming to pry."

165

"Of course, we would be thankful for any information that would make our stay inoffensive to the nation."

"It's such a little thing, but it is good to be cautious." Here he pulled at his beard a bit. There was a brief moment of indecision. He straightened in his chair and looked directly at Samantha.

"Is there any special reason you are driving that kind of truck with darkened windows?"

"Why yes, we were going to rent another vehicle, but it was not air-conditioned, so I chose this one. Is it a problem I should know about?"

"Oh no, nothing really important. It's just that government officials use it a lot. I guess you could say it is their favorite way to get around. It is a handsome auto. I thought, perhaps, you knew someone who had recommended it."

"No, I have it because of my tirade at the rental counter in the airport, and my determination not to drive in this heat if I could help it."

"The weather here in Antigua is quite pleasant, only if you drove to Guatamala City, would you find warmer weather."

"Well, we didn't know that. It seemed quite warm when we got off the plane. Perhaps, we won't require air-conditioning after all." Almost got us in a trap, thought Samantha. Now, he won't know if we have business in Guatamala City, or not. Good.

They exchanged "good-byes" and "thank yous" and "come agains." Mr. Zayyat took them to the door. He handed the file to the young man, speaking to him rapidly in Arabic. Then he smiled and saw them out. The Mayan escorted them to their SUV, and with his sleeve rubbed at the door handles to remove any smudge he may have left there, smiling obsequiously.

"Joe the Oilman! Yusuf al Zayyat!" Julie was incredulous. "How would you know that?"

"Because I know Arabic, at least enough to get by on. Remember, I traveled the oil fields with my dad, and we spent a lot of time in Saudi Arabia. Kids pick up a language fast. And by the way, he mentioned to the young man, there at the last, that if we should call again he would not be available."

"Wow! And he was smiling. The smiling oil man. What a hoot." Julie began laughing and shaking her head. Samantha slowed down as they approached the side of the building and looked at something.

"He also told that receptionist guy to bring the "public" file. So, I'm thinking there may be two files."

"Well, while you were listening to Arabic and saying your initial hellos in his office, I was noticing the hardware. Looked pretty up-to-date. I've memorized the log-on procedure by watching that cute guy in the front office at his laptop.

"Should we want to go there, and I'm hearing you may want to do just that, then we might find another digital file or even a private file belonging to your dad. If we had his personal Secure I.D. card we could use the numbers and get to his personal files. I'll be able to get into the company, but I would need passwords, I.D.s that sort of thing to find stuff from your dad, if he left anything."

"What kind of card?"

"It's really thicker than a credit card, but that's what they call it, a special card with changing numbers. There are six LED numbers and they change every 15 seconds. You have to enter the numbers in the computer when it asks for them after you log on and you have 15 seconds to do it, then a new series lights up. Battery life is five years. So watch for it when you go to the crash site. Of course, they may have found it somewhere in his personal effects. If so, we're out of luck on that."

"I just wish there was some way I could look for that other file."

"Breaking into that office with those barred windows, heavy doors, and two ferocious dogs should be a snap." Julie shook her head again. "Honestly, Samantha, you are the most indomitable person I've ever met."

"Well, let me do some thinking. By the way, beneath his charm I thought he was a little nervous. Ill at ease. I really noticed it when he talked about the SUV. I'll have to give that some thought too."

"I doubt if he has two gorgeous gals call on him every day of the week."

"Yeah, maybe you're right. In the meantime, I'm going to look up an Internet café and do a little research."

"I'll go with you. Remember, I'm a computer whiz."

"You're a godsend, Julie, let's go load up on some calories and get with it. Then we've got to do some sight seeing, but no more volcanoes."

"How could we ever do without guidebooks?" said Samantha as they headed toward the magnificent cathedral laid out in 1680. She read that they were approaching the finest and largest church in all of Central America. The quakes in 1717 and 1773 damaged it severely, and it was left in ruins. Samantha and Julie walked into the soaring and roofless nave and marveled at the dedication of the people who resisted giving in to quake after quake.

"Remember, if you still want to break into that Fort Knox building, dedication doesn't always win you know."

"Who knows? Getting past a couple of dogs won't be as hard as trying to rebuild this."

They looked at the famous fountain standing in the center of the Plaza de Armas. "I think they tried to farm fish in it," said Julie leafing through her own guidebook. "No, no, wrong fountain, the fish fountain is in a monastery which also fell to a quake."

"I was in an earthquake in India earlier this year. Buried all night. No fun."

"Please tell me all about it tonight at story hour. Your life is totally unbelievable."

"Look at this," pointing in the book at a tremendously heavy float. "It starts at the church where the fish fountain is. It has a huge statue of Jesus carrying a big cross. It takes eighty men to lift it and then they have to maintain a walking rhythm so that it looks as if Jesus is walking. It'll be in the procession on Good Friday."

"I'll have to see that before I go see Trak."

The afternoon went by and the charm of the city worked its

way into their minds and hearts.

"I just love it here, don't you?"

"I bet Joe the Oil Man loves it a heck of lot more than Guatemala City."

"Look over there, two volcanoes. One is smoking away. Wait. Wait. Yes, it's Fuego blowing steam at that other volcano, whose name is...here it is, Acatenango. A mouthful.

So, enough of the guidebook. I'm putting it away and just enjoying the scenery. Let's see if any stalls are open. O.K.?"

To Samantha, everything looked peaceful. And yet the ruins surrounding them spoke of destruction. Mother Nature couldn't be trusted.

Chapter 34

Sometimes I love intrigue. Not always. Sometimes its such a bore to dance around in masks pretending we don't know the faces behind them. Sex can be a fantasy too. Real faces are better and so is real sex. −From Samantha's Journal

"Samantha, it's hammock time. Beer time. Follow me. I've got some news from my uncomplicated, totally dedicated archaeologist and lover."

Julie grabbed two beers, handed one to Samantha and headed outside. The sun was long gone, but the after effects of pink and lavender tinted the sky. The once brilliantly colored bougainvilleas dozed, muted and shadowy, along the thick stucco walls. The two women climbed into one large hammock with their feet at opposite ends.

"This is better than two hammocks. We don't have to talk so loud either. First, all is cool for Trak and me this week-end. I shall lovingly wear him out until he puts me back on a bus. I swear, I could just eat that boy up sometimes. But, being manless, you need not hear of my coming moments, nay, hours of ecstasy."

"And I will not need a play by play description after you return either. So, skipping to the breaking news..."

"O.K., so there we are yakking away and I'm assuring him my goal this week-end is to fuck the Mayan alphabet right out of his head, oops, sorry. Anyway, as we talked I happened to mention that the heat wasn't so bad, especially driving the SUV. Well, you could have sworn the line had been cut. I said Trak, you still there? And he said, 'Faux pas, big time' and went on to say that what we were driving, and he couldn't imagine how we got it in the first place, was the vehicle used by practically everybody who could get you disappeared."

"Get you disappeared?"

"Yeah, that's what they call it down here. Troublesome folks are 'disappeared.' Then he went on to say there was a systematic 'cleansing' here resulting in the hundred or so unidentified bodies discovered monthly in stream beds, by the roadside, in the gutters, in the fields, and even in out-door toilets. These are the 'disappeared ones' who have done something displeasing to one of the ruling factions or maybe nothing at all, but the order has come down to rid this fair country of their presence."

"So, let me guess. Driving around in our red SUV with tinted windows means we're connected to one of those factions, right?"

"Right. Which explains why traffic is so nice to us. But someone might start nosing around, and Trak says we better get rid of it before someone puts us on a list."

"Good God! Joe the Oil Man knew this and didn't tell us."

"That's another thing, Trak said. Guatemalans get information, but they hate to hand out any. Too scared. What a country. He said there's the DIC, the Department of Criminal Investigation, hold it, I made notes." Julie rummaged in her jeans pocket and produced folded paper, making the hammock swing.

"Almost too dark to see, but I think I can make it out. Yes, here, the DIC. Belongs to the National Police. They run around looking like civilians, definitely can alter your life-style in a hurry. Another group is the G-2 which is military intelligence, and they run around with 'civies' on too. There's the border police, the regular police, and the soldiers. They get to wear uniforms unless they don't want you to know they are in the security forces. They're all connected. Sort of a love-hate relationship. And they all have goon squads, also called death squads, that carry out executions.

Even the political parties have private militia ready to wipe out rivals. Torture is rampant. Their number one job seems to be to keep the rich, rich, and the poor, poor. Guatemala is armed to the teeth thanks to the U.S. and others. The enemies, get this, are the people of the country. And we're right in the middle of it. Kind of exciting, eh, Senora?"

"O.K. first thing in the morning, I'll take the SUV back and get something less noticeable. Hey, you did good Julie." A moment went by.

"Julie, you didn't sign on for this cloak and dagger stuff. That's my problem not yours. I think after the week-end you better fly out of here." Another moment as the two Red Roosters tilted.

"Samantha, I'm here to help and I'll do just that. Guatemalan bad guys haven't messed with the likes of us. They're the ones in trouble."

"Spoken like a true nit-wit. O.K. and thanks from a bigger nit-wit. I really appreciate it Julie. Now, lets finish the beers and hop out of this sling and do some planning before we attack the next bunker."

"Or get disappeared."

"Over my dead body."

Chapter 35

I watched the sun come up in Antigua today and bring to glorious life the multi-colored blooms of bougainvilleas all along a stucco wall of white, so beautiful. –From Samantha's Journal

Just after daybreak, a red SUV with tinted windows lurched out onto the cobblestone streets of Antigua and took the highway toward Guatemala City. The morning was muggy and warm. Samantha dreaded the ride back with no air-conditioning. The tops of the two volcanos she could see on her right had their tops lopped off by heavy gray clouds.

The guide books said this was the dry season; if so, she'd sure hate to be driving when the rains really came down. Worrisome splatters on the windshield gave the wipers plenty of work.

She ran over in her mind the tasks of the day. Two were daunting. Get rid of the SUV first thing. Easy. Check for flight records at the airport for March 10 last year. Probably non-existent. See if any maintenance records for the plane could be found. Not likely.

As the sun rose and rain moved away, she could see the city take shape. Mist and dirty banks of fog still clung to the higher buildings and the hills. Trees looked like ghosts.

Even with the air conditioning on she recognized the odors she and Julie had experienced when they landed last Sunday. Now that she had learned there could be "disappeared bodies" joining the smoking garbage in the city's ravines, she found it hard to take a deep breath.

At Samantha's insistence, Julie would be busy in Antigua doing touristy things. She was determined to keep Julie out of harm's way as much as possible. The less they were seen together, the better.

The attendant at the rental agency greeted her warmly as she drove in, obviously thankful to have the SUV back and honestly relieved when he saw not one dent or scrape.

Samantha chose the 4-wheel drive pickup again. After a couple of days she had accepted the heat better. If Guatemalans could stand it so could she. Actually, it wasn't all that hot, just muggy. Sweat was just sweat. Perfectly natural stuff. She did get two thick colorfully woven seat mats which would allow some air circulation between them and the plastic.

She had the windows deeply tinted, even though the cost was high. Once the job was finished the windows would be doubly appreciated, keeping out the direct sunlight and keeping out prying eyes. So, it wouldn't be so bad she kept saying to herself, while smiling at the attendant who couldn't seem to do enough for her now, at a price, of course.

Samantha drove to the airport's parking area. She noticed the large number of air terminal soldiers, each carrying an efficient-looking assault rifle. The uniformed young men stood about, eyeing arriving and departing passengers. Something warned Samantha to walk purposely and to look straight ahead as if she knew exactly what she was doing.

———————

It took half an hour to find out she was in the wrong building. Once in the right place, she bumped against the stucco wall of non-information. She received blank stares, hunched up shoulders, but ever-present smiles. Did they have flight plans or her legs on their minds? She could have made a fortune on that bet she thought. She had offered to pay. No luck. No takers. She turned to leave.

"Senora, I think I can help. Tell me as much as you can." A small man, with a drooping mustache, and some sort of airport insignia on his sweat-stained shirt, motioned her to him, his palm turned downward and the fingers scratching at nothing. Eagerly, Samantha listed what she knew. She told the man how important it was to her while waving a wad of quetzals. Not discreet enough. He laughed.

"Ah Senora, that will not be necessary." But she knew it was.

He made a call and soon he asked her to follow him. So, he'd probably rape her, then throw her abused body into the nearest ditch. Samantha sighed, and followed anyway.

They climbed stairs. He went first, which encouraged her. She remembered a very proper friend relating how she had preceded a friendly wine merchant up a steep flight of steps in a wine cellar and half-way up sensed all was not right. She turned just in time to see two cupped hands ready to attach themselves to her well-formed derriere. Lesson: Don't go first.

On the landing, and through a door, she saw a young woman at a desk. Behind her, like stacks in a library, were cartons of thick books.

One such book lay opened at her desk. The clerk pointed to an entry for Samantha to read. On the morning of March 10, 2000, a flight plan was filed by a Martin King. His route went south of the city to a private facility, then to an unknown destination. The plane was a 1980 Cessna Citation. She jotted down the registration number.

There was no record that the twin-engine jet had crashed. Mr. Zayyat had not mentioned the scheduled stop at the private airstrip. Did it belong to the company? Did her dad pick up someone there? Or leave someone? Or deliver and receive some cargo? Too many questions.

Samantha thanked the airport employees. She insisted on a gift of quetzals for them both, placed discreetly this time in the pages of the thick book. She felt elated. Two tasks now completed. As she left, she felt the heat of the sun battling the soggy weather. Sweat wasn't so bad. Everybody looked damp and warm. Clammy and sticky. She was one with the Guatemalans.

She decided there was nothing to be gained by trying to find the maintenance records, so she crossed that task off her list. Besides, the logical place for them would be in the oil company's office.

As she drove off, she saw a building near the airport for airplane sales. A totally unreasoned and unscheduled idea took root, and blossomed in an instant. Inside, she made inquiries and soon a man in a light-colored guayabera approached with a pleasant, but questioning expression. His pale-blue, bloodshot eyes peered at her, ready for a snap judgement. Women don't buy planes. Samantha offered her hand.

"Samantha King."

"Javier Rodriguez."

"Is there some place where we could talk in private?" Reluctantly, he led her to a small office, and turned on an ancient fan that shoved the humid air around the room. She pulled at her skirt to free it from a sweating thigh. He noticed. She tugged some more.

"I represent a company that prefers to remain anonymous. We wish to buy a high performance plane that would require only one pilot. There are what might appear to be strange conditions. The company is not concerned with registration. Indeed, we would prefer it to be unregistered.

If the plane is in good condition, and privacy about the transaction is maintained, the company will pay a premium in US dollars, cash."

"What kind of plane did you have in mind?"

"A late 70s or early 80s Cessna Citation." There was an audible scraping against the concrete floor heard above the churning fan blades. He pursed his lips as if to whistle, but if he did, Samantha could not hear it.

"They're kind of scarce, right now. I don't know if I can help with that."

"We're patient. There will be an efficient and sensible inspection procedure. I, myself, will do the inspecting. Maintenance records are to be up-to-date and all scheduled maintenance to have been completed. We're not interested in the logs of the previous owner or owners.

"Avionics have to be excellent. Upgraded engines would be attractive. We don't care about the decor as long as it is in reasonably good condition. Good exterior. Nothing fancy. And again, we would prefer an unregistered aircraft, but if that's a problem, we can work around it. I will make the decision to purchase and will pay in cash in US dollars as I said."

His chair squeaked.

"So, what are we talking about? The premium price you mentioned?"

"Four million."

"I don't know."

"That's over twice what a plane that age and in good condition would bring, and I think given the circumstances, it's more than a fair price. Remember, cash. No records. No receipt. We'll fly it out without a flight plan. Think it over. If we can do business, I'm in Antigua for a few days at this number.

One more thing, any mention of this conversation to any government agency or any security group, and I'll know about it. The deal will be off. I hope we can help each other, Mr. Rodriguez."

Samantha stood, offered her hand, then smiled, and walked to her truck. Her knees wanted to tremble. They received a stern and silent lecture.

Chapter 36

I remember seeing a photo of the earth from four billion miles away. It looked not much larger than the head of a pin. Empty space surrounded it. I thought how awesome. How marvelous. What alien would believe such a tiny blue dot could hold so many squabbling people? -From Samantha's Journal

A woman knocked on their door right after Samantha and Julie returned from breakfast. Samantha cracked the door and the young woman said there was a call for a Senora King. She would have to take it in one of the public phones in the lobby.

Samantha shook her head as the messenger left.

"If it's that aircraft sales guy he moved fast."

"Well, I guess you know how to find out." Julie's broad wink made Samantha laugh.

"Right, Ms. Know-it-all. If you'll hold the fort, I'll scamper up there. Be back in a jiff."

In less than five minutes Samantha returned. She saw Julie's questioning look.

"Gotta use the bathroom. Hold on, and don't go anyplace."

In addition to heeding nature's call, Samantha needed time to think.

The phone call had made her nervous. Mr. Rodriguez had found a plane, a 1980 Cessna Citation through some "very private" contacts. Located in a private hanger, at an unused part of the field with its own tarmac.

How interesting he would know the number for a public phone booth. Maybe such things were common. Maybe there was even a directory. Why hadn't she given him her cell number? No way. Too much intrigue already without a Mr. Rodriguez calling her anywhere in the world.

If she had been thinking, she would have changed her name. But how would he have called her at the hotel? "No one with that name is registered." The point: She hadn't thought at all. She could have done better. Impromptu ideas came bundled with a myriad of problems. She should have slept on it, but what was done was done.

So, now what? He wanted an immediate inspection. She'd said tomorrow. If her instincts were right, this could be big. If not, then at least she could think of her dad in a plane such as this one. Maybe sit in the pilot's seat. After all, she was inspecting it, and of course, like any of her wary real estate buyers, she could turn it down without giving a reason.

Maybe it would work. What about Julie? Would she come? Sort of a getaway truck driver. She shook her head at the thought of starring in a foreign movie. A covert operator. More like the Keystone Cops, except here she might get "disappeared." Samantha dried her hands. She would let Julie decide.

The directions were thorough. She and Julie would drive to the old hanger; Samantha would be met by someone called Manuel. Julie would stay in the truck and watch. Samantha would have two hours, if needed, to look the plane over. The maintenance records would be there, too. The previous owner's name would be blacked out.

Mr. Rodriguez would not be there and she was not to call him, or come by the office, no matter what. The time of arrival would coincide with the busiest time of day for the airport.

"The more things going on, the less time anyone has to wonder about you, Ms. King. I'll call you later in the day for your decision, around six if that's convenient."

The hanger needed repairs. Weeds, gray-green and wiry-looking, proliferated. No clumps of bougainvilleas here. The metal roof sagged, and she heard a creaking. Clearly, it had seen better days. The tarmac was crumbling here and there and would need a walking inspection before using it for a take-off. The main airport was a good two miles away. For a minute Samantha thought she was actually in the market for an anonymous twin-engine jet. "I'm probably going to use it in the drug trade," she muttered to herself as she got out, exchanged a thumbs up signal with Julie, and walked toward an open door. She cupped her hand over her nose, as a small cloud of smelly smoke reached her.

"What if my uncle could see me now." Samantha took quick short breaths to minimize the encroaching stink. Her uncle had said it wouldn't hurt for her to sniff around while down here. Get some answers to questions he couldn't ask. Had he actually said sniff? She hoped not.

And where would Emerson be right now? Gazing at his paintings, polishing his repaired and beloved Jaguar? Jaguars roamed here in the jungles, where she would soon be going, if she got out of this part of her adventure. The sun beat down today more than usual, and she felt especially hot and sticky. She wore jeans since she would be crawling over and under the Cessna. She wanted the inspection to look authentic. She shook her head and sneezed.

"Buenas tardes. Senora King?"

"Si. Manuel?"

"Si, adelante por favor."

"Gracias."

Manuel beckoned Samantha to enter the gloomy interior. Dim lights glowed in the cavernous building. There, in the middle, sat a beautiful silver Cessna Citation. Long and sleek with a graceful jet engine nacelle on each side of the fuselage near the high vertical stabilizer. The wings were swept back and seemed to yell out speed.

The plane sat level on its tricycle landing gear. It looked poised for take-off. Samantha regretted not being able to buy it and fly it away. Actually, she could buy it, but like a lot of things, it was not the initial cost, but the upkeep that would eat up every saved rainy-day dollar. And if she did buy it she would pay no more than 1.5 million, certainly not four.

She motioned for Manuel to come closer. He seemed almost

boyish with unruly black hair, large black eyes and the Mayan high cheek bones. He smiled warmly. She noticed he still had most of his teeth. She smiled back. She asked that the boarding steps be lowered. She clamored up and went inside. She turned on the lights. She moved toward the passengers' section.

The cabin seats, in plush creamy leather, gave off a clean fragrance and a leathery smell at the same time. She touched them and realized the presence of smoky blue, purple with red overtones. Then something flashed in her mind, and she left before examining the cockpit area.

She walked carefully down the steps and surveyed the tail. She had glanced at it earlier, but she had neglected to notice something. Something not there. No registration letters and numbers. The graceful knife-like stabilizer soared high above the gray oil-smudged floor.

The registration would have appeared toward the base of the stabilizer, in large letters and numbers, but still several feet above her.

Samantha asked Manuel for a set of stairs to inspect the tail area. Soon he returned, pushing in front of him a large network of aluminum pipes and bars that would reach the tip-top of the stabilizer and rudder if Samantha so desired. She would not need to go that high.

The scaffolding was wheeled into place and she made her way upwards, checking this and that, getting closer to where the registration should have appeared.

By stretching she could touch where some of the numbers would have been painted. Someone had done a thorough job taking them off, which of course, was exactly what she had expected, for if her hunch was right, she could solve part of the puzzle of her dad's crash. The registration had not been removed because of her request. It had been done earlier. "Thank you synesthesia," she murmured.

Relying on her gift of merged senses to guide her, she traced the skin of the stabilizer with the tips of her fingers. With one hand she grasped one of the metal bracings of the scaffolding.

She could feel her heart beat increase. She could hear it in her ears. She wondered if Manuel watched her. She glanced down, but he had disappeared, although probably within shouting distance. Good.

She almost caught herself humming the tune about black being the color of someone's true love. Black, of course, being the paint color of the registration. While she traced, her mind played with the words "true love."

Would she ever know it? Why wasn't she in London making love to Emerson? How crazy to be thinking of love now. Concentrate, Samantha!

Her mind snapped suddenly back to the smooth skin of the Cessna. Yes, yes, she felt the paint, although it appeared invisible to her eyes. A fuzziness, a fog cover clung to the paint or rather, where it used to be. She could not reach far enough to feel the whole registration number, but definitely could trace several numbers and letters. Enough. She wiped sweat from her brow and reached in her jeans pocket for a folded-up piece of paper.

The hangar was like an oven. She certainly wouldn't be taking the full two hours to do an inspection, especially not if what she suspected would pan out. Her hand shook a little as she unfolded the damp paper. She dropped it! She watched as it flopped this way and that on its way through the gloom to the floor below.

Julie drove. Samantha had to admit that Miss Amber could really drive. The pickup had a powerful engine and Julie put the accelerator to the floor as she gunned away from the hangar. Samantha watched Manuel grow smaller until a bend in the road "disappeared" him. They sped back to the highway leading out of Guatemala City.

Thankfully, the rancid and sour smelling area was "disappeared" too. Julie barely slowed as she plowed through the rubble of the land slide they had inched through last Sunday.

"I can see I need to take driving lessons from you if I ever want to take up delivering boot-leg whiskey. My heart was in my mouth in that hangar and it's still in my mouth on this road. You are good. Really good." Samantha shook her head while Julie laughed.

"That's what you get for leaving me in this fucking truck baking in the sun for nearly an hour, I'm wringing wet and the faster I go the cooler I get. It feels great."

"Yeah, sweat's not so bad in a strong breeze, and we still smell better than parts of Guatemala City."

"How in the hell can anyone live there with all that stink, day in and day out?"

"Like having an abusive husband, you get used to it, and it only seems strange to others; besides, I bet when the wind's right, it smells better."

Julie pushed the accelerator to the floor again, and the pickup leaped forward.

"If a man ever hit me, not even really hard, he'd be in that garbage pit back there making some worms very happy," she yelled above the roaring engine.

"Hear, hear and well put. And speaking of hearing, do you want to hear what I discovered? I'm still shaking, but I can't talk over all this noise. Slow down and get back to a breeze, please."

"Will do. Sorry, lost my head, but it just pisses me when spouse abuse rears its stupid head." The pickup slowed.

"Well, I'll be damned. Your dad's plane. Are you sure?"

"As sure as I can get. The numbers and letters I felt matched the ones I scribbled down from the flight plan."

"Felt?"

"Oh, I haven't told you, I'm a synesthete. I'll let you in on this marvelous gift of mine tonight. Just trust that what I say is true."

Samantha filled Julie in on her experiences in the hangar and how she had traced some of the letters and numbers with her finger tips though the paint was no longer visible.

Julie said, 'wow' several times as Samantha went on telling how she had flown a similar plane with her dad in Saudi Arabia and had actually taken it up herself, zoomed around for a time and came in for a bumpy landing.

The Arab workers at the airport kept waiting for the pilot to come out after she skipped down the steps in her school girl uniform, a short black skirt and a white blouse. One bearded mullah had glared at her and scolded her dad for letting her run around naked.

"Fantastic. You're unbelievable!

"Dad thought it hilarious. He also said I shouldn't fly anymore without proper training and a license. Anyway, Julie, seeing that plane today brought back the wonderful times with my dad, and it made me all the more determined to get to the cause of his death.

If he didn't crash that plane, then what did happen? He was killed or at least died. I know that. But how? Why? Believe me, this little country down here is going to come up with some answers or else."

Chapter 37

I enjoy the give and take between Trak and Julie. The preoccupied archaeologist meets the savvy business executive. The past and the future sparking in the present. -From Samantha's Journal

The bus ride to Copán from Antigua traversed rugged country, hills, valleys, cultivated land. Campesinos trudged along the edges of the highway. The bus did not slow. The driver seemed unaware of the parade of fragile flesh and bone so near to his heavy, speeding wheels. The men and women, dressed in bright colors, stooped beneath their loads of firewood, corn, textiles, or fruit. They had plenty of time to think during the slow trek from fields to city markets.

Julie wondered if they thought at all, but if they did, what would they think about? Where to spend the evening? In the open around a small fire as the temperature dipped into the 40s? Did they have something to eat? A warmed-up tortilla? A parched ear of corn?

There could be more important concerns to think about. What to do with the money received from the sale of their wares? Essential things to buy that could not be made or grown. Enough to buy a beer or two, even though warned in the village not to squander a single quetzal? Did their feet hurt?

Did they despair that this was the absolute last trip in those falling-apart sandals? Would the sore on the left leg ever heal? And the new pain and ache in the stomach, would it get worse until it would be impossible to walk to the doctor's clinic located eight miles away? Perhaps the pain would be followed by death. Expected and accepted.

At the border, the bus driver negotiated with the police, money changed hands. Laughter. Everyone transferred to another bus. Julie had thought it would be a through trip. Maybe she had boarded the wrong bus in Antigua.

No problem. She transferred to a bus and a driver that looked remarkably like the one she arrived with, and of course, the passengers were the same. On the highway now to Copán, more trudging campesinos and campesinas. Guatemala, now Honduras. More U.S. military in Honduras. Would that make it better or worse, or would it matter at all? In all of this apparent poverty and intrigue, Julie concentrated on seeing Trak, giving him a big kiss, a prelude to other good things.

It was a little too warm as the sun rose in the sky. She felt the sweat on her body. Her legs were slick. She had decided on wearing a short green skirt to greet Trak. She had not counted on the male passengers' eyes peering at her and craning to see farther up her thighs. She would wear jeans on the way back. But for now, let them look.

The bus entered the dusty quaint town of Copán. Flowers and vines crowded against each other out of window boxes and from on top of pastel-painted walls. Bronzed Indians with high cheek bones, prominent noses, and black eyes watched the bus as it stopped. Tourists sprinkled themselves among the Indians. Tourists from all over, Julie surmised.

Trak had told her that the ruins, not far from the town, attracted thousands of visitors each year, especially around Christmas and Easter. Sort of a two-quetzals-with-one-stone idea. See the ruins and join the celebrations of amalgamated Christian/Mayan religious beliefs graphically displayed in the villages and towns. The sky smiled down blue, clear, and unseasonably warm. Julie felt her legs sliding against each other as she descended the bus steps.

She saw Trak. She could tell he had seen her too, and he seemed to be having difficulty looking above where her skirt ended. Maybe she had overdone it. Nah. They embraced, sweat and all. He sweated too, she noted. Trak retrieved the suitcase, and the hotel being so close, they walked to it, got the key to the room Trak had secured, and walked down an outside corridor where the multi-colored sensuous blooming profusion of flowers bathed them in rich perfume and seemed to shout "make love, make love." Trak opened the door. No air-conditioning. Julie clicked on a big fan and the sudden blast of air felt wonderfully cool. Should love-making wait until the temperature dropped in the evening? Could she wait? What a question.

"Do I have time to go to the bathroom, Trak?"

"Uh, oh yes, of course, I'll wait right here."

"Well, I hope so. See you in a sec." And she was soon back in the room and into his arms. She moved easily against him.

"Sorry I'm so wet. Just feel my legs, they're really slippery." Since he hesitated for a micro-second, Julie put his hand between her thighs to prove her point. That was a good time for a hungry kiss, sweat and all.

Trak's eyes were bright and eager-looking as he told Julie about his work translating glyphs.

"I can hardly wait to show you. I brought some to work on while you're here. Tomorrow I'll take you on a tour, and you'll get to meet my research leader. You'll like her; she's really nice."

"She?"

"Dr. Emily Deboreaux. Yes, she's super. Helps me and says I'm a real asset. I go over and work sometimes most of the evening translating. She's brilliant."

"Go where? Go over where?"

"Julie, Dr. Deboreaux is not like what you're thinking at all. We work at her office because she's got air-conditioning. You'll see it's all right. Dr. Deboreaux, a famous Mayan authority, would certainly not be making eyes at a lowly graduate assistant."

Examining that sentence, Julie had a feeling that if Trak were a full professor, then maybe Dr. Emily would make eyes at him. He didn't say he wouldn't be interested if she did. The business world had taught her to read between lines and protect your back at all times.

She felt bad that those thoughts threatened the happiness of her time with Trak this weekend. She drummed the words of assurance on her heart. "There's nothing happening here." He didn't say she was fat or ugly, though.

"Trak, please forgive the green monster in me. I guess I worry you wouldn't notice someone trying to take you away from me until after you got married. I know that's not true and yes, I'd be happy to meet Dr. What's-her-name tomorrow."

"Dr. Emily Deboreaux. You'll see she's professional, through and through."

"Cool. What color is her hair?"

"Sort of a reddish brown, I think."

"Blue eyes?"

"Julie stop it. You're making a mountain out of a mole hill."

"You're right, my sweet lover. Come kiss me and make me forget I ever said anything, and then I'll tell you about my adventures with Samantha."

"Man, Julie, you're dealing with dangerous stuff. This is no Spielberg movie you're in. I think you better get home and the sooner the better. Samantha's wild ideas don't have to be yours."

Trak stood outside the bathroom, drying with a large towel. Julie had finished folding her towel turban-like around her head. She leaned against the bathroom's doorway, naked, waiting for him to turn around.

They had made love for two hours and had jumped into the shower. Julie had begun sharing her escapades in Guatemala City and Antigua as they showered together. Trak had become agitated as they talked, but not in the way she preferred. Trak turned toward her.

"Aw, dammit, Julie, you know I can't talk with you standing there like that. Get something on. I've got to talk to you about this...please Julie.

"O.K., I'll slip on some shorts and a halter top, but I'm not promising to keep them on for long. So, talk fast."

"Julie, I thought you knew Central America boils like a pot, and it's a mess. Tourists are welcome and even protected, unless they roam around at night, and Julie, anyone, who pokes around like you're starting to do, ends up in a pine box."

188

"They don't box you up here. Just dump you in the ravine and let you smolder with the rest of the garbage."

Trak looked incredulous at this remark. He got up and paced the floor.

No more love-making that evening.

"Why can't people have a conversation, even a little disagreement, and still go on and fuck each other? What's the big deal? I came to make love. I want you Trak. I need you. Can't you see that?"

"Julie, you really have me worried. I can't act like nothing's wrong. You and Samantha will live (or die) regretting what you're doing."

"O.K., stay a monk the rest of the night. I'm sorry you're worried, but I'm a big girl. I'm going to stand by Samantha as long as she needs me. I don't rush into your play pen to protect you against snakes, bugs, disease, and who knows what all, do I?" She almost included skirts.

"Do we have to fight, Trak? Just accept the fact I'm an independent, hard-headed cuss who loves you a lot. Just don't try to control me O.K.? Now, if you're too upset to get it up you can at least give me a hug, and we'll both shut up." A buzzing fly landed on the wall as if it were a spy.

Trak and Julie felt much better Sunday morning. At least Julie felt better, and she thought Trak was less preoccupied than usual. They held hands as they began the tour of the Ruins. The ruins enthused Trak. He could hardly wait to show Julie around. Last night had been fun after all.

Julie had pulled Trak into the shower and turned on cold water. The tropical sweat dissipated and a cool glow had taken its place as the evening temperature began dropping. Julie had asked to be close for warmth, Trak had obliged and nature, as Julie was fond of saying, had its way with them.

"I'm really glad you're here, Julie, and I apologize for being a worrywart last night. I know you can take care of yourself."

"Hey, no apology needed. I'm the hard-headed stubborn bitch

and I think it's damned nice to know you care what happens to me. I'd hate to try to break in another lover when you're just the most important thing that's happened in my life. I really need to kiss you Trak."

"Now? Here?"

"Yep." And she did. His face flushed with pleasure and a small amount of embarrassment.

"I'll sure get ribbed if any of the staff saw that. But I'll have to say it was pretty nice. Nice enough that I feel the need to return it and to heck with onlookers."

"Here? Now?"

"Oh shut up." He kissed her soundly, and she locked her arms about his neck and kissed him again.

"Julie, we gotta stop. We'll have to forget the tour if you keep doing that."

"I'm ready to forget the tour." Julie guided his hand to cup her breast.

They heard footsteps and turned around.

"It's Emily, er, Dr. Deboreaux. Let me introduce you."

Julie appraised the woman. Very much a woman in her early forties or late thirties. So hard to tell anymore, a well-put-together woman with a lot of reddish-brown hair. Trak had gotten that right, and big brown eyes, a straight nose, a mouth that Julie bet used to know how to pout and was now just full and sensuous and maybe sensual, too.

"Dr. Deboreaux I would like you to meet my very close friend, Julie Amber, down for a visit. Julie this is Dr. Emily Deboreaux."

"Please, call me Emily, and we're delighted you are here. Trak is always talking about you, and I must say you will be proud to know Trak has been the highlight of this research effort."

"And please call me Julie and I know he appreciates your support, and he has told me how you have helped him with translations...." She wanted to add, "all night," but bit her tongue and smiled instead.

"So, you two are seeing the Ruinas. Would it be imposing if I walked with you for a ways?"

Yes, thought Julie, I knew it. I knew it. You've got designs on my man.

"Cool, Please join us." And so the morning went by and Julie felt as though she were the net on a tennis court as balls of information whizzed back and forth.

The reading she had done, hoping to show Trak that she, indeed, was interested in his chosen field, quickly became useless as theory after theory rocketed by without touching her. Then the net captured a ball.

"Julie, look at this stela, it's Stela A." Trak pointed to a 20-foot towering column of carved stone, that leaned slightly.

"It's sort of an information stela. The glyphs or carvings coming down from the top when translated name the four large classical cities of the Mayan culture.

"Let me guess, Copán, Tikal, Calakmul and Palenque."

Dr. Emily and Research Assistant Trak gaped at Julie in wonder.

"And lower down are glyphs, or carvings as you said, depicting the four sacred world directions. Let's see, those must be...," squinting studiously for effect at the lower glyphs, " yes, west, east, north and south."

Trak laughed.

"You have been studying. And here I thought you were just a run-of-the-mill tourist." He patted her arm. Julie knew she was at the edge of her Mayan knowledge. About all she had left centered on the ritual playing in the ball court and a few comments about the hieroglyphic stone stairway erected by the leader Smoke Shell in the eighth century. Kindergarten stuff to archaeologists.

———————

Julie had been truly amazed at the complexity of these ancient cultures. She and Samantha had read how in the past twenty years tremendous progress in deciphering the hieroglypics had opened these civilizations for the world to see and appreciate. Breathtaking, really.

Dr. "Emily" and Trak were discussing human sacrifice and ritualized blood letting, when she refocused on them. The subject shifted to a piece of news, a discovery near Tikal, another of the great cities, which Julie had memorized to impress them. Tikal was in Guatemala. And near Tikal was the gradual unearthing of what was a pre-classical city called Cival.

"The amazing thing, Trak, Cival while falling in the preclassical period...," that would have been prior to 250 C.E., thought Julie, trying to keep up intellectually.

"Well," Dr. Emily of the flashing eyes, went on.

"I have news on the QT that Cival looks just as grand as the classical cities and it dates, are you ready?...," and her voice dropped low enough for Julie to strain to hear it, "200 B.C.E or earlier! And it reached its peak by 150 B.C.E.! Excavations are already showing a monster city with the same markings as classical cities: complex iconography, grand palaces, polychrome ceramics and writing."

Julie thought Trak would fall over. Dr. Emily of the great figure, looked suddenly at Julie.

"Please, Julie, you must forget or at least not mention what I have just said to a soul." Then, she touched Trak's arm, much to Julie's annoyance.

"Trak, there's your future. Your future in this ancient past." She paused perhaps thinking of this oxymoronic statement, decided Julie. Then, "Doc Brown Eyes" put her hand on Trak's shoulder!

Gad, how much more of this...and what do they do late at night while translating? 'Oh Trak, that is such a good translation, I have to kiss your cheek and pat your butt...' Arrrrggggh, thought Julie, even though she knew she smiled spinelessly and with the appropriate countenance of wonder and disbelief at the news of this out-of-sync city.

Julie watched as the siren witch goddess with the reddish-brown hair looked at Trak with her huge soulful eyes and opened those sensuous pouting lips.

"I judge a couple of years yet, before it's written up. I know the group in charge. I want to go and be a part of it, and I know Julie would want you to be a part of it too, wouldn't you Julie? I mean something like this is a once-in-a-life time opportunity, right Julie?"

Why am I being drawn into this, steamed Julie, biting her tongue. What am I supposed to say? "Yes, why don't you take my sweet naïve Trak and fornicate with him deep in the Guatemalan jungles for years and raise little Guatemalans?

Julie heard raucous bird calls at the jungle's edge. She peered at the too–green grass lying like a lush carpet around the ancient monuments. The whole place reeked of intrigue, human sacrifice, scheming home-wrecking Doctors of Archaeology, and seduced graduate assistants.

"Uh, yes, yes, of course, what a chance. And I'm sure Trak will give it careful thought, won't you darling?" She never called Trak darling or sweetheart. He appeared taken aback. She put an arm around his waist and hugged him to her. So there.

Julie lay on the bed in the one-story Copán hotel with her skirt and blouse on. Her shoes off. She wondered if Trak had noticed she had removed her bra a few minutes ago. Her breasts were a bit lower without it, but still quite fulsome and her nipples poked at the thin blouse fabric. She liked the feeling of the cloth rubbing against her bare skin.

Julie sighed and looked at Trak, reading, scribbling, translating probably. Just four feet from heaven and he didn't know it. She wondered if Dr. Emily Deboreaux had a bed in her office? Would she lie on it and watch Trak translating?

His eyes had been eager and bright as he talked of that new city that was so old. A great opportunity, but for whom? Dr. Emily Pouty Lips maybe. Julie would fight for her little fella. He was hers and hers alone.

They had made love twice yesterday and early this morning before it got so warm. She wanted him again. After the tour they had gone to a local restaurant for some spicy Honduran food. She hoped it might have an aphrodisiac effect. Worked for her. Not, apparently, for her lover. Maybe if they made love enough, he wouldn't be tempted by Dr. Emily Brown Eyes. But it takes two to tango, and right now she was the only one wanting to dance.

The fan made four more swings. The sheaf of papers on Trak's table riffled with each pass. He stared at the mysterious glyphs, no doubt pondering their meaning. Maybe the message would be "Make love to Julie, you dodo head." Probably too much to hope for.

Instead of the expected cool front, the forecast promised sultry. Julie felt sultry all right. Surely, Trak could see she wanted him. Maybe not. Crazy preoccupied archaeologists. Why couldn't she have fallen for a normal red-blooded, sex maniac like her mother kept picking out for her: "He's so nice, such a gentleman."

No, Trak had hooked her good and getting unhooked never entered her head. She had to admit the very thing that interfered with their love-making was the thing she so much admired about him: his unwavering dedication to his work. He would do great things, she just knew it.

In the meantime, she would have to short-circuit that dedication for a couple of hours. The weekend would soon be over. Did she know what to do? She did.

"Trak, put down your papers. Put something on them so they won't blow away and come over here and sit beside me. Put the fan directly on us, no oscillating."

She waited patiently. Extraneous information took awhile to penetrate.

"Oh. Oh yes, Julie, sure I'll be right there." Aha, contact. Now for the follow up.

"Trak, please stop working. Put something on those papers, and I'll take care of the fan. O.K.?" Not as much waiting required at stage two.

Julie rolled over and stood up, grabbed the fan, untightened the gizmo that made it oscillate, pointed it at the bed, picked up one of her shoes and placed it on the pile of documents on Trak's table and took him by the hand and led him back to the bed. Easy when you knew how. And now the fun part began.

"Trak, tell me very succinctly what a 'ruin' is."

"Well," looking thoughtful, "I guess it would be some sort of building, or artifact that is decaying because of disuse or some sort of neglect."

"What would you do if you could be the very first to come

194

upon such a site? How do you think that would make you, as an archaeologist, feel?"

"Absolutely marvelous. A once-in-a-lifetime experience."

"So, let's suppose you are walking along and you see this hill, like, let me raise my knee up and it'll be the hill and you see it." Julie, lying on the bed, raised her knee. Her skirt slipped down her tanned and glistening thigh. Trak looked at the 'hill' and swallowed without speaking. Julie smiled. The boy was coming around.

"Now you are on top of the hill. So put your face on top of the hill." He did. "Now, you are there. Tell me what you see." Trak had his lips pressed against her knee. He kissed the top of it twice and the little hollow on the side of the knee. Julie knew he had caught on, but the game wasn't over and she wanted him totally committed to excavation.

"So, go on, what do you see?" He swallowed again. He kissed her raised knee again. Her smooth tanned knee.

"I see the rest of you."

"No, no, no, that won't do. You see ruins, remember? Ruins are spread out before you, but guess what?

"What?"

"The jungle is obscuring them, silly. You will have to clear away the jungle. Do you want to start clearing a little right now?"

"Right, the jungle. I see miles of jungle. Probably covering the most beautiful ruins in the world, long neglected, needing restoration, a one-man job." He laughed. She laughed.

It took a little ingenuity, but it was always worth it. The erotic approach. Marvelous indeed. Trak cleared the jungle away. What lay before him were hills and valleys, small depressions, a hidden arroyo, and a grove of trees, no doubt hiding an exquisite temple. There were wells to taste. Slippery mounds topped with small pink buildings. He was so excited by his "discovery" he just had to kiss them, a lot. Sweat pooled in Julie's belly button, no, not a belly button, a spring of crystal clear water. Now he was in the game. She could join him and the sheaf of papers would remain undisturbed for the rest of this luscious evening. But there was one more thing.

She pulled a canister out from under the pillow. Whipped

cream topping. The evening temperature was now deliciously cool.

Julie flipped the fan switch to low. She pretended to shiver.

"Guess what, my archaeological lover? A sudden snow storm is coming, and you will be trapped in these beautiful ruins until spring."

Chapter 38

Sometimes, I think of Emerson as my other half. So, why do I get along better with my half? Were you just pulling my leg, Plato? –From Samantha's Journal

Antigua.   Saturday morning. The temperature just right. Samantha swung her legs from the bed, stood up, stretched and headed for a tepid shower. She stood under the stream of water for several minutes, careful not to get any in her nose, ears, mouth or eyes. She was certain the hotel didn't supply bottled water for the showers. One could not be too careful.

By now, Samantha guessed, Trak probably wondered what had hit him. Good for Julie. She knew what she wanted and that was Trak. And she meant to keep him. Samantha had to stop thinking about what those two horny little animals were doing.

Still on that general topic, Samantha wondered if Emerson was worth conniving for. Part of her wanted to keep him. Part of her remained noncommital. But she also knew that the noncommital Samantha disappeared like the Guatemala fog at mid-day, as soon as she was within touching distance. Loving had to be more than sex. She knew that too.

What were the qualities that drew her to him? What drew him to her? Dare she wonder about that? She turned over those qualities in her mind, trying to stay away from sex.

He was fun. He had a keen wit. He wanted her. Oops, strike that. He was as good at his business as she was at hers. He appreciated art, good food, literature. He dressed well. He was boyish and also mature. He was impulsive and yet sensitive. It struck her that those same qualities in herself might have attracted him to her. She felt fulfilled when they were together. But he also drove her bonkers. He would probably say the same thing about her. Maybe one couldn't love deeply without some frustration. There would be no way to really figure it out. The answer could simply be time.

Maybe she should show up and say "I've come to live with you for awhile." On the face of it that could be the practical solution. After six months of rubbing shoulders and other parts daily, facing problems, talking, laughing, and maybe even crying occasionally, they would know. But that approach certainly seemed cold and calculating.

Maybe she could contrive to do some business in England. They would have more opportunities to see each other, and that might help them decide if they wanted to live together. They could sleep in the same bed, eat breakfast, do the laundry. Calculating still, but possibly more romantic. He could show up in the states and do the same thing.

Why did she have to do all the planning? Work out the logistics? If he did show up, would she feel restricted, pressured, manipulated, and controlled? Probably. Maybe more than probably. She smiled thinking of the two of them trying to make room for the other in their ego worlds.

Life can be so wishy-washy when it comes to straight-ahead commitment. She could test it by talking about the possibility of being in England for an extended period of time and see how he responded. Eager, restrained, silent, over-joyed? She would listen closely.

Samantha dressed, opened the door to the pink and lavender dawn, the heady perfume of flowers, and walked to the hotel's restaurant for breakfast.

She didn't think that Mr. Rodriguez would call one of the public phones so early, and she was right. Once out watching the processions she would be unreachable.

After her breakfast and out in the street, she heard the sounds of a crowd. When she reached Calle de los Pasos, she saw that the cobblestones had been covered with intricate designs made from colored sawdust, fresh flowers, and greenery. People lined the nar-

198

row sidewalks waiting. Soon there appeared a traditional Easter float carried on the shoulders of women.

They walked directly on the newly created carpet of flowers. A band playing mournful funeral music accompanied the women. The procession had left San Francisco Church and would proceed down the Calle de los Pasos to El Cavario Church, commemorating the 1,322 or 1,367 steps Jesus purportedly took on his way to his crucifixion. At each of the 14 stations of the cross special prayers and meditations would be offered.

After the procession, the vendors followed, selling candy, balloons, and small religious mementos. Behind them came the clean-up truck. The ruined carpet would be cleared away so that a new one could be constructed that night for a new procession the following day. That would go on all week. As the days went by, the number of processions would increase. She was glad the handbook she had purchased contained so much information.

Samantha walked to the Saturday mercado. She thought about the tumult surrounding the creation of those street carpets. The pace would increase tremendously as Holy Week drew nearer. There would be a lot of activity in this part of Antigua until late into the night, maybe all night.

After lunch, Samantha returned to the hotel for a siesta in the hammock. Maybe she would read more about the Mayan culture in preparation for going to Copán with Julie the following weekend before Easter.

Sipping on a cold Red Rooster, she read awhile, but her mind kept returning to the carpets. The word "perfect" formed in her head, and she spoke it quietly and confidently.

———————

Sunday was a busy day. Too busy to watch processions, marvelous as they were. She visited shops and stalls and accumulated things the ordinary tourist wouldn't begin to think about. But no one seemed to care or notice the strange items purchased by the gringa.

Julie arrived. Samantha took one look at her radiant face.

"You may describe your week-end, but only in three words.

Got it? I don't want to hear anything about it unless you can say it in three words, then we've got work to do."

Julie bent over laughing and Samantha could not help smiling. It did seem kind of funny. Julie straightened up sporting a ridiculous look on her face.

"All right, three words and here they are: Whipped cream topping." For a second Samantha didn't react, then she fell back on the bed, groaning, trying not to laugh.

Chapter 39

A dare-devil I am not...who am I kidding? –From Samantha's Journal

"The call came Sunday at lunch time," said Samantha. "Mr. Rodriguez wanted to know my decision. I was prepared. I told him I was satisfied with the plane, and the company had accepted my recommendation, and we were ready to move forward, except for a small, inconsequential political problem. It might take a week to work through. I told him if he could get a buyer on that Cessna, to go ahead and sell, then rustle up another one.

"Actually, the company wouldn't mind an upgrade, I said. More powerful engines for one thing. But if the one I looked at was still available by next week, and the problem had gone away, then we'd do business. If things didn't work out, he could look for another Cessna Citation in the late 80s.

"The company might add a few more million depending on what he found. Then I said I thought the company wouldn't be out of this mess until May, which should give him enough time to find a better plane."

"What did he say?"

"What could he say? Wouldn't you wait around for a half month and make more money? He thanked me all over the place and was delighted to do business with me and my company."

"And by May, we'll be outta here, right?"

"Right."

"And now Julie, dear, I have this plan I want to run by you. First, meet some powerful 'night-night' pills. And here's some chorizo we'll keep in the fridge until Wednesday, which is just about the busiest night of the year in Antigua. All the police will be watching the crowds make those beautiful carpets for Thursday and Good Friday."

"You're going to do it aren't you? Break into the office! I knew it! I just knew it!"

"You got that right. And now, Julie, look at this nice, long, hemp rope. And this cute little flashlight and this cute little camera which I brought with me from the states."

"So, where's your skin-tight costume?"

"Good point. Black would be good. I'll get something tomorrow. And I almost forgot gloves."

"You're really going to do it, I can't believe it. How are your nerves?"

"O.K., but I don't know about later. And the irony, all this detective stuff may lead us nowhere."

"Samantha, you're engaging in criminal activity, and it may lead to a dark and dank cell."

"Hey, thanks, I needed that. I'm not breaking and entering. I'm just entering. And I'm not robbing. Just acquiring information."

"Stealing information."

"I don't care. Somebody in that oil company, probably Joe the Oil Man, knows he did wrong, and from what I've learned down here, if it's help I want, I'll look at my own business card."

"Me too."

Chapter 40

As a kid I read about that howling hound coming across the moors with the fog everywhere, and this guy kept right on walking to his doom, I wanted to scream at him to run, run, run! –From Samantha's Journal

Dusk on Wednesday. In the west the last vestiges of another warm day lingered with faint lavender streaks and weakening fingers of flame.

"We'd better go, I want to get there before it's totally dark."

Julie drove the truck, skirting the gathering crowds coming to decorate designated streets with their vivid and short-lived carpets of flowers. For Samantha and Julie, Monday and Tuesday and most of today had been filled with rehearsals, testing for flaws, nervous eating, drinking, and wandering about.

Now, the hour was at hand. The truck growled and thumped over the cobble-stoned streets at the periphery of Antigua. The crowds were near the center of the city, just as Samantha had hoped. Few cars. Just an occasional low wattage light casting a yellow gleam in the approaching darkness.

They drove past the GUASAUCO offices. They couldn't see any lights shining through the large wrought iron doors. Julie parked a half-block away.

"O.K. stage one." Samantha whispered. She reached for the bag containing chorizo balls. The meat had an additional ripe aroma since she had purchased it Sunday. She had made the balls today and inserted the number of pills in each which the pharma-

203

cist had guaranteed would put her noisy dogs to sleep, allowing Samantha a good night's rest.

"Gracias, mucho gracias," Samantha had agreed that dogs could be a problem, but she liked them around too. The pharmacist had smiled as he handed her the package. Had he suspected anything? Probably. No one in Guatemala or anywhere down here ever said anything without a hidden agenda. So, it was just the prattle of a wife getting ready to lethally dose a wayward husband? What did it matter?

Trying her best to blend with the building, Samantha walked the short distance along the narrow sidewalk. Darkened clumps of bougainvilleas, swept over the wall, causing her to bow her head at times.

She came to the small alley-way that served as a narrow street alongside the wall of the office headquarters. She looked through the darkness to examine once more the cage of wrought-iron that jutted out from the window. She and Julie had inspected it quickly on drive-byes on Monday.

"Good, so far," breathed Samantha.

She reached the gates at last and sighed with trepidation and relief. She took hold of the bars and after a second to get control of her nerves, caused the wrought iron to jangle. Nothing. She did it again. Then she saw two shadows coming along the inside walls of the courtyard, one on either side.

No growling, no barking, just slipping along. With a ferocity that made her jump back, the two Rottweilers lunged at the gate with flashing teeth, which she could see quite clearly in the fading light. Their deep growls vibrated against her chest.

As they lunged again, she recovered, opened her bag and tossed two balls through the gate. The dogs ignored them. She tossed two more that landed squarely in front of them. The growling stopped. They sniffed at the meat. One bolted down a ball just like the wolf-dogs in Greenland had done.

The other Rottweiler found two balls and swallowed them quickly. The balls she had thrown were gone. Had one dog got three or had they both swallowed a pair each?

This time she tossed she was careful to make sure both dogs ate. Then the final two balls left her smelly hand. If she held her hand through the bars, they would eat that too. She shuddered at the thought.

Samantha and Julie waited in the hotel room. An hour dragged by.

"Better wait two. Make sure those dogs are sound asleep. I heard the band playing. Everyone will be watching and listening and helping to lay those flower carpets too. No one will be in our part of town until dawn."

"You're right, Julie. It's just that I want this whole thing to be behind me. I had some bad dreams last night. Means I'm nervous, I guess."

"Tell me."

"Someone, probably me, came upon a hungry lion. He licked my hand, then gently bit it and began eating it. I understood, and patted his head with my other hand. After all, hunger is a terrible thing. An officer arrived, and I pleaded that the lion's life be spared." Samantha shifted her position on the bed.

"I tugged the lion into the back seat of the patrol car, the kind with a protective screen sealing off the front seat. Well, I sat there with the lion nibbling away, and we drove off, going to a zoo. He had eaten nearly up to my elbow, so I asked if we could stop at a convenience store for a couple of pounds of hamburger. The rest of my arm was spared. I woke up."

"That's weird, Samantha. Some shrink would love that one."

"Oh, that's not the half of it. After that dream, I dreamed of the lion again. This time I was naked and he took a bite out of my butt. He kept on eating, again gently, and I allowed it. When he finished I had no butt left at all."

"Wow, a butt eater," said Julie. Samantha laughed.

"Those are the craziest dreams I've ever had. What do you think they mean?"

"It means stay away from hungry lions and keep your butt covered. No, wait, I'm getting a handle on this. You're in a wild country that is going to nibble on you without your knowing it and your waking response (your rational brain) is to CYA."

205

"Perceptive, perceptive, dear Julie. No wonder I like you. How about splitting a Red Rooster?"

Clad in a black rebozo she had purchased at a stall, that sold dark clothing for the Good Friday processions, Samantha felt totally invisible. Religiously invisible. It was now 10 p.m. The city was wide awake in its center and fast asleep everywhere else.

Again, Julie drove to the GUASAUCO building and stopped a half-block away. Samantha hurried to the gates and jangled them three times. Nothing. She saw a dark mound about ten yards away. A sleeping Rottweiler. She couldn't see the second one, but assumed he was having great dreams too. By daylight, both should awaken and feel quite rested.

Filled with nervous energy, she ran back to the car and got the rope, flashlight and camera, knotted the rebozo around her shoulders and slipped on latex gloves.

"This is it. Come back in 30 minutes. If I'm not out, drive away and come back in 15 minutes. If that doesn't work do it again."

"And then?"

"And then we'll go back to the hotel."

"Samantha, if they catch you, I'll do everything I can to get you out, and that's a promise."

"Damn, Julie, you're going to make me cry. Thank you, thank you. Samantha closed the pickup's door and made her way up the street. Things would work out.

Back at the gates, Samantha clanged the iron again, but the other dog was nowhere to be seen. She shrugged and walked around to the alley to the barred window. She coiled the rope on her shoulder, grabbed at the protruding cage and pulled herself up enough to get a toe-hold in the fenestrated metal.

From there it was an easy climb to the top of the cage and in seconds she stood on it, the top of the wall just another three feet up, a snap for one in her physical condition.

She tied one end of the rope to the top of the cage, then tossed the rest up and over the wall. She bound her hands in the rebozo and leaped for the top of the wall, hoping there was no glass. None. Why bother with broken glass anyway when two Rottweilers guarded the grounds? Unwrapping the rebozo she made her way carefully across the tile roof.

A loose tile cracked and skittered. She waited while her heart drummed on impatiently. At the edge she looked down.

The rope dangled at least four feet from the ground. Damn, and I thought I had plenty. Oh, well, it's reachable and that's a relief. She climbed down the rope and landed on the cobblestones with more noise than she wanted.

She stood motionless, the black rebozo wrapped around her. Her heart pounded, but nothing stirred. She hurried across the courtyard. Above her, Samantha's star friends winked. A cooling breeze circled the enclosure.

The two sedans were missing, but the mud-splattered truck remained. A dark hulk of machinery. She wondered if she could start it. Power enough to crash through the gates if she needed to. CYA. No lions about.

The blacker space set in the wall loomed. The door. The open door. Just as the Mayan had said. Doors were left open. The dogs would watch everything. Would the absent dog be in there? Should she shut the door or try to? Would that signal an alarm? She hadn't thought of that. Leave it open. No sense taking a chance. She hoped both dogs stayed asleep.

Only thirty minutes allowed. Time to get to work. First the big file cabinet in the outer office. Unlocked. Hooray! She held the tiny flashlight in her mouth. Alphabetical folders. King, Martin. Not there! What? How could that be? Another file cabinet across the room. King, Martin. Nothing. No more filing cabinets. either. What to do? Don't panic.

Think. Not enough time to go through every file in four drawers of each cabinet. She returned to the first cabinet.

"Oh, dad, I'm letting you down, help me." She took a deep breath and out of the recesses of her mind, she remembered. Arabs don't file people under surnames which are genealogical, geographical or nick names to them, but under the given name. Eureka! Under "M", Martin King!

She laid the file on a desk top and steadied her hands. Then page by page with her tiny digital camera flashing a page-sized light she snapped away. In five minutes she finished. The public file was hers.

She doubted if anything of importance lay buried in this file. No file in the second cabinet. On to the inner office. New territory. No filing cabinets there and the desk was locked. So, how does he open it? Carries a key. And if he misplaces it? A back-up. There has to be a back up. She felt the desk. One drawer opened. A small ring of keys. She tried them all.

Nothing fit the file drawer. "This is not the way it happens in spy movies. Why is everything being so difficult?"

Tempted to tap into her peculiar relationship with the Higher Power with her special greeting, she stood up and lightly brushed against one of the wall hangings. She felt an out-of-place color. Not only did she sense the orange of cotton and the smokey blue and red plum of wool, there was an additional presence, a small presence of blue and pink. Steel? She pushed the hanging to one side and there on a small nail was a key.

"If this one's a trick you're going to get an earful for sure." She glanced at the ceiling.

The key fit and the drawer opened. She thumbed immediately to Martin King. No Martin King, but there was an M.K. She took it out. There were emails, letters. Scribbles. Documents. She photographed everything.

Suddenly, she was aware of the suffocating heat. No A/C at night, of course. And the building had not cooled off yet. What breeze there was couldn't reach her down the hallway. She clicked her small flashlight and looked at her watch; she had five minutes. She returned the file, locked the drawer and replaced the key behind the hanging textile. This was more like it, and she breathed a thank you toward the ceiling. She heard an answer: toe nails clicking on the tile floor down the hallway.

Samantha stood still. She could only stare at the door of the inner office as the clicking toe nails entered the long tiled corridor. The Rottweiler paused before each opened office door along the way. Then the clicking would begin again. Two offices, three along the corridor? She couldn't remember. Did it make any difference?

Then in the darkness, in the void of the open door, a darker presence. The Rottweiler stood there, blocking the lower half of the entrance. Rottweiler: a German breed that rivals the mastiff in size and strength. Probably used to kill lions, crocodiles, and elephants, thought Samantha.

The huge dog waited. Menacing. When would it attack? Would she see the flashing teeth before they sunk into her flesh? What good would her martial arts skills be against a 200 pound giant with muscles of steel and trained to kill?

She flicked on her tiny flashlight to see the time. She didn't know why. She was as good as dead and no one would care what time she had been mangled beyond recognition. Her 30 minutes would be up in three minutes. She pictured Julie waiting then driving on to return and to return again. She had asked, "Then what?"

Samantha turned the tiny beam of light on the dog. The eyes looked at her and they didn't look at her. She remembered an old man in Southeast Asia with that same look. Her dad had taken her to an opium den where the air was close and sweet. And there that old man, nearly skin and bones, had looked at her and had not looked at her. "He's in another world," her dad had said.

"The Rottweiler's in another world," breathed Samantha. The sleeping potion still held him in a dream world. A dream world that would soon become the real world as the effects of the sleeping-pill-laced chorizo continued to wear off. She walked slowly toward the dog. He didn't move, but he got bigger with each step. It took all the will power Samantha could muster to continue walking, walking. The office became an immense stadium, and it would take her forever to reach that door and possibly death.

She reached it. Nothing happened. She walked by the Rottweiler, barely brushing against him, for there was not enough room in the doorway to do otherwise. She thought about reaching out her hand and patting the huge head and saying something like "nice doggie." Instead, she walked as fast as her two legs could carry her without breaking into a run. "If I run, I may fall. Don't run. But walk fast. Faster, dammit."

She could hear the toe nails coming along behind her. A steady clicking, not in a hurry. Yet. She reached the courtyard. Camera and flashlight in her jeans. Black rebozo clinging around her shoulders. She wanted to fling it away, but she wanted nothing left behind that would tip off the people in the morning that someone had been there. Nothing that is, unless it was her chewed-up body.

Samantha could hold back no longer. Her long legs broke into a galloping run. "If you're going to run then sprint. Sprint!" But her legs preferred galloping like in a dream where you run in slow motion and the evil ones are zooming after you at the speed of light.

Then, a roaring. It came from the farthest corner of the courtyard. The other Rottweiler, fully awake. Now her legs decided sprinting wasn't such a bad idea after all. The rope. The rope. There! As she came close, the image of the moors and the hound of the Baskervilles added an adrenaline rush to her already burning muscles.

She leaped as high up the thick hemp as she could and swung her legs up above her head just as the massive animal grabbed at her, snatching a mouthful of rope instead. A wild wolf-like wail broke from his throat as his 200 pounds of muscle and bone let the world know he wanted only one thing: that pretty intruder's neck in his jaws.

Swiftly, Samantha scaled the rope. Then she tugged at it to free it from the animal. Impossible. She skittered along the edge of the tiled roof and he let go of the rope to follow her. She yanked it up out of his reach. Then, she wondered if she were about to faint. "Not now. I'll faint later."

Samantha turned and scrambled back to where the caged window waited. She slipped over the wall, felt for the railings at the top of the cage, found them, lowered herself, untied the rope, threw it on the street below, and, with shaky knees and quite a bit of sweat soaking her through, made it to the ground. She gathered up the rope and the rebozo and walked to the broader street. No truck. No Julie.

She grabbed her flashlight. She had made it in exactly 30 minutes. So where in the hell was Julie? An accident? Picked up? Out of gas?

She slumped against the wall. After all she had been through, and now, no Julie. Two minutes went by then three. Then a pickup turned onto the street. Parking lights only. The truck! Samantha ran to meet it, opened the door and jumped in, and Julie roared off.

"Got stopped by the police. Wanted to know why I was out. Said I was on my way to meet a gentleman. Asked them what DIC meant since my gentleman friend had mentioned it. They got real friendly after that, but I gave them a handful of quetzals for the hell of it. They wanted to know if I had a trailer stashed somewhere."

"Trailer?"

"Yeah, apparently this truck's got a monster hitch back there."

"So, Samantha, how'd it go?"

"Piece of cake, but as soon as we get back to the hotel I wouldn't say no to a cold Red Rooster or two."

"Cool."

Chapter 41

A little victory now and then fuels the soul...or could that be fools the soul? –From Samantha's Journal

Euphoria reigned as Julie downloaded the camera files to the laptop, then viewed them page by page.

"Beautiful," said Julie. Only two pages seemed to be out of focus.

"Nothing I can do about those two. I didn't load the software for that job. What do you want to do next, Samantha?"

"Before I call it a night–and I'm exhausted–I want to read through everything one time, take a shower then hit the sack."

"I'll read with you."

It took two hours to read each line of every letter, memo, email and hand written note. Some of it scribbled in Arabic. A note mentioning $2M and a line with $35K CC and P-140 Big Difference, scrawled in Arabic. On another memo the short message: Q. $1M per year. Quota!! Renegotiate. Too much! Again in Arabic.

Like miners searching for the dark grains of gold, Samantha and Julie sifted and sloshed through the photos for useable information. An insurance settlement of $1.5 million for the crashed Cessna was noted, causing Samantha to say "Aha, fraud."

Julie peered at the next page.

"Didn't he just say degrees and minutes of longitude and latitude?"

"I think so. Wait until I...." Samantha dug into her attache case. "Here it is. Plus latitude 14 degrees and 30 minutes north and minus longitude 88 degrees 50 minutes west...why, what did you find?"

"Just the piece of information that made that break-in worthwhile, that's all. In addition to what he gave you, here are seconds for the longitude and seconds for latitude."

"Which means," said Julie, "instead of wandering in miles of forest, we can get it down to a Sunday walk in the park with our GPS. All we have to do is a conversion to decimals. Way to go."

"And," said Samanatha, "I didn't break-in, I climbed in and the doors were open." Julie shook her head.

As Samantha reviewed the pages, she would occasionally wipe at a tear as various paragraphs talked of her dad, his job description, his years of employment, how he had been the company's liaison with OPEC. There were copies of brief letters from the company to her and to Stuart King about the crash and a notice about shipping the ashes.

During breaks, Samantha told Julie what had happened at the office. At the end of the account, both women were wide awake.

"Wow, Samantha, you amaze me. By all rights you should be dead by now."

"I should have checked out how big those guys were before I fed them the hors d'oeuvres. I had just enough sleepy stuff to give them a refreshing nap. If we had waited another hour, I would've been the entrée. No two-ways about it.

In spite of the adrenalin still flowing, Samantha felt a big yawn coming on.

"I need to go to sleep. I think I've had enough excitement for one night. Thank you for being there for me. I couldn't have done it without you." And Samantha got up and gave Julie a hug.

"Glad to have been of service, you little hard head. This trip will make my journal entries very interesting to my biographer someday. Now, go take your shower. I want one too."

––––––––––––

The early morning sun streamed through the hotel's restaurant windows. Many of the tables were empty. Too early for most of the guests. Breakfast was ordered, and with full cups of Guatemalan coffee cradled in their hands, Samantha and Julie examined options.

"I think it would be a mistake to find a place to print that stuff off," said Samantha.

"You're right. Wouldn't want a hard copy on us if we got raided. Of course, copied or not, it's still on the laptop and they'd sure take that."

"Not on there for long, I hope."

"Let me suggest using something neat I brought with me, Samantha. It's a device that allows us to go wireless off somebody else's network. We simply drive around until we locate a signal, log on with our wireless set-up while sitting in the comfort of our steamy truck, and we send the whole batch of stuff you "discovered" to your uncle, just like that."

"You can do that?"

"A snap. Well, not exactly. We'll have to locate an unprotected network, and I can find it with the gizmo I brought from home. We can try here, and if it doesn't work, we'll have to go to Guatemala City."

Driving by the few buildings used as offices in Antigua produced no signal, so packed with a map of Guatemala City, the laptop, Julie's signal hunting device, and an ice chest with beers and bottled water, they roared along the highway. Julie drove.

"If we're lucky we can get in and get out again before the city warms up." Samantha spoke over the sound of the powerful engine.

"Man, can this baby move." Julie punched the accelerator.

"Like your hair."

"This is my dotcom executive hairdo." Julie laughed. The braids of her long golden brown hair had been wound around her head.

"We'll roll up the windows when we get to G.C. We can open the vent and with the windows cracked it won't be too bad as long as we're moving. And when we find a signal, we'll hope for a big tree nearby to park under." Samantha was thankful for the seat mats. Good air circulation. She almost felt comfortable.

Soon the city smell from the smoking ravines reached them. Rot, decay, diesel smoke, and rancid butter fought for dominance.

"The smell du jour. Great place to go on a diet. Can't stand the thought of food, can you? Ah, avenues north and south and calles east and west." Julie swung onto the Avenida La Reforma and drove north up the tree-lined multi-laned avenue toward the U.S. Embassy.

"Probably got a firewall on their systems, but won't hurt to check and we can try other streets." Julie deftly merged with early morning traffic. Tall cypress trees shrouded in polluted fog flanked the avenue. It would be midday before warm breezes cleared the air.

"We're in Zone ten," said Samantha, "the ritzy part. But it smells to high heaven today."

"Hold on, we're making a signal. Good. Good. I'll pull into a side street, and we'll see if we can piggy-back."

Julie shut the engine down. The side street, while still busy and not as wide as the boulevard, did have a tree.

Samantha handed the booted laptop to Julie who got busy with the wireless hook-up procedure.

"Hooray, we're on-line. Here, attach the files." She handed it back for Samantha to type in a brief message to her uncle and clicked through the dialog boxes to send the attachments. So far so good. At last all was ready, and she clicked 'send' and off went the files winging their way to Texas.

"Uncle Stu will have something to read over his morning coffee."

"Fantastic! Let's get out of this hell-hole and back to Antigua before we are mush," said Julie.

"We'll keep the files on the hard drive until we hear from him and then...what's the matter?"

"You remember that red SUV you rented? Well, its cousin just made a U-turn and is coming up behind us. Roll up your window."

Chapter 42

I played cops and robbers in Guatemala City...how many suburban housewives can say that? They may live longer though. -From Samantha's Journal

The red SUV stayed behind them as Julie maneuvered through the traffic going south back to Diagonal 12 leading to Antigua. She changed lanes, increased her speed, slowed down, speeded up, changed lanes again, but the SUV stayed where it was, two car lengths back.

Samantha watched through the pickup's tinted rear window and voiced a hope that the SUV wasn't following them after all."

"Don't take that to the bank. Trak told me..., damn, get outta the way! I'm coming through!" Julie hit the accelerator, and they sped through a light that had turned red.

"Trak told me they do that to intimidate. Shit. The sonofabitch went right through that red light, too. He's got us in his sights all right." Julie careened around a slow-moving car. The powerful engine roared.

"Don't worry about my driving. My brother raced, and I learned a lot from him." The SUV narrowed the space between them. The darkly shielded windows of the SUV hid the passengers from view.

"The Unseen pursued by the Unseen," Julie said. "Samantha, we gotta lose those guys. They'll confiscate our lap-top whether we erase those files or not. I bet they tracked us when we hooked onto that signal. It's time to say bye-bye to those suckers. Get out the map and navigate. I want to go back north. What's another through avenue?"

"Seven Avenida is on your right and goes all the way to the

Old City. Maybe a six-mile stretch. You going to race him all the way north?"

"Nope, I'm going to lose him temporarily at the next stop light. Then we'll turn onto Diagonal 12. He'll think we're high-tailing into the country. Instead, we'll double back on Seven. Here goes." Julie hit the brakes at the light. The SUV behind them screeched to a halt, bumped the tail gate and hitch, then backed off.

Julie gunned the engine, punched in the 4-wheel drive and slammed the truck into reverse. The trailer hitch connected with the SUV's radiator at about 10 miles per hour. With blue smoke coming from her spinning tires, Julie shoved the SUV backwards into the traffic and continued pushing until the SUV turned sideways. A bus coming up to the light couldn't stop in time and hit it.

Drivers around them fought their steering wheels. Tires squealed. Cars slid. "Incredible," gasped Samantha, inhaling clouds of diesel smoke and the smell of burning rubber.

Julie jerked the truck into first gear and stomped on the accelerator. Her wheels smoked and she flew, sliding through the intersection, barely missing a delivery truck.

"Cool."

She turned right at Diagonal 12 and then back north on 7 Avenida as planned. She forced the truck in and out of traffic as she barreled along at 60 miles per hour at times, slamming on the brakes, sliding, gunning the engine. Samantha hung on.

"Where do race-track drivers learn this?" she yelled above the noise of the tires and the engine and the honking horns.

"They don't. My brother, see, he's an accountant, drove in demolition derbies and let me help out sometimes."

"I don't believe this. O.K., I think I feel better. Go for it." Samantha started calling off streets. Julie kept shaking her head until Samantha called out Diagonal 2.

"That's it. How far?"

"Three more miles maybe from where we are."

"Turn around and see if you can see them. If you spot anything, we'll zig-zag onto side streets if we have to."

"Nothing, nothing. You walloped him good."

"Yeah. His radiator will never be the same."

"Wait! I see something flashing back there. It's another SUV.

Different color!

Julie put the truck into a sideways slide, goosed the engine and shot off into a narrow street. She hit the brakes just inches from a sidewalk stall where a terrified vendor covered his face with his hands, fearing the worst.

"That was too close." Julie drove on, more slowly now on the crowded street where stalls butted up against each other and where buses and cars and trucks squeezed by. Blue and black smoke hung in the air. All around, throngs of people shopped for the brightly colored shawls, jackets, textiles, and trinkets.

The truck snorted through the narrow cobblestoned street, the tires vibrating and humming against the rough stones, sometimes squealing when a brief space of a few yards opened. Samantha could see palm trees in the distance. And there in an open court-yard a jacaranda tree. Bystanders in colorful costumes gaped at the growling pickup.

Julie continued northward. Finally she ventured back to 7 Avenida and roared north, then shot past the intersection called Ruta 2. The next intersection would be Diagonal 2 and when it jumped into view she slid into it and revved the engine to maintain torque and zoomed northwest.

"Now what?"

"Now watch for a way to get back to Diagonal 12."

"Great. Here's a diagonal going southwest, that should do it. Turn on Avenida Bolivar."

"Perfect. There it is, I think. That sign said del Ferro...something. Anyway it's going the right way. So off we go. Now just to make sure we've given our boys the slip, we go into the byways once more and head west and south and pick up Bolivar or whatever the hell it is, in a mile or so."

The truck thundered into the side streets again. Chug holes appeared causing the pickup to lurch and splash muddy, souring water. A smelly open sewer burbled on the side near a crumbing sidewalk. The sewer contained human waste, rotting food, and congealing pools of old oil sludge, iridescent in the sunshine. The

218

signs of extreme poverty bore in on Samantha.

Questioning looks came from large dark eyes. People hugged the walls as Julie sped past. Here and there, pepper trees, pines, cedars, and the ever present bougainvilleas tried to hide the misery of struggling lives.

Samantha had a sudden feeling of sadness for the poor of the world. The Inuit in Greenland, forgetting their cultural roots, the teeming masses of the desperately poor of India and Africa. Now, the back streets of Guatemala City were added to the list.

Samantha thought of the luxury hotels they had just passed in their mad dash out of the City, the ten-story Camino Real with its white lattice-work exterior wrapped in a semi-circle of welcome for those with the money to stay there, the soaring office buildings, the buildings of government, the shops in Zona ten, the Viva Zona which could be described as the creme de la creme of the shopping places in Guatemala City. How could a world justify this economic dichotomy?

She noted how her own lifestyle was so luxurious, knowing it would continue, but wondering what she could do to help those who had nothing.

"Julie, when we hit Bolivar and connect with 12 let's take this truck back to the airport and get something else. I have a feeling they'll be watching for this pickup."

"Good thinking," said Julie, wiping beads of sweat from her face.

Samantha paid for the truck rental and an added an extra hundred dollars for the scrapes on the tail-gate and rented a small blue Toyota. She also made arrangements to leave it in Antigua the next day, Good Friday, although the attendant said that was against the rules. Another $50 and the rule got changed. And wonder of wonders, the sedan was air-conditioned!

Julie was still in a race-demolition-derby mode, so Samantha drove back to Antigua at a moderate speed as Julie slowly came back to earth.

"Man what a rush! We should go back and do that again tomorrow." She pounded the dash with her fists and laughed.

"That's the most fun I've had since I tore up my brother's car in Oklahoma."

Samantha smiled and shook her head. It had been a harrowing experience and certainly no laughing matter. The Security Forces played for keeps down here. But in spite of that, she had to admit it had been exhilarating.

And they had accomplished their mission. While the two of them had been playing hide and seek with the Security Forces, Uncle Stu had the files and no doubt at that moment was poring over them with his CIA expertise.

"Damn, we forgot the ice-chest and the beers in the back of the truck."

Chapter 43

Today I didn't look at the sky. Cloudy, blue? I didn't notice the flowers or see a single bird...I was too busy being agent 007, Ms. Bond. –From Samantha's Journal

Near Antigua, Samantha pulled over, but kept the engine running and the A/C on.

"Forgive me, Julie, but my background in dealing with paranoid buyers is sending me signals. So, let me tell you what I'm thinking."

After a few minutes, Samantha pulled back onto the highway. They parked two blocks from the hotel, and Samantha walked to the lobby. She asked for messages. There were none. She then said they would be leaving the next day at check-out time (1 p.m.) for a week's stay at Lake Atitlan, a beautiful resort area and a favorite place for tourists, located just west of Antigua. Since they would have several things to do, Samantha wanted to pay in advance and did so.

Meanwhile, Julie was at an Internet Café looking for a message from Samantha's uncle. It came, but did not mention receiving any files. He said the birds had arrived at the condo he'd built. Good flock of them. She memorized it and deleted it. She joined Samantha, and they walked the corridor to their room. Samantha said the birds would have been martins, and the condo was a bunch of bird apartments on a pole.

"So, he's telling us the Martin King files arrived and safely at home." The heat of the afternoon intensified the flower perfume.

Everything looked peaceful. They opened the door to their room and went in. Julie was ready to comment, but Samantha held up her hand. All was quiet save the buzzing of an inquisitive fly.

"The first thing I'm going to do is shower the dust and grime off this poor body. Next time let's use the Internet Café to send our articles. That was too much trouble, and the story would have made it to the magazine soon enough anyway."Julie followed Samantha's cue.

"I don't know what came over me. When that car bumped us I accidentally hit reverse instead of forward, and then I just panicked. Do you think we ought to report it? I'm still shook up."

"We'll ask the embassy tomorrow before we check out. If we have to take our lumps we'll do it. They did hit us first."

"Probably a male driver."

"Hah! O.K. take your shower, I want one too."

Samantha turned on the shower full force. They stood close to the shower curtain.

"If we're bugged this should drown it out. Sorry for the inconvenience. Everything looked O.K., Julie, except I didn't leave the rope coiled that way, and one of the suitcases has been moved."

"Maybe the maid?"

"Maybe, but she hasn't touched anything before. I think we've been invaded and bugged. By the way, good job on the conversation. Another thing my buyers watch out for are transmitters."

"Transmitters?"

"Yeah, the enemy puts a tiny transmitter on something you carry around with you, and it transmits your location. The room is probably bugged, and we could have a little electronic parasite, ready to go with us when we travel.

"While you take your shower, I'll do a fast search and rely on my synesthesia to tell me if there's something that doesn't belong. There may be more than one transmitter as well as the bug. Lot of people have been caught just by finding one and thinking they were safe." Samantha slapped the shower wall, in case someone was listening for activity.

"If we can't find them we'll just leave everything except what we had with us today and some thoroughly gone over essentials and blow this place early like we planned."

"That was a neat message your uncle sent."

"Yes, my Texas good ol' boy and smart-as-a-whip uncle. I love it."

Everything was piled on one bed, except what they had with them in Guatemala City.

Samantha walked close to the curtain.

"When you get out, get dressed and run those errands. With just one of us in here, we won't be expected to talk."

"Right on."

She was half-done with no results when Julie, saying how wonderful it felt to be clean, also announced she wanted to visit a stall and buy some more stuff and would be back in thirty minutes.

Samantha found only one transmitter which bothered her. In addition to the transmitter, she searched for the bug. Her hand swept across a brightly-colored textile hanging on the wall. Her impression did not jibe with the colors she was expecting. She pulled the textile away from the wall and found the bug stuck to the wall.

"Damn wall hanging is leaning, drives me nuts. O.K. I'll fix that and you'll never hang crooked again," she said out loud. She banged the wall a couple of times with a heavy ashtray and then smashed the bug.

She couldn't believe how everyone seemed to think the last place anyone would look for something was behind a textile wall hanging. "Real creative minds down here." Julie returned and waved a questioning hand at Samantha.

"It's O.K., I found the bug, and I've sent it to the Big Listening Room in the Sky."

"Whew, that's a relief, I was about to run out of conversational topics. Here's the deal. I got a van to meet us down at the corner. Private. Like you said. We're to be there at 7 in the morning. Direct run to Copán. Maybe three hours.

And here's the extra rebozo, black of course. Tomorrow, being Good Friday, there will be a lot of these around."

"Great. I'll go turn in the car just before closing, but I'll say I may want it again around noon. They'll think that's crazy, but gringas are supposed to be crazy. Maybe they won't report it.

"With these humongous shawls on we're going to be religious Indians in the morning?"

"That's the plan."

"Tallest damn Indians in Guatemala."

"We'll bend over and scrunch down."

"I need a beer."

Chapter 44

**Every once in awhile I am overwhelmed with relationship long-
ings and the memory of my dad. Maybe that's why I run even
when no one seems to be chasing. –From Samantha's Journal**

Finding only one transmitter yesterday rankled Samantha.
Giving up the search, she decided they would take only what they
had with them in Guatemala City and leave everything else. They
had their money, passports, laptop, GPS and a change of clothes.
Samantha had gone over the clothes inch by inch. As they stepped
out the door, the sun light peeked over the horizon and a beam
sparkled as it hit Julie's neck.

"What's that?"

"My locket? Trak gave this to me last year. Surely, you don't
want me to leave it behind?"

"You didn't wear that yesterday. Let me look at it. Open it."
Julie fumbled and fidgeted, clearly annoyed, but did as she was
asked, although the asking sounded more like a command to her.
Inside the locket, another transmitter.

"Well, I'll be damned, how dare they touch my locket?"
Samantha retrieved the transmitter and was about to toss it back in
the room when a campesina came walking by, clad in a black rebozo and carrying an open woven bag.

Samantha called to her, saying good morning and asked if she
would be going to the processions. She was. As they talked
Samantha slipped the transmitter into her bag. The woman's hair
was glistening black, but several teeth were missing and those remaining were discolored. Old already in body, but not years.

After the woman walked on, Samantha and Julie got out their
rebozos, draped them over their heads and shoulders and scrunched

down enough not to be stared at.

"One transmitter stays in a suitcase. Means we're still there. One transmitter says we're watching processions. What could be better than that?"

"Do hunched-over rebozo-clad women wear white athletic shoes and blue jeans?"

———————

The van rolled through the rugged countryside. Campesinos and campesinas walked alongside the highway on their way to the processions and the city markets. The air-conditioned van and the occasional informative monotone remark by the driver, Roberto, made Julie and Samantha want to doze.

"We just had too much excitement to enjoy a nice quiet ride."

"You can say that again," said Julie stifling a yawn.

"Maybe we'll be hijacked. Actually, I'm not breathing really easy until we're over the border. We've been pretty smart, but remember, outwitting the police here is like trying to take advantage of a used-car dealer."

"You're right. I bet we were of minimum interest. Other than my doing a number on that SUV, we haven't caused anyone grief, as far as they know. If they thought we were dangerous, we'd be dead, I bet."

"A bet I wouldn't want you to win."

At mid-morning they arrived at El Florido. What once had been a bumpy road, had been paved, resulting in a comfortable ride for most of the way. The border police hardly glanced at the rebozoed women. The driver's credentials checked out O.K. and soon the van was on its way for the short ride into Copán.

"Nothing could have been easier."

"Hope you're not too disappointed," smiled Samantha. "We should have let you drive. We could have been here hours ago."

"Now you're talkin'. Wait until I tell my brother."

"You know, Julie, I'm wondering about my choice of friends. Seems like my really good female friends all drive like bats out of hell. Why do you think that is?"

"Cause, maybe you'd still be in hell if we didn't get you out."

"Good point. I like that. Thanks. Let's stop and get something for Trak to nibble on besides you."

"And it better be just me and not Dr. Emily Bordello.

Trak engulfed Julie with a definite look of hunger in his eyes, hunger not assuaged by the two spicy-meat tortillas Samantha and Julie had bought from a street vendor. Dr. Emily Deboreaux had been called back to Texas and sent to a conference in Europe. The news caused Julie's eyes to sparkle.

Samantha could see that if she were not careful she might get caught between smoldering volcanos not unlike those in Guatemala. She excused herself to visit a guide company.

Within an hour, Samantha had made arrangements. The guide looked at the coordinates and agreed that the place, though rugged and on the side of the great mountain, posed no serious problem. It could be reached with two to three days of hiking.

They would be taken by pickup truck to a drop off point, then it would be hiking through the jungle to the site. Piece of tortilla.

Trak and Julie disappeared. Samantha attached herself to a tour, in order to visit the spectacular ruins of the great Mayan civilization.

A sharp pang invaded Samantha's heart as she joined the group of strangers. She felt alone. After awhile, she left the tour and sat on a bench. The jungle, ready at anytime to absorb these ruins again, seemed to emit sounds of life and longing. She heard a howler monkey far off. An eerie calling sound. "Well named," she thought. The animal was joined briefly by another. They stopped howling. Too early yet. Soon the howlers would greet the dusk with their Evensong. The thousands of tree frogs would tune up to present the evening concert, not Brahms, not Beethoven, but perhaps something from Shostakovich or Schönberg, although, some could argue the frogs never progressed beyond the tuning-up phase. Whatever. Come the dawn the instruments would be put away, until the next evening.

"Perhaps, I too, am just tuning, tuning, and not yet playing a theme, developing it, embellishing it, moving it to a satisfying close."

Samantha saw the face of Ben. Ben Kruger, a young man with a future so promising, had searched for his theme in life, maybe as a rabbi. He brought Samantha stability, understanding, humor, enduring and beautiful friendship, but not physical love. What was love anyway without those ingredients? Essential ingredients. Yet, she still hungered for something more.

Had she found it with Emerson Jacque? She had tried. She wanted to try still, but it was so up and down, so wearing as well as exciting, she wondered what really drove her to be with him. Mother Nature's idea of a cruel joke? Hormones could not substitute for love, could they?

Samantha knew she was too old to give serious thought to conceiving, bringing a new life into the world; true, other women had done it at her age. Maybe she should. Perhaps that call of nature explained her sexual hunger. But what of love? Was this love or just the prime directive at work? Samantha shook her head. Love had to be more than strong physical attraction, wonderfully distracting and consuming as that was.

Also, it seemed to Samantha, it had to be more than birthing a new life, although that would be wonderful or devastating depending on one's point of view. Love was cherishing. Love was the willingness to sacrifice, as the wedding ceremony says, to have, to hold, whether in sickness and in health, forsaking all others. Did she honestly feel that way toward Emerson? Did he feel that way toward her? Did he not love London and his Jaguar more? Did she not love her lifestyle more?

She sat there. A breeze teased at her hair. Peaceful. Gentle, but unsettling. The grounds grew quiet now since most of the tourists had moved on. Soon, the keepers would want her to move on too. Time to move on. It seemed her whole life was just a moving on. On to what? She looked at the monuments scattered about and the carvings on the stelae. The successful attempt to tell a story, to let the future generations know what had gone before. Freed at last from the jungle, they had waited for someone to unlock their tales. It was being done at last.

The giant egos of long-dead rulers, who sought to escape oblivion through stone carvings–glyphs, had achieved their goal. If they had not built these buildings, if they had not laboriously invented ways to communicate, they would have never appeared on the pages of history.

Poor, backward Central America, once the home of the greatest of the civilizations of the western hemisphere, now struggled for survival without glory. Surely the descendants of the great Maya must feel some pride, some recognition of their once-upon-a-time greatness. Surely, as the years marched on, the children of the Maya would reclaim that greatness.

Was not that part of the reason she wanted to stand at the place of her father's death, an attempt to place him again in her memory and the memory banks of the world? In a way, she would carve his life upon some stela for the world to see and wonder at. He was a great man. Her father. Tears streamed down her cheeks.

"Dad, I love you. I am so sorry I could not say it because of my stubbornness. I will not let you die unknown and unloved in the jungles of Honduras. If you have died with secrets to tell, I shall find them and release them into the world. I shall avenge your death, if someone caused it, or I shall die trying.

"Dad, I am coming to you. Help me find you again. I love you so." Samantha felt herself trembling. The air was cooler now, but it was not the cooling air that caused her shaking. She rose from the bench and began the walk back into town and to her hotel. The howlers announced the symphony of the evening and the orchestra tuned up.

Tomorrow, Samantha and her guide would begin preparing for the journey she both dreaded and demanded. Despair and deliverance. Revenge and resolution. Love and forgiveness. In the jungle maybe she would find out about her dad and perhaps answers about life itself.

Chapter 45

Justice and hurricanes don't seem to mix well. It's a mystery why God is exempt from playing fair. –From Samantha's Journal

Early morning clouds hovered on Saturday, chased away later by a burning sun in a blue sky. A lazy breeze came and went. The appearance of clouds and the brief splatters of rain that had made the foliage dance promised that the rainy season would soon descend on the country. Mud would become a daily topic.

Samantha hoped she and Julie would be long gone when the heavens finally opened, and long, long gone before the hurricanes came through. In Honduras, the gigantic hurricane named Mitch still marked the land three years after it had roared through the countryside.

With winds of 200 miles per hour, it had slammed into the northern coast, developed into a tropical depression, and dumped torrential rains on Honduras, Nicaragua, and Guatemala. Whole villages disappeared in rivers of mud.

Nearly 10,000 people had perished. Disease and hunger were rampant. Over a million people displaced. Loss of life appeared greatest in Honduras, already one of the poorer countries in the world.

"Good going, God. Kick 'em while they're down."

For most of the day, Samantha met with her guide, Juan Espinosa, a thick-bodied man with black shiny hair. His black eyes and leathery brown skin stretched over high-cheek bones. His prominent nose revealed his Mayan heritage. It looked Roman to Samantha.

He approved of most of her purchases. She had a small tent, a water resistant sleeping bag, a backpack, insect repellant, first aid supplies, including three bottles of ethyl alcohol, and mole skin in case of blisters, extra socks, extra pants, and long-sleeved shirts, a water repellant vest, a water-proof poncho, two pairs of sturdy boots, and a couple of hats.

Also mosquito netting. They carried pills for water purifying. There would be plenty of water, where they were going. The mountain area birthed eleven rivers on its flanks.

Dried food concoctions, light and durable, would sustain them. They could be brought to life by adding water. She brought a small digital camera, not her "spy" camera she had used in the oil company offices, compact binoculars, some Benadryl tablets, and ointment for bites and stings, tape, cord, a small saw, a machete, her GPS, and a cumbersome satellite phone good only as long as the satellite whizzed by overhead from horizon to horizon.

Someday, surely they would work out a better system. In a money belt, she would carry a goodly supply of US dollars as well as lempira, the Honduran money currency at about 17 to the dollar. Juan had suggested the shoes she bought in Austin remain behind along with a lot of her other earlier state-side purchases he deemed unsuitable.

Juan would carry cooking supplies, some dry firewood, matches, and lighter fluid since it was always wet on the mountain. The rest of his equipment copied Samantha's with the exception of the money belt.

There was an uncomfortable orientation for them both as Juan explained they would carry no toilet paper and how one could manage without it. Samantha felt herself blushing while trying her best to keep a straight face.

Other topics included poisonous vines, snakes, bugs and the dangers of being infected through cuts because of the organisms on the forest floor. If they got into trouble, they could hike out to one of the surrounding primitive villages.

The villages would be extremely poor, and Juan suggested that Samantha should bring pen flashlights, knives, needles, thread, anything useful (not candy), as gifts. Although not as used to foreigners as those on the northeast side of the mountain, the campesinos would be friendly. Samantha bought several items to take.

East of them, the semi-permanent U.S Air Force Base near Comayagua could be reached, though it would be quite a hike, but Juan shook his head, obviously not wanting to consider that at all. Amazing to Samantha how only the rich loved the presence of the U.S. military in Central America.

Samantha thought of taking a fifth of whiskey, in case of boredom, and decided against it. Too bad she knew it was worthless against a loving bite from the Barba Amarilla, one of the snakes she would watch for as she scrambled over roots, stones and through vines.

She wanted to start early the next day, Sunday, but Juan, whose belief system included Catholic and Mayan practices, stated that starting on Easter would bring disaster to their enterprise. They would wait until Monday. On Sunday, Samantha had breakfast and lunch with Trak and Julie, wandered around, watched a procession, stayed fidgety, and retired early. She had stared at the ceiling for a couple of hours it seemed, before realizing the night gave way to dawn and her little bedside clock said, "Get Up."

Samantha bolted from bed, showered, dressed and almost too nervous, ate breakfast with Julie. Trak stayed in bed, recuperating, Samantha guessed. She told Julie over tortillas, chorizo, huevos, frijoles, and numerous cups of strong coffee, not to worry if she didn't hear anything for maybe ten days or so.

She and Juan might have to spend a lot of time searching, even though the coordinates were much narrowed thanks to her "enterin" last week. Julie would remain at Copán until Samantha returned, and they would go home together.

Julie had a plan of her own.

"If Dr. Emily does return she will find only a husk of a man remaining. Trak will be totally uninterested in any other member of the opposite sex except moi."

"And, of course, you won't go into detail about it to me."

"You have my promise. No titillating tales for you."

232

Juan came by with truck and driver. They would travel some fifty miles to the southern side of Cerro de las Minas, the mountain of Celaque. From there she and Juan would hike up the southwestern flank, using a very primitive trail.

Eventually, they would leave the trail and strike off into the wilderness to reach the crash site. Maybe two days away.

Then the search would begin. Samantha fully expected all evidences of the crash to have been cleared away by villagers. She hoped she would find something, if no more than a scrap. At the end of their search they would hike out to a neighboring village, and Samantha would hook up her satellite phone to call Julie for transportation back to Copán.

Samantha hugged Julie and Trak. He had arrived at last and was apologetic for sleeping so late. Samantha took her place in the truck, between driver and guide, on the wide bench seat. The equipment got heaped up in the open bed. The engine started. More waving. Samantha turned and watched as the figures grew smaller, then, resolutely she faced the insect-spattered windshield, ready for the mountain and her dad.

Chapter 46

...and a good time was had by all. –From Samantha's Journal

Rather than the northern, much longer paved road, circling eventually back through Santa Rosa de Copán, not to be confused with Ruinas Copán, the driver chose the shorter fifty miles of dirt road leading to Belén Gualcho.

There he would leave them at a trail head, leading from the southwest to the summit of El Castillo, the locals' name for Cerro de las Minas. The trail was seldom used by gringos, said Juan with a friendship smile of white teeth. The drive through the rugged country kept Samantha's neck well-exercised as the truck tried to miss holes, fallen tree branches, and the odd boulder.

It was exhilarating. She breathed deeply of the fresh air and green perfumes. Good workout and I'm sitting down, she mused.

Bits of information bounced back and forth as the truck leaped from rut to rut. Samantha enjoyed the repartee. Local idioms challenged her, but she held her own, and they laughed together as she repeated some and probed for a like idiom in English.

"So, hacer buenas migas con alguien, or making good crumbs with someone, means to get along well with someone?" They laughed and agreed. She offered her own.

"We hit it off!" she said in Spanish which only caused puzzled looks and then laughter when she explained. It became a game.

Juan or the driver, Justino, took turns yelling out an idiom like la última gota que hace rebosar la copa, literally "the last drop that makes the glass overflow" became the English idiom 'the last straw,' but when said in Spanish, she received more puzzled looks and then the laughter again as she interpreted the meaning. They examined idiom after idiom. The time sped by and in two hours that seemed like thirty minutes, they arrived at Belén Gualcho and the trail head.

They unloaded the supplies and checked the contents of the backpacks one more time. Good cheer filled the air, then as Justino said goodbye to Juan he commented in an Indian dialect how lucky Juan was to have such an edible fruit he might get to nibble on while on the journey. Samantha recognized a few of the words and certainly got the drift of the sentiment. Just macho guy talk, she realized, but even so, she thought it wise to clear the air of any false hopes.

She looked around and found a four-inch diameter piece of wood, well-seasoned and about three feet long. She picked it up and walked up to Justino.

"Hold this, Justino, por favor." She positioned the stick so that he held it out from his chest at arm's length gripping each end with a hand. She told him to hold it like a statue.

"Be like stone. Don't move. Don't flinch. Ready?" Justino smiled and stood as she told him, but clearly he had no idea why.

In front of him and with Juan looking on, she whirled suddenly and struck the limb with her foot. The branch broke in two, and a startled Justino looked at the pieces in his hands. No one spoke.

Samantha laughed, took the pieces from Justino and tossed them away.

"That's just in case Juan tries to nibble on any fruit."

A moment went by as Justino and Juan looked at each other. The Spanish translation of their Indian dialect suddenly struck them and they pounded each other on the back.

"You one fine lady," said Justino still laughing.

"No need worry," said Juan wiping at his eyes.

Chapter 47

It just shocks me how much I take for granted...like snow and toilet paper. –From Samantha's Journal

Samantha and Juan stood in the make-shift road next to the village of Belén Gualcho, and waved at Justino, probably still laughing and shaking his head, until he and his pickup   disappeared back up the road in a cloud of dust.

Deciding there was no need to visit the village, they hoisted their backpacks and headed up the trail. Juan stopped, and with his sharp machete, chopped two saplings into springy walking sticks.

"We get better ones later when climb harder." He led the way up the faint trail. He swung his machete at the encroaching foliage, striking at small limbs, a vine, and an impudent and opportunistic shrub that had sprouted since the last party had come through. This back trail, he explained, was serviceable, but not as easy or well-traveled as the one leading from Gracias to the peak from the other side of the mountain.

Samantha looked in the direction of the mountain, but could see nothing, except a bank of puffy, gray clouds. In the immediate foreground of a half-mile or so, she saw the beginnings of the ridges they would scramble over. The sun shone down, warming their packs. The temperature felt comfortable at around 75 degrees, but the presence of humidity and the exertion of climbing soon caused sweat to sting Samantha's eyes.

"Stop, Juan, I need to do some adjusting." She slipped out of her backpack, searched through it and found a bright scarf to tie about her head. She also sipped some water from one of the three bottles of water she carried that had to last until they reached a stream. Juan carried six bottles.

"At least the mosquitos aren't out yet."

"Tonight, dusk." Juan readjusted his own pack.

Samantha liked the sound of Juan's voice, the mixture of Indian dialect with Spanish, low and soft, but was not particularly enthralled with the subject matter. They had covered only a quarter of a mile. The park's boundary still lay nearly three miles in front of them. One mosquito had not waited for dusk before sampling Samantha's blood type. She put on more repellent.

The trail became a roller coaster except it continued to rise as each up and down segment receded behind them. At the three-mile point they stopped to catch their breath and to look around. This was the official beginning of the park.

The trail, still faint, continued to wend its tree-studded way in front of them, no doubt a continuation of what they had just experienced, small canyons and outcroppings that plunged and ascended into deeper depressions and higher and more jagged hills. Samantha felt a cooling breeze and hoped that too would remain during the afternoon.

"First stop important. Make sure things fit. Say hello to body. Say, 'Body, we go for walk, wake up.'" Samantha laughed at this, but it was so true. Three miles and her legs sent out distress signals. She knew they would fall in line with a few more miles.

As she rested, she smelled the sharp fresh scent of the pines which were now thicker and bigger, thanks to being farther away from a village, and therefore, not as easy to harvest. Oak and sweet gum mixed with the pine trees. The undergrowth was thicker where they stopped, too.

Vines snaked everywhere climbing over everything, making it difficult to differentiate trees from their clinging and suffocating guests.Hidden in the foliage, birds whistled and clucked. She saw one dart through an open space. She neither heard, nor saw, any other wildlife, excepting some beetles and some colorful butterflies. One large butterfly had brilliant blue wings and came quite close to her.

They had been walking three hours and it was nearly one in the afternoon. They rested for a few minutes, ate high energy bars, and drank more water.

Juan had said they needed to reach the perimeter if they were going to make Chimis Montaña, a village at about 6,500 feet elevation, west of El Castillo and the cloud forest plateau. They had made the perimeter, all right, but unfortunately, over an hour behind schedule and the minutes continued to mount as they sat on their packs in the patchy sunlight.

Samantha wiped her face with her eyes shut, hoping when she opened them there would be a Sealy Posturepedic mattress plopped on the trail. No such luck. Once they arrived at Chimis Montaña, they would ask about a plane crash the year before.

Depending on the information, they would double back to the coordinates and begin a systematic concentric search. It would be similar to a grid search except in place of a square grid they would employ a spiraling circle with the coordinates as the common center.

They sat on their backpacks looking at the huge trees, the vines, and the butterflies, nudging insects away that threatened to climb up boots. They talked, getting to know each other. Samantha learned that Juan had been happily married for six years and already had four children. A girl had died at the age of two, and Juan and Gloria had grieved greatly.

"She like flower. Always smiling, laughing. I miss little face." His dark eyes looked out on the forest, but without seeing the trees, Samantha knew, looking instead for a little girl to come squealing with delight, running up the trail to her father. Juan gave his face a hard rub, rose to his feet, and put on his backpack.

"We go now." Samantha struggled to her feet, too. She could tell her muscles would be a bit stiff in the morning. She heaved on her backpack. Juan was already ten yards in front.

The afternoon turned tough. The temperature dropped, but the humidity increased. Samantha didn't know for sure if she was sweating or just collecting mist. They stopped for a few minutes after each hour of effort.

The trail became slippery with mud. A strong earthy smell of decaying wood and rotting vegetation, while not exactly displeasing, made it hard to breathe deeply. The forest seemed alive.

238

More birds could be heard, and once, as they sat quietly resting Samantha heard a rustling.

"Could be peccary. Could be anteater. Could be tapir. Could be fox." Then, with a mischievous look in his eyes, "Could be jaguar." Juan laughed. "No worry Senora, no jaguars here. Maybe jaguar tomorrow." Again he laughed.

Samantha told him about being robbed by monkeys and about the rattlesnake she had found on her cabin path at the ranch. It was her turn to laugh.

"Must watch for snakes. Some bad."

The afternoon wore on. They grabbed at roots and vines when the trail got steep. Boots slipped in the mud. The speed of one mile per hour dropped down and down until it seemed they barely moved along some of the trail. It was obvious to both that the village would not be reached. Soon dusk would be upon them. Juan called a halt.

"We camp here. Village too far. Three hours tomorrow."

Off came the packs. The temperature, because of the humidity, seemed a lot lower. Was it 40 degrees or was it 60? Samantha felt cold, no matter what the actual temperature was. She watched Juan, appreciatively, as he built a fire. Starting first with some of the dry wood he had carried, he got the blaze going, then fed in the cut-up damp broken branches he found by the trail. As the damp pieces dried out in the heat, they blazed also. The fire sent billows of white smoke up into the trees for awhile.

They put up their tents and cleared a space around the fire to keep an eye out for snakes and insects that might want to crawl to its warmth. Samantha heard the whine of a mosquito and sprayed on DEET before a landing could take place.

The smoke from the fire kept insects away too. She liked the smell of the crackling and hissing wood. Far off, she heard the roaring of a band of howler monkeys. The sound carried for several miles.

Juan found a small stream which would later become Rio Aruco, but was now little more than a trickle from the misty flanks

239

of El Castillo. He boiled the water over the fire although he thought it unnecessary, but since he needed hot water anyway to bring their dried pouched food back from the dead, the boiling was a moot point.

Eagerly and in silence, they spooned up a pouch apiece. The emptied biodegradable pouches were buried. Samantha went off with her can of DEET and the spade to dig her own hole. She carried some of the boiled, but now cool, water along.

It would be her first attempt to do what billions of people around the world had been doing for thousands of years. The only addition was the DEET which she would spray on at the right time, as Juan had instructed her to do.

"Forget, and mosquitos bite." he had said.

The experiment was a total success. Goodbye toilet paper, at least for a few days. So simple. So clean. Tomorrow morning there would be a very quick sponge bath in the stream. She would be renewed. Primitive did not have to mean uncomfortable.

"Tomorrow, when we reach Chimis Montaña, maybe the people will know where the crash happened and will lead us straight to it. Right Juan?"

Juan remained silent for a moment, stirring the embers of the fire.

"Si, Senora, maybe. You find plane. Maybe. You miss father, no?"

"Si."

Samantha told Juan about how they had traveled the world, and how much her father had meant to her, and how they had become estranged.

"I never leave Honduras. I think I go Guatemala City, but too big. Too far. Happy in Honduras. My home. Good wife and good children. I die here."

Samantha asked him about his children, three boys, growing like weeds, and how they wanted to go to the Big North, their name for the U.S.

"They want see snow. Explain me snow."

So, Samantha talked of snow. Snow high enough to bury a bus, and how cold it could be and about snowmen and snow balls.

"I see ice on mountain after cold night sometimes. Snow like that?"

Samantha talked of the flakes floating down so soft and white and sometimes so thick that one could not see.

"Like cloud on ground on mountain?"

"Si, like a white cloud on the ground and when the cloud leaves, the ground is all white and still."

"Maybe I go with boys and wife, Gloria, and we see."

The fire burned low, the embers barely glowing. They zipped up their tents. The temperature dropped more, enough that the sleeping bag felt good. Samantha lay there listening to the forest noises, thinking about other fires in fireplaces, and the wonderful experiences she associated with them, also the pain.

She wondered what Emerson might be doing at that moment in London. It was nine in the evening in Honduras, so three in the morning in London? She was suddenly too tired to figure it out. She closed her eyes.

A soft shadowy light filtered into Samantha's tent followed by a chorus from the howler monkeys. The new day had begun. She stretched, thought about going to the stream, but how could she soap and rinse and dry and DEET herself quickly enough to fend off mosquitos? No, alcohol on a wash cloth would work just fine, and she could stay zipped up in her tent.

Clean clothes still dry in waterproof bags would be great to put on too. If Juan got a big fire going, they could dry yesterday's clothes before they left. If not, then they could wash and dry them at the village. Better idea. Juan would not want to build a fire big enough for drying anyway. The village was three hours away. Easy. And they could make it back to the crash coordinates in time for the next camp.

Squeaky clean and clad in dry clothes, Samantha unzipped the opaque lining of the door, leaving only the insect screening intact.

She could now see out without the bugs getting in. But something wanted in. A rather big something.

As she looked, transfixed, eight long, hairy legs moved slowly up the netting. It was the largest tarantula Samantha had ever seen, a full twelve inches across. Samantha had some experience with tarantulas in Texas. She knew the eight eyes were on top of the head, so she was unseen. She could be heard and felt, however, if she touched the tarantula through the netting.

A bird-eater tarantula. She had read about them. Authorities said they didn't actually eat birds, but they could kill and eat a full-grown mouse. If this spider found a bird's nest, then a bird eater tarantula could do exactly what its name implied. Baby birds were smaller than a mouse.

And this spider could climb. The bite though painful, wasn't poisonous. "My finger would just get infected and fall off." So, what to do? Yell for Juan? Nope.

She thumped the spider carefully and it bounced to the ground. So far, so good. She quickly unzipped the tent door, stepped out, but not close enough to threaten, and cause the tarantula to rear up and dislodge its barbed hairs at her, or grab some part of her anatomy in those huge fangs.

She picked up a piece of charred wood from the fire, and gently pinned the spider with it. She reached down with her other hand, and grabbed between the carapace and abdomen. When she had a secure hold, she released the stick, and lifted the giant straight up off the ground with the usual amazing result.

Once off the ground, a tarantula doesn't know what to do. So, it does nothing. Legs stick out and paralysis seems to set in. However, if one leg barely touches something, even slightly, then things can get interesting in a hurry. For now, touching nothing, the legs shot out, in this case a foot across. Samantha didn't want one of those legs inadvertently touching her jeans. Slowly and carefully, she walked down the trail for 30 feet and released the spider about six inches off the ground and quickly stepped back.

The tarantula turned around to face this perceived threat, and reared up to send a barrage of hairs, to no avail since Samantha had back-pedaled with alacrity, and was well out of range. She looked up to see Juan staring at her, as she walked back to camp.

"You not afraid of spider?"

"No, Juan, we have tarantulas in Texas, just not that big." He shook his head and smiled with a look of disbelief and pride.

"You one fine woman, all right. I glad to be guide."

"Juan, some people eat them. Like big hairy crabs. Roast the hair off. Crunchy. A lot of protein. Use the fangs for toothpicks when you're finished."

"You make fun, no?"

"That's the truth. Want me to go back and get that beauty? We can build a fire and have a feast." They both laughed, knowing they'd rather jump from the top of a forest tree lining the mist-shrouded trail than crunch one single tarantula leg between their teeth.

Chapter 48

...a flying quetzal...emeralds and rubies winging.   –From Samantha's Journal

They made good time and entered Chimis Montaña by ten. The village was small. The campesinos welcomed them. The children crowded around, giggling bashfully and staring. Samantha made arrangements for their clothes to be washed and dried over a fire. The air was so damp they would never dry otherwise.

She wondered how one lived in a place where the humidity stayed around 98 percent day after day. Good for the skin apparently. The villagers complexions glowed.

A family offered them chicken, beans, and some tortillas. An early lunch or a late breakfast. What did it matter? Several cups of coffee worked wonders. Samantha was able to use the local latrine, but stayed with the water approach. Really a good idea.

Back home in Texas she could see an addition to the bathroom. A bidet. An influx of bidets would certainly alter the paper economy. But she knew, when given the chance, it would be back to the roller on the wall, even with a bidet. Wonderful cocktail party conversation starter, she decided.

The villagers denied knowing anything about a plane crash last March, even though Samantha had not mentioned the month. Whatever they knew remained locked within the community. Juan said this was not unusual.

"They think better keep quiet. No one get hurt." But for whatever reason, Samantha got no information. Smiles and noddings continued, however, and it was a welcome respite from the daily hiking. She gave out some flashlights, knives, needles and strong thread which were gladly received.

"I'm sorry we didn't find out what they knew, but they were so gracious. And the clothes we wore yesterday are perfect. Smell that wood smoke."

Juan agreed. They packed and walked back the way they had come. After an hour on the trail, Juan signaled a stop and pointed east.

"We close to cloud forest plateau. You no want to climb El Castillo. Take too long. Plateau good. Must see. You go? Camp there tonight. Leave early. You decide."

Samantha thought this over. A big part of the reason for coming to Honduras in the first place: a closure, a peace, a final letting go. Perhaps a few hours, a stress-free time in the cloud forest would be just the thing to do.

"Gracias, Juan, you are so right. Si, let's do it."

They headed due east. For awhile it was rugged going and several times the machete had to cut a path.

"We be close to head waters of Rio Mocal. No hikers this side of plateau, you will see."

"Maybe a bath in the river?"

"Si, maybe mosquitos."

By two that afternoon they topped a final ridge, having pulled themselves over vines and roots and out of sucking mud. It had seemed to take forever. Then, suddenly, they were there. A park. Practically no underbrush. A diffused light filtered through the solid green canopy 100 feet above. A fine mist made everything spooky and timeless.

A land of fairytales. Where were the princesses and knights? Where were Alice and the Queen of Hearts? Welcome to the forest of Tolkien's middle earth, and hobbits, and magic rings. Giant oaks were covered with vines and gorgeous orchids. Butterflies with colorful wings wafted among the blooms. Samantha heard the plaintive calls of the quetzals. Juan pointed.

245

"Look," he whispered. She followed the line of his hand and there far above she saw the quetzal. It's tail, three feet long, the feathers, an iridescent green with white below. The body and head had dark and light green, also iridescent like the tail. The breast, a deeper green and below that on the lower body, a brilliant red patch flashed like a ruby.

The bird held still, showing off? Then, the wings spread and off it flew, its undulating tail flashing green and white in the mist.

"He eat avocado."

"Amazing," breathed Samantha, "think what he'd look like in the sunlight."

"Si. But soon gone, I think."

"Si. Like the bison in my country. Almost annihilated before we woke up, but a big ol' buffalo never looked that magnificent."

"Feathers used in ancient ceremony of Maya."

"The sacred bird of the Mayan peoples. Crazy, how we try to appropriate the beauty and the strength of an animal to give us power."

Samantha followed Juan into the tree-covered plateau. The scene was exactly the same no matter which way they turned. The tall oak trees standing as in a well-kept park paved over the sky with their own sky of green.

A breeze whispered and a constant dripping could be heard. And off, off as far as she could see in the mist, tree after tree after tree. Each one huge, some, several feet in diameter. She felt like crying. She did cry, she felt the hot tears coursing down her cheeks merging with the tiny droplets of mist already there.

"It's a church. It's a cathedral. I could die here, oh so happily. I hope my dad got to see this before he crashed. Maybe he walked here after the crash. Yes, I would like to believe that." Her heart felt so full, yet so broken.

She took off her backpack in order to sit, to gaze, to drink in the renewal offered by these silent giants, not individual trees but one great organism celebrating its life, a life that should never end and the quetzals, which looped from tree to tree trailing their fairy dust tails, should also always live there. Emerald and ruby gems flying among the stalwart oaks clothed in orchids.

In the stillness Samantha and Juan wandered about.

"Some people who live here get lost and walk many days."

"I can see why. I'm not good at directions even when there are signs pointing the way."

They selected a place for the tents. Juan built a fire to prepare their meal. He produced several tortillas from the village. Surely the temperature had dropped to the forties. Samantha sat close to the burning logs, smelling the wood smoke.

"Fantastic Juan. A real feast. Let me make coffee. And no mosquitos. Guess we should knock on wood? And where is the river you mentioned?"

"Over there, not far. You take swim. I watch for you."

The dusk came quickly. They sat about the fire, poking it, adding more wood, desiring to maintain the feeling of extreme aloneness together, as if they were the only two people on the face of the earth. Samantha liked Juan a lot. A loyal guide.

He could be a friend. They talked of their respective childhoods. Juan was shocked at the places Samantha had gone with her father and the things she had done. She was enthralled with the peaceful quotidian lifestyle he and his family had lived for generations. They talked of the plight of the campesinos in all of Central America and what might be done about it.

"Most time it hopeless to change. We grow, get married, have children, hope they don't die and have enough to eat, clothes to wear, a home. Not too bad. Little more be better."

"Like what, Juan?"

"Like no fear. Like land, maybe. Little farm. Enough for family. Sell things we grow. Buy things. You know."

"How about a television set?"

Juan laughed out loud. He settled down. Then he thought about it again and laughed even louder.

"You funny person. I like you. My wife would like you, you must come see us when we have lots of beans and a television." Here he hit the ground and laughed some more. Samantha realized it was a silly question, worse, a flippant question, and she felt bad about it.

247

But she laughed with him as Juan shook his head. Maybe someday the poor of the world would have a better life. A television, his family did not need. Land he needed, and education, and health, for his children. She wanted to visit his family; and maybe she would one day.

The next morning with the thick mist swirling through the majestic oaks, they hiked to the river. Clear, cold, a feeder creek for the river lower down. Samantha had brought her change of clothes. Juan stationed himself around a bend and stood watch. Would he peek? She thought not, but if he did, so what? She stripped off her clothes, found a place to enter where the bottom looked smooth and maybe a foot or so deep. She gasped when the bottom turned out to be four feet down not one. In the current she lost her footing and her body met the clear icy water all at once.

She would have yelled, but her head went under. She came up sputtering and fought her way back to the bank. She clambered out and grabbed her towel. She felt startlingly alive. Samantha dressed quickly and called to Juan.

"Good bath?"

"Fantastic, but colder than snow!"

He laughed, remembering their earlier conversation. They purified some water, packed up their supplies, and set off to find the coordinates.

By noon they had arrived at what the office file indicated as the center point. The tall oaks were long gone, replaced by underbrush and smaller vine enveloped trees. The plateau had given way to hummocks, chasms, hills, and ridges.

Brilliant ferns, with a heritage reaching back 60 million years, stretched their slender green stalks as high as 45 feet.

What a gardener back home wouldn't give for those ferns. She and Juan continued slogging through the mud. Samantha could not see the sky because of the suffocating foliage. How would they ever find the wreckage in something like this, assuming any of the pieces still remained?

Systematically, Juan set the circular course agreed to and in thirty minutes completed the first circle. Nothing. They began the next circle twenty yards wider than the first. Again, nothing. They did discover a small stream where they stopped to rest and review.

Out of the corner of her eye Samantha detected movement nearby. She motioned to Juan and they moved away as a Brown Tamagas snake, deadly poisonous, made its way to the stream, slipped in and disappeared.

"Well, I'm glad my swimming hole didn't have one of those."

Juan kept watching, but the snake did not reappear.

"Bad snake, Senora. He bite, we die."

That night at dusk a roving group of howler monkeys decided to make tree nests nearby, and the raucous roaring reminded Samantha of Sixth Street in Austin on a Friday night.

When the howlers got settled, the cricket frogs took up the call and were joined by unidentified players.

There were flutes, door creakings, woodwinds, trumpets, bassoons, bass fiddles, chain saws, violins, and even a couple of bass drums beating counterpoint to something going 'ploop, ploop.' Samantha imagined she was attending her middle school orchestra tryouts. She slept in spite of the cacophony.

She opened her eyes with a start as the howlers greeted the dawn with a series of deep grunts then let loose with their wake-up roars. Juan just laughed as he made breakfast. The howlers left to find their own breakfast. A cup of strong coffee put Samantha in a much better mood.

"Maybe today, Juan, we'll find something."

"Si, maybe today. Look like rain."

Samantha saw nothing but green leaves. She wasn't about to be a tourist and ask why he thought it would rain. The day turned out to be just like the day before.

She listened to the incessant chopping sound of the sharp machete, sloshed through mud occasionally, flipped bright green beetles out of the way, and was amazed at the beautiful colors and the squawking of a Scarlet Macaw.

"I should take you back to Uncle Stu," she said to the brilliantly colored bird. Juan warned her not to touch the cute little red frog with blue-black polka dots sitting on a moss-covered log.

"Touch and you dead, Senora. Don't touch."So, she didn't. It didn't rain, just dripped, just an infernal drip, drip, drip. Maybe that was rain. They were on the fourth or fifth or the twentieth circle, Samantha had lost count.

Thanks to her watch she knew it was Thursday, the nineteenth of April, and 2 p.m., thanks to her watch. A horrendously humid day that looked like and felt like every other damned day in that green hell. Patience seeped away as the mist seeped in. She had given up on dry clothes.

Thanks to alcohol baths, she was clean. She had plastered on moleskin on ankles and toes as they became tender. She knew enough not to wait until a blister formed. A broken blister would invite parasites and infection.

After wiping sweat from her neck, she paused and looked up at the dense canopy of green. Something sparkled up there.

"Juan, Juan, come here. Quick. I think I've found something. And it's not green!"

Sure enough, about 80 feet overhead, stuck in the upper branches of a vine-covered tree, high enough to catch some sunlight, flashed something that didn't belong. Samantha ditched her backpack and trained her binoculars on it.

"Juan, it's part of a plane's tail. We've got to get it down."

"That way up there. No way to get, I think."

Samantha shot him what she thought could have been a dirty look, but she was too excited to be angry. She cleared a small space with her machete and looked up at the shining tail again and then at the vine-covered tree and back at Juan.

"I'm going to climb that damn tree and I'm going to get that tail down here and that's all there is to it."

Juan looked aghast, first at Samantha, who was preparing for the climb, then at the tail and then at 80 feet of tree.

"Senora's crazy. You break neck. Blame me. Not good guide."

Samantha grabbed a pen in the innards of her pack and a small notebook. She scribbled away.

"There, Juan, I said you told me not to climb the tree and I said I am going to anyway. You are not at fault. And I signed it. Now

250

let's see how I can do this." Juan, as instructed, cut away the underbrush close to the tree. Samantha walked around it peering at
the thick green vines.

"Ants," said Juan quietly. Correct, there were thousands running up and down the vines. Probably fire ants like in Texas.

"They'll sting the hell out of me all right." She rummaged in
her pack and pulled out her latex gloves, then with cord she had
Juan tie her cuffs tight. She pulled on the gloves. She put mosquito netting over her hat and wound a scarf around her neck.

Satisfied she could see enough through it, she turned her attention to the blue jeans. There could be no exposed skin anywhere.

"O.K. Juan, spray this alien with a bunch of DEET and make it
good. I'll hold my breath and shut my eyes when you get to my
head. O.K. go."

Samantha sneezed twice.

"Woo, what a trip. O.K. that should slow them down a little.
Here I go." She grabbed a vine, dug her boots in and climbed 15
feet before stopping to catch her breath. Juan watched with open
mouth.

"You wild woman. You scare me good."

"Thanks for the pep talk. So far only one sting."

Samantha grabbed the tough vine again and climbed as if she
were ascending a thick rope at her fitness gym. Her vine began
pulling loose and it seemed Juan's prediction of a broken neck
might come true. She quickly grabbed another one and undaunted
by her narrow escape, continued up.

At forty feet she reached the first limbs. It was easy after that.
Fifty, sixty, seventy, eighty feet, and there she was, at the same
height as the tail. She stepped out on the limb while clutching another just above it, then she shook the limb she was holding and
danced up and down on the one where she stood.

The tail moved, but remained stuck. She shook the limbs again
and again. But the tail refused to budge. She walked out farther
and began to dance up and down some more. A loud crack re-
sounded in the forest and as Juan watched in horror, the lower limb

gave way and left Samantha hanging eighty feet above the forest floor.

She did nothing for a few seconds, then she began swinging her lower body to and fro. With each swing she gained momentum until with a great lunge her boots hooked the limb she was holding onto. Her arms and hands ached from fatigue. She crooked her elbows over the limb for a few moments. Her legs encircled it. The relief of that brief rest for her fingers was all she needed. Samantha again gripped the limb with her hands.

Crawling upside down like a sloth, she inched her way back to the main trunk. As she reached comparative safety, the aircraft tail decided it had met its match. It sailed and crashed through the branches landing near an astounded Juan below. Victory.

She climbed down carefully, but once on the ground ran quickly to Juan. She was covered with ants. Juan brushed the frenzied creatures from Samantha's clothes as much as he could.

"I've got to get out of these. Get my other clothes and hurry!" She immediately tore at her coverings and clothing until she was stark naked in front of a completely demoralized Juan who was trying to proffer the clean set of clothing and at the same time refrain from looking.

"Dammit, Juan, look. See if there are any more ants on me. Look at me. I won't attack you. Hurry! Hurry!" He did as he was told. He found some on her back, and brushed them off touching her skin lightly as he did so. He found a couple on the back of her neck and one in her hair and some on her shoulder. Those he flicked off as well, again touching her each time.

She took care of her front and ran her hands over her butt and the backs of her thighs. She knew he would not venture there, the poor man could only stand so much. Finally, she bathed in alcohol, took some Benadryl, applied the ointment and got dressed. Juan had remained silent during the entire ordeal. And as soon as possible he had turned his back.

"Hey Juan, it's all right now. Turn around, I'm dressed. And thanks, I couldn't have done it without you. Now, lets look at that tail."

"This scrap of tail did not belong to a Cessna Citation."

As if that were a surprise.

"Juan, see these horizontal indentations? You find them on Piper Cherokees. If this is the plane that crashed, then dad switched planes at that airstrip outside Guatemala City." She talked to Juan as if he were a co-investigator. His eyes were large and confounded, but she needed to talk her way through the evidence.

"This tail doesn't prove he was flying. Wait. The smell. Explosives. This plane was blown up. I can smell the bomb material. So, one thing for certain, this plane didn't run out of fuel." Samantha hurried over to her GPS and noted the compass reading.

"If this had been the plane he was in, then he would have been on a northerly course headed for Belize or an easterly course headed for the airbase at Comayagua. Let's try Belize first. So, the tail is blown off and we're headed in that direction." Samantha pointed north. "The plane would have crashed in a mile or less. Let's go."

Cutting through the clinging underbrush, they worked their way northward until Samantha dropped to her knees.

"Look, Juan, glass. And here's a piece of metal. Not much." She looked around and up at the canopy. It appeared solid. She studied the trees and finally spotted a broken limb hanging, unable to fall because of encircling vines.

"It came in through there and crashed here. Someone has cleaned this crash site up. I wonder why? Mr. Oilman said GUASAUCO didn't even try to find it. Country too rugged. Too busy. Well, somebody got here and nearly everything is gone, but this is it all right."

Then, Samantha sobbed as she realized that it was on this spot her dad had crashed and died. She kept looking for more pieces of the crash through her tears. Juan looked too. They searched now in silence.

She found nothing else. Still too many questions. Not enough answers. Maybe the files sent to her uncle would help. Her pilgrimage had come to an end. This was the closure she had wanted and needed. She knelt for a few moments, more tears. Through the shimmer she looked at the trees, the vines, the magnificent ferns.

"I'm so sorry dad. Please forgive me. I love you. Rest in peace, my father." She cried softly as Juan stood off to one side watching and waiting.

"O.K. Juan, let's set up camp. But not here."

Juan led Samantha out of the tangled undergrowth to a more open area. There he set up the tents and started the fire and prepared a simple meal. They ate in silence. Samantha retired to her tent and lay there for a long time seeing and not seeing. Images of Martin King flipped through her mind like an old TV news program. News about her dad. Who he was. What he had done. His legacy. Survived by his brother and his daughter.

"I'm not through, dad. If they murdered you, I will find them." She closed swollen eyelids, but the news program in her head continued.

Chapter 49

...unspeakable. Horrible. –From Samantha's Journal

The howler monkeys did not do their thing the next morning, but Samantha woke at dawn just the same. She always consulted her watch to make sure. Yes, dawn. Hard to tell under the green canopy. Morning. Noon. Afternoon. All looked the same. Dawn was just a bit lighter and dusk a little darker.

Quickly, she bathed in rubbing alcohol, getting her washcloth soaking wet and rubbing it through her hair, and then over every inch of her body. Hard on the skin, but disastrous for any tiny microbe, animal or plant trying to establish a colony on her territory.

For a few minutes flies, ants, and mosquitos turned up their noses at her too. She would catch up on the intensive lotion regimen later. At a spa. Yes. Samantha dressed in the clothes Juan had dried for her over the fire and went to find a secluded spot to relieve herself.

Back at camp and feeling better, she greeted Juan and thanked him again for being so helpful the day before. He brought the fire back to life and put on the pot for coffee. It would be their last breakfast. They could stop cutting their way through the jungle and follow a trail to one of the area's villages today, and Samantha could make her satellite calls.

After breakfast, they broke camp and put on their backpacks. Time to go home with Julie. See her uncle. Talk with Emerson. Time to get back to work and sign the lease for the new offices in the World Trade Center. September would arrive too fast. She had a lot to do. She would pursue the murderers of her dad from the Texas ranch with help from her uncle.

Musing about her future, Samantha did not hear the footsteps until too late. Juan cast a fearful look as men with machetes surrounded them.

"Who are you and what do you want?" Samantha knew being tired and cranky shouldn't show when greeting strangers, but this morning, she couldn't help it. Adrenaline pumped through her system, but the backpack slowed her sufficiently and made any kind of defense impossible. Besides, there were too many, and she didn't really think it wise to go up against machetes.

Two of the men knocked her to the ground. Someone ripped off the pack and before she could react her arms and legs were pinned, then bound securely. Dirt and mud from the trail caked her lips and she spat to clear them. The men turned her over. She saw Juan kneeling, his hands tied behind his back.

"Please tell my wife I was a good guide. Tell my children...." In total shock, Samantha watched the machete slice through the air. Juan's head rolled in the dirt and a great gush of blood came from his neck where his head had been a moment before.

His body remained upright in the kneeling position for a time as if wondering what had happened. Then it toppled over and the dirt and mud turned dark as the blood left his body and seeped into the earth. Juan's eyes remained open for a few moments then shut. Samantha knew she would throw up, and she did. The men around her laughed. They untied her legs and pushed her along the trail, blindfolded with a rag that smelled of blood and rancid butter.

Chapter 50

It's ironic when something seems to be over. A door finally closes, then someone comes along and bashes it in. I couldn't believe what was happening. Juan dead. I'm kidnapped. – From Samantha's Journal

A nightmare. No other way to describe it. A horrible, sickening, nightmare. It hadn't happened. It wasn't happening. She would awaken soon, and it would be all right. The blindfold did its job. She could see nothing. Did she walk? Did she fall? Did it matter?

Vines snagged Samantha's arms, and roots grabbed at her boots. She fell a lot. Each time, she was lifted roughly back to her feet. Her knees felt bruised. Her shoulders ached. Her head throbbed. She could not catch herself, as she lurched to the ground. Her hands, bound behind her, were becoming numb.

After awhile, her malaise lifted, and anger began to course through her body. She stopped. She was pushed from behind and she lashed out with a boot and felt it thud against something soft and heard a cry of pain. Now, she would be killed. She didn't care.

"I'm not moving until the blindfold is off! Kill me you miserable excuses for men! Woman killers! I spit on your mothers who brought you into the world! You are all sons of bitches! Do you hear? You are lower than snakes! I curse you   to death!" Her voice rang out. Silence. No one touched her. One voice spoke from a distance. The voice grew louder. She heard footsteps coming closer.

"The one who injures her will die at the hands of our Great One. Take off her blindfold. You will be whipped if she has bruises from falling. You are curs as she said."

There were mutterings. Someone took hold of her blindfold roughly. She heard the sound of a machete whistle through the air and a scream.

"You cut off my hand! Socorro! You cut off my hand!"

Samantha felt a warm stickiness hit her leg. There was considerable activity. She stood without the slightest movement, expecting the worst. Instead, she felt her bonds cut, and a gentler hand undid the blind fold.

"Tie that no good's arm so he won't bleed to death. The next one who harms this woman will lose his head."

When she had adjusted to the light, she looked into the eyes of her powerfully built benefactor. He was naked from the waist up. Numerous scars traced across his arms and chest. Whoever had caused them would no longer be walking the earth, she guessed.

"Es muy terrible, forgive us, we act like animals and not Mayans," he said, wiping clean his machete.

"These animals killed my guide, who was also a Mayan and married with three sons who will now come to avenge him." Samantha rubbed her hands together and shook her head then turned and faced the sullen group.

"You are not men, you are cowards! Stand up to me one by one with your bare hands, and I will kill each of you, and pull off your balls, and stuff them in your mouth!" No one stirred.

Her benefactor smiled with angry-looking eyes.

"What is done is done. I can not bring back your guide. It would not have happened if I had been there. Lo siento. Now, go with us to meet our Great One. You will see what we do to regain our heritage. You are important to us and our gods. If you refuse, I, myself, will kill you." His eyes bored into hers, and she recognized his strength and strange commitment.

"I will go with you. Thank you for releasing my hands and taking off my blindfold. I don't suppose I could have my machete back?" No answer. Humor did not register in his eyes.

"O.K. take me to your high and mighty." Inside, she seethed with anger and could not shake the image of poor Juan kneeling on the path. Outwardly, she made no show of emotion that might signal weakness. The group slogged on until nightfall. Her tent was brought to her, and she set it up. A guard went with her and stood close enough to see her head as she relieved herself near the trail. Back in camp she asked for her backpack. Scar Chest said no. She negotiated for dry clothes, a comb, a cloth, some band-aids, and the alcohol.

"No drink."

"No, not for drinking. Bad for the stomach. I use it for bathing."

The items were granted. She could hardly wait to dive in her sleeping bag, but before she could, a hand scratched at her tent door.

"Here. Take it."

"Gracias." A metal bowl with tortillas and beans came through the door as she unzipped it partially. A cup of coffee followed. She ate every bean and every scrap of the corn tortilla, drank the coffee, put the bowl and cup outside, zipped up the tent, and instead of diving, she crawled painfully into her sleeping bag and lost consciousness.

Sounds of the men in the morning awakened her. She paid no attention to birds that morning. She had no interest in great ferns, vine-covered trees or colorful butterflies. Samantha unzipped her tent and pointed at the bushes. The same guard as the previous evening took up his post.

The day turned into a monotonous repeat of the day before. She had little energy for the trail, most of it still being used to stoke fires of hatred and determination. As dusk approached the pace quickened and soon she could see into a small valley and a grouping of thatched huts in front of which small fires flickered. She was led to one hut and told to enter the small doorway.

"You will stay here until sent for," the Scar Chest said.

"There will be a guard at the door." As she entered, a woman followed with a lighted candle. The floor was packed dirt. There were no windows. The ceiling of branches and leaves reached up at its center to nine or more feet where a hole allowed the cook-fire smoke to escape. A wood plank bed, one foot above the dirt, braced against a wall. An old packing crate to sit on. Near the bed, a pot with a lid for the call of Mother Nature, Samantha supposed. A five-gallon can of water in another corner.

In the center, hearth stones in the form of a triangle, a Mayan custom having something to do with the triangle of stars in Orion, and the beginnings of the earth and sky. She and Julie had read about it, and here she was experiencing it first hand, not liking it at all.

Off to the side, some wood. Two pots for cooking. A stone slab for tortillas. A concave grinding stone. A man came to the door and tossed in her sleeping bag, yesterday's damp clothes, and her tent. Nothing else.

The woman placed the candle on a stone in a puddle of hot wax she had allowed to drip from the flame and there it stood, firmly fixed sans holder. Beside it she laid some matches, a bag of beans, a bag of roasted whole coffee beans, and a bag of corn. The coffee beans and the corn would need grinding. That would certainly give her something to do. So, all the comforts of home. The woman did not look Samantha in the face, but did pause for a moment looking at the floor when Samantha whispered "Gracias."

It occurred to Samantha that her abduction was no accident. Someone had planned to bring her here. She questioned the scarred man's show of concern over Juan. That had been planned too. Maybe even the "good cop, bad cop" routine was staged, though she could hardly think of anyone purposely losing a hand to make a point.

"Have I been abducted for ransom?" she murmured to herself, careful the guard outside did not overhear. She went to the hut's door, and there he stood, not with a gun, just a machete. She asked about her backpack and said she needed it. The guard called out, and soon another man she had not seen before showed up. She explained why she needed the supplies in the pack. He listened and presently came back with it, minus the binoculars, the machete, the pen and notebook, the satellite phone, the camera, and her GPS. Understandable.

After he left, she took a hidden small knife from her boot, cut cord, strung it for her clothes. Got some water in a pot and with a little soap, and a rinsing and wringing, hung up yesterday's clothes. She built a small fire. Put water on in another pot to boil. She hoped the candle would last long enough for her to make coffee. Quickly, she ground some coffee beans and soon had a steaming cup of very strong coffee to drink.

Making the coffee had kept her mind busy. She had little time to think about Juan or her predicament. She would persevere. Always had. Always would. She undressed, poured alcohol on a cloth and gave herself the full body treatment, including her hair. She dressed again as though ready to hit the trail. She stretched the sleeping bag over the wooden bed and lay down. She decided to let the candle burn down rather than face total darkness.

She must have dozed off. For how long? She didn't know. Samantha lay there, not moving, trying to keep her mind totally blank. In a semi-conscious dream, the kind she could control, she saw a lion approach her. It began to nibble on her neck. At first she didn't mind, then the nibbling began to hurt. She awakened with a start, slapping at the spot.

A large bug landed on the dirt floor, she was on it in an instant grinding it with her boot. The stripes and stink-bug type body could only belong to an Assassin bug. Quickly, before giving in to scratching the bleeding bite she poured alcohol on her cloth and swabbed the bite area thoroughly. Surely, the parasites would be killed.

She and Julie had studied the Assassin bugs in Austin while getting ready for their trip. The bug sucked it's victim's blood and defecated near the puncture, leaving parasite-infested feces ready to enter the blood stream as the victim scratched or rubbed the itching bite.

The result: Chagas Disease. A debilitating illness that could cause death within days. A healthy adult usually weathered this acute phase, and the symptoms would disappear. During the months and years that followed, the parasites would invade nearly every organ of the body causing increased weakness often ending with fatal heart and digestive tract failure.

"Damn, damn, damn!" She yelled. The guard stuck his head in

the door, hunched his shoulders, smiled and backed out. Samantha looked at the thatched roof.

"Probably hundreds of the damn things up there, just waiting for me to go back to sleep."

She grabbed her tent and set it up on the floor, threw in her backpack and sleeping bag, got in, zipped it up and fumed.

In the morning, she awoke to the sound of grinding corn. She looked out the tent door and there the woman, who had lighted her way with a candle last night, knelt before the grinding stone, preparing tortillas. A small fire blazed and a pot of water boiled ready for the crushed coffee beans. Already dressed except for her boots, Samantha put them on, laced them up and crawled out.

Chapter 51

**I kept thinking of the outside world. Of Emerson. Of the
ranch and the people I loved. I was scared and mad most of the
time. I didn't admit it, but there seemed no way out. –From
Samantha's Journal**

It was now around eight o'clock, Samantha guessed. Surely
she could talk her captors into restoring her watch. It would help
somehow to know the time and the day. She sat on the packing
crate. She did not want to pace, as that would cause dust to rise
from the dirt floor.

The woman had prepared a breakfast of beans, tortillas and
coffee, and Samantha had been grateful. Apparently, she would
not have to prepare her own food, although a little work might
keep her mind occupied. On the other hand, without work, she
would be free to think and plan. She needed a plan to escape. She
would escape. She had no doubt about that.

Samantha touched the side of her neck. She felt a slight bump.
She got a clean cloth from her backpack and wetted it with alcohol
then rubbed the site of the puncture. The itching subsided. She
knew that if she had not killed all the parasites last evening it
would be too late now. Still, the thought of the bug's feces entering her blood system caused her to wet the cloth and rub again.
She felt no after effects from the bite–probably too early. Another
thing to worry about, as if she didn't have enough on her plate already.

She forced herself to rehearse what had happened from the
moment she and Juan were surrounded to the present, examining
every detail, probing for any weakness of her captors she may have
overlooked.

After preparing her breakfast, the woman gathered Samantha's clothing from the clothesline. In a mixture of Indian and Spanish, she said she would wash them and dry them. In a few minutes she reappeared and made off with the chamber pot. Would it be too much to hope she would rinse it too?

Not exactly the Stanhope. The concierge would get a kick out of Samantha's room service, if she lived to make it back to New York. "Of course I will," she hummed through clenched teeth. She got up and moved carefully about the hut, inspecting it without disturbing the floor dust.

Satisfied there was no easy way out except by the door where the guard was posted, she sat back down on the rough crate and thought again of the Indian woman, a campesina, a poor peasant of the back country.

Her name: Maria, just like her uncle's beloved cook and house manager in Utopia. Her uncle, now so far away. A wave of homesickness swept over her. Samantha shook her head and refocused on the Honduran Mayan, Maria.

Shy last night. Different this morning. The tasks seemed more of a burden. Her eyes vacant. Sad. Yes, Maria was sad and maybe scared. But why? If Samantha asked what was the matter would Maria say anything? Could she help Maria? Perhaps Maria could be of help too. Just then, as if summoned, the woman came through the hut's opening. She carried Samantha's clothes, neatly folded. Her eyes were downcast, and her face seemed drawn and suddenly old.

"Good morning, Maria, my it is a little nippy this morning. Thank you for starting my fire for me."

Maria put the clothes on the bed and mumbled a reply which Samantha didn't hear well enough to understand. She did understand that Maria was still upset over something. Her eyes, opaque, dark, and looking only at the floor, spoke eloquently of

264

loss and fear.

After a moment's hesitation, Maria moved close to Samantha.

"I must not talk to you. Forbidden." She motioned toward the doorway where the guard stood.

Then, there was a look of determination.

"Maybe whisper." She looked searchingly into Samantha's eyes. Samantha gave the O.K. sign and reached to pat Maria's arm.

"Now, I will grind corn and prepare more beans," Maria said out loud. She got the sack of corn and emptied some on the grinding surface of the flat rock. Samantha sat cross-legged near Maria ignoring the dusty floor. She leaned close and smelled her earthy scent, dried sweat, and yesterday's cooking grease.

"I am very unhappy," Maria whispered. "They have 'disappeared' my husband." Her words were a mixture of Spanish and Mayan dialect, but Samantha had no trouble understanding the words.

"When did this happen?"

"Last night late, after I came to you. They came and asked him to go someplace, and he did not come back."

"Who came?"

"Some men in our group, but who live in another village."

"Surely he will return soon."

"No, a woman told me this morning he is dead in the forest." Here Maria began to rock back and forth stifling a sob.

"The Great One ordered it. My husband displeased him."

"Why? What did he do?"

"He cut off the hand of the brother of the Great One."

Samantha's breath stopped for a moment.

"Your man, did he have several scars on his chest?"

"Yes, he was with the men who brought you in."

Samantha told Maria what had happened. At the end of her story she looked into Maria's eyes.

"Your husband was a good man and tried to help me." Samantha did not say that he also promised to kill her if she didn't do as she was told.

Maria finished with the corn and the beans.

"I must go now. I will be back to cook for you in a little

while," Maria whispered. She got up quickly and walked through the door.

Samantha, mindful of creepy-crawlies, put her clean clothes inside her tent and zipped it up. She made herself sit on the crate instead of pacing about stirring up dust.

Trak and Julie would not begin worrying for a few days yet. There was no way she could contact her uncle, certainly not Emerson. So, what are you doing today Emerson, polishing your Jag? When she had been entombed in the rubble of Bhuj after the earthquake, everyone had seemed so far away.

True, Emerson had found her, although she was in no mood to lay eyes on him again, after running out on her in Paris; still, he had saved her from death, and she had to admit she had been at the end of her rope, no water, and Mr. Dewani, dead beside her.

"I'm waiting Emerson. Come through that damned door with commandos or Special Forces and liberate me." Samantha shook her head and felt a small smile. Nope, not this time. This time it would be up to her. Maybe Maria could help. If she could only think how. Think. Nothing came to mind. She would think some more.

She heard voices outside and then in came a fat woman, who had eaten too many carbs in her life, and the guard.

Samantha wanted to ask about Maria, but surmised it would not be wise to mention Maria's name. Instead, she rose from the crate, stood straight, towering over the guard and the woman stranger.

"Where's the other woman," then a thought, "the silent one–the one who can't speak?" Samantha noted surprised looks on both Mayans.

"She's not coming back. The Great One knows she talked to you and that was forbidden." Samantha laughed.

"By the way, I thought you said talking was forbidden, but you're talking to me. Shall I report you to the Great One whoever in hell he might be?"

The guard and the fat woman exchanged glances of anger and fear.

"And yes, when do I get to meet the Big Boy?" The pair glowered at her.

"You must not say bad things about the Great One."

"O.K., I'll shut up, and in the meantime, I want a great dinner of tortillas, beans and coffee and rustle up a tomato while you're at it." The two turned and left without answering.

Chapter 52

You know, I think I missed looking at the stars most of all. If I could only see the stars I could get through it. Waves of despair engulfed me, but I didn't let on. Hell No! –From Samantha's Journal

Tired and bored, Samantha faced the coming evening. The dinner of tortillas, beans and coffee, no tomato, the eternal menu, had come and gone. She was just ready to duck into her tent for an alcohol bath and sleep when the fat woman and guard appeared again.

"No go to bed. Take bath. See Great One."

"Well, it's about time. I'll take my bath in the tent and be with you in a jiffy."

"No. Bath special. You wait."

Two men came in carrying a large oblong wooden tub. They sat it on the dirt floor. They left and in came a woman with a large container which proved to be filled with hot water. She was followed by two more women, also with large containers of hot water. Small rugs were placed near the tub. The guard went out, leaving only the fat woman.

"You give me clothes. Take bath."

"What if I don't want a bath?"

"Guard come in and make you."

"O.K., just checking."

Actually, Samantha could hardly wait to lie down in the tub of hot water. The woman watched with interest as the clothes came off. Once in the tub Samantha tried mightily to contain a loud sigh of pure pleasure and failed. Two women entered with brushes and soap. They knelt down outside the tub and vigorously soaped and brushed Samantha from top to bottom.

They left and reappeared with two large containers. More hot water? The fat one told Samantha to stand up and the two containers were emptied on Samantha's head. Ice-cold water. Samantha wanted to yell. She coughed instead to hide her shock. "Just like my shower at home, hooboy," she said in English, wiping at her face. The women remained totally impassive.

The fat woman motioned Samantha to step out of tub. The two women rubbed her dry with large towels. Then massaged her with a delicious aromatic oil and dried her again.

"Comb hair."

Samantha pointed to her backpack in the tent and in due course, she found a comb, toothbrush and toothpaste. She asked for a small basin of water. The women watched. Apparently she passed inspection. She supposed she would now put on her clean clothes and go meet Mr. Mystery Man.

"You wear this," said the woman and she held out a robe or rebozo long enough to cover her body to the ankles. It was intricately woven, colorful with strange figures, and scratchy, but in a nice way, and its warmth was certainly welcome against the deepening chill of the forest. There would be no underclothes. "Oh, well, when in Rome...," Samantha noted.

"Put these on," and a pair of guaraches dangled from the the woman's hands. The sandals were made of dried plant fiber and when she slipped them on, Samantha found them quite comfortable.

"You ready. We go now."

At last Samantha slipped through the small door and stood in the darkness which enveloped the enclave of huts. She could see smoke spiraling up from this or that hut. The forest surrounded everything, dense, a protection for some and a threat to others. Somewhere out there Scar Chest, Maria's husband, had been killed for looking out for her.

The guard led, and Samantha followed. The fat woman padded heavily along, behind. In a few moments they stood before a much larger hut where two guards were posted. There the trio waited while one of the guards ducked inside, presumably to announce their presence, judged Samantha. They waited for what seemed like hours, but surely only minutes elapsed. The guard reappeared and motioned for Samantha to enter.

Partitions sealed off portions of the hut, creating a small hall-way or corridor at the end of which a drapery decorated with several odd motifs blocked what lay beyond. The guard stopped.

"This is an honor for you. No one enters here, unless very special. You special. Close eyes and walk in. Do not look until the Great One tells you to look." The message was in Spanish and Indian dialect.

Samantha decided to forego a sarcastic reply. She closed her eyes, almost, parted the curtain and walked as though blind for three steps, then stopped. After a few seconds during which with her squinted eyes she could make out candles and a throne of sorts, a deep voice in Spanish boomed.

"Open your eyes and approach the Great One."

Standing there, she had felt carpeting. Now, she could see the entire room was carpeted. The structure in front of her had a chair or seat on it. A man arrayed in robe and quetzal head dress sat there.

An ancient Mayan ruler would receive her. A foreign film. A fictitious documentary gone awry. She began walking toward the Mayan throwback. On his right stood a man, also in a flowing robe, and on the Great One's left stood Maria! She wore a robe as well.

What was Maria doing here? Did she belong to the Great One now that her husband was dead, killed by this very man or men under his command? Maria stood without blinking and gave no hint of recognition. She stared straight ahead, her expression un-readable.

"We are pleased you have been sent to us by the great gods and ancestral kings of the Mayan peoples. We welcome you as a sign that our progress has been approved. Venga! Venga!"

Samantha approached the makeshift throne as requested. Sent by gods? A sign of approval? Am I living in the right century? Samantha decided not to respond and waited in silence.

At a signal, the robed man and Maria walked toward the curtained door.

"Send in a chair for our guest." Samantha continued to stand and remained silent.

"You must be tired after your long journey, but you look so much better than my loyal subjects described, my dear. Ah, here is a chair. Please be seated, and we shall talk." The Great One used perfect Spanish.

Samantha heard a chair being placed close behind her, and turned in time to see a young Mayan man slipping back through the curtain. She was tired, but had not realized how tired until the Great One mentioned it. Grateful for this small favor, she sat down. Tired in body, but her mind raced with thoughts, plans, questions, anger, and some fear.

"You wonder why you are here." A statement or a question?

"Ah, if you could only know and appreciate what your coming will mean to all of us. We are poised on the cusp of destiny. You will help us move to the next phase of our rebirth and integration. You will be blest and remembered throughout our new history even as I shall be remembered as the Mother-Father of the completed Mayan state and the preeminent Keeper of Days."

This had gone on long enough. Either this man was a megalomaniac suffering from delusions of grandeur or simply a con man seeking to grab power and wealth while bamboozling these poor peasants. Depending upon his reactions to what she was ready to say, she would know where she stood and what she might or might not be able to do.

"First, I want to thank you for the chair and for the nice bath. Gracias. However, neither would have been necessary had you not abducted me in the jungle, sliced off the head of my Mayan guide, and thrown me into a vermin-infested hut. If the gods sent me to you, I wager they were Arabic and not Mayan."

An almost imperceptible glint came and went as she spoke the last sentence.

"Arabic?"

"Yes, do you speak Arabic? I do. I talked with some folks a week or so ago and believe it or not they described you among themselves not realizing that I understood their language. To them

271

you are a pig at a trough and they await the day when you are fat enough to butcher."

"Guard!" A man ran in.

"Take this woman back to her hut." Samantha was hurried from the room. On the outside again, her original guard and woman were given instructions. They marched back single-file with Samantha in the middle, but at a faster pace.

In her hut, the tub, rugs, and towels were gone. The woman took the large rebozo from her and returned Samantha's clothes. Then, showing no emotion and saying nothing, she walked out. A new candle on the rock, stuck to its own wax, flickered, settled down, and burned with a steady flame.

Inside her tent, Samantha inched her way into the comforting bedroll and gazed up at the mesh, stretched across the top of her house within a house. She wished dearly she could see her friends, the stars; so far, the evening skies had remained cloudy.

Remembering her outburst, she had to smile. I don't think that was the dumbest thing I've ever said, but it's pretty close, she murmured to herself, hunching her shoulders. She sighed and waited for sleep. There would be plenty of time to worry tomorrow.

Chapter 53

**At the time it was just a bad dream, day after day. I think I
was numb most of the time...like a sleeping cat with ears swiv-
eling...listening. –From Samantha's Journal**

The second full day proceeded as the first. Breakfast, lunch,
the occasional visit by the fat woman to empty the chamber pot,
grind corn, wash clothes, the swatting of two or three mosquitos.

The only daylight available came by way of the open top of the
conical roof and the small doorway through which all kinds wildlife could crawl, slither or fly.

At first, Samantha watched the open door warily, ready to
pounce on any unwelcome wildlife visitor, but after a while, boredom set in, and she hardly glanced in its direction anymore. She
wished for something to write on, and a pen, or at least, a book to
read.

She was forced to think, and this she did. She tried to figure out
why the Great One had been so angry. She reckoned that instead
of a con man, she was dealing with a fanatic who would brook no
criticism, even from the likes of Joe the Oilman.

Of course, she had not heard any such conversation take place
and only used it to shake up the Great One, but maybe not quite
that much. Now, the question became what to do next?

She could try to interest the Great One in some sort of ransom
demand; the money could help in his "progress" toward a Mayan
state. She would try that as a last resort. Perhaps, she could just
talk him out of holding her. After all, she was here on a personal
pilgrimage to bring closure to the death of her dad.

If he had any semblance of humanity in his veins surely he
would let her go. Her outburst yesterday evening might work

against her. What did she mean "might?" What was that old saying about killing the messenger of bad news? She had not done her cause any good. Not that he would kill her. Back to the ransom.

That must be it. Wonder how much I'm worth? Perhaps he would be happy with ten thousand or even fifty thousand dollars. Should I hold out for a higher ransom to bolster my self-respect? Maybe a million. Hey! I'm worth every penny. She had to smile at her thoughts.

The light waned as another night approached. Dinner was over and the cricket frogs tuned up for the nightly chorus. At dusk she had heard some howler monkeys far off getting ready to bed down for the night.

Again she was thinking about the alcohol bath and the bedroll inside the zipped up tent, when in marched the fat woman followed by the two men carrying the tub, and the ladies with the hot water, cold water, soap, brush, towels, rugs, and the colorful rebozo and sandals.

"Let me guess. Bath time. The Great One seeks another interview. My hair would look better if I could see what I'm doing."

The woman with her retinue went about their duties and totally ignored Samantha's attempts at conversation. The only words spoken came at the end.

"We go now. Vamonos!"

Samantha, cleaned within an inch of her life, slathered in oils, rubbed to a lustrous sheen, brushed and wrapped in the beautiful rebozo robe, walked to the doorway.

"As the song says, At Last."

She stepped carefully into the night shod in her guaraches and padded along behind the torch-carrying guard and in front of the fat woman. Samantha needed to know the woman's name and the guard's, too, since by now she was beginning to think of them as family. If they wouldn't cooperate, she would be forced to make up two names. Assuming she survived the night, she would get on it first thing in the morning.

274

As she walked along, the images of Paris and Emerson, flickered in her mind. Just a few short months ago, they had walked, sat by the fireplace, the prelude to being touched that night in bed, Emerson's tentative hand reaching for her in the near darkness and how she had hungrily moved into his arms.

The rebozo caressed her oiled thighs and slipped back and forth against her breasts, her erect nipples responding to the scratch of the warm loose fabric. Time seemed to stretch out and double back. Some things seemed so far in the past, while others seemed like they had happened only a few days ago.

So much had happened: the death of her colleague, followed by her sexual awakening and the insatiable lust for Emerson, the ensuing despair when he vanished on the night when she would have given herself to him again. Rapturously. Chocolate had swirled about her as they made love the night before and that second night promised a room full of chocolate.

She interrupted her thoughts to glance up at the stars, but again, a smothering overcast barely topping the surrounding forest hid them from her.

She sighed, feeling suddenly lost and vulnerable. She could not face the Great One in such a mental state. Focus. Focus. I must focus and repair the damage of last night. I can do it. I will deliver. He will not win. Her steps were firm. She planted each foot resolutely one after the other on the path. She rehearsed her arguments which would surely free her from this Honduran nightmare. The torch seemed to burn brighter, and soon, the large hut loomed before her. "Second night, get it right," became her mantra as one of the guards at the doorway bent slightly to enter and announce her presence.

"So, your friends think of me as a pig, almost ready for slaughter." His voice carried his anger.

"They are not my friends. So what if they are lies? Why punish me for what they said? A plane crashed near here a year ago. I

275

am investigating that crash. The pilot died. It may not have been an accident. Perhaps you know something about it?"

He shifted in his seat. His robe opened enough she could see the well-muscled calf of his left leg. A large knife sheath tied to the lower leg shone in the candlelight. Samantha steeled herself not to gasp. Was it possible? Her dad's oversized knife?

"A plane crash? I know nothing of what you say."

"Too bad, maybe there would be a reward for some straight answers." Samantha did not expect anything to come from this exchange. If the knife belonged to her dad, then Mr. High and Mighty knew something. She turned her attention to his seat as he stood briefly to rearrange the robe. As she suspected, it had come from a plane and, if her memory served her, it belonged to an old Piper Cherokee. She needed no more information from the Great One. Obviously, he knew of the crash. He and his "crew" had been charged with clearing the site of any evidence.

They had probably taken the body of her father to a far away village from where it was transported back to Guatemala. Only a portion of the Piper's tail had eluded them, lodged in the canopy out of sight. Things were becoming clear and her prospects for living to a ripe old age, suddenly, seemed shaky. She would fight.

"Since you know nothing of the business I was sent here to investigate, I would like to leave as soon as possible, before someone comes looking for me which could prove uncomfortable for you."

"Ah Si, I wish it were that simple, my dear, but you see, there's the matter of your guide's unfortunate end. Que triste! Would you not report it and make my life uncomfortable anyway?"

"I can assure you there would be no benefit to me or to my company by getting involved. It was a dreadful thing that happened on the trail, but the reality is I must overlook it and issue a report of a vanished aircraft, then my work will be done and if I ever come back to Honduras, I will have lost my mind."

"You have a bad feeling about our country. That is regrettable. I believe it is destined for great things, and I believe you will have a part to play in that destiny."

"And if I decline the part?"

"Well, you see, you don't really have a choice. I would hope that you will accept your role with good cheer. You will be honored and remembered for what you are about to do."

Then the Great One recited a passage from some ancient source, using the language of the old Mayans. She and Julie had read the most recent version of the Popol Vuh, the story of beginnings for the Mayan civilization. It was considered the Mayan Bible. This recitation seemed to be from an earlier more poetic version.

"So, do you know anything about what you just heard?"

"I believe it is from the Popul Vuh, but a version I am not acquainted with."

His gaze told her he was quite surprised and for a moment he just sat and looked at her. Then he smiled.

"Excellent. You are informed. What I quoted was from the Quiché version copied by Francisco Ximénez around 1700. The original Council Book has been lost. The Light that Came from Beside the Sea was its name among others. For those who knew how to read it all things were as clear as the vision of the first four humans before the gods took away their powers. All wars were forecast as well as famines, deaths, quarrels, everything in the sky and in the earth could be seen in the Council Book.

"So, you have the Spanish invaders to thank for preserving it."

"Si, after they did their best to destroy it."

He mused for awhile. Then the Great One motioned that Samantha should come closer. His stocky body radiated power. His generous and humped Mayan nose dominated his swarthy smooth-shaven face. As before at their "meetings" he wore the brilliant feathers of the quetzal. Hieroglyphics decorated his dark red robe. His was a commanding presence.

"Have patience, my dear, I shall reveal to you the mysteries and the wonders of our great opportunity soon, very soon. Entiende?"

He breathed deeply as if he could smell the aroma of the oil the women had rubbed into Samantha's body. She had grown warmer beneath the folds of the rebozo. Despite her sense of danger, she felt a rising excitement. It would be her wit against his. Would he be a worthy opponent? What was she thinking? This was no time for games. Her life could be at stake.

"No, I don't understand."

Samantha awoke to screaming. She dressed quickly and crawled from her tent without lacing up her boots. The fat woman, now named Ramona by Samantha since she had refused to offer her real name, knelt motionless before the grinding stone. She had been preparing breakfast. Samantha knew it was useless to ask what was happening. She could hear an intermittent whacking and murmurs from several voices, but above all this the piercing sound of screams sent a shudder down her back. She moved to the door. The guard had left. His new name, Ra, after the Egyptian sun god, since he led their procession with a blazing torch. She peered out, then wished she hadn't.

In the middle of the compound, people were milling about, quite agitated, and making a chanting-like noise. Tied to posts were two men and a woman. Tunic-clad men stood around them, each with a long whip, taking turns lashing the bound bodies. Blood splattered the robes and ran down the backs and faces of the prisoners. The screams grew less as the robed men hit ever harder, lacerating the flesh. Soon, only exhausted moans and whimpering groans came from the lips of the beaten trio. The onlookers grew silent.

The Great One suddenly appeared and strode into the circle. The crowd of thirty or so backed away, bowing toward him as he turned about looking up beyond the tops of the mist-shrouded trees surrounding the enclave of huts. He had on a heavy black tunic that covered him from shoulders to his knees.

Samantha got a better look at the large knife sheath tied to his leg just below the knee. She was too far away to make sure, but it looked like the sheath that Jason kept his knife in. The Great One paraded about and in a strong voice led the crowd in a chant which Samantha could not understand. It was eagerly adopted, and soon everyone shouted it against the walls of the forest.

At the height of the frenzy, the Great One reached for the

sheath and pulled out the gleaming blade, nearly a foot long, not counting the handle. The hilt guard and the flash of gold made Samantha wince. Could this be her dad's knife, after all? A twin knife to the one she had held in Greenland.

Unable to tear her eyes away, she watched as the Great One grabbed the hair of the woman, bent her away from the post, then sliced the front of her neck. A gush of blood pumped quickly upward and then bubbled over her shoulders and subsided. The head of the woman lay upon her back. He wrenched at it, slicing again with the knife until he freed it from her slumped body. A new chant began and the bloody head was placed in a basket.

Cries of despair came from the throats of the two men as the Great One cleaned the knife against his short robe, held it high while the voices and stamping feet of the onlookers seemed almost child-like with excitement. Santa Claus would toss out more candy soon. Gather around. The Great One walked towards the two men. Samantha turned and stumbled back into the hut. She had seen too much.

Nausea overwhelmed her, as it had on the trail when she had watched the beheading of Juan. Without any food, only dry wrenching gags tore at her throat. She collapsed onto the hard bed and doubled up to ease the knotted feeling in her stomach. Ramona still waited, and continued to wait, until at last silence reigned outside. Ironically, Samantha heard a beautiful song from a bird calling from the forest. Another bird joined in the sweet singing.

The ground coffee beans boiled in the blackened pot and the aroma of coffee filled the hut. Ramona slapped some tortillas into shape. Samantha needed a cup of coffee in the worst way. It was as though the strong brew would wipe away the images of the brutal butchering.

Chapter 54

It was at this point I should have known there was a screw loose in his head. A maniac. I still tried to work with him. I was fooling myself. Facing reality seemed unbearable. –From Samantha's Journal

The day seemed endless. For the first time, Samantha found it hard to concentrate on strategies that might get her out of that place. Over and over she felt that paying ransom would be the only avenue of escape, but the logistics and the amount of the ransom eluded her in the storm of emotions which threatened her with complete panic.

The savage execution refused to leave her mind. The woman's poor head just dangling on her back, mouth open in a silent scream, and then the relentless slicing and jerking by the Great One to sever it from her body haunted Samantha.

She clenched her fist and beat on the hard bed to force herself back to a fighting mentality. She would fight! If she had to subdue the entire village, she would do it! Her breathing increased in intensity. She flexed her arms, her legs, her hands. She jabbed and kicked through her martial arts routine, then stretched thoroughly. She sat down on the bed and felt the change taking place.

Strength replaced horror and resignation. Time went by. Deep slow breathing brought peace. More time went by. She felt relaxed as though delivered from some inner turmoil. She had restored her resolve.

Samantha lay down on the rough bed and drifted into sleep at last, oblivious to insects or anything else that might come through the open door. The terrible images became enemies which she subdued as fast as they appeared.

One enemy disguised as a grasping vine tried to snare her, and she struck it and moved to kill it with another blow. But the vine squealed with pain. Samantha bounded from the bed ready to continue the fight only to find Ramona sitting on the floor holding her arm, a surprised and fearful look on her face.

"Oh, I'm so sorry, I didn't mean to hurt you. Lo Siento. Please let me help you. It was a bad dream. I thought you were attacking me...."

Samantha moved toward the woman who now had a genuine aura of terror about her. Ramona struggled to her feet as quickly as her heavy body would allow and still holding her arm, ran from the hut yelling for help.

"Well, I seem to be batting a thousand with the staff."

Now fully awake, she paced between bed, tent and door, heedless of any dust she might be raising. If and when she had another talk with the Great One, she would speak with power. Money could be her power. She would use it. She would win.

Now, she was hungry. Not a good time for her cook to resign. She got the bag of corn and began grinding the kernels. Hard work, but it felt good, although the results didn't seem too appetizing.

"Why did I have to beat up my personal chef?"

Ramona's unhappy bulk filled the doorway. Two men followed, pushing her along. Samantha put her heart and soul into explaining, apologizing and even took an oath not to hurt Ramona again. Reluctantly, Ramona agreed to remain and took over the meal preparation to Samantha's relief. The men left.

Samantha sat on the bed pretending to sort her meager supplies, aware of Ramona casting furtive glances in her direction as if ready to flee should this mad gringa leap upon her again. All signs of haughtiness had disappeared from the pudgy chef. The brief physical attack, unfortunately at Ramona's expense, had topped off Samantha's energy reservoir. She felt ready for anything.

The afternoon passed slowly, as every afternoon did. Samantha longed to walk about. It gave her a new appreciation for what prisoners endure locked in a cell. As she had wished to eat apples

281

in Greenland, so she longed to walk anywhere she wished in Honduras. Samantha longed to be free again. She would not take her freedom for granted ever again, assuming she got out of this mess alive.

After doing more thinking about how to go about the ransoming process, she began contemplating the possibility of the evening bath and the third meeting with the Great One, a murderer.

The procession of tub, rugs, towels, hot and cold water, oil, etc. arrived several hours earlier than before. Nothing was said about the schedule change and soon Samantha was clean and aromatic. When it came time to slip into the ornate rebozo-like robe, she was handed a lighter and much shorter tunic of brilliant blue decorated with hieroglyphics. Longer-legged than the squat Indian women, Samantha realized she now had on a mini-skirt. No one seemed to notice and Samantha didn't care whether they did or didn't. A longer shawl provided insect protection for the procession.

The earlier schedule allowed Samantha to look around more. Some of the people were out and around, cooking, cleaning, making things, talking. Two children chased two other children. Samantha wondered if they had been present at the killings that morning and, if so, how that might affect them as they grew up. Would they think nothing of beheading anyone who got in their way?

At the hut, the guard escorted her to the room. Inside, a surprise. A table covered with a white cloth, displayed plates, glasses, gleaming flatware, lighted candles, and a small center piece of orchids. A serving table stood at one side. Two chairs faced each other. Dining. Unbelievable. Another surprise, the Great One wasn't seated on his "throne" and that afforded her an opportunity to inspect it. Yes, it was definitely one of the seats from the Piper's cabin, and undamaged, and that meant there was no fire when the plane crashed. She glanced back at the dining table. A lot of information to process. Important and confusing. A Piper seat, a dining table...how to react?

Had her dad been alive when found? Had the Great One killed him? Could she find out the truth? Why bother to ask? But not to ask...wouldn't that be worse? A cricket sang in the corner shadows.

The Great One entered the room. He walked towards her, smiling. He too wore a tunic. Not black as the one that morning, but a blue one similar to her own.

"Remove your rebozo, por favor. You will find it quite comfortable in here without it."

Samantha hesitated. How would her bare legs affect him? She shrugged the thought away and took the shawl off as if being scantily clad were no big deal. In silence the Great One stared at her thighs still gleaming from the oil.

"Quite handsome, my dear. I see I did not over-estimate your beauty. Please be seated. We shall eat together as we talk." He clapped his hands and two women came in bearing bowls and platters. Pork chops! And steak! On another platter, a whole chicken with roasted peppers. There were bowls of steaming yellow, green and orange vegetables which she did not immediately recognize in the candlelight, and sliced tomatoes! A bowl of glazed pineapple appeared. Something sweet to eat. It seemed like forever since she had eaten anything with sugar in it. Then came a large bottle of red wine.

Samantha decided the Great One had already imbibed a bit while waiting for her. His voice sounded deeper and slower and his approach to the table overly deliberate, requiring total concentration. Once seated, he raised his full goblet.

"A toast to our common objective, my dear. An objective made perfect by your partish...parcipatation." The stumble over the word, another sign of creeping inebriation. Samantha felt uneasy. The wine could jeopardize the evening. On the other hand it could help. Whatever they discussed today could disappear like morning mist tomorrow. She would have to be careful, the usual admonition, usually ignored.

"Thank you for inviting me to this feast. Everything looks so delicious."

"Tell me, my dear, were you upset this morning? I believe I saw you briefly in front of your dwelling. The guard was negligent to let you witness what was a very necessary lesson."

"Beheadings are necessary?" Samantha gritted her teeth con-

283

trolling her rage. Now, the sight of the food made her feel ill. Obviously, he knew she would watch. Were the lives taken as a lesson for her?

"Yes, necessary. It did pain me to administer the punishment, but if I had not acted, the whole enterprise could have unraveled."

"Enterprise, objective, destiny? My part to play? My great role? I've had it up to here with your empty words. I would like to hear exactly why you go around beheading people, and by the way, when you sliced off that poor woman's head I saw no pain on your face." Samantha stood up and walked to the Piper throne.

"This seat came from a Piper Cherokee plane, the one that went down last year. Yes, I am investigating that crash. You want to know why? Because I think the oil company in Guatemala is responsible for the crash. The pilot in that plane was my father, and if I thought you had a hand in his death you would be dead too." Samantha touched the leather and then, incensed that this drunken maniac had dared use it, she pushed it off the platform, toppling it to the carpeted floor. So much for being careful. In the silence that followed, only the cricket resumed its plaintive song.

The Great One lifted his wine glass, tipped it toward Samantha then gulped down the wine allowing some to spill from his mouth and trickle down his chin and onto his tunic.

He held onto the large goblet, rose slowly, walked to his overturned throne, put it back on the platform and seated himself on it, then called out loudly, and a trembling young woman ran in with another bottle of wine. He waved her away.

" Aguardiente!" He barked the word at her and the frightened woman returned with the sugar cane liquor. Samantha, still seething, stood her ground. He threw his glass away and drank from the bottle.

"I went to a lot of trouble to have a nice dinner for you and to prepare you for greatness, but you have refused to cooperate and you are not appreciative. So, you want to know everything? Very well, I will tell you your fate. It won't take long." He swallowed another mouthful of the sweet liquor.

284

"I had nothing to do with that pilot's death. He was dead when we arrived. You say he was your father. That means nothing to me, all fathers die eventually. But, if he had been alive, we would have killed him as part of the deal. Your showing up was a bonus. A gift of the gods. When I said you were destined for greatness, I meant it.

"I have studied the Popol Vuh," he continued, "the story of our people, the story of Sky-Earth and how all things began and how all things will end. I am close to seeing everything.

A sacrifice done in the old way must be made, a sacrifice of a special woman, the woman I saw in a dream months ago. A virgin of intense spirit. You are that woman. You will usher in the beginning of the new age of our ancestors. You will not have to wait long. The Ceremony of Healing and Transformation will be day after tomorrow. No one can stand in our way."

For a moment, Samantha just stood, saying nothing. Then she spoke quietly, yet forcefully.

"I don't believe what I'm hearing. Healing? Transformation? The Mayan religion returning because you are going to sacrifice me? And may I make a minor but important point here? I'm certainly not a virgin."

The Great One smiled, his eyes narrowing as he drank more of the anise-flavored alcohol.

"You will be. I have but to cleanse you with a holy act and that I shall do before offering your heart to the gods."

Samantha gasped. Delusions big-time. A fanatic. How could she work with such a maniac? Did he mean to rape her? Would he cut out her heart? She felt a tremor beginning and fought against it. She must remain strong. Outwit this human misfit.

"So, you are a great leader with great plans and you have had a great vision. Perhaps you misread your vision. If I am that woman you envisioned, an intense spirit, perhaps I am useful in a more powerful way."

The Great One twisted in his seat, his eyes heavy-lidded.

"Another way? There can be no other way."

"Alternatives are always possible, even as the gods found out when they first attempted to create humans. The first beings had no arms and could not work to serve the gods. The second experiment used mud and the beings melted. Then the gods tried wood, but they just pretended to be human and today are monkeys. Only the fourth attempt worked when the first four human men were made from corn dough."

"Yes, yes, that is true. What has that to do with us?

"Money."

"Money?"

"Yes. A ransom would provide safety for you and power to reach your objective. A million U.S. dollars." She watched as the dollar amount sank in.

"Someone would pay a million dollars for you?

"Of course."

"Give me the names of those people." Too fast. Too easy. She would stall for time. His words slurred, but underneath she detected a calculated cunning.

"Tomorrow, I will furnish names provided you cancel the ceremony."

"Of course, my beautiful hostage." He tipped the bottle again and wiped at his mouth with his sleeve. He burped.

"You are wise as well as beautiful." His eyes fastened again on her legs. Things were deteriorating rapidly.

"I must go now." She retrieved the rebozo and walked to the curtain. The Great One did nothing to stop her. Samantha's pulse rate increased dramatically as she walked. Just a few more feet. Just two more feet. She parted the curtain and walked quickly to the front of the hut. Ra and Ramona were seated, and jumped up, bumping against each other in their haste to stand. No one had summoned them, and they didn't know what to do.

"Take me to my hut. Vamonos!" said Samantha in a commanding tone, trying to hide her nerves.

Chapter 55

Most folks would jump at the chance to be included in a great celebration, especially, if they were to be the main attraction. I would have let them take my place. Gladly. –From Samantha's Journal

Alone that night inside her tent, Samantha gave herself permission to cry. She was not good at crying. Things had to be pretty important to cry over. This was one of those times.

The ransom would not work. He would kill her. She would make up the names. What did it matter, except to act as if she believed him and watch as he continued preparations for her death. Knowing this, she vowed to escape or die trying. She would fight to the last. The tears stopped. Her stomach grumbled at her for not eating the steak and pineapple when she had the chance.

As she ate the same dreary breakfast the next day, the pretense drama unfolded with the next scene. A man arrived for the names. Samantha handed over a list of twenty fictitious names and fax numbers he had no way of using out here in the middle of nowhere. A comical charade play ending in tragedy? Not if she could help it.

At noon, Ramona told Samantha there would be a big celebration the following day and the entire compound was already busy with food preparation and the making of special garments. Samantha would be on her own for dinner. There would be no bath and oil treatment today either. Some of the haughtiness had returned.

Samantha spent the afternoon sharpening her muscle reflexes, readying herself for action. That night she sponged off with alcohol and climbed into her bedroll, maybe for the last time.

The Great One was sick in the head, a flawed and impaired

brain, a zero in history who could end her life. A con-man tricked by his own game and now a fanatic. She wondered if he realized how well she understood him.

On the other hand, the Great One seemed to know her better than she thought, for on Thursday in the late afternoon, four stocky men rushed into the hut and pinned her to the earth floor even though she had managed one blow that knocked out the first one to reach her.

They tied her and carried her to the Great One's hut. Three women took away her clothes and undid her boots while the men held her. Maria was one of the three. Samantha tried to catch her eye, but Maria refused to look at her. A feeling of great dread began to spread throughout Samantha's body. Again, she was securely tied and wrapped in a woolen blanket and laid on a table.

Dusk turned to night. The distant calling of the howler monkeys died away and the chorus of tree frogs swelled. The four men, including the one she had knocked out that afternoon, picked Samantha up and carried her on their shoulders along a path away from the huts. She treasured the fleeting moments when she caught sight of the stars through the canopy.

The men stopped before a shallow cave with a large opening. A fire blazed at the entrance, and the heat felt good.

They laid her on a large flat stone behind the fire. The slab was warm which meant the fire had been burning for some time.

What would it be like to die? How would it feel to have her heart cut out? How long would she remain conscious? Would she see her heart held high? She hoped not. Surely she would be dead long before that. Maybe it wouldn't be too painful. Maybe just the first awful thrust of the knife. What irony to be killed by her father's knife.

But what bothered her more than death was that mad-man thrusting himself inside her. He would rape her. She saw it in his eyes. Rape: the "holy act" to make her a virgin again.

She would be powerless to stop him. Violated the moment before death. Her last awareness while alive, struggling against an enemy plunging between her legs. The vision would not fade.

The blanket lay around her loosely. A man held each arm and each leg. Women removed the ropes and blanket leaving her spread-eagled and naked on the rock. In spite of the warm slab she shook violently.

The women washed her with warm water, and Samantha wanted to thank them. Ridiculous thought. They massaged her with warm oil. They wove flowers into her hair. The shaking slowed.

While the men held her arms and legs, the women tied her with new ropes, anchoring her body to hooks in the stone. Maria tied Samantha's right wrist, and for one quick moment, looked into her eyes. An intense look. A look of sadness? Samantha looked away. A woman covered her with a light blanket.

Dusk came and went. Night approached. Cricket frogs intensified their ceaseless songs. The wind blew softly against Samantha's face, and she could feel the flowers move in her hair. What kind of flowers had they used? What would Emerson think when he found out she was dead? She thought of her uncle, Aisa, and Christina. What would happen to Duchess? Unable to say goodbye to anyone. Despair flooded her thoughts.

Chapter 56

The mind is peculiar. I faced death, yet the one thing that stuck in my brain was the sound of those kids going "ehhh lep, lep, lep," in their little high-pitched voices. –From Samantha's Journal

Voices chanted from far off. Exotic sounds thousands of years old. A procession of some sort? Would there be a moon tonight? The rope fibers binding her gave the impression of a ripe persimmon color. Samantha felt sad that her synesthesia, that marvelous gift, would die with her.

The chanting continued. In the light of candles she saw the face of the Great One looking at her. He daubed something on her forehead and down her nose. Then he daubed various places on her body. More chanting. She lost track of time. If only she had her watch, but then, how could she see it tied down? An hour? Two hours? More chanting. Prelude to the sacrifice.

Again the face, this time with cheeks distended, then a sudden forceful mist engulfed her as the Great One blew a mouthful of licorice-tasting alcohol at her head. Aguardiente. She gagged as the sweet liquor hit her face. Samantha heard other voices. The children were mimicking the tree frogs.

"Ehhhh, lep, lep, lep. Ehhhhh lep, lep, lep." Small strident voices from very young throats. Samantha wondered what they were thinking about her impending death. "Ehhh, lep, lep, lep. Ehhhh lep, lep, lep." The sounds grew louder. And then something quite odd. Mariachi music. Surely not. But she heard the guitars, a strange sounding violin, drums, maracas, and singing.

The chanting, the children's frog calls, and the music stopped.The Great One stood above her. In his hand the gleaming blade of her Father's knife. Soon it would be over.

In the torch light he pointed the knife in four directions calling upon ancient gods of Sky-Earth. The names rang out. Too many to remember.

As the tiny cricket frogs replaced the children's voices with their dissonant recital, the Great One raised his voice in some sort of a proclamation. Announcing her sacrifice? Announcing his "holy act" to restore her virginity? Would she die still asking stupid questions?

Close at hand she heard the whine of a mosquito, then a tiny stab on her cheek that immediately itched. She could not reach to scratch it. That she couldn't scratch it seemed terribly unfair and callous. She cursed Mother Nature for allowing such torture. Never mind my death, just let one of your insects have a last meal.

Above her, the Great One lowered the knife and put it in its sheath tied to his leg. He looked at her and grinned.

"Now you will become a virgin. Es verdad."

Samantha stared. She had almost forgotten the ordeal she had to experience before being killed. The thought about what was to happen shot through her system like an electric current. Stoic acceptance disappeared. Intense anger fueled her muscles. She tugged on the ropes that held her fast to the rock.

The Great One removed his ceremonial head dress and his ornate robe. In his dark nakedness he knelt above her and placing his hands beneath her lower body, he raised her to meet him. His heavy belly pressed against her and she inhaled a combination of fried peppers and aguardiente fumes.

Then she felt the head of his penis probing. Apparently, he was having some difficulty. Maybe too much alcohol. He had misjudged the athleticism, the sheer strength of Samantha, who twisted away each time he made an attempt to bury himself between her thighs. He had trouble holding her. The women had done a good job rubbing a generous amount of oil on her, and the Great One's hands slipped repeatedly. Each time he jabbed at her, she shifted enough to thwart his attack.

The constant twisting and straining had another effect. The rope around her right wrist had loosened. Maria had tied that wrist. Bless you Maria. Bless you. Now I know why you looked at me. With renewed strength Samantha pulled at the rope, heedless of her wrist, enduring the pain.

The rope relaxed, unraveled, gave way. The hard edge of her hand lashed against his neck, but a sharp pain caused her to scream. He brushed her arm aside. Her wrist, too injured by the rope lacked the power needed to do damage. She almost cried, not from the pain, although that was considerable, but from the betrayal of her body which had failed her when she needed it most.

He laughed as she swatted at him.

"Go on, hit me. It is nothing to me. I shall have you soon. Tanto mejor. Está bueno!" He grunted with a renewed effort, and she felt his penis barely miss its mark and slide up on her stomach. It would be only a matter of time. He would win. And then she would die.

A vision of the ranch in Texas swept into her mind. She saw the half-eaten carcass of the pregnant deer killed by the mountain lion, the look of wonder and resignation in the deer's large brown eyes. "I will not be a victim." Words remembered. She yelled them at her attacker as she struck his neck again. The Great One ignored her effort. Her arm slid down the side of his heaving body and touched the top of the knife's handle strapped to his lower leg.

Her dad's knife. Could she grab it? "I will not be a victim!" continued to ring in her ears. She strained forward to get a grip on the handle. Almost there, but it moved away as he lunged again, closer this time. His breath came in great gasps, but his stocky body continued to overpower her. Samantha despaired at holding him off any longer.

By concentrating on the knife, she left herself defenseless for a crucial second. He was at the door. He pushed it open. He had only to plunge, to pin her to the smooth hard rock. He paused, savoring the moment.

The knife slid from the sheath. Samantha, screaming with pain and anger, rammed the huge blade into soft flesh just under the Great One's rib cage. With no hesitation she drove it in and up, burying it to the hilt and jerking it from side to side. She did not stop screaming. Fury drove her now.

Glazed eyes no longer focused on her as she roared hoarsely at him in her rage. Blood began to gush from his mouth. A shudder

292

went through his body, and the organ that had bludgeoned her so forcefully a moment before, collapsed. Surely she had pierced the stomach and his lungs with the thick blade. The razor-edged tip would have reached his throbbing heart, slicing it and destroying it. He shuddered again, and his eyes went blank. Dead eyes. She was not the deer slain by the mountain lion. She was not the victim. She was the lion.

More blood. It spilled out of his mouth and onto to her face, neck and breasts. Hot. Sticky.

She yanked out the knife. He slid off the slab and onto the ground. She slashed through the fiber ropes that still bound her feet and her left arm. Once loose, she steeled herself for the rush of enraged Mayans who would surely try to kill her.

Samantha got a crazy idea. She snatched the Great One's discarded robe with its hieroglyphic designs and threw it about her shoulders. Blood began to coagulate on her face and down her front. The robe gaped open and the shocked campesinos stared at her naked breasts and stomach smeared with the Great One's blood.

She held the dripping knife high and, hoping she could remember, screamed at the paralyzed peasants.

"Heart of the Sky, Heart of the Earth, Heart of the Sea accept this sacrifice! Sky-Earth gods, the one who would rival your power to see everything is destroyed!"

Samantha could remember no more Mayan god names. She wondered what to do next. She took a deep breath to scream again.

Chapter 57

Almost free is not free, but the vision of freedom while one is still threatened with death can supply strength and determination when one's tank is sitting on empty. –From Samantha's Journal

Instead of screaming, Samantha listened. In the distance, a deep, strong voice could be heard. The people turned as one, and looked at a ghost approaching from the forest. Scar Chest, thought dead by everyone, miraculously had come back to life. They fell down before him, although some fell down facing Samantha.

As he approached, Samantha remembered he had once promised to kill her while on the trail. Would she have to fight him too? She felt drained. He yelled at her, and his voice was heard by all:

"The gods are pleased. You are free!"

Undoubtedly, the most beautiful words she had ever heard. She would put those words on a plaque in her Texas cabin. She turned and walked as steadily as possible back up the trail, at times trying to run then slowing, afraid of falling, afraid of blacking out. She concentrated on walking. The dim light of dawn made the trail barely visible.

She held the knife in one hand and with her other clutched the Great One's robe, holding it around her, grateful for its warmth. She stopped at the jungle's edge to catch her breath and to see if there had been guards left behind. She saw no one. She crossed open ground to the Great One's hut.

It had been her dad who saved her. His knife. She would think that over later. Great feelings of excitement, dread, and relief flooded her head and heart. Her heart! Still intact and beating. The night was no more. The welcome light of a new morning blessed her life but urged her to hurry.

Time was not on her side. The Indians might change their minds. Scar Chest might want to hold her for ransom. Freed from the thought of a gruesome death, Samantha's mind focused on a puzzle she had ignored since she pushed the Piper aircraft seat to the floor.

For a while the puzzle had nagged at her then retreated to her sub-conscious as she devoted all her resources to staying alive. Now it demanded attention. Important or not, she would deal with it right after washing away the caking blood. She hoped the Great One had water in his hut.

Chapter 58

A friend is one who cares. One who never gives up on you. But what if that friend can't find you? I guess I go find her. – From Samantha's Journal

"Do you love me?"

"Huh?"

"It's a simple question. Calls for a simple answer."

Trak rolled over to face Julie. He propped himself up on an elbow and looked at her.

"You woke me up to ask me that? You know damn well I love you. I loved you yesterday. I love you at this ungodly hour, and I'll love you tomorrow and every tomorrow after that." He yawned and slumped down on his pillow. His hand reached to cup one of her breasts.

"Why don't we get married?" She guided his hand to cover an already erect nipple.

"And I'm worried about Samantha. I expected a call before now." She allowed his hand to fall from her breast. Trak raised his head then reburied it in his pillow.

"Even if I were awake, it would be hard to answer both those questions. How about we get married tomorrow right after we find Samantha?"

Julie swatted at his returning hand and sat up, then tried to untangle her hair. Their love making always seemed to take place when it was loose, and generally with devastating results. Not that she was complaining. Trak had been unusually virile last night. She had loved every minute of it and had tried her best to let the whole hotel know of her passionate euphoria.

"Some day you're going to be sorry saying that. I'll wear a wire and get you for breach of contract or promise or whatever and then you'll find yourself a properly married man. In the meantime, you're off the hook and yes, I would like to find Samantha. She's late."

"How late?"

"Today's Friday. She's two days overdue."

"I thought you agreed not to worry if she stayed out longer."

"I know, but I thought she would check in if she needed extra time."

"Have you tried to reach her?"

"Doesn't work. She has to have the phone all set up. So far I haven't been lucky, but what worries me is her not trying to reach us."

"Maybe the phone's just out of order, and she'll surprise us and waltz in here wondering why all the fuss."

"I hope you're right. But if she doesn't come or call soon, get ready for a safari."

Trak closed his eyes then opened them to watch long locks of golden brown hair cascading down Julie's creamy-colored back as she continued working out the tangles.

"Now I know why I love you. I once thought it was because you're smart, beautiful, and talked in non-sequiturs. Without a doubt it was tangled hair that captured my heart."

"And long enough to strangle you."

Julie turned and lay down on him rubbing her breasts against his chest and kissing him soundly.

"See what happens when you give me a compliment? While I cover you up with tangles, could I entice you to re-enlist for some very active duty at this ungodly hour?

By Saturday afternoon, Julie could wait no longer. But what to do? Then she thought of Samantha's guide. She would go to the guide's family to see if perchance his wife had heard anything. Someone may have run into Samantha and through the grapevine, so to speak, the news would have found its way back to Copán.

297

Julie located the neighborhood where the Espinosa family lived. Several Espinosas lived in the area, as a matter of fact. She had to use the name Juan and that he was a guide before one woman pointed out the house. The woman had sighed and hung her head.

Julie walked through a small gate and along a walk bordered by brightly colored flowers. She knocked on the door of the modest light-blue stucco home. A small woman with shining black hair and red swollen eyes greeted her. Three boys crowded around staring and hanging on to her full skirt. The woman, Senora Espinosa, said si, her husband's name was Juan and si, he had left several days ago to be a guide for a gringa. Then she squinted up her eyes and sobbed. Julie didn't know what to do. So, she just waited for the woman to stop crying enough to ask her what was wrong.

Senora Espinosa told how a campesino had stopped by with sorrowful news just a few hours before. The campesino said he had heard from others that on a little-used trail south of El Castillo a man had been killed. His head cut off.

In his pocket was a photo of his family and on the back the names of his wife and children. In the background, buildings looked like the photo had been taken in Copán. She and the children were waiting for the body to be returned to them. They would know for sure then. Here she cried again. This time Julie put her arms around her.

Chapter 59

Seeing misty orchid-covered really tall oak trees in a cloud forest is like a healing prayer...maybe better. –From Samantha's Journal

Early Sunday morning the mist blotted out the tops of the trees forecasting another very humid chilly day. The rainy season was only a few days away, not that it really mattered here near the summit of El Castillo.

Sunday marked the beginning of the third day of hiking for Samantha and she longed for a hot bath, a good night's sleep, some really good food, and a break from creepy crawlies, blood-sucking mosquitos, and cold wet nights.

On the plus side she had felt at peace and restored when she had entered once again the cathedral-like cloud forest. The mighty oaks seemed rooted in eternity. Something one could count on. And beautiful too. The high limbs covered with orchids. Here, she had camped with her guide. Poor Juan. A terrible end for a man who took pride in his job and loved his family so much.

Samantha slept in her damp clothes, wrapping herself in her sleeping bag. She was so very tired. She could have slept around the clock instead of the few hours she allowed herself each night.

Samantha wanted as much distance as possible between her and the Mayans she had left behind. By taking the rigorous trail across the back of the mountain and intersecting the one to Gracias, she may have thrown them off long enough to reach safety. She had hoped they would check nearby villages first.

True, Scar Chest had applauded her actions, but he was only one against many and even he might betray her. Anyway, trekking and camping for three days was better than ending up as Juan had. Absolutely.

She had hoped to use the satellite phone to contact Julie and Trak, but so far it hadn't worked. Probably the canopy was too thick for the signal to reach the orbiting satellite. She would try again when she got to a wide enough open space. Surely they weren't worrying anyway. She was just beginning the fourth day beyond the ten she had allotted for the journey.

Soon it would be the end of April. Spring in Austin. Maybe even the start of an early summer. The beginning of the rainy season in Honduras, maybe a week away. She would have to escape before the roads turned to mud.

At last, she reached the visitor's center of the mountain park. She had eaten the last of her pouched dry food and was almost out of the tablets to purify the river water.

The underpaid caretaker of this immense park gave her some coffee and said that the bus from Gracias would be arriving soon at the stopping place, at least a thirty minute walk or more farther down the mountain. Samantha hoisted her backpack, determined not to have to walk the few miles into Gracias if she could help it.

It was a case of perfect timing. The bus rolled up with the day's load of backpackers eager to try their skill at reaching the summit. It was the best two dollars she had ever spent. Soon she was in the old colonial town of Gracias with a room in the rustic, but charming Hotel Guancascos where she had great views.

A tourist had nodded to her, said good morning in French and when she had responded in his language, welcomed her to Gracias and offered advice not to rent one of the rooms offered farther away from the restaurant.

Smiling at the clerk as he talked, he told her they were very near a wall, behind which, roosters crowed loudly enough to awaken the dead. He had found out the hard way.

Samantha had thanked him and settled in. She shook off the numbing effects of exhaustion for a few more minutes. She had to contact Julie. She ached to talk with Emerson. She wondered if he wanted to talk with her. The satellite phone didn't work, so she tossed it in a trash bin with an appropriate epitaph. She felt the country's phone service might be tapped; therefore she didn't dare try to call Emerson in London. Everyone in Honduras would listen in. She missed him so.

She realized she was near the breaking point and acting irrationally. Why would anyone care who she was and what she was doing in Gracias? Other than Joe the Oilman and the Guatemalan security forces and Honduran police, no one.

Poking fun at her predicament always helped. She took several deep breaths, calmed down and telephoned hoping she wouldn't be monitored. She would only call Julie. Deliver a short message and get off. She asked the clerk at Julie's hotel to go get her immediately.

The clerk hesitated, and Samantha wanted to send a stream of invectives and picturesque bodily threats guaranteed to bar her forever from using the phone service in Honduras, but instead, she said this was a special call and if Julie got to the phone right away, there would be something special for the clerk, too. That worked.

While she waited, Samantha's mind raced. The number one priority: get out of the country. She had made an important discovery in the Great One's hut. She had focused on the puzzle that had bothered her earlier.

Touching the Piper seat the Great One had used as a throne she found in addition to the expected purple and reds of leather, the presence of pink and green, which meant plastic. The colors showed up in one small area.

She had probed with her dad's knife. A sturdy plastic pod was hidden beneath a small slit in the leather, the Secure Identity card which Julie had mentioned as being very important if they were to locate her dad's personal files.

Beside the card, a note addressed to "Ajax" and signed "Sam" and a line about her birthday. While strange, it erased her uncertainties. With Julie's help maybe she could find out its meaning, but at the moment she had found it, it was so precious to her, she had sudden tears.

Earlier, she had explored an adjacent storage area at the Great One's hut and had found water, cleaned her body and the knife, located her backpack, tent and a change of clothes. Her boots. All brought from the hut the Great One had kept her in. A chill had gone through her. If things had gone the way he had planned, no

301

longer would she have needed that small hut.

For a moment, it seemed as though she were witnessing her own funeral. She had gathered up the other items they had taken from her including her sharp machete. At its sight the words "rape and murder" had kept time with her throbbing heart.

"Hello, hello? Julie's voice sounded hoarse.

"Julie, it's me."

"Oh Samantha, where are you? Are you O.K.? We found out about your guide, and we were afraid you had been murdered too or abducted. Tell me where you are? What do you want me to do? Are you hurt? Please, please, say you are O.K.!"

The torrent of words spilled out.

"Hold on, Julie, you're talking too fast. I'll tell you all about it when we're together. I'm O.K. Come to Gracias ready to travel fast. Got that? I mean really quick. I don't want to say anymore on the phone. I can't wait to see you."

"Yes, yes, I understand. I'll be there. See you real soon. Samantha, I'm so relieved you're O.K., I don't know what I would have done if I hadn't heard from you today. Please be careful."

It didn't take Samantha long to arrange a ride to La Entrada, fifty miles back toward Copán. Julie would have to come through there, and Samantha planned to intercept her rather than wait in Gracias just in case someone had been listening in. They would go north and fly out from San Pedro Sula.

So far, Samantha felt no one had tried connecting the dots of the wrecked police car in Guatemala City to the office "entering" and the attempt to find a missing Citation jet, or the death of Juan and the killing of the Great One. Once out of the country, they could still face charges since there were extradition treaties between the three countries. For now they would take it one fast step at a time.

Chapter 60

Hitching a ride at a dusty street corner in Honduras with a true friend and racing against time to board a plane that might not be flying. Too scary. While I waited I made notes in my journal about what had been happening. –From Samantha's Journal

The hotel San Carlos sat right by the highway junction in La Entrada. Samantha waited impatiently in the sun-baked street, hoping Julie would see her before roaring through town. She heard the sound of the wide-open engine, a moment later a pickup appeared, sliding around a bend. It had to be Julie, who else would drive like that? Samantha waved frantically. Julie stopped in a cloud of dust, leaped from the cab and grabbed Samantha in a bear hug. Tears and laughter eased the tension.

Back in the truck, Julie U-turned and with tires creating a storm of dirt and rocks, headed north at the junction toward San Pedro Sula. Samantha laid out the plan and asked about Trak.

"He stayed in Copán to keep suspicions to a minimum.

Wherever we leave the truck he can come get it later. Besides, he told me my driving makes him nervous."

Samantha told Julie about what had happened, leaving out the worst parts that were still too painful to talk about.

As they sped along, Samantha showed Julie the I.D. card she had found and also the cryptic note from her dad. She read it out loud above the roar of the truck's engine.

"Dear Ajax: Can't make your birthday this year, but always remember the date. Sam. Martin King."

"Could be a code. We'll play around with it when we get to San Pedro Sula. If we're lucky we'll have some time before having to board. I was afraid the battery life on the card had run out. The numbers are still working, but it may be on its last legs. We'll want to work with it right away, just in case."

They drove straight to the airport on the east side of the city. San Pedro was the business and financial center of Honduras. The city's offices, shops, hotels, and restaurants were within eight blocks of the downtown square. Venturing east of this area after dark, past the railroad tracks, was not recommended, said the guidebook Samantha read from.

They bought tickets and had nearly two hours to wait. The plane was delayed, but it was a direct flight to Houston. Fantastic! Now, they could try their hand at finding a network to access the Internet.

Julie had brought her little device that could spot a signal. Nothing at the airport. They drove back to the center of the city, and Julie had no trouble hooking the wireless laptop up to the Internet, even though she had to overcome a firewall on a company's network.

Once there she worked her way into the GUASAUCO Oil Company's computer using what she had learned while watching the oil company's clerk in Antigua. Once there she tried MKING as the user name, then tried to concoct a password out of the cryptic note left by Samantha's dad in the plane seat.

By trial and error she successfully combined Sam and the date of Samantha's birthday, coming up with s5a1m63. That worked and Julie was almost there. One more box to fill in. The Secure I.D. Six red glowing LEDs.

She entered them, but not fast enough, and the new series of six numbers flashed on the tiny card's screen. Julie swore under her breath and reentered the new set. At last she was in. She had Martin King's personal files and some of the company's files. Martin King's began with:

"Dear Sam, My days may be numbered here. I have accumulated some damaging material on the company. I should have left with Jason. Hope you have met him. I want you to know I love you and I'm so sorry I have been so stubborn. If I can get out of here, I'll make it up to you. In the meantime if you are reading this, I guess I didn't make it. Get this to Stuart if you can. All my love, Dad.

PDF files were attached to the personal note. Julie downloaded them. Then, following Samantha's directions, she uploaded to Stuart King, Uncle Stu, with a short note from Samantha. They had forty-five minutes left to get to the airport and board. Samantha bit her lip and sent a brief message to Emerson saying she would call him when she arrived in Houston, she so much wanted to talk to him. She signed, I love you, Samantha. Julie raced through the streets.

Once inside the airport, a uniform approached sporting a black mustache. The hearts of Julie and Samantha immediately jumped into their throats.

"Passports, por favor." He studied them while the two women pondered how fast they could run.

"Ah, from the U.S. I have been watching you and saw you had a laptop. I would like to have one someday. Are they hard to learn?" He handed back the passports. Samantha tried her best to have steady hands as she reached for the documents.

"Oh no, not at all. Paso a paso. Very easy and you would certainly enjoy having one, and I hope you get one soon."

" Buen Viaje! And come back to visit again." The two women watched him walk away.

"Man oh man, I nearly peed my pants while you were jabbering back and forth. What were you talking about anyway?" asked Julie.

"He wanted to buy you, but his offer was way too low."

"O.K. that settles it. When I get home I'm going to learn Spanish. Now, before you find another cute guy to sell me to, follow me." Outside, Julie picked up a good-sized rock.

"Damn, I need a screwdriver to get to the hard drive. I don't suppose you have one?"

"How about a metal nail file?"

"Perfect, leave it to you to have your nails in shape while your heart is being cut out."

In a few moments Julie had the hard drive out.

"Let me know if anyone notices us." Julie took the rock and hammered the drive.

"That should work. Should have done this in town and ditched the lap top there. We just experienced some good luck with that uniform.

Julie tossed the hard drive and lap top into a messy and very smelly garbage bin.

"Someone would really have to be dedicated to search through that slop. The stuff on that laptop might have locked us away for awhile. And when that guy stopped us, I thought the game was over."

"Thanks Julie, and I won't even charge you for it. I'll even buy us both new state-of-the-art laptops."

"Cool. One more thing, Samantha, although you didn't mention it, you had a birthday didn't you? May 1. Thanks to my sorting out that password I know your age too. But, I'll never tell. Happy belated birthday and you have no right to look so good."

Julie laughed and raised her glass. They sat in the wide seats of First Class and sipped the two complimentary flutes of sparkling wine. Down below, the great turquoise Atlantic dotted with white-beached islands looked just like one of those photos from a cruise-line brochure.

In Houston she called Emerson. He answered. She cried. They talked. Both accepted the blame for their misunderstanding and their stubbornness. They promised to be in each others arms soon.

Chapter 61

Why I have to go through hell to get answers is a mystery to me. Other folks seem to figure out things without hardly getting out of their backyards. Here's to peace and justice. – From Samantha's Journal

At her uncle's ranch a few days later, in the middle of a golden afternoon, Samantha arrived, and after the hugs, asked about the files she and Julie had sent from Guatemala and Honduras. Her uncle tried to look surprised and said he had received nothing and neither had CIA headquarters. She was about to protest, but noticed his slight smile.

"O.K., let's just suppose that the files did get to you and the CIA, what would have happened, you know, hypothetically?"

"What I'm going to say is purely hypothetical, you understand, but I reckon there would be charges of insurance fraud over a plane that never crashed, and there'll be some serious embezzlement issues. There'd be heavy fines and jail sentences, and Guatemala jails are not pleasant places to end up in.

A connection, at least financially, would no doubt be found between a certain oil company and al Qaeda, a bunch of extremists. One guy especially, Osama bin Laden, formerly from Saudi Arabia. That discovery could be very important. That alone would be worth a big thank you."

"And what about murder by blowing up a plane?" Uncle Stu got up and walked around his desk and paused in front of her.

"Samantha, that sort of thing happens down there all the time, and it's just ignored. I'm truly sorry. However, in this case, an investigation would prove unnecessary anyway." Samantha felt the tears start.

"Uncle Stu, dad loved me. He said so on one of those files you didn't receive. It meant everything to read those words. I've finally made my peace with him. I stood where he died."

"I couldn't agree more, darlin', about the trip being worth it to you. You did a damn good job, even though you must have suffered a lot for it. Your relationship with Emerson probably suffered too. Unfortunately, very little of your discoveries will see the light of day, but that doesn't mean they went unnoticed.

There could be some far reaching consequences because of your actions. You might say some big plans have been interrupted, at least temporarily."

"Uncle Stu, Julie and I did some questionable things, and I'm scared to death we'll be extradited to Guatemala, or Honduras, or both." She couldn't bring herself to talk of killing the Great One.

"Well, darlin', I did hear of some things. I think you'll feel better if I get them out in the open. Among a bunch of car accident reports a police car got wrecked in Guatemala City. The report circulating says a pickup of goons from an outlying town, roared into the city and was raising hell, and the police sacrificed one of their vehicles to head it off. The pickup left the city and the police were sure the goons would never return.

"And there's no official report about any breaking or entering in Antigua. An executive named Yusuf al Zayyat got himself "disappeared." Found his tortured body south of Guatemala City at a small private airfield.

He would have faced a lengthy term behind bars for fraud and embezzlement, so even if he didn't get charged with blowing up a plane, he did get his just desserts. There was a supposed killing in the jungle of a con man who was trying to mount an insurrection. Everyone seemed happy he's gone. Never found his body. So, it's all hearsay."

"Yusuf Zayyat killed. The Great One dead, Uncle Stu, I...,"

"Darlin', just don't say anything. Let's just leave it alone. Some things are better left unsaid." Stuart King walked slowly back around his desk, but didn't sit. He attempted a smile.

"Now, how did you and that young lady get along?" Samantha shook her head to clear her thoughts. Too much information. She focused on her uncle's question, relieved he had shut the door to discussion. Later, she would think through all he had said.

"Julie was absolutely incredible. Essential and steadfast. Without her I wouldn't have made it back." Samantha looked away from her uncle and out the large windows. Mesquite trees waved in the Texas wind.

"There's another thing Uncle Stu.... I know someday I'm going to have to deal with it, but I just don't know how. I may never tell you about it, you probably know some of it, but right now I want and need your support...and your love..., to help me through it. O.K.?"

"You have it Samantha, I would gladly go through the gates of hell for you. And I bet that young man of yours would do the same. You know that. And yes, you know I love you, and yes, I know you got hurt. I just don't know all the details and don't need to. You have my support one hundred percent." He held out his arms to her.

She was very close to crying. She hugged her uncle, burying her head against his massive chest. She felt his beating heart, and his deep breathing. They stood there in silence as she felt his strength warm her.

He squeezed her in a gentle embrace, then gripped her shoulders and held her at arms' length. She looked into his understanding eyes. She knew tears of thankfulness were in hers. His voice rumbled.

"You know what? There's a Quarter Horse standing out there pawing the ground and wanting a ride before supper. Do you think you could handle that? Duchess sure has missed you. Take as long a ride as you want. When you get back we'll sit down and enjoy some of Maria's home cookin'."

Samantha and Emerson talked for hours while she was at the ranch. They planned to be together in London and maybe Paris later that summer. Things seemed to be working out. Samantha was eager to get her new offices opened at the World Trade Center. Autumn in New York, a beautiful time of the year. Her favorite season. She hoped Emerson would be there with her.

Julie and I talked at length about what happened in Honduras when I was abducted. She thought it would be good if I went to a therapist for awhile. I may. I talked with Aisa for a couple of hours about it, and she was very helpful. She was also very excited about being a mother in the fall. Emerson is supportive of me and so is my uncle. I haven't shared details and I don't think I ever will. It doesn't seem necessary, at least not now. I'm not sure men would ever be able to understand what rape or the threat of rape does to a woman. I can honestly say, I am glad that guy's dead. I'd do it again. I feel absolutely no remorse. Maybe I'm wrong about it, but there it is. I'm wondering how I'll be with Emerson. I think I'll be just fine. Different maybe, but just fine. I found my dad, and he found me. I'm pretty sure Emerson really loves me. I'm pretty sure I really love him too.

–From Samantha's Journal.

Printed in the United States
209457BV00001B/36/P